PENGUIN BOOKS

2888

THE PENGUIN BOOK OF
ITALIAN SHORT STORIES

The Penguin Book
of Italian Short Stories

EDITED BY
GUIDO WALDMAN

PENGUIN BOOKS

Penguin Books Ltd, Harmondsworth, Middlesex, England
Penguin Books Inc., 7110 Ambassador Road, Baltimore, Md 21207, U.S.A.
Penguin Books Australia Ltd, Ringwood, Victoria, Australia

First published 1969
This collection copyright © Penguin Books Ltd, 1969

Made and printed in Great Britain
by Hazell Watson & Viney Ltd,
Aylesbury, Bucks
Set in Granjon Linotype

CONTENTS

EDITOR'S FOREWORD

THE process of selecting material for any anthology necessarily involves the discarding of a great deal which could justifiably claim a place. To a great extent, therefore, the anthologist must be guided by his own preferences. Let me confess, and not deny: I have been so guided. A clear, objective criterion has, nonetheless, also been followed in arriving at the present selection: the object has been to give the reader, within the compass of a single volume, a thoroughly representative view of the Italian short story from the Middle Ages to our own time – 'representative' has been the keynote, rather than experimental. (The absence of stories from the seventeenth and eighteenth centuries simply reflects a substantial gap in this field of Italian literature at that period.) The major short story writers from every region of Italy have found a place here, giving the reader some idea of how localized the Italian literary tradition has always been. Great writers whose reputation rests principally on their full-length works have been excluded: the accent is on the short story. In selecting stories within a given writer's opus, the aim has been to show him at his most typical, while also trying to avoid stories already available in other modern anthologies.

The new translations have aimed at being above all readable and fluent, although great care has been taken to ensure that the originals have been without fail accurately reproduced both in meaning and, as far as possible, in style. To the same end, a little very light editing has been done to some of the translations already in existence, with the kind permission of the publishers and (where possible) the translators concerned. For the sake of variety, a few of the medieval and renaissance stories have been reproduced in eighteenth- and nineteenth-century translations where these have been of unusual quality.

I am glad of the opportunity to place on record my debt to Mr Bruce Penman for his capable assistance in the very extensive research underlying this compilation.

London, January 1968   G. W.

ACKNOWLEDGEMENTS

FOR permission to reprint the stories specified we are indebted to the following: the University of California Press for Giovanni Cecchetti's translation of Giovanni Verga's 'The She-Wolf' from *The She-Wolf and Other Stories*; Laurence Pollinger Ltd, the Estate of the late Mrs Frieda Lawrence and The Viking Press Inc (Copyright 1925 by Thomas Seltzer Inc, 1953 by Frieda Lawrence) for D. H. Lawrence's translation of Giovanni Verga's 'Don Licciu Papa' from *Little Novels of Sicily*; Aldo Garzanti Editore for permission to translate Matilde Serao's 'Donna Caterina and Donna Concetta' from *L'Occhio di Napoli*; La Fondazione Il Vittoriale degli Italiani for permission to retranslate Gabriele d'Annunzio's 'La Fine di Candia' from *Novelle della Pescara*; George G. Harrap & Co. Ltd, the heirs of Luigi Pirandello and the International Copyright Bureau for V. M. Jeffery's translation of Luigi Pirandello's 'Limes from Sicily' from *Novelle per un Anno*; Martin Secker & Warburg Ltd and the University of California Press for Ben Johnson's translation of Italo Svevo's 'Traitorously' from *Short Sentimental Journey*; Valentino Bompiani & Co. for permission to translate Corrado Alvaro's 'Gelosia' from *Racconti* (Copyright © 1955 by Casa Editrice Valentino Bompiani); Martin Secker & Warburg Ltd and Farrar, Straus & Giroux Inc for Angus Davidson's translation of Alberto Moravia's 'The Strawberry Mark' from *Roman Tales* (Copyright © 1956, 1957 by Valentino Bompiani & Co.); Peter Owen Ltd for A. E. Murch's translation of Cesare Pavese's 'Wedding Trip' from *Festival Night and Other Stories*; Aldo Garzanti Editore for permission to translate C. Emilio Gadda's 'L'Incendio di Via Keplero' from *Novelle dal Ducato in Fiamme*; and Giulio Einaudi Editore for permission to translate Italo Calvino's 'L'Avventura d'un Lettore' from *Racconti*.

Every effort has been made to trace copyright holders, but in a few cases this has proved impossible. The publishers would be interested to hear from any copyright holders not here acknowledged.

PART I

MEDIEVAL AND RENAISSANCE

L'Anonimo Toscano

From IL NOVELLINO

IX, X, XXXI, LXXXV, XCI, XCVI

NEWLY TRANSLATED BY
GUIDO WALDMAN

L'ANONIMO TOSCANO

The 'Anonymous Tuscan Author' of the *Novellino*, or *100 Novelle Antiche*, probably lived in Florence in the late thirteenth century. If so, he would have been Dante's contemporary, a generation older than Boccaccio. When he wrote, Italian had not yet displaced Latin as a serious literary language. A few stories from the *Novellino* were translated by Thomas Roscoe in his book *The Italian Novelists*, 1836.

IX

Concerning an unusual law-suit and judgement given at Alexandria

In Alexandria, which is in the Levant (for there are twelve Alexandrias, which Alexander founded the March before he died); in Alexandria, then, there are alleys where the Saracens live who sell cooked foods; and people search out the alleys with the freshest and most delicate fare, just as among us people search out drapers. One Monday a Saracen cook, called Fabrat, was at his stall, and a Saracen pauper came along with a piece of bread in his hand. He had no money wherewith to buy from him; he held his piece of bread, however, over the steaming pot until it was saturated with the fragrance given off by the food, then he took a bite of it; and in this way he finished his bread. Fabrat was doing little business this morning; and, feeling that an injury was being done him, he laid hands on the pauper and said to him:

'Pay me for what you have taken from me.'

The pauper replied: 'I have taken nothing from your stove other than steam.'

'Pay me,' repeated Fabrat, 'for what you have taken from me.'

The quarrel reached such a point, and the question at issue was so thorny and unprecedented, that it came to the ears of the Sultan. So unusual was the case that the Sultan called together his wise men and sent for the two. He formulated the question. The Saracen wise men set to refining on the issue, and some found many reasons for maintaining that the steam did not belong to the cook: steam cannot be accounted a nutriment, nor is it of any substantial utility; he need not pay. Others said: the steam was still connected with the food; it was in his keeping and emanated from his property, and the man makes his living by selling; and whoever takes from him is expected to make payment. Many opinions were propounded. This, in the end, was their advice: 'Since the one means to sell his wares, the other to buy, do you, just Lord, enact that fair payment be made for his wares, according to their value. If his cooking-stove is to yield him money in accordance with the utility of its products, as he has sold steam, which is the subtle part of his cooking, have one coin struck against another, Lord, and decree that payment be made from the sound that comes from it.' And so did the Sultan decree.

X

Concerning a sound judgement given by Schiavo of Bari as between a burgess and a pilgrim

A burgess of Bari went on a pilgrimage, and left three hundred silver pieces with a friend on the following conditions: 'I am leaving, as God wills. Should I not return, you will donate them for my soul; if I do return before a certain time, you will give me back what you want.'

So he departed on his pilgrimage, and returned within the appointed time, and asked for the return of his silver pieces.

His friend answered: 'What was our agreement?' The pilgrim repeated their agreement.

'Quite correct,' said his friend; 'Here are ten silver pieces I want to give back to you; I shall keep the two hundred and ninety.'

The pilgrim became angry and said: 'What kind of bargain is this? You are defrauding me of what is mine.'

His friend blandly replied: 'I am not defrauding you; if I am, let us go before the magistrates.'

They appealed to Schiavo of Bari. He heard both sides and summed up the altercation. Here was his judgement, which he delivered to the one withholding the silver pieces: 'Return the two hundred and ninety silver pieces to the pilgrim, and let him give you back the ten you have repaid him, for this was the bargain: "You will give me back what you want." The two hundred and ninety silver pieces that you want, therefore: give them back. The ten which you did not want, you may keep.'

XXXI

About a story-teller of Messer Azzolino

Messer Azzolino had a story-teller, and would make him tell stories during the long winter evenings. One evening the story-teller happened to be particularly sleepy, and Azzolino asked him for a story. The story-teller began to relate a story about a farmer who went to market with a hundred silver pieces to buy sheep, and bought two per silver piece. On returning with his sheep, a river he had crossed had become swollen with heavy rains. Standing on the bank he saw a poor fisherman with his boat, but it was so small that it would barely hold the farmer and one sheep at a time. So the farmer put out with a sheep and began to row; the river was wide. And he rowed and he rowed and he rowed. The story-teller fell silent. And Azzolino said: 'Go on.' And the story-teller replied: 'Let the sheep get across, then I'll go on.' As the sheep would take years to cross, he had plenty of time to sleep.

LXXXV

About a great famine at Genoa

Once upon a time there was a great famine in Genoa; and nowhere were so many vagabonds to be found. So they assembled some galleys and hired crews for them, and proclaimed that all the poor should go to the quayside and they would receive bread from the Municipality. An astonishing number foregathered – this was because many who were not needy went in disguise. And the officials said: 'There is no way of ascertaining which these are, but let the townsfolk go aboard this boat, and the strangers aboard that one; and the women with children aboard those others.' Everyone went aboard. In a trice the sailors set hands to the oars, and conveyed them all to Sardinia. There they landed them, where there was abundance; and in Genoa the famine ceased.

X C I

How a man confessed to a friar

A man confessed to a friar and said that he had joined a crowd of people in looting a house. 'I was meaning to find a hundred gold florins in a chest; but I found it empty. So I don't believe I have sinned.'

The friar answered: 'Certainly you have, just as though you had found them.' This vexed the penitent exceedingly: 'In God's name, what do you advise?' he asked.

'I cannot absolve you,' replied the friar, 'unless you make restitution.'

'Willingly, but to whom?'

'Bring the florins to me,' said the friar, 'and I shall donate them to God.'

The penitent gave his word and left. And, with confidence restored, he returned the next morning and, as they were conversing, told him that he had been sent a fine sturgeon and that he would send it to him for dinner. The friar thanked him warmly. The penitent left, and did not send it. The next day he returned to the friar in a very good mood. The friar said: 'Why have you made me wait so long?'

'Oh, have you been expecting it?' asked the other.

'Yes, of course.'

'And has it not come?'

'No.'

'Well then it is just as though you had received it.'

X C V I

About Bito and Messer Frulli of San Giorgio, in Florence

Bito was a Florentine; he was handsome, a gentleman of breeding, and he lived at San Giorgio across the Arno. There was an old man called Messer Frulli, who owned a very good property above San Giorgio, and he lived there with his family practically all year round; and every morning he sent his maid down with fruit or vegetables to sell on the piazza by the bridge. And he was so miserly and suspicious that he prepared the vegetables in batches and counted them out to the maid, and reckoned up how much they should fetch. His most serious warning to her was not to stop in San Giorgio as the women there were thieves. One morning the maid was passing with a basket of cabbages. Bito, following his plan, had put on his richest fur gown; and sitting outside his door, he called the maid, and she at once went to him. Many women had called her first, but she would not go to them.

'How much are these cabbages, my good woman?'

'Two of these batches for a sixpence, sir.'

'Very reasonable. However, as I am alone, with only my maid, for all my family is in the country, even one would be too much for me; and I prefer them fresh.'

Now medals, valued at two for sixpence, were currency in Florence at the time; so Bito said: 'Give me one batch now. Give me a sixpence, too, and take this medal; and next time I'll take the other batch.' This seemed fair to her, and she consented. Then she went to sell the others in accordance with her master's instructions. Returning home, she gave the money to Messer Frulli. He counted it several times but always came out a sixpence short. He told the maid. She replied: 'It cannot be.' He flew into a rage and asked her if she had stopped in San Giorgio. She tried to deny it, but he so pressed her that she said: 'Yes, I stopped for a fine gentleman, and he paid me scrupulously. And I still owe him one batch of cabbages.'

Messer Frulli answered: 'How then do we account for the missing sixpence?' On further reflection, he realized the fraud. He roundly scolded the maid, and asked her where the man lived. She told him exactly, and he recognized that it was Bito, who had already played many tricks on him. Still smarting, he rose early next morning, hid a rusty sword under his cloak and went to the piazza by the bridge; there he found Bito seated in the company of good folk. He raised his sword and would have struck Bito had not someone held him by the arms. An astonished crowd gathered, not realizing the cause. Bito, too, was quite terrified until, recollecting what it was all about, he began to smile. The people crowding around Messer Frulli asked him what had happened. He told them, and so great was his distress that he could scarcely speak. Bito called for order and said: 'Messer Frulli, I want to make my peace with you. Let us say no more about it. Give me back my sixpence, and keep your medal; and keep your batch of cabbages, curse them.'

'I am content,' replied Messer Frulli, 'and if you had spoken like this to begin with, none of this would have happened.' And not realizing that he had been tricked, he gave him a sixpence, took the medal, and left in good spirits. How everyone laughed!

Franco Sacchetti

From LE TRECENTO NOVELLE

XXXI, LXIII, LXXI, CLXI

NEWLY TRANSLATED BY
GUIDO WALDMAN

FRANCO SACCHETTI

FRANCO SACCHETTI (*c.* 1335–*c.* 1400) was a Florentine by adoption, if not by birth. His fame rests on his *300 Novelle*, not quite up to the easy brilliance of the *Decameron* but streets ahead of the *Novellino*. He was born just too late to have known Giotto, but the legend of Giotto and the shield must still have been fresh. He could well have had personal experience of the war between the Genoese and the Venetians, which was concluded to Venice's advantage in 1381. Being a Guelph, he would have approved of Bonamico's trick on the Bishop of Arezzo. A number of the stories are translated by Thomas Roscoe in his book *The Italian Novelists*, 1836, and a selection translated by Mary Steegman was published in 1908.

From LE TRECENTO NOVELLE

XXXI

Two ambassadors from the Casentino are sent to Bishop Guido of Arezzo; they forget their message, and the bishop's reply, and on their return meet with honours for a mission well performed.

If the ambassador in the last story proved a voluble orator after a little wine, in this one I shall show how two ambassadors who had only poor memories almost lost what little they had, through drinking good wine. When Bishop Guido ruled over Arezzo, the communes of the Casentino appointed two ambassadors to lay certain requests before him. They were instructed as to what to say to him, and late one evening they received orders to set out the following morning. Returning home, therefore, that evening, they prepared their bags and the next morning they set out on their journey. When they had gone some miles, the first said to the second: 'Can you remember our message?' The second said that he could not. The first said: 'Oh, I was relying on you.' And the other: 'And I on you.' The first looked at the second, saying: 'A fine state of affairs! What now?' 'Listen,' said the other: 'We'll soon reach the inn for lunch, and there we can put our heads together: we're bound to recall it to mind.' 'A good idea.'

Onward they rode, lost in thought, and at the hour of Terce they reached the inn where they were to stop for lunch; here they cudgelled their brains till lunch time without any success. At table they were served a delicious wine. The ambassadors, who found wine more to their taste than the retention of messages, plied the bottle with a will. The glasses were filled and refilled and cheers! cheers! – by the end of the meal, far from recollecting their mission, they could not even recall where they were, and they went off to sleep. They slept a good while and awoke in a stupor. Said the first to the second: 'Do you yet remember our business?' 'Not I,' answered the second; 'I remember that our host's wine is the best I ever tasted; after lunch I can't remember a thing till now; even now I scarcely know where I am.' 'It's the same with me. Well, what shall we do? What shall we say?' Finally one of them suggested: 'Let us stay here today; and tonight (for night, as you know, sharpens the mind), we are bound to remember.' Thus agreed, they continued there all day, frequently drifting into reveries which had an unforgettable bouquet. That evening at supper they attended more to their cups than to their trenchers, and by the end of the meal they could scarcely recognize each other. They went to bed, and snored all night like pigs. Getting up the next morning, the first one said: 'What shall we do?' 'I can't remember last night at all,' answered the other, 'so damn me if I'll ever remember the message.' 'Well, well, here's a fine state of affairs. I don't know what it is, whether it was that wine or what, but I've never slept so soundly as I slept last night in this inn – I simply couldn't wake up.' 'What the devil can this mean?' asked the other. 'Let us mount our horses,' he continued, 'and be off; perhaps it'll come back to us on the way.' So they left, frequently asking each other as they went, 'Have you remembered?' 'No.' 'Me neither.'

In this way they came into Arezzo and went to the inn. Here they kept drawing each other aside in their room, their hands pressed to their cheeks, but they could never remember the message. Hopelessly the first one suggested, 'Let us go, God help us!' 'Yes, but what shall we say?' 'Well, it's no good staying here,' said the first. They set out, at all events, and went to the bishop; coming into his presence, they fell to their knees, and in that position remained, proceeding no further. The bishop, a man of considerable personality, got up and went to them, and took them by the hand, saying: 'Welcome, my sons; what news?' The two looked at each other: 'Go on; *you* say!' But neither spoke. Finally the first one said: 'My lord, we have been sent as ambassadors to your Lordship by your servants from the Casentino; and those who sent us, and we their ambassadors, are men of no polish at all; and they gave us their message in haste one evening – and somehow or other they explained it badly, or else we couldn't make it out. They warmly entreat your Lordship that they and their communes be commended to your Lordship – a plague on them for sending us and on us for coming!' The good bishop laid his hand on their shoulders and said: 'Go now, and say to my children that I shall always do the best I can for them. And to spare them the expense of sending ambassadors in future, let them write to me any time they need something and I shall answer by letter.' So they took their leave, and departed.

On the way, the first said to the second: 'Let's take care not to have the same trouble going back as coming.' 'Oh, what do we have to remember?' asked the second. 'Indeed yes, we must think,' continued the first; 'we shall have to tell them what message we gave and what reply was made to us. If our people knew how we forgot their message, and we returned to them like a pair of half-wits, far from sending us on further embassies, they would never confer any office on us again.' 'Just let me think,' said the second, who was the more astute; 'I shall say that when we had given the bishop our message, he graciously and readily offered to promote their interests in every way; and in earnest of his goodwill he suggested that, to save them expense, whenever they needed him they should, for their peace and tranquillity, write him a plain letter and forget about embassies.' 'A good idea,' said the other; 'now let us ride faster, the sooner to get to that wine of ours.' So, spurring their mounts, they reached the inn, and their first inquiry to the boy who came out to their horses was not about the host, nor about what there was for dinner, but they asked after that excellent wine. 'Better than ever,' said the boy. Here, therefore, they restored themselves a second time not less than the first, and before they left, the wine diminished and the cask was drained to the last drop – for many drinkers arrived, like wasps to a honeypot. Reluctantly, therefore, the ambassadors took themselves off and returned to those who had sent them. They were better at memorizing the lie they had invented, than the truth they set out with; they had made such a fine harangue, they said, before the bishop – Cicero and Quintilian were left in the shade, so they implied. They were much commended, therefore, and from that day forth many offices came their way, for often they were entrusted with the care and supervision of the public funds.

LXIII

The great painter Giotto is given a shield to paint by a man of no account. He scornfully paints it in such a way as to put the man to shame.

Everyone must have heard of Giotto, and of his unsurpassed stature as a painter. Learning of his reputation, a common artisan, who needed a shield of his painted, possibly in preparation for assuming a public office in his village, went straight to Giotto's shop. He had the shield brought in after him, and going up to Giotto, he said: 'God save you, master; I would like you to paint my arms on this shield.' Giotto looked the man up and down, and all he said was: 'When do you want it?' The other told him. 'Leave it to me,' said Giotto. The man departed, and Giotto was left reflecting; 'What can this mean? Can someone have sent him to me for a joke? Well, well – I've never been asked to paint a shield before. And this man comes along, a mere nobody, and tells me to paint his coat of arms for all the world as though he were of royal birth! Assuredly I shall have to make him a new kind of emblem.' So thinking, he set the shield before him, sketched out his design, and instructed one of his apprentices to complete the painting – which he did. The painting consisted of: a helmet, a gorget, a pair of vambraces, a pair of gauntlets, a breastplate, a pair of greaves and thigh-pieces; a sword, a dagger and a spear. When the worthy man of anonymous ancestry came back and asked, 'Master, is that shield painted?' Giotto replied, 'Indeed it is; go and fetch it.' The shield was brought, and the gentleman-by-proxy started looking at it, then asked Giotto: 'What daub is this you've painted for me?' 'It's always a daub when it's time to pay!' answered Giotto. 'I wouldn't give you four ha'pennies for it.' 'Well, what did you ask me to paint?' 'My arms.' 'Aren't these they?' asked Giotto. 'Is anything missing?' 'All very well ...' returned the other. 'All very bad, you silly dolt,' exclaimed Giotto; 'If anyone asked "Who are you", you'd scarcely know what to answer. And you come here and say, "Paint my coat of arms." If you were one of the Bardi family that would be another matter. What are your arms? Whence are you? Who were your ancestors? Shame on you! Grow up first, before you start talking of arms as though you were Charlemagne in person. I've put a complete suit of armour on your shield; if there's anything missing, say, and I'll have it painted on.' 'You've insulted me,' said the other, 'and you've spoiled my shield.' He left and went to the justices to lay a complaint against Giotto. Giotto appeared and laid his own claim against the other in the amount of two florins for the painting: the other, meanwhile, was claiming as much from him. The justices heard both sides; Giotto argued the better, however, and they decreed that the man should take his shield painted as it was and give Giotto what he claimed, for he was in the right. So he had to take the shield and pay and was discharged. So, for not having measured himself, this man received his measure; for every nobody wants his coat of arms and his family tree, and among them are some whose fathers were found abandoned on a doorstep.

LXXI

An Austin friar preaches a Lenten sermon in Genoa on how the Genoese should wage their war.

Not many years ago, finding myself at Genoa in Lent, and going, according to custom, to church in the morning, I went to the church of San Lorenzo, where an Austin friar was preaching. It was at the time of the war between the Genoese and the Venetians, and the Venetians had just soundly defeated the Genoese. Now, as I drew closer and lent an ear to catch his words, these were the holy words, the lofty ideals which I heard him propound. He was saying: 'I am a Genoese; and if I did not speak my mind to you, I would feel greatly at fault; do not take it amiss, then, if I tell you the truth. You are like donkeys: the donkeys' natural tendency when they are in a group and one of them is struck with a stick, is for all of them to scatter in all directions, such is their cowardice; and this is just their nature. The Venetians are like pigs; they are called Venetian swine, and they behave just like pigs: when they are huddled together in a group, and one of them is struck or belaboured, they all draw together and run against the one who hits them, for this is their natural tendency. And if ever these similes seemed appropriate, they seem so to me now. You beat the Venetians the other day, and they closed in so as to defend themselves and attack you; and they put to sea with all those galleys and you know what they did to you; and you fled all over the place without any common plan and with only a handful of armed galleys while they had almost twice as many. Don't sleep, bestir yourselves: fit out so many that you can, if need be, not only put to sea but enter Venice.' He concluded with these words: 'Don't take it amiss; I would have burst if I had not been able to vent my feelings.' Having heard this sermon I returned home, leaving the rest for the others to hear.

I chanced to be in a gathering of merchants later the same day, in a group that included Genoese, Florentines, Pisans and Luccans; the conversation turned to men of valour, and a Florentine sage called Carlo degli Strozzi was saying: 'You Genoese are undoubtedly the best warriors and the most valorous men in the world; we Florentines should stick to manufacturing wool and pursuing our commerce.' 'Ah, there's a reason for that,' I put in. 'Is there?' they all asked. And I answered: 'When our friars preach at Florence, they admonish us about fasting and prayer, and how we must forgive, and how we must seek peace and not make war. The friars who preach here teach quite the opposite, for this morning I happened to be in San Lorenzo and I listened to an Austin friar preaching; and the teachings and examples the people here could listen to were these': and I recounted what I had heard. They were all amazed: then they discovered how right I was from one who had heard as I had, after which they conceded I was right, and everyone thought it a most original sermon.

And thus are we often schooled; so greatly, indeed, is our faith enhanced when friars such as he go into the pulpit, that only God can account for their prudence and their discretion.

CLXI

Bishop Guido of Arezzo has Bonamico paint a story; a monkey defaces by night what he has painted by day, with the results that ensue.

Painters have always produced their share of remarkable men, among whom there used to be, so I have heard, a Florentine painter called Bonamico, his surname being Buffalmacco; he lived in Giotto's time and was a very great master. Excelling as he did in his art, he was summoned by Bishop Guido of Arezzo to paint a chapel, when this bishop was lord of Arezzo; Bonamico therefore went to the bishop and settled the terms with him. Once the question of how and when was agreed, Bonamico set to work. He painted some saints for a start, and towards Saturday evening, he interrupted his work. Now there was a monkey, or rather a great ape, belonging to the bishop, which had observed the behaviour and activities of the painter while he was on the scaffolding: he had watched him mix the colours and handle the pots of paint, emptying in the egg-yolks, then take up the brushes and rub them against the wall – all this he had taken note of. And to make mischief, as they all do (which is why, as she was particularly mischievous and destructive, the bishop had a wooden ball tied to her leg), this monkey went into the chapel on Sunday when everyone was at dinner; she climbed up one of the supports of the scaffolding on to the painter's platform; there she picked up the paint pots, spilled them one into another, then broke and mixed in the eggs, then took the brushes and sniffed them; to dip them into the paint and smear them all over the completed figures was the work of a moment. In no time at all, therefore, the figures were all besmirched, the pots of paint all knocked upside down and in a terrible mess.

When Bonamico returned on Monday morning to complete what he had started to paint, seeing his paint pots knocked over on to their sides or upside down, and his brushes thrown all over the place, and his figures all besmirched and besmeared, he at once thought that some Aretine must have done it, out of envy or something. He went to the bishop and told him that his painting had been ruined. The bishop was filled with indignation. 'Bonamico,' he said, 'go and restore what has been defaced; when you have done so, I shall give you six men with falchions, and I shall have them lie in wait with you in a hiding-place there and whoever comes, let them have no mercy but cut him to pieces.' 'I shall go and make good the figures as soon as I can,' said Bonamico, 'and when that is done I shall come and tell you, and then it can be done as you say.' And so deliberating, Bonamico set to repainting the figures all over again a second time, after which he told the bishop. The bishop therefore immediately assembled six men armed with falchions, and ordered them to go with Bonamico into a hiding-place near the painted figures; and if anyone came to deface them, they were to cut him to ribbons at once. So Bonamico and the six men with falchions lay in wait to see who would come to spoil the paintings. After a while they heard something rolling about in the church and at once recognized that these must be the people who came to deface the figures; the rolling, however, was the ape with the ball tied to her feet. She made straight for one of the supports and climbed up on to the scaffolding where Bonamico painted; here she stirred up the paint pots one by one, emptying them one into another, and took the eggs and broke them open and sniffed; then she took the brushes, first one then another, and brushed them all over the wall, making a thorough mess. Seeing this, Bonamico laughed till he was ready to burst; and turning to the men with the falchions he said: 'We don't need falchions – you can be off. It's all too clear: the bishop's monkey paints one way while the bishop wants this to be painted in another. Go and put your weapons away.' They came out of their hiding-place and approached the scaffolding on which the monkey was, whereupon she drew herself up and frightened them away, thrusting her muzzle forward; then she made off.

Bonamico went to the bishop with his henchmen and said: 'My father, you have no need to send to Florence for a painter, for your monkey insists that the paintings be done in her own style; indeed, she is such an expert painter that she has twice corrected my work. However, if anything is due to me for my efforts, I pray you to give it to me, and I shall return to the city whence I came.' When the bishop heard this, much though he disapproved of the way the painting had suffered, he could not restrain his laughter at the thought of so absurd an occurrence. 'Bonamico,' he said, 'you have repainted these figures so often that I want you to repaint them once again. And to teach this ape a real lesson, I shall have her put in a cage right where you are working; there she will see you paint without being able to do anything about it; she will stay there until the painting has been finished for some days and the scaffolding taken down.' Bonamico again agreed; he made ready for his work, and no sooner was a cage knocked together than the monkey was put inside. The faces she made and her performance as she watched the painting were incredible; still, what was she to do about it? A few days later, the work was finished and the scaffolding removed, and she was released from her prison; for several days she would return to see if she could not mess up the painting as before; but seeing that the scaffolding and the ladder were gone she had needs attend to other things. The situation afforded the bishop and Bonamico many days' amusement.

Then the bishop, in order to compensate Bonamico, took him aside and asked him to decorate his palace with a lifelike eagle bestriding a lion which it has killed. Said Bonamico: 'Very well, my Lord Bishop; but I must be well screened with matting so that no one can see me.' 'Not with matting,' said the bishop; 'I shall have it done with boards in such a way that you will be quite invisible.' And so he did. Bonamico assembled his pots of paint and other necessaries, closeted himself and began painting; but he set about it quite contrary to the bishop's instructions, making an enormous, fierce lion astride a disembowelled eagle.* And when he had finished it, keeping his working area locked the whole time, he told the bishop that he needed some paints and wanted to have his working area securely locked in his absence while he went to Florence for them. On hearing this, the bishop gave orders that the place be locked and bolted

* Translator's note. The point here is that the lion was the emblem of Guelph Florence, the eagle that of Ghibelline Arezzo; painter and bishop therefore belonged to opposing camps.

till Bonamico returned from Florence. So Bonamico left for Florence.

The bishop waited day after day and Bonamico did not return to Arezzo (for he had finished the painting and had left, resolved not to return to it); when, therefore, the bishop had waited several days and realized that Bonamico was not coming back, he told some of his servants to go and break open the screen of boards and see what Bonamico had painted. So they broke in and saw the finished work; whereupon they returned to the bishop and said: 'The painting has been done in such a way that the painter has executed your orders meticulously, in reverse.' 'What do you mean?' He was told. So, just to be sure, he went to look and, having seen for himself, he was so enraged that he issued a warrant for Bonamico's banishment and for the seizure of his goods and sent to Florence to threaten him. To those bearing the threats Bonamico answered, 'Tell the bishop he can do his worst; if he wants me he'll have to send me his mitre.'

The bishop, then, after witnessing Bonamico's behaviour, had banished him; but, considering the matter further, like a wise master, it seemed to him that Bonamico had done the right and proper thing – so he lifted his sentence and effected a reconciliation. Indeed, he frequently sent for him, and treated him as his intimate and faithful servant for the rest of his life. And so it often happens that lesser men can gain an advantage over their betters by dint of subtlety, and win their friendship just when they most expect to excite their enmity.

Giovanni Boccaccio

From THE DECAMERON

II.4, III.2, III.10, VII.4

NEWLY TRANSLATED BY
BRUCE PENMAN

VI.4, VIII.10, IX.6

TRANSLATED BY
E. DUBOIS (1804)

GIOVANNI BOCCACCIO

GIOVANNI BOCCACCIO (1313–75) was a Florentine. With Dante and Petrarch he succeeded in establishing Italian (the Tuscan variety) as the enduring literary language, doing for Italian perhaps what Chaucer did for English. His fame rests principally on *The Decameron*, the prototype of a thousand imitations: it is a joyful, uninhibited work in which, in the course of 100 stories, the life of fourteenth-century Italy is vividly depicted. More translations must exist of *The Decameron* than of all other Italian prose works put together. The most recent complete translation is Richard Aldington's, 1957. A paperback selection was also published in 1962.

From THE DECAMERON

SECOND DAY, NOVEL 4

Landolfo Ruffolo, reduced to poverty, becomes a corsair, is captured by the Genoese and suffers shipwreck; he finds safety on a box full of richest jewels, obtains refuge with a woman of Corfu, and returns home a rich man.

It is generally said that the coast between Reggio and Gaeta is the pleasantest region of Italy; that part of it overlooking the sea near Salerno, which the inhabitants call the Amalfi coast, is full of little towns, of gardens and of springs – full, too, of rich people who pursue their trade as merchants with incomparable vigour. Among the rest is a town called Ravello, famous to this day for its wealthy citizens, in which there formerly lived one Landolfo Ruffolo, a man of extraordinary riches, who was not content with what he had, but tried to double it, and so came near to losing all his fortune, and his life into the bargain.

Landolfo made up his accounts like a true merchant, bought a large ship, loaded it entirely at his own expense with a variety of goods, and set sail for the island of Cyprus. He there found many other ships carrying the same commodities, so that he had to sell his cargo very cheap – almost, in fact, to give it away in order to be rid of it – which brought him very near to ruin.

In great distress at this, Landolfo did not know what to do, seeing that his vast wealth was suddenly reduced almost to poverty; and finally he resolved that he would either die, or restore his losses by piracy, rather than return as a beggar to the town he had left as a prosperous merchant. He found a buyer for his big ship, and putting together the money he got for her with the sum realized by his cargo, he bought a slim little vessel, fit for his purpose, armed her and equipped her with the best of everything needed for piracy, and set out to acquire the goods of other people – especially those of the Turks. And fortune was much kinder to Landolfo the pirate than she had been to Landolfo the merchant.

About a year later, he had taken so many Turkish prizes that he found he had not only recovered his trading losses, but more than doubled his original fortune. He had learnt his lesson from those early losses, however, and realized how lucky he had been; so that for fear of a second disaster, he convinced himself that his present wealth ought to be enough for him, without any question of wanting more, and resolved to make the best of his way home with what he had acquired; and as he was still fearful of trade, he had no mind to employ any more of his money in that way, but set sail in the little vessel in which he had gained his new fortune.

But when he reached the Archipelago, a great sirocco arose, directly contrary to his intended route, which made the sea so rough that his little ship could not be expected to ride it out, and he was glad to get into a sheltered bay, formed by a small island, to wait for better weather. Landolfo had not been there long when two large Genoese merchantmen, coming from Constantinople, struggled into the bay after him, to avoid the same tempest.

When the Genoese saw the little ship, they placed themselves so that she could not get out to sea; and when they understood that she belonged to Landolfo, whom they knew by name as a very rich man, they followed their greedy and piratical inclinations, and resolved to make her their prize. They landed some of their men, well armed with cross-bows and other weapons, and stationed them so well that no one could leave Landolfo's ship without being shot; and the two large vessels, towed by their long-boats and helped by a favourable sea, were brought alongside Landolfo's ship, which was quickly and easily taken, and its crew captured, without the loss of a man. The Genoese took Landolfo on board, removed all the cargo out of his vessel, and sank her, leaving him with a single poor ragged coat and no other possessions.

The following day the wind changed, and the Genoese set sail, on a westerly course, and had a good voyage all that day; but when night came on a storm blew up again, the sea grew very rough, and the two merchantmen were separated. And such was the force of the wind, that the ship which carried the unhappy Landolfo drove with the utmost violence towards the island of Cephalonia and struck a reef, where it broke to pieces like a glass smashed against the wall. And since the sea was full of floating cargo, chests and planks, as generally happens on these occasions, those of the poor wretches on board who could swim endeavoured to get hold of whatever floating objects came their way among the mountainous waves and the pitchy blackness of the night.

Among them was poor Landolfo, who the day before had indeed wished for death a hundred times, as a fate preferable to returning home a beggar; but now that he saw death close at hand, he changed his mind, and when a plank came his way, he grasped it firmly, in the hope that if he delayed his fate, God would send him some effective help; and riding upon it as well as he could, while the sea and the wind drove him backwards and forwards, he lasted out until the morning. Looking around him by the light of day, he could see nothing but cloud and water, except for a floating box, which drove towards him from time to time, much to his dismay, for he feared that it would dash against him. He kept pushing it away with his hand, though he had little strength left in his body.

But in the end a sudden squall of wind swept down from the sky, and struck the box with such violence that it drove against Landolfo's plank and overturned it, sending him far below the surface; and when he struggled up again, with fear lending strength to his weary limbs, he found that his plank had been carried far away by the waves, so that he doubted whether he could reach it again; and swimming over to the box, which was much nearer, he managed to rest his chest upon it, and held it upright as well as he could with both arms. And in this manner, driven to and fro by the sea, eating nothing because he had no food, and drinking much more than he desired, not knowing where he was nor seeing anything but the waves, he passed the whole of that day and the following night.

By the next morning Landolfo was almost converted into a sponge, and was clinging with both hands to the sides of the box in the very attitude of a drowning man clutching at his last hope; and at last, either through the will of God or the force of the wind, he was cast up on the shore of the island of Corfu, where by good fortune a poor woman was scouring her dishes with salt water and sand. When she caught sight of him floating in towards her, she had no idea what he could be, and backed away with a startled cry.

Landolfo was past speech, and could see very little, so he did not call out to her; but as the sea brought him nearer to the shore she made out the shape of the box, and looking more closely she saw two arms laid over it, and then a face, so that she knew that this was no sea-monster, but a man. So she had pity on him, and wading out a little way into the sea, which was now calm, she took him by the hair and pulled him and the box to shore. She released the box from his grasp, not without some difficulty, and gave it to her young daughter to carry; and then she carried him like a child to her village, and put him into a bath, and chafed him and washed him with hot water until the vital warmth returned to his limbs, and with it a little strength. In due time she took him out of the bath, and fed him up for a day or two with nourishing food and wine, until he was well enough to know where he was. Then the good woman thought it was time to give him back his box, which she had kept for him, and to tell him that he might now provide for his departure.

He remembered nothing about the box, but took it when the good woman offered it to him, thinking that it might serve for his expenses for a day or two; but he was disappointed to find how light it was; however he broke it open when his hostess was out of the way, and found a great quantity of precious stones, some set and some loose. He knew something about jewels, and when he looked at them he saw that they were very valuable, which comforted him greatly, and he praised God for not having forsaken him. But as he had been twice buffeted by fortune already, and was fearful of a third mishap, he judged that great care would be needed to get these things safely home; and so he wrapped them up as best he could in some old rags, and told the woman that he had no further use for the box, which she might keep if she would give him a sack in return for it.

She was very glad to do this, and Landolfo, thanking her a thousand times, swung the sack over his shoulder and left her house and he found a ship to take him over to Brindisi, and another to take him along the coast to Trani, where he met some silk merchants from his own town, who clothed him out of charity after he had told them his whole story, except for the chapter of the jewels; and when he said that he wanted to go back to his own home, they gave him a horse, and arranged for him to return to Ravello in the company of some other travellers.

Once safely at home, he thanked God for his deliverance; and opening his sack, he inspected the contents more carefully than he had done before, finding so many valuable stones, that even rating them below their proper value, he was twice as rich as when he left home. When he had found a buyer for the jewels, he sent a good sum of money to the woman at Corfu who had taken him out of the sea and treated him so kindly, and another to the merchants at Trani who had helped him and given him clothing; and he lived handsomely on the remainder, without having any more mind to trade, for the rest of his life.

THIRD DAY, NOVEL 2

A groom sleeps with the wife of King Agilulf; the king secretly finds him out and marks him by clipping his hair; the groom clips the hair of all the other grooms and so escapes disaster.

King Agilulf of the Langobardi, like several of his predecessors, set up his royal residence in the North Italian town of Pavia. He had married the widow of the previous king – a most beautiful lady, of great wisdom and virtue, though not altogether lucky in love. At a time when the Langobardi were living in peace and prosperity, through the wise and just rule of King Agilulf, one of the queen's stable grooms – a man of the humblest possible birth, but in all else fit for far nobler employment, and no less tall and handsome than the king himself – fell desperately in love with her majesty.

Though he had little learning, he had enough to know that his love was outside the bounds of all reason, and he was wise enough to tell no one about it, nor even to let the queen read the truth in his eyes. And though he lived without hope of ever obtaining favour in her sight, he could not help glorying in having fixed his affections so high. Burning with love, he outdid all his companions in every service that he thought might please the queen. And so it happened that when she went out riding, she more often chose the horse that was in his care than any other; and this he thought the greatest of all honours, never leaving her stirrup, and happy beyond words when he could touch her clothes.

But we often see that love increases as hope grows less, and this was what happened to the unfortunate groom; so that in the end he found it unbearable to conceal his feeling in this manner, without any hope to sweeten the pill; and as he could see no other end to his love, he often thought of death as the only solution. And when he came to consider how he should end his life, he decided that it must be in a way that would show that he died for the love he had so long borne towards the queen; and he went on to resolve that it should also be in a way which would give him some chance of obtaining his heart's desire. So he did not seek to prove his love to the queen in words, or by writing to her, which would have been to no purpose, but by trying to gain access to her bed with a trick. And there was no other means of doing this, but by finding a way to impersonate the king, and so to gain admittance to her bed-chamber. He knew that the king did not always sleep with her.

Wishing to see in what dress and manner his majesty went to visit the queen, the groom hid himself several nights in a great room of the palace, which lay between the two royal bed-chambers; and one night he saw the king come out of his quarters clad in a great cloak, with a torch in one hand and in the other a stick, with which he knocked a couple of times on the queen's door; it was at once opened to him, and the torch taken out of his hand, without a word being said. Having seen all this, and also observed how the king returned to his room, the groom decided to do the same. He provided himself with a cloak similar to the king's, and a torch and a stick, and when he had washed himself well, so the odour of the stables would not offend the queen's nose or arouse her suspicions, he hid himself in the same place as before.

And when he saw that everyone was asleep, and that the time had come to obtain his heart's desire, or the welcome release of a death earned by a memorable act of daring, the groom lit his torch with a flint and steel he had with him, wrapped himself up well in his cloak, made his way to the queen's bed-chamber, and knocked twice with his stick. The door was opened by a sleepy serving woman, who took the torch from his hand and put it out of the way; and without saying anything to her, he slipped through the curtain, threw off his cloak, and got into the queen's bed. He embraced her eagerly, but at the same time behaved as if he were a little vexed over something; for he knew that the king always insisted on silence when he was irritated for any reason; and so, without a word being said on either side, he had his will of the queen, and that not once but several times. And then, though he was very sorry to leave her, he began to fear the consequences of staying too long, and so he got up, took his cloak and his torch, still without a word, and went straight back to his own bed.

No sooner was he gone than the king got up and went along to the queen's bed-chamber, which surprised her greatly; and when he got into bed and greeted her very cheerfully, she took courage from his evident good humour to say:

'My dear lord, what is happening tonight? You have only just left me, and that after staying with me much longer than you generally do; and are you here again already? What can you be thinking of?'

Hearing these words, the king at once concluded that she had been imposed upon by someone who had assumed his person and his habits; but he had the wisdom and the quickness of wit to reflect, that since neither the queen nor anyone else knew what had happened, it was better that she should remain in ignorance. This would have been quite beyond many a stupid husband, who would have exclaimed: 'What do you mean by saying that I have just left you? Who has been here? Where did he go? Who was he?' This would have distressed the lady for nothing, and perhaps also made her want to repeat the experiment. By his silence, the king avoided all scandal, whereas by speaking out he would have brought shame on his own head.

After a few moments, the king replied, with more outward calm than he really felt:

'Madam, are you surprised to find me man enough to come back to you again after so short a time?'

'Of course not, my dear lord,' she said, 'but I beg you to think of your own health.'

'I believe you are right,' said the king, 'and I will go back to my own room without giving you any further trouble.'

Full of wrath and indignation against the villain who had injured him, the king put on his cloak and went out, resolving to go quietly and find out who it was; for he thought the man must be a member of the household, and knew that in any case he could hardly have got out of the palace.

So he took a small light in a lantern, and went to a long narrow loft, situated over the palace stables, where nearly all his household slept, and supposing that whoever the offender was, his pulse and heartbeats could hardly have had time to return to normal after all his exertions, the king began very quietly to examine them all, putting his hand on each man's chest in turn, from one end of the loft to the other.

Everyone else was asleep, but the groom who had been with the queen was still wide awake, and when he saw the king coming, and realized what method of investigation was being used, he was so afraid that his heart, which was already beating loudly because of his recent exploits, began to beat more violently still, though he was sure that the king would kill him at once if he noticed it. Various plans passed rapidly through his mind, but when he saw that the king had no weapon with him, he decided to pretend to be asleep, and see what the king would do.

His majesty had now laid his hands on many of his servants, without finding cause to suspect any of them; but when he came to the groom and felt how strongly his heart was beating, he at once said to himself: 'This is the man.' But as he did not want anything to be known of his plans, all he did at the moment was to take out a pair of scissors he had with him, and cut off part of the groom's hair, which they wore very long in those days, so that he would know him again in the morning; and then the king returned to his own room.

The groom knew very well what had happened, and had sense enough to understand why he had been marked in that way; and so he got up a few moments later and went down to the stable for one of the pairs of scissors that they used for their horses; and then he went round the whole loft clipping a similar piece of

hair from the same place on the head of every one of his com-
rades, and went back to bed without being noticed by anybody.

In the morning the king gave orders that his whole household
should assemble while the palace gates were still shut; and as
they all stood bareheaded before him, he began to look among
them for the man he had marked; and when he saw that nearly
all of them had been shorn in the very same way, he was amazed,
and said to himself: 'This fellow may be of low conditon, but
he is of no common understanding.'

The king saw that he could not achieve his object now without a far-reaching scandal, and since he did not want to incur
a great disgrace for the sake of a petty revenge, he thought it
best to admonish the guilty man for the future in a few words
which would leave him in no doubt that his crime was known.
And speaking to them all generally, he said:

'Whoever has offended, let him do so no more – and now go
about your business.'

Another master would have subjected them to every kind of
torture and inquisition; all in order to bring out into the open
something much better hidden from view – something whose
discovery could never lessen his disgrace, however fully he
revenged himself, but would rather have doubled it, and brought
dishonour on his lady.

All who heard this speech were amazed, and speculated among
themselves at great length about the meaning of the king's
words; but not one of them understood it correctly, except the
man for whom it was intended. And he was wise enough never
to reveal the secret during the king's lifetime, and never to
gamble with his own life in such a way again.

THIRD DAY, NOVEL 10

*Alibech becomes a hermit; Rustico the monk teaches her how
to put the Devil in Hell; later she becomes the wife of Neerbale.*

Among the citizens of Gafsa, in Barbary, there was once a very
rich man, who had several children, including a daughter – a
girl of great beauty and gentle manners – whose name was
Alibech. She was not a Christian herself, but there were many

of the faith in Gafsa, and she had often heard them praise the Christian religion and the service of God; so that one day she asked one of them what was the best way to serve the Deity, without worldly impediment. The man replied that God was best served by those who fled from the things of this world, like the hermits who went to live in the lonely desert of the Thebaid.

Alibech was a simple girl, about fourteen years old, and it was no serious vocation, but a mere childish whim, that made her secretly set out the following morning, alone and without a word to anyone, towards the desert of the Thebaid. Though the journey was long and laborious, she stuck to her purpose, and in a few days time she reached those holy solitudes. Seeing a hut in the distance, she went up to it, and found a hermit standing at the door, who was very surprised to see her there, and asked her the object of her search. She replied that God had inspired her to seek a place where she could serve Him, and a master who could teach her how best to do so.

The good man saw how young she was, and how beautiful, and began to fear that the Devil would lay a trap for him, if he accepted her as a pupil; so he praised her virtuous intentions, gave her a simple meal of roots, wild fruit, dates and water, and then said:

'My child, there is a holy man not far from here, who is a far better teacher of the things you wish to learn than I am: you must go to him.'

And he sent her on her way.

But when she reached the dwelling of the second recluse, he gave her the same advice as the first, so that she went on a little further, and came to the cell of a very devout and virtuous young hermit, named Rustico, to whom she told the same story. And this time she was not sent on her way, nor referred to another teacher, for Rustico decided to put his constancy of purpose to a searching test, and kept her with him in his cell. And when evening came, he set aside a place for her, and made her a small bed of palm leaves, on which he told her to sleep.

But it was not long before he felt his virtue under heavy assault from the forces of temptation; and finding that he had seriously overestimated his strength, he did not resist more than two or three attacks before giving ground, and admitting defeat;

and then he set aside all thoughts of holiness, of prayer and of spiritual discipline, and began to let his mind dwell on Alibech's youth, and her beauty, and to wonder how he should behave, and what he should do, when the time came, to prevent her from realizing that he was having his will of her like a common lecherous rake. He asked her a few questions, and found out that she had no experience of men, and was as innocent as she looked; and then he soon thought of a way to persuade her to serve his pleasure under the pretence of serving Heaven. First of all he proved to her with many instances how bitter an enemy the devil was to God; and then he went on to show that the most precious service that anyone could render the Deity was to put the devil in Hell – back into the place to which he had been damned by the Almighty.

Alibech asked him how this could be done, and Rustico replied:

'You will learn the answer in a minute, if you follow my example in all that I do.'

He began to take off the few clothes he was wearing, until he was quite naked; and she did the same – then he knelt down in an attitude of prayer and made her kneel opposite him.

Now Rustico's desires were more inflamed than ever, seeing her in all her beauty, and he began to bear witness to the resurrection of the flesh; so that Alibech looked at him in great surprise, and said:

'Whatever is that thing sticking out in front of you, Rustico? I am sure that I have nothing like it.'

'My child,' said Rustico, 'this is the devil of which I have been speaking. Do you not see how he torments me, so that I can hardly bear it?'

'Then I must praise the Lord,' said Alibech, 'for I see that I am much more fortunate than you, not having a devil like that.'

'That is true,' said Rustico, 'but there is something else that you have and I have not – something that you have instead of the devil.'

'Whatever is it?' asked Alibech.

'The thing that you have,' replied Rustico, 'is hell – and I firmly believe that God has sent you here for the salvation of my soul; for whenever this devil begins to torment me, if you will have pity on me, and allow me to put him in hell, you will give me unspeakable consolation, and do God the greatest possible service – if, that is, your reason for coming to this place is really the one you have given me.'

'Father,' replied the girl in perfect good faith, 'since I have this hell, let it be as you have said, whenever you like.'

'Blessed shalt thou be, my daughter,' said Rustico. 'Come then, and let us put him in hell, so that he may leave us in peace.'

And with these words, he led her to one of their beds, and showed her what attitude to adopt when incarcerating the enemy of God.

The girl, who had never put a devil in hell before, felt some discomfort on this first occasion, and she said:

'I can see, Father, that this devil must be really wicked, and a great enemy to God – he hurts quite badly even in hell, when he is put in there.'

Rustico replied:

'My child, it will not always be thus.'

And he repeated the incarceration six times before they rose from the bed; so that for that time the devil's pride was humbled, and he was glad to be left in peace.

But his pride returned in full vigour several times in the next few days, and Alibech was always obediently ready to cure it again; so that in the end the sport began to please her, and she said to Rustico:

'Those good people in Gafsa certainly spoke the truth when they told me how sweet a pleasure it was to serve God, for I cannot remember ever doing anything which gave me such happiness and delight as putting the devil in hell; and I really think that anyone who devotes his time to other things, instead of to the service of God, must be a stupid beast.'

After this she would often go to Rustico, and say to him:

'Father, I came here to serve God, and not to live in idleness; come, let us put the devil in hell.'

And while they were doing so, she would sometimes add:

'Rustico, I cannot think why the devil keeps on escaping from hell; for if he were as happy to stay there as hell is to welcome him and hold him, he would never come out again at all.'

The girl invited Rustico to the service of God so often, and encouraged him so warmly, that she overtaxed his strength, and he started to feel cold among flames that would have burnt another man; and so he began to tell her that it was not right to punish the devil, nor to put him in hell, except when he raised his head in pride.

'And we, by the grace of God, have so humbled him,' he added, 'that his one prayer is to be left in peace.'

These words silenced the girl for a time; but when she saw that days were going by without Rustico asking her to put the devil in hell, she said:

'Rustico, your devil may be well punished, so that he gives you no discomfort; but my hell will not leave me in peace, and I really think that you ought to help me to calm the fever of my hell with your devil, just as I helped you to humble the pride of your devil with my hell.'

Living on a diet of roots and water, Rustico found it difficult to respond to her appeal; and he told her that many devils would be needed to bring complete peace to hell, but that he would do what he could. And so he satisfied her from time to time; but so rarely that it was like tossing beans into the mouth of a hungry lion; and the girl began to complain that she was not being allowed to serve God as well as she would have wished.

But while this discord arose between Rustico's devil and Alibech's hell, through too much appetite on the one hand, and too little strength on the other, there was a terrible fire in Gafsa, in which Alibech's father perished with his other children and all the rest of his family, so that she was left heir to all his wealth. There was a young man in Gafsa named Neerbale, who had wasted his fortune through extravagant hospitality, and when he heard that Alibech was still alive, he set out to look for her, and found her before the court could sequester her father's estate on the ground that he had died without leaving any heirs; and much to Rustico's delight and her dismay, he took her back to Gafsa and married her, sharing the inheritance of her father's vast wealth. But before the wedding, it happened that certain ladies asked her in what way she had served God in the desert, and she replied that she had served Him by putting the devil in hell, and that it had been very wrong of Neerbale to prevent her from continuing in that service.

'But how do you put the devil in hell?' asked the ladies.

Partly with words and partly with gestures, she showed them what she meant. And they laughed so heartily that they are probably still laughing to this day, and said:

'There is no cause for sorrow in this, Alibech, no cause at all; just the same thing happens here in Gafsa, and you can trust Neerbale to join you in rendering exactly the same service to God.'

And as the story passed from mouth to mouth through the city, it became a proverb that the best service we can offer to God is to put the devil in hell; and the same saying has crossed the sea to Italy and is still popular among us.

SEVENTH DAY, NOVEL 4

Tofano shuts his wife out of the house one night and she, unable to gain entrance by her entreaties, pretends to throw herself into a well, throwing in a large stone. Tofano comes out of the house and runs to the well, whereupon she goes into the house and locks him out, covering him with abuse.

A rich citizen of Arezzo, called Tofano, married a very beautiful girl, whose name was Ghita; and soon after the wedding, without knowing why, he became extremely jealous of her. When she noticed this, she was indignant, and asked him the cause of his jealousy on several occasions; and as he was unable to produce any reasons for it that were not of a general and unsatisfactory kind, she decided to give him a sharp dose of the medicine he so stupidly feared.

Having noticed that a certain young man, whom she liked well enough, had been paying particular attention to her, Ghita discreetly began to show signs of response. Soon they were so well agreed together, that it only remained to put their agreement into practice; and she started to consider how this could be done. Among her husband's bad habits was that of drinking too much, and she now began to show approval of his vice, and cunningly encouraged him in it whenever she could. And soon she reached the stage of being able to get him to drink himself insensible almost whenever she liked. It was when he was soundly drunk, and safely asleep, that she had her first meeting with her lover; and many other meetings followed, without any fear of disturbance. Her faith in Tofano's drunkenness grew so strong that she not only welcomed her lover into her own home, but would sometimes go and spend most of the night in his house, which was not far away.

As Ghita continued in this way of life, her wretched husband began to think it strange that she encouraged him to drink, but drank very little herself; and this led him to suspect the truth – that she made him drunk so that she could do what she liked while he was asleep. And he tested the accuracy of this notion, when he came home one evening, by acting and speaking like the most drunken sot in the world, although he had drunk no wine that day at all. His wife was taken in, and as she thought he would sleep well enough without any more to drink, she put him straight to bed. And then she went off to her lover's house, as she had done on several previous occasions, and stayed with him until the middle of the night.

When Tofano realized that she had gone out, he got up and locked the front door of his house, and took up his position at a window from which he could see his wife when she came back, meaning to leave her in no doubt that he knew what she had been doing; and he waited there until she returned. When she did finally come, and found the door locked, she was very disturbed, and began to try to force it open.

Tofano watched her for a little, and then said:

'Madam, you are wasting your time – I will not let you in. Go back to the place where you have been; and make up your mind to it that you will never come back to my house, until I have celebrated your exploits as they deserve, in the presence of your family and the neighbours.'

His wife began to implore him to open the door, saying that she had not been where he supposed, but had been sitting up with a neighbour's wife, because the winter nights were long, and she could not sleep right through them, and hated to lie awake by herself.

But her words had no effect, and the foolish husband seemed resolved that no one in Arezzo should remain in ignorance of his shame.

Seeing no result from her entreaties, she had recourse to threats, and said:

'Unless you open the door, I will make you the most miserable man that ever was born.'

'And just what can you do?' asked Tofano.

Love had sharpened her wits, and she replied:

'Rather than put up with this undeserved disgrace, which you are trying to fasten on me, I will throw myself into the well; and when my body is found in the water, no one will doubt that you did it in one of your drunken fits; and then you will either have to go into exile and lose all you have, or stay and be put to death as the murderer of your wife – which will be no more than the truth.'

But this also made no impression on Tofano's stupid resolution. And finally his wife said:

'I cannot stand your hateful cruelty any more – may God forgive you! My distaff I leave by your door – please let it be put away in a safe place.'

He heard her run off towards the well – the night was so dark that a man would hardly have known his neighbour if he passed him in the street. Then, crying 'Heaven forgive me!' she picked up a large stone that lay near the well, and dropped it into the water.

Tofano heard a great splash, which convinced him that she really had thrown herself into the well, and he picked up a rope and bucket and ran out to help her.

Meanwhile Ghita had hidden herself near the door, and as soon as she saw him running out to the well, she got back into the house and locked him out. Then she went to the window, and softly called out:

'You ought to take more water with your wine, instead of getting drunk and then swilling water from the well in the middle of the night.'

Realizing that he had been tricked, Tofano came back to the house; and finding it locked, he told her to open the door.

She had been speaking quietly before, but now she raised her voice.

'You loathsome drunk!' she shouted. 'You are not coming in here tonight if I have anything to do with it. How can I be expected to put up with this sort of behaviour any longer? The time has come for me to let everyone know what kind of man you are, and what hours you keep.'

Tofano lost his temper, and began to shout and to swear at her, so that his neighbours, and their wives, woke up and came to their windows to ask what was the matter.

Ghita began to weep.

'It is my wretched husband here,' she sobbed, 'who either comes home drunk every evening, or goes to sleep in some tavern and comes home in the middle of the night like this! For a long time I put up with it patiently, which did no good at all, and now I can stand it no longer. So I am trying to shame him out of his drunken ways by locking him out of the house.'

Then Tofano was fool enough to tell everybody what had really happened, with terrible threats against his wife.

'Now you can see what sort of man he is!' said Ghita to the neighbours. 'I wonder what you would say if I were standing out there and he were looking out of this window! You really might believe him then. But see how his mind works! He is trying to tell you that I have been doing the very same thing that he has just done himself. He did try to frighten me just now by dropping something heavy into the well – I only wish he really had fallen in and drowned himself! Then all that wine inside him would have been well and truly watered!'

The neighbours and their wives all began to blame Tofano, and told him he was a brute to speak like that about his wife; and before long the disturbance spread from house to house, until it reached the ears of Ghita's relations, several of whom came to see what was happening. They heard the story first from one of the neighbours, and then from another; after which they seized Tofano and beat him black and blue. Next they went into the house and carried off Ghita herself and all her property, and went back home, threatening Tofano with worse to follow.

Tofano saw that his jealousy had done him no good; and as he was still very fond of his wife, he got some of his friends to act as intermediaries, and persuaded her to come back and live in peace with him, promising that he would never be jealous again: and after this she was free to do whatever she liked, provided she kept it secret from him.

As the proverb says:

> When a fool is wronged, he will
> Come to terms – and pay the bill.

SIXTH DAY, NOVEL 4

Chichibio, cook to Currado Gianfiliazzi, by a sudden reply which he made to his master, turns his wrath into laughter and so escapes the punishment with which he had threatened him.

Lauretta being silent, Neiphile was ordered to follow, which she did in this manner: – Though ready wit and invention furnish people with words proper to their different occasions; yet sometimes does fortune, an assistant to the timorous, tip the tongue with a sudden, and yet a more pertinent reply than the most mature deliberation could ever have suggested, as I shall now briefly relate to you. Currado Gianfiliazzi, as most of you have both known and seen, was always esteemed a gallant and worthy citizen, delighting much in hounds and hawks; to omit his other excellences, as no way relating to our present purpose. Now he having taken a crane one day with his hawk, and finding it to be young and fat, sent it home to his cook, who was a Venetian, and called Chichibio, with orders to prepare it for supper. The cook, a poor simple fellow, trussed and spitted it, and when it was nearly roasted, and began to smell pretty well, it chanced that a woman in the neighbourhood called Brunetta, with whom he was much enamoured, came into the kitchen, and being taken with the high savour, earnestly begged of him to give her a leg.

He replied, very merrily, singing all the time, 'Madame Brunetta, you shall have no leg from me.' Upon this she was a good deal nettled, and said, 'As I hope to live, if you do not give it me, you need never expect any favour more from me.' The dispute at length was carried to a great height between them, when, to make her easy, he was forced to give her one of the legs. Accordingly the crane was served up at supper, Currado having a few friends along with him, with only one leg. Currado wondered at this, and sending for the fellow, he demanded what was become of the other leg. He replied without the least thought, 'Sir, cranes have only one leg.' Currado, in great wrath, said, 'What the devil does the man talk of? Only one leg! You rascal, do you think I never saw a crane before?' Chichibio still persisted in his denial, saying, 'Believe me, Sir, it is as I say, and I will convince you of it whenever you please, by such fowls as are living.' Currado was willing to have no more words out of regard to his friends, only he added, 'As you undertake to show me a thing which I never saw or heard before of, I am content to make proof thereof tomorrow morning; but I vow and protest, if I find it otherwise, I will give you something to remember me by, if you live to remember it.'

Thus there was an end for that night, and the next morning Currado, whose passion would scarcely suffer him to get any rest, arose betimes, and ordered his horses to be brought out, taking Chichibio along with him towards a river where he used early in the morning to see plenty of cranes; and he said, 'We shall soon see whether you spoke truth, or not, last night.' Chichibio, finding his master's wrath not at all abated, and that he was now to make good what he had asserted, nor yet knowing how to do it, rode on first with all the fear imaginable: gladly would he have made his escape, but he saw no possible means, whilst he was continually looking about him, expecting every thing that appeared to be a crane with two feet. But being come near to the river, he chanced to see, before anybody else, a number of cranes, each standing upon one leg, as they use to do when they are sleeping; whereupon, showing them quickly to his master, he said, 'Now, Sir, yourself may see that I spoke nothing but truth, when I said that cranes have only one leg: look at those there if you please.' Currado, beholding the cranes, replied, 'Yes, sirrah! but stay awhile, and I will show you that they have two.' Then riding somewhat nearer to them, he cried out, 'Shoo! shoo!' which made them set down the other foot, and after taking a step or two, they all flew away. Currado turned to him and said, 'Well, you lying knave, are you now convinced that they have two legs?'

Chichibio, quite at his wits' end, nor knowing scarcely what he said himself, suddenly made answer, 'Yes, Sir; but you did not shout out to that crane last night, as you have done to these; had you called to it in the same manner, it would have put down the other leg, as these have now done.' This pleased Currado so much, that, turning all wrath into mirth and laughter, he said 'Chichibio, you say right, I should have done so indeed.' By this sudden and comical answer, Chichibio escaped a sound drubbing, and made peace with his master.

EIGHT DAY, NOVEL 10

A certain Sicilian damsel cheats a merchant of all the money he had taken for his goods at Palermo. Afterwards he pretends to return with a greater stock of goods than before; when he contrives to borrow a large sum of money of her, leaving sham pledges for her security.

How much they were all diverted with the queen's novel, it is needless to say; and it being now ended, Dioneus began in this manner: – It is certain that those stratagems are the more entertaining, the more cunning and artful the person is who is imposed upon by them. Therefore, though the other novels have been agreeable enough, yet I think to relate one that will please you better; inasmuch as the lady outwitted was a greater mistress of those devices, than any of the persons beforementioned.

It was formerly a custom, and may be still, in seaport towns, for all the merchants that come thither, to bring their goods into a common warehouse, under the keeping of the community, or else the lord of the town; when they give a particular account, in writing, of the nature and value of them: the goods are kept under lock and key, and the account entered in a register, for the merchants to pay the accustomed dues, as all or part are sold, and delivered out of the warehouse. From this register, the brokers are informed both of the quantity and quality of the goods, and also who are the owners, to treat with for them, either by exchange, truck, or sale. This was the way at Palermo, as well as in many other places, where was likewise great plenty of handsome women, not overstored with modesty. And yet, to all appearance, many of them were grand ladies, and pretended to a character: who, making it their whole employ to shave and even skin such men as fell into their clutches, no sooner did they see a strange merchant, but they would inform themselves from that register, both of the nature and value of his goods; when, by their amorous wiles, they would endeavour to bring him to their lure, which they often did; and some have been cajoled out of part of their goods; others have lost ship, goods, and body, to boot, so finely have they been touched over by these cunning shavers.

Now it happened, not long since, that a certain young Florentine, called Niccolo da Cigniano, though more usually Salabaetto, arrived there by way of factor, with as much woollen cloth, which had been left unsold at the fair of Salerno, as might be worth five hundred florins; and having given in his account to the officers, and laid his goods safely up in the warehouse, he was in no great haste to dispatch his business, but took a turn up and down the town to amuse himself. Being a personable young man, one of these female extortioners, that we have been speaking of, called Madam Jiancofiore, having heard something of his affairs, soon took notice of him, which he perceiving, and supposing she was some great lady who had taken a fancy to him, resolved to conduct the affair with the utmost caution; so without saying a word to anyone, he used to take his walks frequently by her house. She was soon sensible of this, and when she thought his affection towards her fully secured, under pretence of languishing for him, she sent one of her women to him, an adept in that sort of business, who told him, with tears in her eyes, that her lady was so in love with him, that she could get no rest night or day; therefore she desired very much, whenever he would do her that favour, to meet him at the public baths; and with these words she took a ring out of a purse, and gave it him as a token. Salabaetto was overjoyed at the message; so taking the ring, and looking lovingly at it, and kissing it, he put it upon his finger, and said, 'If your lady loves me as you say, be assured she has not misplaced her affection, for I love her more than I do my own life, and shall be ready to meet her at any time and place she shall appoint.'

She had no sooner reported his answer, but she was posted back to tell him at which bath her mistress would meet him the following evening. Accordingly, he went thither at the time fixed, and found it engaged for that lady's use. He had not waited long before two women slaves came, the one laden with a fine cotton mattress, and the other a hamper full of things. This mattress they laid upon a bed in one of the chambers, covering it with a fine pair of sheets, curiously edged with silk, and over the whole was spread a rich Grecian counterpoint, with two pillows, worked in a most delicate manner; after which they undressed and went into the bath, and cleaned it very carefully. The lady now came attended by two slaves, and after some sighs and embraces, she said, 'My dear Tuscan, there is nobody could have obtained this favour from me but yourself; you have set my heart afire.'

So they went naked into the bath together, and with them two of the slaves; here she let no one but herself wash him, using soap scented with musk and gilli flowers; then she had herself washed and massaged by her slaves. The other slaves then brought two fine sheets, smelling of nothing but roses, in one of which they wrapped Salabaetto, and in the other the lady, and carried them to bed, where, after they had lain some time to perspire, those sheets were taken away, and they were left between the others. After this, they took out of the hamper silver canisters of rose, orange, and jessamine water, which they sprinkled upon the bed, and presented them with sweetmeats and rich wines, by way of collation: he all the time thought himself in paradise, wishing heartily that they would go away, and leave him in possession of his mistress. At length, at their lady's command they departed, leaving a taper alight in the chamber. Then they lay a long while in each other's arms, much to Salabaetto's delight, it seeming to him that she was deeply in love with him.

After they had lain a convenient time, the servants returned, and put on their clothes, and when they had taken some more refreshment of wine and sweetmeats, and washed their hands and faces with orange-water, as they were going to depart, she said, 'If it be agreeable to you, I should be vastly pleased if you would come and sup with me, and stay all night.' When he, supposing himself as dear to her as her own heart, replied, 'Madam, whatever is pleasing to you, is entirely so to me; now, therefore, and at all times, I shall be ready to obey your commands.'

So she went home, and had her apartment richly set out, and provided a costly supper for him; who accordingly went thither as soon as it was dark, and was very elegantly received; and after supper they went into a chamber, scented with costly odours, where was a most noble bed, and everything besides that was grand and sumptuous. All which made him conclude, that she was some very great and rich lady. And though he had heard various reports about her, yet he would not believe them for the world; nay, had he been convinced of her tricking other people, he could never have been made to believe that she would serve him so. He slept with her then all that night growing ever more inflamed, and the next morning she made him a present of a fine wrought belt and purse, saying to him, 'My dear Salabaetto, fare you well; and from henceforth be persuaded, as you are entirely to my good liking, that my person and all I possess are at your service.' He then took his leave with great satisfaction, and went to the place where the merchants usually resort.

And continuing his visits to her without any expense, and becoming every day more enamoured, it happened, that he sold his cloth, and gained considerable profit; which she being immediately apprised of, not from himself, but other hands, as he was with her one night, she seemed to express a more than ordinary fondness for him, and would needs make him a present of two beautiful silver cups which he refused to accept; having had divers things of her before, to the value of at least thirty gold florins, without being able to persuade her to accept of a single farthing. At last, after she had set him all on fire, as it were, with this extraordinary love and liberality, she was called out by one of her slaves, as she had contrived beforehand, when she returned in a little time full of tears, and throwing herself down upon the bed, she seemed to grieve most immoderately.

Salabaetto was under the greatest astonishment, and taking her in his arms, he began to say, 'Alas, my dear heart, what is it that has happened to you thus suddenly? Tell me, my life, I entreat you, do.' She at last replied, 'My dear lord, I know neither what to do, nor what to say. I have just received letters from Messina, wherein my brother informs me that, though

I pawn all I have, I must, without fail, remit a thousand florins of gold within a week; otherwise, he must inevitably lose his head. Now I find it impossible to raise the money upon so short a notice: had I but a fortnight, I could procure it from a place, whence I could command a greater sum; or I could sell some of my lands: but as it cannot now be done, I wish I had been in my grave rather than lived to know this trouble,' and she continued weeping; whilst Salabaetto, whose love had taken away his understanding, thinking that her tears were real, and what she said was true, made answer, 'Madam, I am unable to furnish you with a thousand; but with five hundred I can, as you think you will be able to pay me in a fortnight: and it is your good fortune that I happened to sell my cloth yesterday, otherwise I could not have spared you one farthing.'

'Alas,' quoth the lady, 'then have you been in want of money? Why did you not speak to me? For though I have not a thousand, I have always a hundred or two to spare for you. You deprive me of the assurance to accept your proffered favour.'

He, quite captivated with these fine speeches, made answer, 'Madam, you shall have it nevertheless; had I been in the like circumstance I should have applied to you.' – 'Ah me!' she replied, 'I am convinced of your most constant and entire love towards me, to supply me with such a sum of your own accord: I was yours before, and now am much more so; nor shall I ever forget that it is to you I am indebted for my brother's life. But Heaven knows I accept it very unwillingly, considering that you are a merchant, and must have occasion for a great deal of ready money; but being constrained by necessity, and assured also that I shall be able to return it at your time, I will make use of it; and I will pawn all my goods rather than fail in my engagement to you.' With these words she fell down, weeping, in his arms. He did all he could to comfort her, and stayed with her all that night; and the next morning, to show what a liberal lover he was, and without waiting for any further request, brought her the five hundred florins, which she received with laughter at her heart, though with tears in her eyes, he looking only to her simple promise.

But after she had got the money, the times were soon changed; and whereas before he had free admittance to her as often as he pleased, now reasons were given that he could not get a sight of her once in seven times that he went; nor did he meet with those smiles and caresses, nor with the same generous reception, as before. Moreover, the time limited was past, and one or two months over, and when he demanded his money he could get nothing but words by way of payment. Whilst he, now sensible of the arts of this wicked woman, as well as of his own want of sense, and knowing that he had no proof against her, but what she herself would please to acknowledge, there being no witness and nothing of any writing between them, was ashamed to make his complaint to anyone, both because he had notice of it before, and also on account of the disgrace which he must undergo for his monstrous credulity; so he continued uneasy and disconsolate to the last degree. And receiving frequent letters from his masters, in which he was required to get bills of exchange for the money, and remit to them, he resolved, to prevent a discovery, to leave the place, and he embarked on board a little vessel, not for Pisa, as he should have done, but directly for Naples.

At that time lived there Signor Pietro dello Canigiano, treasurer to the Empress of Constantinople, a very subtle, sensible man, and a great friend to Salabaetto and his masters, to whom he made his case known, requesting his assistance in getting himself a livelihood, and declaring that he would never more return to Florence. Canigiano, who was much concerned for him, replied, 'You have done very ill; very ill indeed have you behaved yourself; small is the regard which you have showed to your principals; too much have you expended upon your pleasures. It is done, however, and we must remedy it as well as we can.' Then, like a prudent man, he considered what course it was best to take, and acquainted him with it. Salabaetto was pleased with the scheme, and resolved to follow it; and having some money of his own, and Canigiano lending him some, he made divers bales of goods well packed together, and procured about twenty casks for oil, which he filled, and returned with them to Palermo, where he entered them as on his own account in the register, with what value he pleased to put upon them; and he laid them up in the warehouse, declaring, that they were not to be meddled with till more goods of his should arrive, which he was daily expecting. The lady hearing of this, and understanding that the goods he had already there were worth two thousand florins, and that what remained to come were rated at three thousand more, began to think that she had as yet got too little from him; therefore she thought of returning the five hundred, to come in for a better part of the five thousand, and accordingly she sent for him.

Salabaetto went, having now learnt guile, whilst she, seeming to know nothing of what he had brought, appeared wonderfully pleased at seeing him, and said, 'Now, were you really vexed because I failed giving you your money at your time?' He smiled, and replied, 'In truth, Madam, I was a little uneasy, since I would pluck my very heart out if I thought it would please you; but you shall see how much I was offended. Such is my regard for you, that I have sold the greatest part of my estate, and have brought as much merchandise as is worth two thousand florins, and I expect from the Levant what will amount to three thousand more; resolving to have a warehouse, and to abide here, for the sake of being near you, as I think nobody can be happier in their love than I am in yours.'

She then replied, 'Now trust me, Salabaetto, whatever redounds to your benefit is extremely pleasing to me, as I hold you dearer than my own life; and I am glad you are returned with an intention of staying, because I hope to have a great deal of your company; but it is fit that I excuse myself to you, in that sometimes you came to see me, and were not admitted, and at other times not so cheerfully received as before, and besides this, for my not paying you the money according to promise. Now you must know that I was then in very great trouble and affliction, and upon such occasions, be one's love what it will, one cannot look so pleasantly as at another time: I must tell you likewise that it is a very difficult thing for a lady to raise a thousand florins, people impose upon us in that manner, without ever minding what they promise; so that we are forced to deceive others. Hence it is, therefore, and for no other reason, that I did not return you your money; but I had got it ready just as you went away, and would have sent it after you, had I known where to have found you; but as I did not, I kept it carefully for you.' So sending for a purse, which had the very same florins in it that he had delivered to her, she put it into his hand, saying, 'See, and count if there are five hundred.'

Never was Salabaetto so overjoyed as at the present time; so telling them over, and finding there were just five hundred, he replied, 'Madam, I am convinced that what you say is true; but let us talk no more about it, you have done your part, and I assure you, upon that account, as well as the love I have for you, that whatever sum of money you shall want at any time, if it be in my power to supply you, you may command it; as you may soon see upon trial.' Thus their love being renewed, in word at least, he continued artfully his visits as before; while she showed him all the respect and honour that could be, expressing the same fondness as ever.

But he, willing to return measure for measure, being invited one night to sup with her, went thither, all sad and melancholy, like a person in despair. When she, kissing and embracing him, would needs know the cause of all that sorrow. He, having suffered her to entreat him for some time, at last said, 'I am undone; for the ship which had the goods on board, that I have been expecting, is taken by the corsairs of Monaco, and put up at the ransom of ten thousand florins, one thousand of which falls to my share, and I have not one farthing to pay it with; for the five hundred which you paid me, I sent instantly to Naples, to lay out in cloth to be sent hither; and were I to offer to sell the goods I have here, as it is an improper time, I must do it to very great loss, and, being a stranger, I have nobody to apply to; so that I know neither what to say nor what to do; and if the money be not sent immediately, they will be carried into Monaco, and then they will be past redemption.'

She was under great concern at hearing this, reckoning a good part of it as lost to herself; and considering how to prevent the goods being sent to Monaco, at last she said, 'Heaven knows how much my love for you makes me grieve for your misfortune. But to what purpose is that? Had I the money, I would instantly give it you; but I have not. Indeed there is a person that lent me five hundred florins the other day, when I was in distress, but he expects an exorbitant interest, viz. no less than thirty in the hundred. If you will have the money of this man, you must give him good security. Now I am ready to pledge my goods here, and pass my word as far as that will go to serve you; but how will you secure the remainder?' Salabaetto knew the reason of her proposing this piece of service, and that she herself was to lend the money; so, being well pleased, he returned her thanks, and said, that, let the interest be what it would, his necessity was such that he must agree to it: then he added, that he would make a security by his goods which he had in the warehouse, and that they should be assigned over in the register to the person who advanced the money, but that he would keep the key, as well for the sake of showing them, if anybody should want to see them, as to prevent their being exchanged or meddled with. The lady replied, 'You speak extremely well, the security is sufficient,' and at the time appointed she sent for a broker, in whom she put great confidence, when she told him what he was to do, and gave him a thousand florins, which he carried straightaway to Salabaetto, who assigned over his goods to him at the custom-house, and they were entered in his name; thus they parted, having both countersigned the documents.

Salabaetto now immediately embarked with the fifteen hundred florins, and went to Pietro dello Canigiano at Naples, from whence he remitted to his masters at Florence the entire account of what he had made of their cloth; and having paid Pietro and everyone else what he owed them, they laughed very heartily together at the trick put upon his Sicilian mistress. From thence, resolving to trade no longer, he went to Ferrara. In the meantime, the lady, finding Salabaetto was not at Palermo, began to wonder, and grow half suspicious; and, after waiting two months, and hearing nothing of his return, she made the broker force open the warehouse, when first she tried the casks, which she supposed had been full of oil, and found them full of seawater, with a small quantity of oil at the top, just at the bunghole. She then looked into the bales of goods, only two of which had cloth in them, and the rest were stuffed with coarse hurds of hemp; in short, the whole was not worth two hundred florins. So she, finding herself thus imposed upon, was under great affliction for a long time, with regard to the five hundred florins that she had restored, and much more for the thousand she had lent, often saying, that whoever had to do with a Tuscan, had need have all their eyes about them. Thus she became a common jest afterwards, having found to her cost that some people have as much cunning as others.

NINTH DAY, NOVEL 6

Two young gentlemen lie at an inn, one of whom goes to bed to the landlord's daughter; whilst the wife, by mistake, lies with the other. Afterwards, he that had lain with the daughter, gets to bed to the father, and tells him all that has past, thinking it had been his friend: a great uproar is made about it; upon which the wife goes to bed to the daughter, and very cunningly sets all to rights again.

Calandrino, who had so often diverted the company, made them laugh once more: when the queen laid her next commands upon Pamphilus, who therefore said, Ladies, the name of Niccolosa, mentioned in the last, puts me in mind of a novel concerning another of the same name; in which will be shown, how the subtle contrivance of a certain good woman was the means of preventing a great deal of scandal.

In the plain of Mugnone lived an honest man, not a long time ago, who kept a little shack for the entertainment of travellers, serving them with meat and drink for their money; but seldom lodging any, unless they had nowhere else to go and were his particular acquaintance. Now he had a wife, a very comely woman, by whom he had two children, the one a dainty girl of about fifteen or sixteen years of age, still unmarried, the other a baby boy not yet one year old, whom his mother still fed at the breast. The girl had taken the fancy of a charming young gentleman of our city, one who used to travel much that way: whilst she, proud of such a lover, by endeavouring, with her agreeable carriage, to preserve his good opinion, soon felt the same liking for him: which love of theirs would several times have taken effect, to the desire of both, had not Pinuccio, for that was the young gentleman's name, carefully avoided it, for her good name as well as his own. Till at last his love growing every day more fervent, he resolved, in order to gain his end, to lie all night at her father's house; supposing, as he was acquainted with the state of the house, that it might then be effected without anyone's privity. As soon as he conceived his plan, he straightaway put it into effect. Accordingly he let a friend of his, named Adriano, into the secret, who had been acquainted with his love; so they hired a couple of horses one evening, and having their portmanteaus behind them filled with things of no moment, they set out from Florence; and, after taking a circuit, came, as it grew late, to the plain of Mugnone; when turning their horses, as if they had come from Romagna, they rode on to this cottage, and knocking at the door, the landlord, who was always very diligent in waiting upon his guests, immediately went and opened it. When Pinuccio accosted him, and said, 'Honest landlord, we must beg the favour of a night's lodging, for we designed to have reached Florence, but have so managed, that it is now much too late, as you see.' The host replied, 'You know very well, Pinuccio, how ill I can accommodate such gentlemen as yourselves; but, as you are come in at an unseasonable hour, and there is no time for your travelling any farther, I will gladly entertain you as well as I can.'

So they dismounted, and went into the house, having first taken care of their horses; and as they had provision along with them, they sat down and supped with him. Now there was only one little chamber in the house, which had three beds in it; namely, two at one end, and a third at the other, opposite to them, with just room to go between. The least bad and incommodious of which the landlord ordered to be sheeted for these two gentlemen, and put them to bed. A little time afterwards, neither of them being asleep, though they pretended it, he made the daughter lie in one of the beds that were made, and he and his wife went into the other, whilst she set the cradle with the child by her bedside. Things being so disposed, and Pinuccio having made an exact observation of every particular, as soon as he thought it a proper time, and that everyone was asleep, he arose, and went softly to bed to the daughter, and got in beside her; she welcomed him gladly, albeit with some trepidation, and so he continued with her to his great satisfaction. In the meantime, a cat happened to knock something down in the house, which awakened the good woman, who, fearing what it might be, got up in the dark, and went where she had heard the noise.

Whilst Adriano rose by chance, upon a particular occasion, and finding the cradle in his way he removed it without any design, to beside his own bed; and having done what he rose for, went to bed again, without taking any care to put the cradle back in its place.

The good woman, finding what was knocked over to be of no moment, never troubled herself to strike a light, to see farther about it, but after scolding the cat, returned groping to the bed where her husband lay; and not finding the cradle, 'Bless me,' she said to herself, 'I had like to have made a strange mistake, and gone to bed to my guests!' Going farther then, and finding the cradle which stood by Adriano, she stepped into bed to him, thinking it had been her husband. He was awake, and treated her very kindly, without saying a word all the time to undeceive her. At length Pinuccio, fearing lest he should fall asleep, and so be surprised with his mistress, after having made the best use of his time, left her to return to his own bed; when meeting with the cradle, and supposing that was the host's bed, he went farther, and stepped into the host's bed indeed, who immediately awoke; and Pinuccio thinking it was his friend, said to him, 'Surely, nothing was ever so sweet as Niccolosa! never man had so much pleasure from a woman, and I tell you I have been her guest six times since I left this bed!' The host hearing of this, and not liking it over well, said first to himself, 'What the devil is the man doing here?' Afterwards, being more passionate than wise, he cried out, 'Pinuccio, you are the greatest of villains to do as you have done; but I vow to God I will pay you for it.' Pinuccio, who was none of the sharpest men in the world, seeing his mistake, without ever thinking how to amend it, as he might have done, replied, 'You pay me? What can you do?' The hostess, imagining that she had been with her husband, said to Adriano, 'Alas! dost thou hear our guests? What is the matter with them?' He replied, with a laugh, 'Let them be hanged if they will, they got drunk, I suppose, last night.'

The woman, now distinguishing her husband's voice, and hearing Adriano, soon knew where she was, and with whom. Therefore she very wisely got up, without saying a word, and removed the cradle, there being no light in the chamber, and prudently drew it to her daughter's bed, and crept in to her;

when, seeming as if she had been awoke with their noise, she called out to her husband, to know what was the matter with him and the gentleman. The husband replied, 'Do not you hear what he says he has been doing tonight with our daughter?'

'He is a liar,' quoth she, 'he was never in bed with her, it was I, and I assure you I have never closed my eyes since. Therefore you were to blame to give any credit to him. You drink to that degree in the evening, that you rave all night long, and walk up and down, without knowing anything of the matter, and think you do wonders; I am surprised you do not break your neck. But what is that gentleman doing there? Why is he not in his own bed?' Adriano, for his part, perceiving that the good woman had found a very artful evasion, both for herself and daughter, said, 'Pinuccio, I have told you a hundred times that you should never lie out of your own house; for that great failing of yours, of walking in your sleep, and telling your dreams for truth, will be of ill consequence to you some time or other. Come here then to your own bed.'

The landlord hearing what his wife said, and what Adriano had just been speaking, began to think Pinuccio was really dreaming; so he shook him by the shoulders to rouse him, saying, 'Awake, and get thee to thy own bed.' Pinuccio, understanding what had passed, began now to ramble in his talk, like a man that was dreaming, with which our host made himself vastly merry. At last he seemed to wake, after much ado; and calling to Adriano, he said, 'Is it day? What do you wake me for?' 'Yes, it is,' quoth he, 'pray come hither.'

He, pretending to be very sleepy, got up at last from the host's bed and went to Adriano's. And in the morning the landlord laughed very heartily, and was full of jokes about him and his dreams. So they passed from one merry subject to another, whilst their horses were getting ready, and their portmanteaus tying upon them; when, taking the host's parting cup, they mounted and went to Florence, no less pleased with the manner of the thing's being effected, than with what followed. Afterwards Pinuccio contrived other means of being with Niccolosa, who still affirmed to her mother that he had been dreaming. Whilst she, well remembering how she had fared with Adriano, thought herself the only person that had been awake.

Gian Francesco Straparola

From THE NIGHTS

VIII.2, IX.5

TRANSLATED BY
W. G. WATERS (1894)

GIAN FRANCESCO STRAPAROLA

GIAN FRANCESCO STRAPAROLA (late 15th – mid 16th century) was born at Caravaggio (whence also the painter), near Milan. His collection of stories *Le Piacevoli Notti* (*The Agreeable Nights*) was published *c.* 1550 at Venice. He is said to have originated the story of Puss in Boots. The complete collection was translated by W. G. Waters in 1894.

From THE NIGHTS

Two brothers who are soldiers take to wife two sisters. One makes much of his wife, and is ill-rewarded by her disobedience. The other mis-handles his, and she does his will. The former inquires of the latter how he may gain his wife's obedience, and is duly instructed thereanent. Whereupon he threatens his wife with punishment, and she laughs in his face, and ultimately makes scoff at him.

The learned and prudent physician, when he foresees that a certain disease will manifest itself in the human body, adopts those remedies which in his estimation promise fairest to preserve life, without waiting for the distemper to make itself apparent, because a new wound heals more readily than an old one. And a husband when he takes to himself a wife – I must here crave forgiveness of the ladies – should act in precisely the same fashion, that is, never to let her get the upper hand, lest, when some time afterwards he may wish to keep her in order, he may find such task beyond his powers, and be forced to follow in her wake for the rest of his life. Such in sooth was the case of a certain soldier, who, wishing to induce his wife to mend her ways, after he had too long delayed to assert himself, had to put up with the consequences of this failing of his to the day of his death.

No great time ago there lived in Corneto, a village near Rome, situated in the patrimony of St Peter, two men who were sworn brothers; indeed, the love between them was just as great as it would have been supposing they had been born of the same womb. Of these one was called Pisardo and the other Silverio, and both one and the other followed the calling of arms, and were in the pay of the Pope; wherefore a great love and friendship sprang up between them though they did not dwell in the same house. Silverio, who was the younger in years and was under no family restraint, took to wife a certain Spinella, the daughter of a tailor, a very fair and lovely maiden, but somewhat over-flighty in humour! After the wedding was over and the bride brought home, Silverio found himself so completely inflamed and dominated by the power of her beauty that it seemed to him she must be beyond comparison, and straightway he fulfilled any demand that she might make upon him. Thus it came to pass that Spinella grew so arrantly haughty and masterful that she took little or no reck of her husband. And in time the doting fool fell into such a state that if he should ask his wife to do one thing, she would forthwith do something else, and whenever he told her to come here, she went there, and laughed at everything he said. Because the foolish fellow saw nothing except through his own foolish eyes, he could not pluck up heart of grace enough to reprove her, nor seek a remedy for his mistake, but let her go her own way, and work her own will in everything, according to her pleasure.

Before another year had passed away Pisardo took to wife Fiorella, the other daughter of the tailor, a damsel no less comely of person than Spinella, nor less sprightly in her disposition. When the wedding-feast was over, and the wife taken home to her husband's house, Pisardo brought forth a pair of men's breeches and two stout sticks, and said: 'Fiorella, you see here this pair of men's breeches. Now you take hold of one of these sticks and I will take hold of the other, and we will have a struggle over the breeches as to who shall wear them. Which one of us shall get the better of the other in this trial shall be the wearer, and the one who loses shall henceforth yield obedience to the winner.' When Fiorella heard this speech of her husband's, she answered without aught of hesitation in a gentle voice: 'Ah, my husband! what do you mean by such words as these? What is it you say? Are not you the husband, and I the wife, and ought not the wife always to bear herself obediently towards her husband? And, moreover, how could I ever bring myself to do such a foolish trick as this? Wear the breeches yourself, for assuredly they will become you much better than they will become me.' 'I, then,' said Pisardo, 'am to wear the breeches and to be the husband, and you, as my dearly-beloved wife, will always hold yourself obedient to me. But take good care that you keep the same mind and do not hanker after taking the husband's part for yourself, and giving me the wife's, for such licence you will never get from me.' Fiorella, who was a very prudent woman, confirmed all that she had hitherto said, and the husband, on his part, handed over to her the entire governance of his house, and committed all his chattels to her keeping, making known to her the order he desired to have observed in his household.

A little time after this Pisardo said to his wife: 'Fiorella, come with me. I wish to show you my horses, and to point out to you the right way to train them in case you should at any time have to put your hand to such work.' And when they were come into the stable he said, 'Now, Fiorella, what do you think of these horses of mine? Are they not handsome? Are they not finely tended?' And to this Fiorella replied that they were. 'But now see,' said Pisardo, 'how docile and handy they are.' Then picking up a whip he gave a touch now to this and now to that, saying, 'Go over there; come here.' And then the horses, putting their tails between their legs, went all together into a group obedient to their master's word. Now Pisardo had amongst his other horses a certain one, very beautiful to look upon, but at the same time vicious and lazy – a beast upon which he set but little store. He went up to this horse, and dealing it a sharp cut with the whip, cried out, 'Come here; go over there,' but the beast, sluggish and sullen by nature, took no heed of the whip, and refused to do anything his master ordered, lashing out vigorously now with one leg, now with the other, and now with both together. Whereupon Pisardo, remarking the brute's stubborn humour, took a tough, stout stick, and began to baste its hide therewith so vigorously that he was soon out of breath with fatigue. However, the horse, now more stubborn than ever, let Pisardo lay on as he would and refused to budge an inch; so Pisardo, seeing how persistent was the obstinacy of the brute, flew into a violent rage, and grasping the sword which he wore by his side he slew it forthwith.

Fiorella, when she saw what her husband had done, was mightily moved with pity for the horse, and cried out, 'Alas, my husband! Why have you killed your horse, seeing that he was so shapely to look upon? Surely it is a great pity to have slain him thus.' To this Pisardo replied, with his face strongly moved by passion, 'Know then that all those who eat my bread and refuse to do my will must look to be paid in exactly the same coin.' Fiorella, when she heard this speech, was greatly distressed, and said to herself, 'Alas! what a wretched miserable woman I am! What an evil day it was for me when I met this man! I believed I had chosen a man of good sense for my husband, and lo! I have become the prey of this brutal fellow. Behold how, for little or no fault, he has killed this beautiful horse!' And thus she went on, grieving sorely to herself, for she knew not to what end her husband had spoken in this wise.

On account of what had passed Fiorella fell into such a taking of fear and terror of her husband, that she would tremble all over at the very sound of his footsteps, and whenever he might demand any service of her she would carry out his wishes straightway. Indeed, she would understand his meaning almost before he might open his mouth, and never a cross word passed between them. Silverio, who, on account of the friendship he felt for Pisardo, would often visit the house of the latter, and dine and sup there, remarked the manners and carriage of Fiorella, and, being much astonished thereat, said to himself: 'Great God! Why was it not my lot to have Fiorella for my wife, as is the good luck of my brother Pisardo? See how deftly she manages the house, and goes about her business without any uproar! See how obedient she is to her husband, and how she carries out every wish of his! But my wife, miserable wight that I am, does everything to annoy me, and uses me in as vile a fashion as possible.'

One day it chanced that Silverio and Pisardo were in company together, talking of various things, when the former spake thus: 'Pisardo, my brother, you are aware of the love that there is between us. Now, on this account, I would gladly learn what is the method you have followed in the training of your wife, seeing that she is altogether obedient to you, and treats you in such loving wise. Now I, however gently I may ask Spinella to do anything, find that she always stubbornly refuses to answer me, and, beyond this, does the exact opposite to what I ask her to do.' Whereupon Pisardo, smiling, set forth word by word the plan and the means he had adopted when first he brought his wife home, and counselled his friend to go and do likewise, and to see whether he might not also succeed, adding that in case this remedy should not be found efficient, he would not know what other course to recommend.

Silverio was much pleased with this excellent counsel, and having taken his leave he went his way. When he reached his house he called his wife at once, and brought out a pair of his breeches and two sticks, following exactly the same course as Pisardo had recommended. When Spinella saw what he was doing, she cried out: 'What new freak is this of yours? Silverio, what are you about? What ridiculous fancy has got into your head? Surely you are gone stark mad! Don't you think everybody knows that men, and not women, should wear the breeches? And what need is there now to set about doing things which are beside all purpose?' But Silverio made no answer and went on with the task he had begun, laying down all sorts of rules for the regulation of his household. Spinella, altogether astonished at this humour of her husband, said in a mocking way: 'Peradventure, Silverio, it seems to you that I know not how to manage a house rightly, since you make all this ado about letting your meaning be known?' But still the husband kept silence, and having taken his wife with him into the stable, he did with the horses everything which Pisardo had done, and in the end slew one of them. Spinella, when she saw this fool's work, was convinced in her own mind that her husband had in truth lost his wits, and spake thus: 'By your faith, tell me, husband, what crazy humours are these that have risen to your head? What is the true meaning of all this foolishness you are doing without thinking of the issue? Perhaps it is your evil fate to have gone mad.' Then answered Silverio: 'I am not mad, but I have made up my mind that anyone who lives at my charges and will not obey me shall be treated in such fashion as you have seen me use this morning towards my horses.'

Whereupon Spinella, when she perceived the drift of her besotted husband's brutal deed, said: 'Ah, you wretched dolt! It must be clear enough to you that your horse was nothing but a poor beast to allow himself to be killed in this manner. What is the full meaning of this whim of yours? Perhaps you think you can deal with me as you have dealt with the horse? Certes, if such is your belief, you are hugely mistaken, and you put your hand much too late to the task of setting things in order after the fashion you desire. The bone is become too hard, the sore is now all ulcerated, and there is no cure at hand. You should have been more prompt in compassing the righting of these curious wrongs of yours. You fool! you brainless idiot! do you not see what damage and disgrace must come upon you through these doltish deeds out of number of which you have been guilty? And what profit do you deem you will get from them? None, as I am a living woman.'

Silverio, when he listened to the words of his shrewd wife, knew in his heart that his effort, through the doting affection he had hitherto spent on Spinella, had miserably failed; so he made up his mind, greatly to his chagrin, to put up patiently with his wretched lot till death should come to release him. And Spinella, when she perceived how little her husband's plan had turned out to his advantage, resolved that if in the past she had worked her own will with a finger she would henceforth work it with an arm; for a woman headstrong by nature would sooner die a thousand times than go aside aught from the path which she has deliberately marked out for herself.

NINTH NIGHT, FABLE 5

The Florentines and the Bergamasques convoke their learned men for a disputation, whereupon the Bergamasques, by a certain astute trick, outwit the Florentines their opponents.

I would remind you, comely ladies, that, however great may be the difference between men of wisdom and letters and men who are gross-minded and sensual, it has now and then come to pass that sages have been worsted by men of small learning. Is not indeed a clear proof of this set forth in the Holy Scriptures, where we may read how the simple and despised apostles confounded the understanding of those who were full of knowledge and wisdom? Also I will strive to set this plainly before you in this little fable of mine.

In times long past (as I have often heard tell by my grandsires, and perchance you may have heard the same) it happened that a number of Florentine and Bergamasque merchants were travelling together, and (as it not seldom occurs) they fell to discussing and divers matters. Now, as they were passing from one subject to another, a certain Florentine said: 'Of a truth you Bergamasques, as far as we can judge, are mightily stupid and thick-headed, and, were it not for the little traffic in merchandise which you exercise, you would be good for nothing on account of your coarse-grained tempers. It happens indeed that Fortune allows to you a certain degree of success as merchants, but this favour of hers is assuredly not granted to you by reason of your keenness of intellect, or of any learning that you may have gotten, but rather because of your rapacity and avarice, which cause you to be very sharp-set to grasp the smallest gain. In good sooth I know no men who are more gross and ignorant than you.'

On hearing these words a certain Bergamasque came forward and said: 'Now I, for my part, maintain that we Bergamasques are worth more than you Florentines according to any reckoning you like to bring forward. For although you Florentines may be gifted with a smooth and wheedling speech, which delights more than our own dialect the ears of those who listen, still in every other respect you are a long way inferior to the men of Bergamo. If you will take the trouble to make candid observation, you will find there is no man amongst our people, whether of high or low degree, who has not contrived to acquire some knowledge of letters. Beyond this, we are all of us always ready and eager for the prosecution of any great-souled enterprise. No one can say that a disposition of this sort is commonly to be met with amongst you Florentines, except perhaps in the case of a few of you.' Hereupon there arose a great contention between one party and the other; the Bergamasques not being willing to give way to the Florentines, nor the Florentines to the Bergamasques, each one speaking up for his own side; until at last a Bergamasque merchant arose and said: 'What is the good of all these wrangling words? Let us put the matter to the proof and make due provision for the holding of a solemn discussion, for which we will, Florentines and Bergamasques alike, let come together the very flower of our learned men, and in this wise it may be clearly demonstrated which of us holds the first place.' To this proposition the Florentines forthwith gave their assent, but after this there still remained to be settled the question whether the Florentines should go to Bergamo, or the Bergamasques to Florence; wherefore, after much discussion, they agreed to settle the question by casting lots. So having prepared two ballots and put them into a vase, they drew one out, which drawing proclaimed that the Florentines should go to Bergamo.

The day for the discussion was fixed to be the calends of May, and, this point having been decided, the merchants went back to their respective cities and referred the whole matter to their wise and learned townsmen, who, as soon as they heard what was proposed to be done, were greatly pleased thereanent, and set to work to prepare themselves for long and subtle disputations. The Bergamasques, like the astute and crafty folk they were, began to lay plans how they might best contrive to overreach the Florentines and to leave them covered with shame and confusion; thus, after having convoked all the learned men of the city, grammarians, rhetoricians, lawyers, canonists, philosophers, theologians, and doctors of every other faculty, they chose out of these the men of keenest wit, and bade them keep themselves in readiness at home, in order that they might do service as the rock and fortress of the city's reputation in the forthcoming dispute with the Florentines. The rest of the learned doctors they caused to be dressed in ragged clothes, and then bade them go out of the city and bestow themselves at different places along the road by which the Florentines must pass, directing always to speak with them in the Latin tongue. Therefore these learned men of Bergamo, having dressed themselves in coarse clothes and gone down amongst the peasants of the plain, set themselves to work at divers sorts of labour — some dug ditches, others delved the earth with pickaxe and shovel, one man doing this thing, and another that.

While the Bergamasque doctors were labouring in this fashion, so that anyone would have taken them to be mere peasants, lo and behold! the chosen Florentines came riding past in great pomp and splendour, and when they noticed these men working in the fields, they cried out to them: 'God be with you, good brothers!' Whereupon the peasants answered: *'Bene veniant tanti viri!'* The Florentines, thinking they were making some joke, said: 'How many miles have we yet to cover before we shall come to the city of Bergamo?' And to this the Bergamasques answered: *'Decem, vel circa.'* When the Florentines heard this reply they said: 'Brethren, we address you in the vulgar tongue, whence comes it that you answer us in Latin?' The Bergamasques replied: *'Ne miremini, excellentissimi domini. Unusquisque enim nostrum sic, ut auditus, loquitur, quoniam majores, et sapientiores nostri sic nos docuerunt.'* Having left these men behind, the Florentines, as they continued their journey, saw other peasants who were digging ditches beside the high road, and, coming to a halt, they spake to them thus: 'Ho, friends! ho, there! may God be with you!' To which greeting the Bergamasques answered: *'Et Deus vobiscum semper sit!'* 'How far is it to Bergamo?' inquired the Florentines; whereupon the others answered: *'Exigua vobis restat via.'* And after this reply they went on from one manner of discourse to another, till at last they began to dispute together on questions of philosophy, concerning which these Bergamasque peasants argued with such weight and subtlety that the Florentine doctors were hard pressed to answer them. Then, struck with astonishment, they said one to another, 'Of a truth it is a marvellous thing that these clownish fellows, who must spend all their time labouring at all manner of rural tasks, should be thus excellently instructed in polite letters.' Then they rode on towards a neat and well-kept hostelry, standing at no great distance from the city; but, before they had come thither, a stable varlet advanced to meet them, and invited them to alight at the inn, saying: *'Domini, libetne vobis hospitari? Hic enim vobis erit bonum hospitium.'* And, for the reason that the Florentines were already wearied from the long journey they had made, they gladly dismounted from their horses, and, when they would have gone upstairs to go and repose themselves, the innkeeper came forward and spake thus, *'Excellentissimi domini, placetne vobis ut praeparetur coena? Hic enim sunt bona vina, ova recentia, carnes, volatilia, et alia hujusmodi.'* Hereupon the Florentines were filled with greater amazement than before, and knew not what to say, forasmuch as all the people with whom they had conversed spoke Latin as if they had studied it from their earliest days.

A little after this there came into the room a serving-maid, who was, in sooth, a certain nun, a woman of great knowledge and learning. She had been well instructed as to how she should bear herself at this juncture; wherefore she addressed them saying: *'Indigentne dominationes vestrae re aliqua? Placet, ut sternantur lectuli, ut requiem capiatis?'* The Florentines were utterly overcome with astonishment at these words of the serving-woman, and straightway began to talk with her, and she, after she had discoursed on many matters, using always the Latin tongue, brought forward for debate the subject of theology, and spake thereanent with such universal knowledge that every one of those who heard her was constrained to give her the highest praise. While she was thus holding dispute with the Florentine doctors there entered one dressed as a furnace-man, and swart with coal-dust, and he, hearing the discussion which was going on between the serving-maid and the strangers, contrived to interpose a speech of his own, and put forth an interpretation of the Holy Scriptures so learned and erudite that all the Florentine doctors declared that they had never before listened to any discourse which excelled it.

When this controversy had come to an end the Florentines withdrew to get some rest, and the next day they took counsel amongst themselves whether they should return to Florence at once or go on to Bergamo. After much wrangling they came to the decision that it would be wiser to go back straightway. 'For,' said they, 'if such deep learning is found amongst field-labourers and innkeepers, and male and female servants, what must we expect to meet in the city itself, where men are always more accomplished than in the country, and given to nought else than the prosecution of learning from one year's end to another?' As soon as they had come to this decision, without hesitating further, and without having ever seen the walls of the city of Bergamo, they mounted their horses and rode back to Florence. In this wise the Bergamasques, on account of this wily stratagem of theirs, contrived to outwit the Florentines, and ever since that time the Bergamasques have enjoyed a privilege, granted to them by the emperor, to travel securely in all parts of the world without hindrance.

Anton Francesco Grazzini

From LE CENE

I.I

NEWLY TRANSLATED BY
BRUCE PENMAN

ANTON FRANCESCO GRAZZINI

ANTON FRANCESCO GRAZZINI (1503–84) was a Florentine, and a founder member of the Crusca Academy, whose special concern was to protect the purity of the Italian written language, something very close to the heart of the Florentines, who had effectively originated it. He is principally remembered for the stories published under the title *Le Cene* (*The Repasts*). A handful of the stories figure in Thomas Roscoe's *The Italian Novelists*, 1836. D. H. Lawrence translated 'The Story of Doctor Manente' (*Le Cene*, x.2).

Raiffeisenkasse
6311 **Wildschönau**, Bez. Kufstein
reg. Gen. m. u. H.

Kauf-Abrechnung
Note of purchase
Décompte d'achāt

BU
V
D

Wir kaufen von
We bought from
Nous avons acheté de

Paß-Nr.

Paß-Ausstellungsort

Frohnweiler 9598

Datum	Kurs offiziel rate cours officiel	Schilling

Kommission und Spesen
Commission and charges
Commissions et frais

Bar-Auszahlung
payment in cash
paiement en argent comptant

Konto
account
compte

} S

Raiffeisenkasse
6311 **Wildschönau**, Bez. Kufstein
reg. Gen. m. u. H.

From LE CENE

I.I

Salvestro Bisdomini, imagining that he is bringing to the doctor the urine of his sick wife, brings instead that of his healthy maidservant; on the doctor's prescription, he goes to bed with his wife and cures her; and to the maidservant he gives a husband, for she needs one.

Not many years ago, there was a very learned and skilful physician in Florence, whose name was Dr Mingo. He was an old man at the time of this story, and tormented by the gout, so that he seldom left his house. To pass the time, however, and to help his friends, he would still occasionally write a prescription. He had one young friend called Salvestro Bisdomini, whose wife fell ill. Salvestro consulted several doctors; but, far from curing her, none of them could even diagnose the disease, and in the end he went to see Dr Mingo. He told him all about her illness, and explained that all the doctors who had seen her had taken an extremely gloomy view of the case.

Dr Mingo was very sympathetic, and told his friend how sorry he was, but added that he must not give way to despair.

'These terrible pains that women have,' he said, 'are rather like a sudden blow on the elbow, which hurts very badly, but soon passes off. So don't be afraid – you aren't going to lose her.'

Salvestro, who was an exceptionally loving and devoted husband, was not convinced, and begged him to prescribe something for her.

'If only I could come and see her,' said the doctor, 'we could do something, but as it is ... well, never mind, bring me a specimen of her water tomorrow morning, and if I can see a way of helping her, you may be sure I will do my duty.'

He asked a few more questions about the details of her illness, and then went on:

'The specimen must be taken as soon as possible after five in the morning. It must be kept separate, and brought to me for examination a few hours later.'

Salvestro thanked the doctor warmly, and went back home, feeling much happier. As soon as he had finished his dinner, he told his wife that he wanted to take a specimen of her water to their old friend on the following day, and explained that the sample must be one passed at or just after five in the morning.

His wife was very pleased, as she was most anxious to recover her health.

Salvestro called their young maidservant – a girl of twenty-two or so – and told her to look after the details. He lent her his alarm clock, and set it for her, and told her that as soon as it went off she must get up and collect the first specimen of urine that her mistress passed, and put it in a special jar.

Salvestro went off to sleep in another room, leaving the maid to look after his wife, and get her anything she wanted during the night, which was their normal arrangement. The alarm went off at the right time, and the maid, whose name was Sandra, got out of bed and waited until her mistress made up her mind to get up and pass water. Then Sandra poured the specimen very carefully into the jar, which she placed on the floor next to a cupboard, and hurried back to bed.

When she woke up in the morning, she remembered that she must be ready to give the specimen to her master as soon as he asked for it; so she jumped up and quickly went to the place where she had left the jar. To her horror, she found that it had somehow been knocked over, perhaps by the cat, and the specimen was all over the floor. She could not think what excuse to make, and was very frightened. She knew that Salvestro was inclined to be hot-tempered, and was afraid he would scold her, and perhaps beat her too. As she happened at that moment to want to make water herself, she decided to replace the specimen in that way, and soon had the jar half full again.

Soon afterwards Salvestro came and asked for the specimen, and Sandra carried out her plan, giving him a sample of her own water instead of that of the invalid. He took the jar without the slightest suspicion, hid it under his cloak, and sped off to his friend's house. Dr Mingo examined the specimen, and was very surprised at what he saw.

'She doesn't seem to have anything wrong with her at all,' he said.

'I only wish you were right,' said Salvestro. 'Poor thing, she can hardly turn over in bed.'

Still unable to see any kind of illness in the water, the doctor turned to his friend, and gave him a long medical disquisition, with quotations from the best authorities, which ended in a request for a second specimen the following morning.

Then Salvestro went off to work, leaving the doctor very puzzled.

That evening, when Salvestro had returned to his house and had his dinner, he made the same arrangements with Sandra as the previous night, and went to bed. Once again, the alarm clock went off at the appointed time, Salvestro's wife provided her specimen, and the maid poured it into the jar and went back to sleep.

Early in the morning, she woke up again and began to think the matter over. She was alarmed by the thought that if the doctor saw a real specimen of her mistress's water, he would notice the difference and guess what had happened. She bitterly regretted what she had done the day before; Salvestro would be very angry, she thought, and would get the truth out of her. Then she would either lose her job, or get a sound thrashing. In the end she thought it best to throw away the new specimen and fill the jar up again as she had before; and she jumped out of bed and did so.

She was a typical Casentino girl, about twenty-two years old, as I think I said before; not tall, but well-covered, with a good waist, and very dark hair; fresh and firm to the touch, but with a bad complexion, rather too red in the face. Her eyes were big and shining, and projected a little, so that sometimes they seemed ready to shoot out of her head, and sometimes they seemed to send out sparks. She was a hard-handed peasant girl, fit to grind at the mill after harvest; a stout-hearted mare, who would pull anyone out of the mud.

In due course Salvestro asked her for the jar, and went off with it to the doctor's house. Dr Mingo looked at the specimen, and looked at it again, even more amazed than the day before.

He could see nothing in it at all, except for certain signs of hot-bloodedness.

'Salvestro,' he said with a smile, 'tell me the truth – how long is it since you slept with your wife?'

'This is no time for joking!' said Salvestro indignantly. But when the doctor repeated the question, he said it was more than two months.

'I see,' said the doctor, and after thinking it over for a minute, he decided that he had better see a third specimen.

'Cheer up, my dear fellow,' he said. 'I think I know now what is wrong with your wife; and if my idea is correct, we shall soon be able to get her right again. Let me have another specimen to-morrow morning, and then I'll tell you what to do.'

Salvestro went happily home to tell his wife the good news, longing for the next day to come, so that he could hear what must be done to restore his dear companion to health. After dinner, he sat up with his wife for some time, trying to cheer her up; and then he gave the maid the same instructions as before and went off to bed.

Sandra's mind was made up – to avoid the detection of her past two acts of folly, she would repeat them a third time. So the following morning she again gave Salvestro a specimen of her own water instead of her mistress's; and he took it along to the doctor as quickly as he could. Dr Mingo looked at it, and saw that it was as clear and bright as ever.

'Come here, Salvestro,' he said, turning to him with a smile. 'If you really want your wife to get better, as you say you do, you must have intercourse with her. I can find nothing wrong with her, except hotbloodedness, and intercourse is the only cure for that. I must insist on your doing it, the sooner the better, and making every effort to serve her as vigorously as you can. If it doesn't work, there's no hope for her.'

Salvestro had complete faith in the doctor, and promised to do his duty. He left his friend with many thanks, and eagerly awaited the night which was to enable him to drive away his wife's sickness, and restore her fully to health.

Evening came at last, and he ordered a very good dinner, which was served on a little table in her bedroom. He asked a friend of his to join him – a cheerful and amusing man, full of witty sayings – and they had a very pleasant meal. Then he said good night to his friend, and told Sandra to go and sleep in her own room, so that he was left alone with his wife. Still joking and laughing, he began to take off his clothes. His wife watched in terrified amazement to see what he would do next. Soon he was stark naked, and, jumping into bed beside her, he began to kiss her, hug her and fondle her. She was appalled at this, and said:

'Good heavens, Salvestro, what does this mean? Have you gone out of your mind? What on earth are you trying to do?'

'Keep still, you silly girl, and don't be afraid,' said Salvestro. 'I'm curing you.'

And then he started to get on top of her, and she began to scream.

'You unfeeling brute!' she cried. 'Have you decided to murder me like this? Can't you wait for my illness to finish me off? It won't be long now anyway. Do you have to hurry me into the next world in this disgusting way?'

'What do you mean?' said Salvestro. 'I'm keeping you alive, sweetheart; this is the right treatment for your trouble. Our friend, Dr Mingo, told me so, and you know he's the best doctor in the world. Just keep quiet, and keep still, and we'll soon have you up and about again.'

She screamed and tried to defend herself, covering him with reproaches and abuse; but as she was very weak, she could not resist his entreaties and his superior force for long. So they celebrated the rites of holy matrimony; and though she had resolved to lie perfectly still, as if she were a statue, she presently found herself participating to the full. Her husband held her tightly in his arms, and she really began to feel that he was infusing health into her veins, as he had said he would. The nausea and exhaustion of fever suddenly left her body, the heaviness and confusion left her brain, and the fatigue and slackness left her limbs. She felt light and free, as if all pain and discomfort had been flushed away with the generative fluid.

After the first encounter, both of them lay still for a little, to get their breath back. But Salvestro had the doctor's words at heart, and was soon ready for a second bout, which was followed not long after by a third. Then they fell into an exhausted sleep. Salvestro's wife had not been able to close an eye for the previous three weeks, but she went straight off to sleep this time. She did not wake up for eight hours, and then only because her husband began to fondle her again in preparation for the fourth assault, which took place in broad daylight. Then she went back to sleep, and did not wake until eleven o'clock.

Salvestro got up, and brought her grapes and preserved fruit with his own hands, as if she had just had a baby. Though it was the middle of the morning, she ate more than she had eaten for the whole of the previous week, and with much better appetite.

Next Salvestro went round to the doctor and told him exactly what had happened, omitting no detail. Dr Mingo was very pleased, and told him to keep it up.

Salvestro went off to attend to certain business affairs, but he was back at home in time for the midday meal. He had ordered a fine, fat roasted capon, and he and his wife happily ate it together. There was nothing wrong with her appetite now – nor with her thirst.

In the evening they had an excellent dinner, and then went to bed together; and this time she felt no repugnance or fear, but a serene confidence in the rightness of the medicine. Salvestro continued the treatment for the next week, and did his best to keep his wife happy; and, to cut a long story short, in five or six days she was up and about, and in another three or four days after that she had got her strength and colour back, and was as well and pretty as she had ever been before, to her great delight and that of her husband. They returned due thanks to heaven and to their old friend Dr Mingo, whose powers of observation and diagnosis had saved her from so deadly an illness, by such an agreeable remedy, and restored her to perfect health.

Soon afterwards the time of carnival arrived, and one evening Salvestro and his wife were sitting by the fire in the best of spirits, laughing and cracking jokes. Remembering how the confusion over the specimens had been the saving of her mistress's life and her master's happiness, Sandra came out with the whole story, exactly as it had happened. After their first astonishment, they laughed at her tale until the tears came into their eyes.

The very first thing Salvestro did the following morning was to go round to Dr Mingo's house and tell him all about it. The doctor was beside himself with amazement, and said that it was a most fascinating case. He reflected that Sandra, by an action which might have been expected to do her mistress a great deal of harm, had unwittingly been the cause of her recovery, and he could not help laughing a little. He told all his visitors about the case, as if it had been the story of a miracle. And he wrote it down in his book of prescriptions, as a general recommendation for women between the ages of sixteen and fifty, that in all cases of serious female illness, where other treatment had failed and the doctors had given up hope, intercourse was a most effective remedy, which would soon lead to a complete cure; quoting the example of Salvestro's wife as a case in point, which had occurred in his own practice.

Next he made it clear to Salvestro that his maidservant, who had done him such a good turn, was in very bad need of a husband. 'Otherwise,' he said, 'she may easily become the victim of some strange and dangerous illness.'

Salvestro acknowledged his obligation towards Sandra by giving her in marriage to one of his workmen. The bridegroom was a strong-backed young fellow of her own age – a new broom well qualified to make a clean sweep, who soon found the shortest road to her affections.

Matteo Maria Bandello

From LE NOVELLE

1.26, III.62

NEWLY TRANSLATED BY
GEORGE BULL

1.28

TRANSLATED BY
PERCY E. PINKERTON (1895)

MATTEO MARIA BANDELLO

MATTEO MARIA BANDELLO (1485–c. 1561) was a Lombard, from near Tortona. Being a courtier in the much-contested Duchy of Milan, his life was full of vicissitudes, and he ended his days as Bishop of Agen in France. He is the best known of the populous school of sixteenth-century 'novelists'; the 214 stories in *Le Novelle* provide a valuable panorama of life in sixteenth-century Italy, as seen from the top of the social scale. With regard to the stories here reproduced: Shakespeare was by no means the only English playwright who went to the Italian 'novelists' for his plots; here is the source of John Webster's *The Duchess of Malfi*. There must be an element of painful autobiography in Cornelio's adventures as an outlaw. The striking thing about the Henry VIII story is that it was published by 1554. Henry only died in 1547 – it is interesting to see how quickly history could turn to legend. A number of the stories feature in Thomas Roscoe's *The Italian Novelists*, 1836. John Payne produced a complete translation in 1890. Percy E. Pinkerton translated *12 Tales from Bandello*, 1895. G. Fenton's sixteenth-century translation was somewhat modernized by R. Harris in 1924.

From LE NOVELLE

1.26

Antonio Bologna marries the Duchess of Amalfi, and they are both slain.

As many of you were able to know, Antonio Bologna of Naples lodged with Signor Silvio Savello when he lived in Milan. Then, when Signor Silvio left, he went to Francesco Acquaviva, the Marquess of Bitonto, who, after his capture in the defeat of Ravenna, was imprisoned by the French in the castle of Milan until, having given strict pledges, he was released and lived in the city for some while. Then the Marquess paid a fat ransom and returned to Naples.

In consequence, Bologna, with three servants, went to live with Alfonso Visconti, and would ride about Milan like a gentleman. He was a man of great prowess and gallantry, very handsome to look at, with a dashing spirit and cutting a splendid figure on a horse. Moreover, he was no mean scholar and he sang very sweetly to his own accompaniment on the lute. I know that some of you here heard him singing, or rather plaintively bewailing the state in which he found himself, the day that Signora Ippolita Sforza and Bentivoglio constrained him to play. In France he had been in the continuous service of the unhappy Federico of Aragon, who after being chased out of the Kingdom of Naples had thrown himself into the arms of Louis the twelfth King of France of that name, who had received him with the greatest kindness; Bologna, on his return from France, went back to live in his own house in Naples.

For many years he had served King Federico as his majordomo. So not long after, he was asked by the Duchess of Amalfi, the daughter of Henry of Aragon and the sister of the Cardinal, if he would enter her service as majordomo. And Bologna, who was accustomed to Court life and very devoted to the cause of Aragon, accepted the proposal and went to her.

The Duchess had been widowed while she was still very young, and now she governed both the son of her dead husband and the Duchy of Amalfi. Still young, active, and beautiful, she was enjoying the pleasures available to one of her condition, and she disliked the idea of marrying again and putting her son under the government of someone else; so she determined that if at all possible she would find some worthy lover and enjoy her youth with him. She saw many of her subjects and as many others again who seemed to be well mannered and courteous, and having scrupulously studied their behaviour and manner it seemed to her there was none the equal of her own majordomo. For in fact he was a very handsome man, tall and well built, with a fine and charming manner and endowed with many splendid talents. So she fell passionately in love with him, and every day she more and more sang his praises and commended his ways, till she was so inflamed that she knew she could not live without seeing him and being with him.

Bologna was no simpleton or sluggard, and although he did not aspire to such heights, perceiving this love of hers, he let it so penetrate into his heart that he had no other care save to love her in return. And so they lived, in love with each other. Then taking a fresh look at things, the Duchess (in order to give as little offence as possible to God and to bar the way in future to any reproach that might be directed against her) determined without telling any others of her love to become not Bologna's lover but his wife, and to enjoy their love quietly together until it was necessary to reveal their marriage. Having reached this decision in her own mind, one day she sent for Bologna to come to her room, and stood with him beside a window, as she often did when she discussed his duties with him; then she began to speak to him as follows:

'If I were speaking with anyone else, Antonio, I should be very doubtful of saying as much as I have decided to reveal to you. But I know that you are a gentleman of high discretion and intelligence, nourished and reared in the royal courts of Alfonso II, of Ferdinand and of Federico, my relations; and so I am utterly convinced and it pleases me to think that, when you have heard the honest explanations I give, you will find yourself of one opinion with me. For if I find otherwise, I shall be forced to suppose that you lack the fine intelligence everyone credits you with. Now as you know, through the death of my husband of happy memory, I was left a widow very young, and have till now so lived that no one, no matter how stern and critical a judge, could as far as the purity of my life is concerned reproach me a jot. And similarly I have so ordered the government of this Duchy that when the time comes that my son is of an age to govern, I hope that he will find its affairs in better order than they were left by my lord the Duke. For as well as my having paid off fifteen thousand ducats of debts, accumulated for past wars by my lord the Duke of happy memory, I have purchased a rich barony in Calabria, and today I owe not a farthing's worth of debts and my household is well provided with all that is necessary.

'Well, it had been my intention to continue living as a widow and, as I have done so far, to spend my days visiting now this estate and now that castle, passing some of my time in Naples, and attending to the government of the Duchy; but now I think that I should change my plans and make another life for myself. And in truth I think that I should do far better to find myself a husband than to do as some women do who incur the enmity of God and the lasting condemnation of the world by giving themselves in prey to their lovers.

'I well know what is said about a certain Duchess of this Kingdom, even though she loves and is loved by one of the chief barons, and I know that you understand me. But to return to my own affairs, you see that I am still young and that I am neither cross-eyed nor a cripple, nor do I have an evil face that must be hidden from the world. I live most comfortably, as you see every day, and so I cannot help entertaining thoughts of love. I would not know how to find a man equal in rank to my former husband, unless I were to marry some child who as soon as he tired of me would drive me from his bed and lead his mistresses there instead. For there is no baron who is both unmarried and of an age suitable for me. And so, having thought about this at great length, I have resolved to find a suitable gentleman and to take him for my husband. But in order to avoid the murmurings of the people and not to fall foul of my noble relations, and especially my brother, the Cardinal, I want to keep the matter secret until the time comes when it can be revealed with less risk.

'The man I intend to take for my husband has an income of about a thousand ducats, and with my dowry, including the additional amount left me on his death by my lord the Duke, can command about two thousand ducats, as well as the household property that is mine. And if I were not able to live up to the rank of Duchess, I should be happy to live as a gentlewoman. And now I should like to hear what you advise me.'

Antonio, having heard this long speech by the Duchess, did not know what to say because, being certain that he was loved by her and himself loving her in no small measure, he had no wish to see her marry while his own love was still not yet gratified. So he remained silent, his face marking his discomposure, and instead of answering he sighed deeply. The Duchess had guessed what her lover was thinking and she was not displeased by this evidence that she was fervently loved by him; and so to put an end to his misery she said to him:

'Antonio, don't be dejected or disheartened for, if you wish it, I am resolved that you shall be my husband.'

Hearing this, her lover returned from death to life, welcomed what the Duchess was proposing with many well chosen words, and offered himself to her not as a husband but as a most loyal and humble servant. Being assured of each other's trust, they spoke at great length together and after much deliberation they arranged to remain together in the best and most secret way that could be devised. The Duchess had a maid in her service, the daughter of her childhood nurse; in her she had always confided her thoughts. So she sent for her, and when just the three of them were together she was married to Bologna in the presence of her maid.

For many years their marriage remained a secret, and almost every night they slept together. And this intercourse continuing to their mutual delight, the Duchess became pregnant and gave birth to a male child. Everything was so well arranged that no one at Court was aware of this, and Bologna had the baby well nurtured and christened with the name of Federico.

They continued to make love together, and the Duchess became pregnant once again and gave birth to a beautiful baby girl. This time they were not able to keep things hidden so well and prevent many from learning that the Duchess had been pregnant and given birth. And when the rumour got about, the story came to the ears of her two brothers, namely the Cardinal of Aragon and the other. And, having heard that their sister had had a child, but not knowing who the father was, they determined not to put up with the shame of it and began with great diligence to spy in every possible way on every move and act of the Duchess.

With the Court full of rumour and with people in the service of the brothers doing nothing but spy out what had happened, Bologna feared that the maid would reveal how matters really stood, and so one day when walking with the Duchess he said:

'You know, madam, the suspicions that your brothers have concerning this second birth of yours and the relentless way in which they are trying to find out the whole truth. I am very much afraid that they may have some clue as to my role and that they may one day have me killed. You understand their nature better than I do, and you know how ruthless one of them is. And since I do not believe that they would ever treat you cruelly, I am sure that were they to have me killed that would be the end of the matter. So I am resolved to go to Naples, and, once my affairs are settled there, to go on to Ancona, where I shall be able to arrange for my money to be sent to me. And I shall stay there till we see that your brothers have tired of their suspicions. After that, time will be our counsellor.'

For a long time, the two spoke together. Finally, grieved beyond words, Bologna left her and arranged his affairs, leaving them in the hands of a cousin of his, as he had decided, and went to Ancona. And there he lived as a gentleman, and was suitably attended. He had brought his son and daughter with him, and he had them brought up with the greatest care. The Duchess, whom he had left pregnant for the third time, could not bear to live without her dear husband, and she suffered so intensely that she almost went out of her mind. And after endlessly fretting to imagine what would happen, fearing that if this third birth should be brought to light her brothers would make life impossible for her, she determined that she would rather rejoin her husband and live with him as an ordinary gentlewoman than keep the title of Duchess without him.

And there are those who would say that love is not the most powerful thing! But who are they who would maintain such an opinion? Truly, its force is greater by far than anything we can imagine. Do we not see that every day love works the most rare and marvellous effects in the world and that it conquers everything? Indeed, it is often said that to love in moderation is impossible. For when it wishes, love makes kings, princes and great nobles fall a prey to the basest of women, and even become their slaves.

But let us leave this argument and return to our story. Once she had determined to go to her husband in Ancona, the Duchess secretly forewarned him of everything. At the same time, she sent to Ancona all the money and belongings she could. She then gave out that she had vowed to go to Loreto. And, having made all necessary preparations and arranged for the care of her son who was to stay behind as Duke, she set out on the journey, well and honourably escorted and with a long train of mules. She reached Loreto, where she had High Mass sung and offered rich gifts to the holy and ancient shrine; and as everyone was expecting her to return to the Kingdom, she said to them:

'We are only fifteen miles from Ancona and we understand that it is a beautiful and ancient city; so it would be only fitting to spend a day there.'

All agreed to the Duchess's suggestion, and so, with the mule train going ahead, the whole company took the road to Ancona. Bologna, who was informed of everything, had suitably prepared his house for the distinguished company and had had a rich and abundant banquet prepared. His palace was on the main road so that it was necessary to pass in front of the door. The steward, who had arrived in the morning to arrange dinner, was led into the house by Bologna, who told him that he had prepared the dwelling for her ladyship the Duchess. The steward was pleased with this, for although Bologna had withdrawn from Court, nobody knew what his reason had been for doing so, and he was held by everyone in high regard.

When he thought it was time, Bologna mounted his horse

and with a fine escort of gentlemen from Ancona rode about three miles out of the city to meet the Duchess. And when those with the Duchess caught sight of him they started to cry out happily:

'Look, madam, here is our Signor Antonio Bologna!' And all welcomed him most joyously. Bologna dismounted from his horse and kissed the hands of his consort, and then invited her with all the company to his house. She accepted; and he brought her home not indeed as his wife, but as his suzerain. Here, after everyone had had dinner, the Duchess, wanting to take off the mask, and knowing that this must now be done, summoned all her attendants to the hall and spoke as follows:

'Now is the time, noble friends and servants, for me to reveal to everyone what was once done simply before God. Being a widow, it seemed right to me to marry again and to take for my husband one whom my judgement had chosen. So I now tell you that several years ago, in the presence of my maid who is in your company, I married Signor Antonio Bologna, whom you see, and he is my legal husband and with him, because I am his, I intend to remain. Hitherto, I have been your mistress and your Duchess and you have been my faithful vassals and servants. For the future you will devote yourselves to the care of your lord the Duke, my son, and you will be loyal and faithful to him as is his right. You will accompany these damsels of mine to Amalfi, and their dowries are in the bank of Paolo Tolosa, where I deposited them before leaving the Kingdom, and all the documents are at the monastery of Santo Sebastiano with the Mother Superior. For, of all the damsels, I wish for the moment to retain only this maid of mine. Signora Beatrice, who has until now been my Lady of Honour, is, as she knows, well provided for. Nonetheless in the documents that I have mentioned to you she will find adequate provision to marry off one of her daughters who is living with her. If among the servants there is anyone who wishes to stay with me, he will receive good treatment. As for the rest, when you reach Amalfi the majordomo will see to your wants in the usual way. And to conclude, I prefer to live with my husband Signor Antonio than to stay as Duchess.'

All the company were astonished and bewildered when they

heard this. But then it was made clear to each one that she had spoken nothing less than the truth, for Bologna sent for the boy and girl whom he had had by the Duchess, and she picked them up and kissed them as being her children and Bologna's, and all agreed to return to Amalfi, except for the maid and two footmen who remained with their mistress.

There was a great deal of talk and everyone had his say. Then they all left Bologna's house and went to the inn, because no one dared, for fear of the Cardinal and her other brother, to stay with the Duchess once they realized how matters stood; indeed they agreed among themselves that the next morning one of the gentlemen should ride with the post to Rome where the other brother was too, see the Cardinal, and tell him everything. So it was done. The others all departed for the Kingdom. The Duchess remained with her new husband and lived with him as happily as could be. And not many months later, she gave birth to another male child, whom she called Alfonso.

While they were living in Ancona, loving each other more and more every day, the Cardinal of Aragon with his brother, who could not tolerate for a moment their sister being married in such a way, so arranged matters through the Archbishop of Mantua, Cardinal Gismondo Gonzaga (who under Julius II was Papal Legate in Ancona), that Bologna and his wife were driven out by the people of Ancona. They had been there about six or seven months, and even though the legate contrived hard to have them driven out, Bologna for his part worked to such good purpose that the affair dragged on. However, knowing that eventually he would have to leave, and in order not to be caught unprepared, Bologna arranged through a friend of his who lived in Siena to have a safe conduct from the Signoria allowing him to stay there with all his family. In this manner he sent off all his children and so arranged matters that the very day he received from the people of Ancona notice to leave within a fortnight, he with his wife and servants mounted horse and departed for Siena.

When the two Aragonese brothers heard of this, and saw they had been tricked (for they had hoped to capture them by surprise on the journey) they worked on Cardinal Alfonso Petrucci of Siena to such effect that Signor Borghese, the Cardinal's brother and head of the Signoria, had Bologna similarly dismissed from Siena.

Racking his brains as to where to go, Bologna decided to make his way, with all his family, to Venice. So they set out on the journey, travelling through the Florentine territory towards Romagna in order to reach the sea and embark for Venice. On reaching the territory of Forlì, they saw that they were being followed by a large band of horsemen, among whose number were some spies. Fearful and uncertain what course to take, seeing no way of escape, they were at their wits' end. However, fear quickening their pace, they hurried to seek safety in a house that was not far distant.

Bologna was riding a very fast and powerful Arab horse, and he had put his elder son on another, also very good and fast. The younger son and the little girl were both in a litter. His wife was riding a good carriage horse. He and his son could easily save themselves, since they were on such good horses, but because of his love for his wife he could not leave her. But she believed firmly that those who were pursuing them would harm only her husband, and so with tears in her eyes, she begged him to save himself, saying:

'My lord, please leave us, for my brothers wouldn't harm me or our children, but if they could capture you they would deal cruelly with you and kill you.'

And straightway giving him a big purse full of ducats, she continued to beg him to flee, saying that in time perhaps God would grant that her brothers should be appeased.

The wretched husband, seeing that those who were pursuing them were so near there was no chance for his wife to escape, took tearful leave of her, grieving beyond words and spurring his horse, bade his attendants to see to their own safety. Seeing his father take to flight, the son boldly followed him at full gallop, and the two of them, along with four servants who were well mounted, made their escape, deciding to change their destination from Venice to Milan. Those who had come to kill him seized the woman and her little son and daughter and all the others. The leader of the troop, either on the brothers' instructions or on his own initiative, in order to get her to go with him quietly and without protest, said to her:

'Madam, your noble brothers have sent us to escort you home to the Kingdom so that you should undertake once more the care of your son, our lord the Duke, and not go travelling here one day and there another; for Signor Antonio Bologna was the sort of man who, once he had had enough of you, would leave you absolutely destitute and disappear from the scene altogether. Now be of good cheer and do not worry about anything.'

The Duchess seemed to be greatly calmed by these words and she thought that she must be right in saying that her brothers would not treat her or her children cruelly. And in this belief she travelled for some days until they reached one of the castles belonging to her son, the Duke. As soon as they arrived, she with her little children and the maid were held and placed in the keep of the castle. What became of the four of them here did not transpire at once. All the others were allowed to go free. But the Duchess with her maid and the two children, as later became known for sure, were wretchedly put to death in the tower.

The unhappy husband and lover, with his sons and servants, reached Milan, where he stayed for some days under the protection of Signor Silvio Savello, this being the time when Silvio was besieging the French in the castle which he was trying to seize in the name of Maximilian Sforza, as he later did through treaty. From there Savello led his forces to Crema, where he remained for some days. And so Bologna went to stay with the Marquess of Bitonto and when the Marquess left, he stayed in the house of Signor Visconti.

The Aragonese brothers so arranged matters in Naples that the chancellor seized Bologna's property. And Bologna for his part sought only to appease these brothers, not for a moment accepting that his wife and children might be dead. Once he was warned by certain gentlemen that he should take great care for he was not safe in Milan. But he would listen to no one, and I believe, on the evidence of what I learned, that in order to ensure that he did not leave, he was secretly given to understand that he would be reunited with his wife. And so buoyed up by this vain hope and living from one day to the next, he stayed in Milan for over a year.

At that time it happened that one of the noblemen of the Kingdom, who had men-at-arms in the Duchy of Milan, told all this story to our Delio, and moreover affirmed that he had been commissioned to have Bologna killed, but that he had no wish to be a butcher for others, and that he had found means to warn Bologna not to cross his path; he also said that his wife with the children and the maid had most certainly been strangled.

One day when Delio was with Signor Ippolita Bentivoglio, Bologna was playing the lute and singing a verse which he had composed about his own misfortunes. When Delio, who had not known him previously, learned that he was the husband of the Duchess of Amalfi, moved to pity he called him aside and assured him that his wife was dead and that he knew for certain that there were soldiers in Milan with orders to kill him. Bologna thanked Delio and said to him:

'You are deceived, Delio, for I have letters from my people in Naples that the chancellor is about to release my property, and from Rome I am also given to hope that my most illustrious and reverend lord Cardinal is no longer so angry and still less his brother, and that without fail I shall see my wife again.' Delio, realizing how Bologna had been tricked, said what he thought was right and went away.

Those who were seeking Bologna's death, seeing that no result was forthcoming and that the man who had the armed retainers was blowing cold over the enterprise, gave the commission to a Lombard nobleman, exhorting him fiercely to do everything to have Bologna killed.

Delio had told Signor L. Scipione Attellano all the story so far and said that he wanted to put it in one of his *novelle*, knowing for certain that poor Bologna would be killed. And one day when Delio and Scipione were in Milan, near the Monastero Maggiore, they saw Bologna riding a very handsome little pony, on his way to Mass at San Francesco. He had two servants going ahead of him, one carrying a lance and the other a Book of Hours of Our Lady. Then Delio said to Attellano:

'There's Bologna.'

It seemed to Attellano that Bologna was looking distraught and he said:

'My God, he would do better to have another lance instead of that little prayer book, seeing how uneasy he looks.'

Attellano and Delio were just approaching San Giacomo when

they heard a great noise, for, before Bologna could reach San Francesco he was set upon by Captain Daniele da Bozzolo with three fully armed companions and run through and wretchedly killed, without anyone being able to come to his aid. And those who murdered him left in their own good time and went where it suited them, there being no one who cared to chase after them for the sake of justice.

111.62

The many wives of the King of England, the death of two of them, with various other accidents which befell them.

Henry, who was the eighth King of England of that name, took for his wife Catherine, the daughter of Ferdinand of Aragon and Isabella of Castille, rulers who had won the title of 'Catholic' because of their conquest of the Kingdom of Granada and their zeal for the Catholic faith, even though Alfonso (the first King of that name) was called so previously. By this Catherine, Henry had a daughter called Mary, who grew into a gracious and charming young lady of most noble character. Then Henry fell in love with Anne, of the Boleyn family, the daughter of an English knight, whose body was beautiful but whose soul was base and common.

The King's love for this girl, who was one of Queen Catherine's ladies-in-waiting, grew so much and so turned his head that he began to think of getting rid of the Queen and marrying her lady-in-waiting. It is said that the Archbishop of York, Cardinal Wolsey, who at that time administered all the country's affairs, advised him that he might get rid of her and gave him to understand that the Supreme Pontiff would allow a dispensation on the grounds that Catherine had previously been married to his elder brother, and so could not be his wife. But others told the King that he should take care, since the Pope would never dissolve the marriage, seeing that the Pope of the time had granted a dispensation for the union, even though Catherine had been the wife of his brother, with whom the marriage had not been consummated.

So now the King, infatuated with love for Anne and weary

of the Queen, rid himself of her on his own authority, without asking for any dispensation; and indeed the Pope could never have satisfied his wish, by reason of the fact that Catherine was his true wife whom he had married on the authority of the Church: the marriage had been consummated and they had had children, and so they could never be separated.

Endless consultations were held on the subject; there was nobody or person with any reputation for learning that was not asked to compose something on the matter. Not only were such consultations arranged for by the Pope, but the King likewise sent everywhere for them. Generally, however, all the Catholic scholars gave the most cogent reasons for concluding that the King could not rid himself of his wife, and that still less could the Pope dissolve the marriage. Full of ill will and anger, the King drove the Cardinal from Court, and confined him to a certain part of England, and confiscated all his revenues. This led to the Cardinal's death, for when the King subsequently sent for him to be brought to Court he was terrified of being done to death and, it is said, poisoned himself on the journey and expired before he reached London.

As well as the Cardinal, there died many other great prelates and nobles, including that most holy man, the Bishop of Rochester, who was found, after his head had been cut off, to be wearing the roughest of hair-shirts next to his skin. And what shall I say about Thomas More, that master of Latin and Greek and most upright man? But if I were to try to catalogue all those who refused to give way to the unbridled desires of the King, I would be writing another *Iliad*. For he left in the Island not a single friar or monk, and did countless numbers to death, destroying all the monasteries and abbeys and bestowing the bishoprics as he fancied, without any authorization from the Pope.

Henry then married the Anne mentioned before, while Queen Catherine was still living in retirement in a place decided by the King. Unfortunately things that start badly and wickedly never end well. Anne was full of marvellous charms and beauty, but she was also unchaste, because before the King married her (and she confessed as much at the time of her death) she had many times known the feel of a man thrusting his Devil into Hell. And after rising so far as to be an honoured Queen, from being just a little maid, with no regard for the exalted rank which she had so undeservedly attained she abandoned herself to dishonourable and forbidden love affairs.

She lusted after her own brother, whom the King had made a great baron, and many times she lay with him. Not content with such wickedness, she fell in love with a favourite of the King, called Weston, and she gave her body generously to this man as often as possible. But she was so dishonourable and insatiable that things did not end there. She turned her eyes on a baron who frequented the court, called Bretherton, a man of high standing, and she persuaded him too to lie with her. And in order to have someone always with her, and not to have to lose time, she developed such an intimacy with Norreys that this too ended with their sharing in bed the pleasure that men are so eager to have with women.

I see many of you, my lords, marvelling at what I am telling you, and you must perhaps be supposing that I am repeating romances or fables that are made up out of one's head. But I am telling you a true story, for when she was beheaded in the Tower of London, I found myself there too and I heard the charge read out, after she had been led on to the scaffold, and I also saw five of her adulterers beheaded. You have heard me mention four of these. Now I should tell you about the fifth; and you will marvel still more, and with good reason.

There was at the Court a certain Mark Smeton, a lower-class man, the son of a carpenter. He had learned to sing and play various musical instruments, and because of this the King was very fond of him and would often, when he was in bed with the Queen, have him come into their room. And even if he were not there himself, the King would let Mark sing and play to the Queen on her own. Mark knew all about the Queen's love affairs, as did also a certain maidservant called Margaret who gave the Queen a helping hand with her adulterous enterprises. Now the Queen was accustomed, after the King had risen, to call for Mark and to hear him play; but either because she wanted to ensure his secrecy over her relations with the noblemen I have mentioned, or because she wanted to find out if he played as well on his own pipe as he did on the other instruments, she took him again and again in her arms and gratified him with what should have been denied to everyone save the King.

And so this impure Queen amused herself now with one man and now with another, whenever she saw the chance, and yet she never slaked her thirst. The whole Court was suspicious of what was happening, but seeing that the King loved her more than his own eyes no one dared say a word about it, and the adulterers enjoyed happy hunting. The King likewise, not content with possessing the Queen, pursued a love affair with a very beautiful lady-in-waiting of the Queen, and he would often wrestle with her, and it was always her role to lie underneath.

This lady was the sister of the doctor, Antony Browne, whom the King held very dear and treated most affectionately. Then the King discovered how well this woman got on with men and that she enjoyed wrestling with them to try them out and see who had the firmest muscles and toughest back. This disturbed him not a little. So one day he called for her brother and said to him as follows:

'Antony, I am very sad that I must tell you something disagreeable, because I am fond of you and would rather give you pleasure. But for my honour's sake I am forced to tell you what I do now. I wish to bring decency and order to my wife's Court and to rid it of certain practices that displease me. If this is to be done it is very necessary, for many reasons, that your sister should no longer stay there, because whatever I put in good order she would immediately throw into disorder. So take her away from Court and see to her affairs, as I do not want her here at all in future. For the sake of your name and hers, however, I consider that it would be well that she should ask leave from the Queen, when the other ladies and maids of honour are present, finding some excuse for not being able to stay at Court. And I shall tell my wife to dismiss her graciously and honourably.'

Antony thanked the King and said that he would do what he commanded him. And that same day he spoke with his sister, revealing what the King intended and begging her to do what the King had arranged. The lady, who knew about all the Queen's adulteries, replied to him:

'Dear brother, by all means go and tell the King that I shall do just what he commands; but also say I warn him that he should

take care to observe his wife and that he will have much to do if
he succeeds in watching her closely.'

When Antony heard this, it seemed to him too scandalous,
and he demurred from taking any such message to the King
and said she should say something else.

'Nor will I,' said she, 'do what the King commands; and I
shall wait to be publicly dismissed, and that will disgrace both of
us. But if you are wise, you will do what I tell you; and I know
that the King will be obliged to you for it.'

After no little dispute between them, Antony decided to take
the King the message his sister wanted him to. And so, when he
was near to the King, he said:

'Sire, I have spoken with my sister, and she is ready to do all
you wish. But first she wants me to say to you that, as the
humble servant she is, she advises you that you should take care
to observe your wife and that you will have much to do if you
succeed in watching her closely.'

The King, on hearing this speech, felt as if he had been
stabbed and was greatly agitated in his mind. Then, after he had
thought for a while, he turned to Antony and said:

'With this gossip of yours, which is of the highest consequence and importance, you have sown doubts in my mind. But
if your sister wants to live, it is very necessary that she should
make clear to me how my wife has sent me to Cornwall * without my leaving London, for this is what her words seem to
mean. So you will tell her that she must make this clear to me
and that, insofar as she values her life, she should say not a word
to anyone and in no way take leave of the Court.'

Antony returned to his sister and revealed to her all that the
King had in mind. Then she said:

'You'll soon see, my brother, that the King will remain be-
holden to you for what you have disclosed to him on my behalf.
Now I want you to tell him that to confirm how the affairs of his
wife are managed and how he is betrayed by his subjects, he
should order the arrest of Mark the musician and the chamber-
maid Margaret. From these two he will find out far more than I
am able to tell him, since they know more than I do.'

* Translator's note: Cornwall (Cornovaglia): play on word *corno*
(horn). In Latin countries horns are the emblem of cuckoldry.

When he had heard this reply, the King sent for his Constable, Cromwell, who after the fall of the Cardinal was in charge of the government of England and charged him with what he wanted to be done, in accordance with Antony Browne's advice.

It was in the month of April that the King was made aware of these things; and so he ordered preparations to be made for a magnificent tournament on the first of May, in which he intended to joust, and he named the companions he wished to joust with him: namely, the Queen's brother, Weston, Bretherton, Norreys and several other knights, all of whom, armed and on horseback, made a splendid spectacle when they appeared on the day of the tournament as gay, gallant and courageous knights.

On the last day of April, when the Constable was in the Tower, he called Mark to him and asked him if he would accompany him that day to a place of his some two short miles from London. Mark promised that he would. 'Go then,' said the Constable, 'and bring some of your instruments, and we shall have the time of our lives today and this evening, and tomorrow morning early we shall return.'

Mark went off and did what the Constable said, going to the place mentioned with a party of friends, including Antony Browne, but just a few soldiers. They stayed there happily and had a pleasant supper, and after supper they amused themselves with games. The Constable wanted Browne and also Mark to sleep in his room; when everyone had lain down to sleep, two of the Constable's henchmen came in as arranged and seized and bound Mark so that he could not move; and they left him at the mercy of the Constable and of Browne and went away. Then the Constable said to him:

'Mark, the King wishes to know from you all about the practices of the Queen, which he knows you know about. It is far better that you should reveal everything and not have to be tortured because of any obstinacy. In any case, there are others who know about them besides you and have already apprised the King.'

Poor Mark, as scared as a rabbit and imagining that the torturer was already tearing him to pieces, exposed all the adulterers, and himself along with them. The Constable, having put Mark under strong guard, and having made sure that nothing could be guessed in London of his arrest, returned to London in time for the tournament. When the jousting was finished, he declared to the King all that Mark had admitted. Grieving beyond measure and envenomed against everyone, the following night the King had all the adulterers and the Queen and Margaret seized quietly and secretly and lodged in different prisons; and Mark was brought there that same night.

Then, shortly after the charges had been drawn up and it was found that all that Mark had said was true, the King had all five of the adulterers publicly beheaded in London, at the Tower, to the great wonder of the people. And one morning, on the Tower Green, he had the same done to the Queen and Margaret. The wretched Queen, from what was seen, died with great constancy and very contrite over her sins.

The King waited for two years, and then married Jane Seymour, the sister of a knight, who conceived a male child, during whose birth, however, she died. This boy is known as the 'Prince'. After the death of this Queen, Henry negotiated with the Duke of Cleves to take his sister, and he married her and brought her to England. But she remained his wife for three months only, because once when she was in bed with the King, talking of one thing and another, she foolishly let slip that when she was a young girl she had promised one of her own countrymen to take him as her husband. For this the King got rid of her, sending her to stay at a place not far from London, and arranging for her an income of 20,000 ducats.

Having sent packing the woman from Cleves, he married a niece of the Duke of Norfolk, a great nobleman. He kept her for just two years only. For, after a visit to the North of the country, he returned to London after an absence of some days; and on his return he heard that the Queen had made love with a favourite gentleman of his, called Culpepper. And so, after the truth of this had been established, he had them both beheaded at the Tower.

But you should know, my lords, that the King had planned to have his favourite married, and, wanting to give him a rich and noble wife, had so arranged matters that he was publicly

betrothed to this niece of the Duke. And having ordered a great
wedding suitable to such a marriage, the King honoured it with
his presence and fell passionately in love with the bride himself;
after which all he could think of was how he could get her to lie
with him. It seemed to him quite wrong that he should have to
wait for his favourite to lie with her, and only afterwards set
plans afoot to induce her to do what he wanted. So finally he
decided to deprive Culpepper of her and to take her for his wife.
When the wedding feast was over, and Culpepper thought that
he would go to sleep with the woman whom he now loved
deeply, the King in the presence of everyone said to him:

'Culpepper, I want you to be content for the moment to find
yourself another woman – I shall see that you get whom you
want, because this one I want for my own wife.'

What could the wretched bridegroom do? The King then
publicly took her as his wife. Nonetheless between the two former betrothed there remained a certain tenderness that tempted
them to lie together. And being less than cautious in their in-
timacies, they were seen to be kissing each other most passionately in secret; and for this reason, as already said, they were
seized and killed.

Now it happened that one day a widow, who had been married to a knight, having been involved in litigation with the relations of her husband and having failed to get possession of her
property, was advised that at the opportune moment she should
present herself to the King and humbly ask him for justice. And
this is what she did, entering the hall of the King, accompanied
by some of her relations, and waiting there until he came out of
his room; and when he appeared, the woman approached and
knelt before him, handing him her petition and also telling a
few words about her case and weeping as she spoke.

Having heard the widow, the King charged her to come back
after dinner and the King, after looking at her and weighing her
up, said:

'Madam, if it pleases you, we should like to give you a husband.'

Now the woman was about thirty-five years old and, when
she heard what the King said, she answered:

'Sire, I should first want to recover my property and to settle the question of my marriage portion, because I believe that then I should not lack a match suitable to my rank if I wanted to marry.'

'Indeed so,' said the King, 'you have spoken wisely. But we shall give you a man who with little effort will help you to do all that you say.'

'Let it be as you will,' replied the woman.

At this the King held his hand out to her and said:

'If you wish, I mean to be your husband; and in order to avoid delay, let us to the church and there I will marry you as my wife.'

And so the whole Court flocked to the church, where Henry took and married her in the presence of his people, and she is his wife still. True enough, they say that he indulges in intercourse with other women and that almost once a fortnight he goes to visit the woman from Cleves and enjoy two or three days of intimacy with her.

Such then, is the life of Henry VIII King of England insofar as it appertains to women and the Christian religion.

I.28

Of the divers mischances and grievous perils which befell Cornelio for the love of his lady.

Among those Lombard fugitives who came on to Mantua after the famous defeat of the Swiss at Melegnano* was Messer Cornelio. With myself he took up his abode in that city. It is a pleasure to me, having all good cause for it, to speak of him as a most noble and gallant young gentleman of about four-and-twenty, tall, well-made, and of great strength and comeliness. He had his full share of virtues; while, in the gifts of fortune, he was passing rich. His mother, who lived in Milan, and took the utmost pains to save his patrimony intact, always sent him all

---

* Translator's note: The battle of Melegnano, fought on 13 September 1515, when Francis I completely routed the Switzers, and in fact decided the fate of the Duchy of Milan, which Maximilian Sforza had so miserably governed. Marshal Trivulzio termed it 'a combat of giants', in which the very flower of the French nobility took part.

that he needed, so that he could keep a house in Mantua, and was well furnished with clothes, and horses, and serving-folk. Before leaving Milan he fell in love, as lads will do, with a young married lady of high birth and great beauty, whom, that no scandal touch her, we will call Camilla. As a zealous partisan of the Sforzas, when Maximilian Caesar came, Cornelio had done all he possibly could to recapture his fatherland, and he was still in close relationship with Duke Francesco Sforza, often going to Trent, and scheming ceaselessly to bring about the Duke's return to Milan. But with all these plottings and schemings he could never forget his mistress. Indeed, she was in his thoughts by day as by night, and it grieved him far more not to be with her nor see her face than to be banished from Milan.

This Camilla whom Cornelio thus passionately loved was but a girl, not yet one-and-twenty; and of all the beauties in Milan, she was held to be the fairest. And though this mutual liking had led to no grave consequences, Cornelio's long devotion, and the absolute truth and sincerity of his love, caused her to repay this heartily; so she herself was grieved beyond measure at his going, and often bemourned his absence. They had not yet had the chance to speak freely of their loves, but by means of the man who drove her carriage they had often written to each other. The driver was very willing to do their bidding in this, as he had long been in the service of Cornelio's mother. Indeed, had chance favoured them, the lovers would very readily have compassed their desires.

While Cornelio thus lived in Mantua, not as an outlaw, but in great affluence and honour, it happened that a gentlewoman of the city fell desperately in love with him, apprising him indirectly of her deep affection. To the waiting-woman who brought these love-messages he replied with a sigh, 'My good woman, you can tell your mistress that I am under great obligations to her for her courteous tenders of affection, knowing that I am loved by her beyond any merit that is mine. It pains me much that I cannot return her the same, but I am not free to dispose of myself at will, having plighted my troth to another, and, being so bound, cannot loose myself. Of a truth, if I were my own, not another's, I would be hers without fail. Her beauty and engaging manners seem to me worthy of all honour and service, not only at my hands, but at the hands of those far greater than myself. Nevertheless, if she would command my life or my worldly goods, they are at her disposal; these I offer willingly, provided that I fail not in my constancy to her for whom I live and die.'

The messenger brought back this answer verbatim to her mistress; and, dear ladies, you may easily imagine how bitter was her chagrin at being thus refused, if you will only put yourselves in her place. She was a damsel of about six or seven-and-twenty years, to whom the greatest gentlemen in Mantua had paid court, yet, as I afterwards knew for certain, had never loved any one before our friend Cornelio inspired her with such fervent affection.

Touching this, let me tell you what I said to him upon my return from Trent. When he had recounted the whole story, I said, 'My good Cornelio, forgive my excessive frankness, but our brotherly friendship emboldens me to say as much and more if occasion serves. You say that in Milan you have fallen deeply in love, which I believe, for I know how soft of heart are the ladies of Milan, and how prone they are to love. But think you that your mistress differs in aught from other women, or that if, in your absence, she came across any man that pleased her she would hesitate to get such solace as fortune had chanced to offer her? Be sure that there is not a woman on earth who, having an opportunity to amuse herself with a man she likes, omits to profit by it, if only the thing may be done in secret. As you know, I have many relatives in Milan, the Bossa family being both numerous and ancient. Now, I believe my sisters and the rest of my kinsfolk to be made of flesh and blood, like any other women with whom I have had dealings. Compared with you, I am an old man, so that I have tried a good many. Women, my friend, are women all the world over, generally doing that which belongs to their sex. There you go, all day long, fretting your jesses like a hawk, taking naught in the way of pleasure, and believing that she you love does likewise. But, as I think, you are grossly mistaken. Assuming that she loves you, keeps true to you, and does as you do (though I can never believe that she is so silly as to remain with her hands at her waistband), what harm or reproach or slight do you do her if, being now here, you take your pleasure with some other woman? How shall this bring her any hurt? Do here what you like, and as all of us do who, not to seem wall-eyed, lick both sides of the platter, taking what is good when we may, since things left are lost. This gentlewoman here loves you, and tells you so, therefore you ought to love and woo her in your turn. What the devil would you have more? Remember that Dame Fortune wears her hair in front; the back of her head is bald. If she should see that you neglect the chances that she offers you, and she be angered against you, you may say, as they said when Giovanni Galeazzo was encamped about the walls of Florence, and caused races for the mantle to be run on St John's Day, viz. 'The game is up, unless death be our help.' * Therefore, that you be not brought to a like pass, give yourself a good time while you may. Make up to this pretty little gentlewoman; and when we are back in Milan, you can amuse yourself with the other.'

With these and a thousand similar arguments I sought to persuade him, but all my words fell upon deaf ears. He was firmly resolved not to break faith with his lady, and he begged me to say no more to him about this matter. When she got Cornelio's answer, the fair Mantuan was greatly mortified and confounded. However, making a virtue of necessity, she grew calm, and the ardour of her love changed to an intimate sisterly friendship. Even to this day she loves Cornelio as a brother. The first time she spoke to him after getting her answer she highly praised his loyal resolve, and even now, whenever love is the subject under discussion, she always declares Cornelio to be the truest and the most faithful of all lovers.

Laying aside, then, all other loves, Cornelio thought of no one save of his dear lady in Milan, his only consolation being to get letters now and again from her, or to write to her in reply. This seemed to cool the heat of his passion, a faint help, a slight com-

---

* Translator's note: Death, in fact, did come to the aid of the beleaguered Florentines, as their enemy, Gian Galeazzo, fell a victim to the plague on 3 September 1393. It is characteristic of the man that he should have taken the appearance in the heavens of a comet as a presage of his death. 'I thank God,' he exclaimed, 'that He has suffered the signal for my recall to appear in the sky, so that all men may see it.'

fort, perhaps, yet one which in a measure served to while away his time of exile.

One day a letter was delivered to him from his lady-love which gave him much matter for thought, and he felt at a loss how to act. Camilla's husband, as it happened, was obliged to leave Milan for an estate of his in the country, where he would have to remain for some time. Knowing this, she wrote to Cornelio, as usual, an affectionate letter, in which, among other things, were these words:

'See, now, my dear lord, if you and I have not fortune adverse to our wishes, and if we have not good reason to bewail our bad luck, for my husband is about to leave Milan for one of our places in the country, and will be absent for some days. Were you but here while he is away, we might easily be together; but I see no chance of this, and am infinitely grieved that we cannot meet.' A thousand other loving messages followed, of the sort that damsels who love ardently are wont to write.

The letter greatly perplexed Cornelio, and at length he went to see his friend Delio, whom he loved as himself, and who when in Milan had known all about this love matter, as indeed about all Cornelio's other affairs. Putting the letter into Delio's hand he said, 'Read.' Hardly had Delio read the letter than he seemed to guess what Cornelio thought of doing, and said, 'My friend, you want to go to Milan and get your head cut off, an absolutely unreasonable proceeding. I can easily see that this woman wants to cause your death, and make that death an ignominious one to boot, for you know what a grudge the French have against you.'

'You are always harping on such horrors,' replied Cornelio; 'do but listen to me a little, for I should like us calmly to consider this question of my going, and judge which course to take that shall prove the lesser ill. You know how much I love that woman, and what sufferings I have borne in paying court to her, and in doing her loyal service. Yet, in spite of all my efforts to be alone with her, we have never yet had an opportunity for this. Now that her husband is not there, I could easily manage to meet her, and get that which I have so long desired; and, if this came to pass, I should prize the boon far more than aught else which fortune might bring me. What say you, now?'

'My dear Cornelio,' replied his friend, 'you would have us talk over the matter calmly, dispassionately; but I see no way of doing this, for you yourself are so passionately bent upon this woman, and have become so blind as not to see the death that stares you in the face. Therefore you must be ruled by one whose eyes are open. You know that I love you, for you have ofttimes put that love to the test, therefore take heed to what I say; drive these silly fancies out of your head, for all this that you think is a mere will-o'-the-wisp. I advise you as I would have you advise me were I in a like case, viz., on no account go to Milan. Do you forget that you have been proclaimed a rebel, and that all your goods are confiscated? You would hardly be gone from here than they would know of it in Milan. Just now, in Carnival-time, this place is full of masks, and there are many who spy out all that you say and do. Moreover, you have already been warned from Milan that you can do nothing that they do not know there. If, which God forbid! you go thither, and by mischance fall into the hands of the French, not all the gold in the world will save your head. Would you, just for a brief and fleeting pleasure, lose your life? Then, again, how can you be certain of getting there in safety? You would have to pass through Cremona and Soncino, or else by way of Pizzighitone and Lodi. In all these places you are better known than the wayside nettle. Yet, assuming that you travel by disused roads to avoid being seen, what assurances have you, on reaching Milan, that you will obtain of her that which you so hotly desire?

'I believe that, knowing that you could not, and indeed dared not, go to Milan, she wrote thus to show you that she ever bears you in her thoughts and loves you most dearly; for, had she believed that you could with safety come, she would have written differently. Now, supposing that when you arrive she is perfectly ready to do your pleasure, ought you not to reflect what sort of house hers is, and that, though her husband be absent, his household servants are all at home? Don't you know what a grim old woman is her governess, who never leaves her side for an instant, and perhaps even sleeps with her when the husband is away? For just one hour of bitter-sweet toying, would you endanger your life? And if mischance should overtake you in this attempt, what would be said of you, then? Though young, you are deemed wise, with prudence and wit riper than your years might warrant; do not, then, shake the general belief in your discretion. If for the service and benefit of your lord you must needs go to Milan, and if evil betided you, at the least you would win general compassion even from your foes, being praised as the loyal, faithful servant of your master. But, for such a thing as this, besides the hurt, you would only get perpetual reproach and ignominy. My brother, do you keep this life of yours which you value so lightly; keep it for a better use, for a more honourable enterprise than this.'

This advice served to cool Cornelio's ardour not a little, albeit it was much against his will. Being at a loss what to answer, he remarked that night was the mother of thoughts, and that he would reflect further upon the matter before he saw Delio again. So saying, he took his leave. When night came, and he found himself alone, as sleep he could not, he gave rein to his thoughts, turning over all in his mind, and remembering the discussion he had had with Delio. There being no one at hand to contradict him, appetite overcame him; and he determined, though death should be his portion, to go to Milan.

He rose with the dawn and went to see Delio, who was still abed, saying to him, 'Delio mine, I have determined, no matter what befall me, when the day comes, to start at nightfall, and go straight to Cremona, and wait there until the city-gate is opened, when I shall visit the house of our friend Messer Girolamo, and stay with him all day. Late in the evening I must push on to Lodi at Zurlesco, where I shall be privily lodged at Signor Vistarino's. Here also I mean to remain a whole day until evening, when I shall journey on to Milan, arriving there in the third hour of the night. As you know, the Porta Ticinese is open at all hours to any one who can pay the porter a few pence; and, on entering the city, I shall go straight to Messer Ambrogio's.'

When Delio knew of his friend's intention, he used all possible efforts to turn him from his purpose. But though he said all that he knew and all that he could, Cornelio was resolutely determined to go at all cost, adding as a final reason, 'I would fain try my fortune, and, if the thing succeeds, as I desire and hope it may, what more fortunate and happy lover than I? And if it should happen otherwise, this solace at least I shall have, that she whom I love will plainly perceive that my devotion to her was true, and not feigned.'

When Delio saw that Cornelio was determined to run such a risk, and that no remedy might avail to hinder him, he said that, as Cornelio was bent upon going, he had better leave his own servants behind in Mantua, and take with him others of trustworthy character, who were not known in Milan. He accordingly engaged three servants, and got everything in readiness. On the evening appointed he stealthily quitted Mantua, and, taking the route he had already planned, he reached Milan in the third hour of the night and went straight to the house of Messer Ambrogio, his very faithful friend. He bade one of his serving-men knock at the door and tell Messer Ambrogio to come down at once, as there was a gentleman who wished to speak to him. Then Cornelio whistled in such a way that Ambrogio knew it was he; so, coming down, he unbarred the door and said, 'Who's there?' Without answering, Cornelio made a certain sign, when Messer Ambrogio, doubly assured of the truth, caused the torches to be taken inside which he had had brought out with him to light the threshold, and then joyfully welcomed his friend. He took him into a chamber on the ground floor, letting nobody know who the newcomer was, except one trusted servant. It was in the month of February, and for many days there had been no rain nor snow to spoil the roads, so that they were very dusty; with this, Cornelio had had an easy ride.

When morning came Cornelio sent for a tailor, who used to carry letters to him from Camilla. The man was overjoyed at seeing him, and they talked together for a good while. Cornelio then gave the tailor a letter, which he was to take to his lady. When aware of her lover's arrival in Milan, she felt at once glad and sorrowful – glad in the hope of seeing her Cornelio, who loved her and her alone, she was very certain, since he had exposed himself to such peril for her sake; and sorrowful, because in a day or so her husband would return. You must know that in the letter she wrote to Cornelio she mistook the day of her husband's going, so that Cornelio delayed his departure from Mantua over-long. Camilla sent back a note by the tailor,

to tell Cornelio that she would expect to meet him that very day
between the twenty-first and twenty-second hour at the gate of
her palazzo. He was to come masked, and make a certain sign.
At the time fixed, Cornelio (wearing a mask) donned one of
those long coloured dresses then in fashion with Milanese
gentlemen, put plumes in his cap, and, mounting a beautiful
little jennet, rode off alone to Camilla's house. There she stood
in the doorway, talking to some gentlemen, looking lovelier and
more graceful than ever. Cornelio halted, and bowing to the
lady gave the sign, but did not utter a word. Seeing a mask stop
silently near them, and thinking it might be some one who
wished to speak to Camilla unobserved, the gentlemen discreetly
set spurs to their mules and rode off, leaving Cornelio (though
they did not recognize him) a fair field. When they had gone he
reverently saluted the lady, who, amid countless blushes, was for
a long while unable to say a word. Half beside himself for joy,
Cornelio could hardly realize his position as he gazed upon
the supreme beauty of his lady-love. At length, breaking this
delicious silence, they found voice, and spoke much of their
great love, fortune favouring them in this talk; for though many
masks and cavaliers passed along the street, no one, noticing the
lady in close converse with a mask, accosted them, so that they
talked on, unhindered, until the brown dusk fell.

The lady chid her lover not a little for having exposed himself
to so perilous a risk, blaming him moreover for not coming in
time, as she hourly expected her husband. So Cornelio produced
her own letter, and, reading it, showed her that she had mistaken the date of her husband's departure by a week, which
error much dismayed her. Nevertheless she agreed to see Cornelio that night at the fourth hour, when her serving-maid, being in the secret, should at a given signal let him into the house.
If, however, that evening the husband should have come back,
on giving the signal Cornelio would hear the waiting-woman
say at one of the windows of the great hall, 'I am sure that I left
the comb here, but now I cannot find it.'

Upon getting this promise, Cornelio in great glee returned to
his lodging, where he partook of a light meal, and when the
Broletto clock struck four he put on a coat of mail, with gauntlets and sleeves to match, and, taking a sword, set out for his

lady's house. While waiting there for the door to be opened he heard, close by, a great buffeting of armed men, and the noise of many blows. Then one, running past, called out, 'Alack! I am dead!' and fell down in front of Camilla's door, just as the maid opened it for Cornelio to enter. The night was very dark, so that, without a light, nothing whatever could be seen; but the noise of this scuffle had brought some of the neighbours to their windows with lights, and one of them, living opposite, spied Cornelio going into the lady's house, sword in hand. Though he heard somebody fall close at his feet, Cornelio took no heed, not even thinking about this, for his whole mind was set on something else. The maid took him into a room between the postern and the main entrance, where he was to wait till Camilla came. She, hearing that her lover was downstairs, feigned sudden indisposition, and told all her servants to go to bed. Hereupon the men-servants all went out of the house to sleep, as it was Carnival-time, and their master was away, leaving only the old cellarer and two pages, lads of about fourteen years, at home. The women of the house went to their beds; and, when she knew that they were all sleeping, Camilla crept downstairs with the maid, as quietly as she could, to fetch Cornelio up to her chamber.

While all this was going on, the watch happened to pass along the street. The head of the police at that time was a certain Monsignor Sandio, a very tall, big man, such as one seldom sees, who as his lieutenant had one Mombojero.

Having heard of the fray (which was now over), and finding a groom in the service of Signor Galeazzo Sanseverino (Master of the Horse to his most Christian Majesty the King) half dead, and his body still warm, the captain of the watch called up the neighbours, and sought to know from them how the fight began. But these could tell nothing, save that they had heard a great outcry and clash of arms. Then one of them said that he had seen a tall fellow, sword in hand, go into Madonna Camilla's house, at whose theshold the dead groom lay. So the officer went thither, and, knocked loudly, calling out in French. At this the lovers were greatly terrified, as they believed that some spy had found out that Cornelio was there. Camilla had only just joined her gallant in the room below, and was about to give him an

affectionate embrace, he doing likewise, when, lo and behold!
the watch was knocking at the door.

Startled by the noise, Cornelio, quick as thought, clapped two
stools one upon another, and, helped by Camilla and her maid,
climbed up into the chimney, where, planting his feet firmly on
the two great hooks from which pots hang, he kept in an upright position, having his sword in his hand. Then, taking away
the stools, and closing the room, Camilla said, 'Who is there?
Who knocks?' The keys were fetched, and when the cellarer
and other womenfolk, roused by the noise, came up, they opened
the door, and Camilla in her boldest voice cried, 'What do you
want at this hour?' The captain, who had heard that the palace
belonged to a person of quality, answered, 'Pardon us, madam,
if we disturb you at this hour, for we do it unwillingly. I was
told that he who killed the groom, who lies outside your door,
entered in here; and, if this be so, I have come with the watch to
arrest him.' Camilla, who had feared it was her lover they
wanted, was half-reassured at hearing this; and she replied, 'Sir,
I have had my door locked ever since nightfall, as my husband is
away from home, so I know that nobody has entered the house,
as I have kept the keys. But, in order to satisfy you, all the rooms
shall be opened, so you may search.'

So they first of all entered the room where poor Cornelio was
hiding in the chimney, who through the hole at the top watched
the stars and shivered.

Searching here, there, and everywhere, under the bolsters and
under the bed, one of the sergeants, to show what special zeal
was his, struck the rope holding up the canopy over the bed with
his halberd, so that the whole thing came tumbling down. Cornelio kept perfectly quiet, repeating to himself the monkeys'
paternosters.* Leaving this room the fellows searched in every
hole and corner of the house; and when they could only find the
pages and the cellar-man, they went down into the basement.
Thinking the assassin might be hidden inside the casks, they
were desirous to taste the flavour of most of the wines. As often
happens on such occasions, some of the neighbours came in to
see what was going on; among these was the fellow who had

---

* Translator's note: Which means that his teeth chattered with cold
and fright.

told the captain of the watch that he saw the murderer enter the house. Not finding the culprit, the captain decided to take his accuser before the court, believing that he knew more about the matter.

Hardly had the officer and his men got half-way down the street than Camilla's husband came up. Finding the door open, and the neighbours with his wife making a great fluster and buzzing, he was greatly astonished. When Camilla saw him she felt more dead than alive, and cried out, 'Alas! my lord, just look here at what these sergeants of the watch have been doing to this room and to the whole house!' Taking him by the hand, she led him into the chamber where Cornelio was; and in order to let the latter know that her husband had come back, she called out loudly, 'Look, husband dear; look how the rogues have turned everything upside down!' Then she told him why the watch had come; but her husband, being very tired, felt more inclined for rest than anything else, so he said, 'Wife, let us go to bed now, and we will see to these matters in the morning.'

Apprised by his voice of the husband's return, Cornelio for very fright was like to have swooned. Then the neighbours were sent away, the door locked, and the horses taken off to the stables hard by. The husband went up to his room, where he had a fire lighted, and got the servants to undress him preparatory to going to bed, while two of his men lay down in the room where Cornelio was hiding up the chimney, in sore discomfort, and knowing not what to do. Some of the other serving-men had put their arquebuses and partisans here before going to sleep in their usual quarters. Leaving her husband abed, Camilla came down again with her maid to discover if there were any way of setting Cornelio free. When she saw the two servants in bed there, she said, 'You ought not to have put yourself here, as everything is in such a mess.' Then the majordomo came in and said, 'Let them shift, lady, just for tonight as best they may, and in the morning all shall be put straight. Do you go up to bed, for by now it must be midnight.'

Camilla saw that she could give her lover no sort of help so she said, 'I also came down to see that no fire was lighted here, as the chimney top is cracked, and might easily set the house on fire.' With this she went upstairs, still thinking of poor Cornelio. Finding her husband nearly asleep, she lay down beside him, and said, 'You have come home rather late, my lord, for this cold weather.' 'Yes,' he answered, 'I left Novara this morning, expecting to get here by nightfall, but our kinsfolk, the Cribelli, kept me such a time at Buffaloro that I changed my mind, and decided to have supper and sleep at our place on the Navilio. I got there late, and the steward had prepared an excellent supper for us, but asked me to excuse the bad sleeping accommodation, as the beds, which in wartime had been fetched away to Milan, had not yet come back, though I thought they had. So I determined to come on here as soon as we had supped; and, as the roads were good, and the way safe, we did this.'

Cornelio, who had heard all that went on, was now in a greater fright than ever, fearing that, overcome by sleep, he might fall down and be killed by the servants. On the other hand, the icy blasts which blew down the chimney seemed to pierce his very bones. He more than once thought of letting himself drop as gently as possible when those in the room were fast asleep, and so escape; but he was unfamiliar with the house, and knew neither how to get out nor where to hide. Then, again, his feet hurt him greatly, as the hooks were round, and to stand on them for long was most uncomfortable; indeed, he could hardly keep himself in that position at all. Nevertheless, hoping to get away when the morning came, he buoyed himself up with this faint hope, thinking of his lady's beauty, and saying to himself now and again, 'The great discomfort that I now endure is not half as great as that which I ought to suffer for the enjoyment of such beauty and charm as belong to my lady. How should she know that I loved her wholly and solely, if for her sake I did not endure far greater perils and far sharper pains?' So, with thoughts such as these, and helped by ardent love, he set himself courageously to bear all.

In the meanwhile, as we have seen, the captain of the watch took the accuser to the court and brought him before Mombojero, who, after questioning him, threatened him with all kinds of tortures if he did not tell the truth about the groom's murder. But the poor wretch could only repeat what at first he had said; and Mombojero thereupon ordered the watch to go back to the house, and search it thoroughly from top to bottom. So the captain returned thither with his men, and knocked so loud that all in the house heard him. The cellarer got up first, and, fetching the keys, went to open the door, while his master dressed himself. On entering, the officer went straight to the room where Cornelio was, who had heard all, and thought the sergeants were come on some pretext to arrest him. Seeing the two lackeys asleep, and finding halberds and firearms in the room, the captain in a trice had both fellows bound. The steward had only just got out of prison, where he had been kept a long while for wounding a workman. When the man asked what all this might mean, the officer, recognizing him, replied, 'You shall know soon enough, and pay both for this and the other affair as well.' Then, just as the sergeants were going upstairs, down came the secretary, whom they promptly arrested. In great surprise at hearing this, the master of the house, half dressed, met the captain on the stairs, who called out, 'Monsignor, you are a prisoner of the most Christian king!' To say this and to seize him was the work of an instant. They also clapped hands on three or four others, making the very deuce of a rumpus, so that it was as if the Day of Judgement had come. Cornelio, hearing all their din, said to himself, 'God help us! What devilry are they up to now?'

The master of the house tried to make excuses for his servants and himself, saying that he had only returned from the country a little before midnight with his men. But it was in vain to protest, as the watch without further ado marched the whole nine of them off to the courthouse, where they were put in the prisons.

At this fresh trouble Camilla wept bitterly. But as she knew that her husband and his folk were innocent of the murder in question, she thanked God for what had happened, as it gave her a chance to set her faithful lover free. So, after locking the door, and sending her women and the others back to their beds, she went with her maid into the room where poor Cornelio, like the Jews, awaited the coming of the Messiah. Approaching the chimney she dried her tears, and laughingly called up to Cornelio, 'Sweetheart, how are you? What are you doing? You may safely come down now, for God, to prevent a greater scandal, has suffered my lord husband with most of his serving-men to be carried off to the court-house.' Then the maid placed the stools as before, and she and her mistress held them fast for Cornelio to step on. He soon came deftly down, and was gleefully welcomed by Camilla, who took him upstairs to her chamber, where a good fire was lighted. After washing his hands and face, which were all besmirched with soot, Cornelio soon shook off the chill that the chimney had given him, and got into bed beside his mistress, gathering the fruit of his fervent love, and laughed many a time with her at all these misadventures which had befallen him.

Early next morning Camilla had her lover taken to a little room, where everything he needed was fitly supplied to him by the maid; and here, when it was convenient, the lady visited him. Then, having summoned her relatives, she took steps for the release of her husband, informing them exactly how the whole thing had occurred. However, the matter went further than ever they thought, as it became necessary to send a notary to Novara to examine witnesses, and also make inquiries at the village where the hapless gentleman and his crew had supped, to prove the truth of their assertions. In this way six days elapsed before they could get out of prison, and all the while Cornelio passed every night in his lady's company, for fear that, sleeping alone, she might see some disagreeable ghost. Then, knowing the day of her husband's homecoming, she sent Cornelio away betimes, after countless kisses and endearments, when he straightway returned to his lodging. Having dined, he went, masked, to pay his respects to Signor Alessandro Bentivoglio and his lady, Signora Ippolita Sforza. While conversing with them certain gentlemen came in, one of whom told how Mombojero had just been with the police officers to Cornelio's house, having got wind of his departure from Mantua, and of his arrival in Milan; and Cornelio's mother had suffered him to search the house. At this news Cornelio soon bade his friends farewell, and, going back to his lodging, determined to remain no longer in such peril. So, that very night, he took horse and rode back to Mantua, by way of Bergamo and Brescia, not caring to travel by the road that he had first taken, lest haply he might meet some ill-favoured folk by the way.

Giovanni Battista Giraldi

From ECATOMMITI

III.7

TRANSLATED BY
W. PARR (1795)

GIOVANNI BATTISTA GIRALDI

GIAMBATTISTA GIRALDI (1504–73) was a Ferrarese. His Senecan-style tragedies interest the historian rather than the general public, and his reputation is better sustained by his *Ecatommiti* (100 stories), which he began in 1528 and published in 1565. The one chosen here is an outstanding example of Shakespeare's indebtedness to the plots of the Italian 'novelists'. A few stories are in Thomas Roscoe's *The Italian Novelists*, 1836. In addition, there exists W. Parr's translation of the Othello story, 1795.

From ECATOMMITI

DECAD III, NOVEL 7

A Moorish captain takes to wife a Venetian lady; his ensign accuses her to her husband of adultery; he seeks for the ensign to kill the man whom he believes to be the adulterer; the captain kills his wife, and is accused by the ensign, but the Moor does not confess; but, there being clear proof, he is banished; and the wicked ensign, seeking to harm others, miserably compasses his own death.

There was once in Venice a Moor of great merit, who for his personal courage, and the proofs he had given of his conduct, as well as his vigorous genius in the affairs of war, was held in great esteem by those gentlemen who, in rewarding patriotic services, excel all the republics that ever existed. It happened that a virtuous woman of great beauty, called Desdemona, not drawn by female appetite, but by the virtue of the Moor, fell in love with him; and he, subdued by the charms and noble sentiments of the lady, became equally enamoured of her. Their passion was so successful that they were married, although her relations did all in their power to make her take another husband. They lived together in such peace and concord while they were at Venice, that there never passed between them either word or action that was not expressive of affection.

The Venetians, resolving to change the garrison which they maintain in Cyprus, elected the Moor to the command of the troops which they destined for that island. Although he was extremely pleased with the honour proposed to him (as it is a dignity conferred only on those who are noble, brave, trusty, and of approved courage), yet was his joy diminished when he reflected on the length and inconvenience of the voyage, supposing that Desdemona must be very averse to undertaking it. His wife, who valued nothing in the world but her husband, and rejoiced exceedingly in the testimony of approbation so lately shewn him by a powerful and celebrated republic, was extremely impatient for the departure of the troops, that she might accompany him to a post of so much honour. But she was very much vexed at seeing the Moor disturbed; and, not knowing the reason, said to him one day at dinner, 'How can you be so melancholy after having received from the Senate so high and so honourable a distinction?' 'My love for you, Desdemona,' replied the Moor, 'disturbs my enjoyment of the rank conferred upon me, since I am now exposed to this alternative – I must either endanger your life by sea, or leave you at Venice. The first would be terrible, as I shall suffer extremely from every fatigue you undergo, from every danger that threatens you : the second would render me insupportable to myself, as parting from you would be parting from my life.' 'Ah, husband,' returned Desdemona, 'why do you perplex yourself with such idle imaginations? I will follow you wherever you go, though it were necessary to pass through fire instead of only going by water in a safe and well-equipped vessel. If there are dangers in the way, I will share them with you; and, indeed, your affection for me could not be great, if you thought of leaving me at Venice to save me from a sea voyage, or believed that I would rather remain here in security than share with you both danger and fatigue. I insist, therefore, on your preparing for the voyage with all that cheerfulness which your dignity ought to inspire.' The Moor then tenderly embraced his wife, saying, 'May Heaven long preserve us in this degree of reciprocal affection.'

Soon afterwards, having settled his affairs and prepared the necessary stores, he went on board the galley with his wife and his company, and sailed for Cyprus with a favourable wind. He had in his company an ensign of a very amiable outward appearance, but whose character was extremely treacherous and base. He had imposed on the Moor's simplicity so successfully, that he gained his friendship; for although he was, in fact, a very great coward, yet his carriage and conversation were so haughty and full of pretension, that you would have taken him for a Hector or an Achilles. This rascal had also conducted his wife with him to Cyprus, who was a handsome and discreet woman; and, being an Italian, Desdemona was so fond of her, that they passed the greatest part of their time together. In the same company was also a lieutenant, to whom the Moor was much attached. The lieutenant went often to the Moor's house, and dined frequently with him and his wife. Desdemona seeing that the Moor was so fond of him, showed him every mark of attention and civility, with which the Moor was much pleased.

The detestable ensign, forgetting his duty to his own wife, and violating all the laws of friendship, honour and gratitude with which he was bound to the Moor, fell passionately in love with Desdemona, and thought only how he might enjoy her. He dare not, however, avow himself, for fear the Moor, if he discovered it, should instantly put him to death. He sought by all the private means in his power to make Desdemona conscious of his love. But she was so entirely taken up with the Moor, that she thought neither of him nor of any one else; and all that he did to engage her affections produced not the least effect. He then took it into his head, that this neglect arose from her being pre-engaged in favour of the lieutenant; and not only determined to get rid of him, but changed his affection for her into the most bitter hatred. He studied, besides, how he might prevent in future the Moor from living happily with Desdemona, should his passion not be gratified after he had murdered the lieutenant. Revolving in his mind a variety of methods, all impious and abominable, he at last determined to accuse her to the Moor of adultery with the lieutenant. But knowing the Moor's great affection for Desdemona, and his friendship for the lieutenant, he plainly saw that unless his deceit was very artfully conducted, it would be impossible to make him think ill of either of them. For this reason he determined to wait till time and place afforded him a fit opportunity for entering on his wicked design; and it was not long before the Moor degraded the lieutenant for having drawn his sword and wounded a soldier upon guard. This accident was so painful to Desdemona, that she often tried to obtain for him her husband's pardon.

In the meantime the Moor had observed to the ensign, that his wife teased him so much in favour of the lieutenant, that he feared he should be obliged at last to restore him to his commission. This appeared to that villain the proper moment for opening his scheme of treachery which he began by saying, 'Perhaps Desdemona is fond of his company.' 'And why?' said the Moor. 'Nay,' replied he, 'I do not choose to meddle between man and

wife; but if you watch her properly, you will understand me.'
Nor would he, to the earnest entreaties of the Moor, afford any
further explanation. These words had stung the Moor so
severely, that he endeavoured perpetually to find out their meaning, and became exceedingly melancholy. Whereupon, when his
wife sometime afterwards repeated her solicitations that he
would forgive the lieutenant, and not sacrifice the service and
friendship of so many years to one slight fault, particularly as
the lieutenant and the soldier were friends again, the Moor grew
angry, and said to her, 'It is somewhat extraordinary, Desdemona, that you should take so much trouble about this fellow;
he is neither your brother nor your relation, that he should
claim so much of your affection.' His wife, with much sweetness
and humility, replied, 'I have no other motive for speaking, than
the pain it gives me to see you deprived of so excellent a friend
as you have always told me the lieutenant was to you. I hope
you will not be angry with me; yet his fault does not merit so
much of your hatred: but you Moors are of so warm a constitution, that every trifle transports you with anger and revenge.' The Moor, still more irritated by these words, replied,
'Perhaps one who suspects it not may learn that by experience; I
will be revenged for the injuries done to me, so thoroughly, that
I shall be satisfied.' His wife was much terrified by these expressions, and seeing him, for the first time, in a passion with her,
submissively answered, 'I have none but the purest motives for
speaking on the business: but not to displease you in future, I
promise never to speak of it again.'

The Moor, on this new application made by his wife in favour
of the lieutenant, imagined that the ensign's words meant that
she was in love with him: he therefore went to that scoundrel
in a state of great dejection, and endeavoured to make him
speak more intelligibly. The ensign, bent on the ruin of this
poor woman, after feigning an unwillingness to say anything to
her disadvantage, and at last pretending to yield to the vehement
entreaties of the Moor, said, 'I cannot conceal the pain I feel in
being under the necessity of making a discovery which will be
to you so very shocking; but since you insist on it, and the attention which I ought to pay to the honour of my commanding
officer prompts me to speak, I will not now refuse to satisfy

your demand and my own duty. You must know, then, that Desdemona is only displeased at seeing you angry with the lieutenant, because, when he comes to your house, she consoles herself with him for the disgust which your blackness now occasions her to feel.'

These words penetrated to the very bottom of the Moor's heart; but to be better informed (although his previous suspicion made him give credit to the ensign's information) he assumed a threatening countenance, and said, 'I know not what prevents me from cutting out that insolent tongue of yours that has so impudently attacked the honour of my wife.' The ensign then replied, 'I expected no other reward for this friendly office of mine; but since my duty has made me go so far, and my regard for your honour still remains, I tell you again that the case is so; and if her feigned affection for you has blindfolded you to such a degree that you have not seen what is so very visible, that does not at all lessen the truth of my assertion. The lieutenant himself, who is one of those who are not content with their own enjoyments when some other is not made acquainted with them, told me so; and,' added he, 'if I had not feared your displeasure, I would have given him at the time that death he merited. But since the information I give you, which concerns you more than any one else, makes you treat me so very improperly, I am sorry I did not hold my tongue, that I might have avoided giving you offence.' The Moor then answered, in great agitation, 'If you do not make me to see with my own eyes the truth of what you tell me, be assured that I will make you wish you had been born dumb.'

'This would have been easy enough,' replied the villain, 'when he came to your house: but now that you have driven him away for a much lighter reason than that which ought to have banished him thence, it will be difficult to prove it. For though I think yet that he continues to enjoy Desdemona whenever you give him an opportunity, he must necessarily proceed with greater caution now than he did before he had incurred your displeasure. But I do not despair of making you see that which upon my word you will not believe.' They then separated. The poor Moor went home with a barbed arrow in his side, waiting impatiently for the day when the ensign should show him what was to render him for ever miserable. But the known purity of Desdemona's conduct gave no less uneasiness to the villainous ensign, because he was afraid he should not be able to convince the Moor of what he had so falsely assured him. He applied himself therefore to the invention of new malice, and devised other expedients.

I have already said that Desdemona went frequently to the ensign's house, and passed great part of the day with his wife. The villain had observed that she often brought with her a handkerchief that the Moor had given her, and which, as it was very delicately worked in the Moorish taste, was very highly valued by them both; he determined to steal it, and by its means complete her ruin. He had a little girl of three years old that was much caressed by Desdemona; and one day, when that unhappy woman was on a visit to this villain, he took up the child in his arms and presented it to Desdemona, who received it and pressed it to her bosom. In the same instant this deceiver stole from her sash the handkerchief, with such dexterity that she did not perceive him, and went away with it in very high spirits. Desdemona went home, and, taken up with other thoughts, never recollected her handkerchief till some days after; when, not being able to find it, she began to fear that the Moor should ask her for it, as he often did. The infamous ensign, watching his opportunity, went to the lieutenant, and, to aid his wicked purpose, left the handkerchief on his bolster. The lieutenant did not find it till the next morning, when, getting up, he set his foot upon it as it had fallen to the floor. Not being able to imagine how it came there, and knowing it to be Desdemona's, he determined to carry it back to her; and, waiting till the Moor was gone out, he went to the back door and knocked. Fortune, who seemed to have conspired along with the ensign the death of this poor woman, brought the Moor home in the same instant. Hearing someone knock he went to the window, and, much disturbed, asked, Who is there? The lieutenant hearing his voice, and fearing that when he came down he should do him some mischief, ran away without answering. The Moor came down, and finding no one either at the door or in the street, returned full of suspicion to his wife, and asked her if she knew who it was that had knocked. She answered with great truth that she knew not. 'But I think,' said he, 'it was the lieutenant.' 'It might be he,' said she, 'or any one else.'

The Moor checked himself at the time, though he was violently enraged, and determined to take no step without first consulting the ensign. To him he immediately went, and related what had just happened, begging him to learn from the lieutenant what he could on the subject. The ensign rejoiced much in this accident, and promised to do so. He contrived to enter into discourse with him one day in a place where the Moor might see them. He talked with him on a very different subject, laughed much, and expressed by his motions and attitudes very great surprise. The Moor as soon as he saw them separate went to the ensign, and desired to know what had passed between them. The ensign, after many solicitations, at last told him that he had concealed nothing from him. He says he has enjoyed your wife every time you have stayed long enough from home to give him an opportunity; and that in their last interview she had made him a present of that handkerchief which you gave her. The Moor thanked him, and thought that if his wife had no longer the handkerchief in her possession, it would be a proof that the ensign had told him the truth.

For which reason one day after dinner, among other subjects, he asked her for this handkerchief. The poor woman, who had long apprehended this, blushed excessively at the question, and, to hide her change of colour, which the Moor had very accurately observed, ran to her wardrobe and pretended to look for it. After having searched for some time, 'I cannot conceive,' said she, 'what is become of it! have you taken it?' 'Had I taken it,' replied he, 'I should not have asked you for it. But you may look for it another time more at your ease.'

Leaving her then, he began to reflect what would be the best way of putting to death his wife and the lieutenant, and how he might avoid being prosecuted for the murder. Thinking night and day on this subject, he could not prevent Desdemona from perceiving that his behaviour to her was very different from what it had been formerly. She often asked him what it was that agitated him so violently. You, who were once the merriest man alive, are now the most melancholy. The Moor answered and alleged a variety of reasons, but she was not satisfied with any of them; and knowing that she had done nothing to justify so much agitation, she began to fear that he grew tired of her. She once in conversation with the ensign's wife expressed herself thus: 'I know not what to say of the Moor; he used to treat me most affectionately; and I begin to fear that my example will teach young women never to marry against their parents' consent, and the Italians in particular, not to connect themselves with men from whom they are separated by nature, climate, education, and complexion. But as I know him to be the confidential of your husband, whom he consults on all occasions, I entreat you, if you have heard anything that might explain this mystery and be of use to me, not to deny me your assistance.' These words were accompanied with a flood of tears.

The ensign's wife, who knew all (as her husband had in vain endeavoured to prevail upon her to become an accomplice in the murder of Desdemona), but durst tell her nothing for fear of her husband, only said, 'Take care not to give the Moor any cause for suspicion, and do all in your power to convince him of your affection and fidelity.' 'Why, so I do,' said she, 'but to no purpose.' The Moor, in the meantime, did all in his power to prove what he desired not to find true, and begged the ensign to make him see the handkerchief in possession of the lieutenant. Although this was a difficult undertaking, yet the villain promised to do all in his power to give him a satisfactory proof of this. The lieutenant had a woman in the house, who was a notable embroiderer in muslin, and who, struck with the beauty of Desdemona's handkerchief, determined to copy it before it should be returned to her. She set about making one like it, and while she was at work, the ensign discovered that she sat at a window where any one who passed in the street might see her. This he took care to point out to the Moor, who was then fully persuaded that his chaste and innocent wife was an adulteress. He agreed with the ensign to kill both her and the lieutenant; and, consulting together about the means, the Moor entreated him to undertake the assassination of the officer, promising never to forget so great an obligation. He refused, however, to attempt what was so very difficult and dangerous, as the lieutenant was equally brave and vigilant; but with much entreaty and considerable presents, he was prevailed on to say that he would hazard the experiment.

One dark night, after taking this resolution, he observed the lieutenant coming out of the house of a female libertine where he usually passed his evenings, and assaulted him sword in hand. He struck at his legs with a view of bringing him to the ground and with the first blow cut him quite through the right thigh. The poor man instantly fell, and the ensign ran to him to put him to death. But the lieutenant, who was courageous, and familiar with wounds and slaughter, having drawn his sword notwithstanding his desperate situation, and raised himself for defence, cried out Murder as loud as he could. The ensign, perceiving that some people were coming, and that the soldiers quartered thereabout had taken the alarm, fled for fear of being caught, and, turning about again, pretended likewise that he had been brought there by the noise. Placing himself among the rest, and seeing that the leg was cut off, he concluded that though he was not dead, he must die of this wound: and, although he was exceedingly rejoiced at all this, yet he condoled with the lieutenant as much as if he had been his brother.

The next morning this accident was spread all over the city, and came to the ears of Desdemona, who being very compassionate, and not suspecting that this could occasion mischief to herself, expressed the greatest concern for the lieutenant's misfortune. The Moor drew from hence the worst of inferences, and said to the ensign, 'You must know that my simpleton of a wife is almost mad with sorrow for the lieutenant's accident.' 'How could it be otherwise,' said he, 'as he is her life and soul?' 'How,' said the Moor, 'her life and soul! I will separate her soul from her body. I should disgrace my manhood if I killed her not.' And discoursing together if poison or the dagger would be the best, and not liking either the one or the other, the ensign said, 'A method has occurred to me that would satisfy you without creating the least suspicion. The house where you live is very old, and the ceiling of your chamber is broken in many places. Desdemona might be beaten to death with a stocking full of sand, and no marks of this would remain on the body: when she is dead we will pull down a part of the ceiling, and bruise your wife's head; then give out that a beam in falling has done this, and killed her. If you follow this advice you will avoid all suspicion, and every one will believe her death to have been accidental.'

This savage advice pleased the Moor: and waiting for a convenient opportunity, he concealed the ensign one night in a closet that communicated with their chamber. When they were in bed, the ensign, according to his instruction, made a noise in the closet, and the Moor immediately asked his wife if she had heard it? She answered Yes. 'Get up, then, and see what it is.' Poor Desdemona obeyed, and as soon as she was near the closet-door the ensign rushed out, and with the stocking that he had prepared gave her a violent blow on the small of the back. She fell down scarce able to breathe; but with what little force she had, she called the Moor to her assistance. He got out of bed and said to her, 'Most infamous woman, you are now to receive the just reward of your infidelity! – even so are those wives treated who, pretending to love their husbands, are untrue to their beds.'

The poor woman hearing these words, and feeling that she was ready to expire from a second blow that the ensign had given her, said that, 'since the justice of this world was refused her, she attested the Divine Justice in favour of her honour and her truth,' and invoking the Divine Assistance, she was finished by the impious ensign, who struck a third time. Afterwards they placed her in bed; and after breaking her skull, they drew down, as they had determined beforehand, a part of the ceiling. The Moor then called out for help, as the house was falling. The neighbours on this alarm ran thither, and found Desdemona dead under the beams.

Her life had been so virtuous that every one lamented her fate; and the following day she was buried, to the great sorrow of the whole island. But God, who is a just observer of the hearts of men, suffered not so great a crime to pass without the punishment that was due it. So that the Moor, who had loved Desdemona more than his eyes, finding himself deprived of her, began to regret her so extremely, that he almost lost his senses, and went about the house looking for her in every room. Reflecting besides that the ensign had been the cause of his losing along with her all the enjoyments of life, and even his own faculties, that villain became so insupportable to him, that he could not bear the sight of him; and had he not feared the strict and impartial justice of the Venetians, he would have put him openly to death. But not being able to do this with safety to himself, he degraded him from his commission, and permitted him no longer to remain in the company. Hence arose between them the most bitter enmity that can be conceived; and the ensign, the greatest of all villains, studied only how he might be revenged on the Moor.

He went to the lieutenant, who was cured and walked about with his wooden leg, and said to him, 'The time is now come when you may be revenged for the loss of your leg; and if you will come with me to Venice, I will tell you who the assassin was. Here I dare not inform you for many reasons; but there I will be your witness in a court of justice.' The lieutenant, who felt himself violently exasperated against the person, though unknown to him, thanked the ensign, and came away with him to Venice. When they were arrived, the ensign told him that the Moor was the person who had cut off his leg, because he suspected him of adultery with his wife, and that for the same reason he had murdered her, and afterwards given out that she had been killed by the ceiling's falling in upon her. The lieutenant on hearing this, immediately accused the Moor before the Council of the injury done to himself and the murder of Desdemona; and the ensign being called as a witness, asserted the truth of both these accusations, and added that the Moor had communicated to him the whole project, with a view of persuading him to execute both these crimes; and when he had murdered his wife from the impulse of a furious jealousy, he had related to him the manner in which he had put her to death.

The Venetian magistrates hearing that one of their fellow-citizens had been treated with so much cruelty by a barbarian, had the Moor arrested in Cyprus and brought to Venice, where, by means of the torture, they endeavoured to find out the truth. But the Moor possessed force and constancy of mind sufficient to undergo the torture without confessing anything; and though by his firmness he escaped death at this time, he was, after a long imprisonment, condemned to perpetual exile, in which he was afterwards killed, as he deserved to be, by his wife's relations.

The ensign returned to his country, where, still continuing his old practices, he accused one of his companions of having attempted to murder a nobleman who was his enemy. The man was taken up and put to the torture, and, denying firmly the crime laid to his charge, his accuser was also put to the torture; where he was racked so violently that his vitals were injured, and upon being conducted home he died in great agony. Thus was the divine vengeance executed against those who had murdered the innocent Desdemona.

The ensign's wife, who had been informed of the whole affair, after his death thus circumstantially related the story.

Anonymous

RANIERI

TRANSLATED BY
THOMAS ROSCOE (1836)

ANONYMOUS

'*The Anonymous Author of Ranieri*' is included by Thomas Roscoe in *The Italian Novelists*, 1836, with his translations of late sixteenth-century stories.

RANIERI

*Ranieri, a merchant, is entreated by his wife to bring home a
purse full of good sense, from the fair of Troyes; he has great
difficulty in meeting with the commodity, but persisting in the
search, is in the end a great gainer.*

There formerly resided in Desiga, a rich district of Provence, a
man of considerable wealth, named Ranieri. Being wholly devoted to traffic, like most merchants, he spent a great part of his
time in travelling from place to place, and had thus succeeded
in realizing by his prudence a fortune, which he daily increased.
In other matters, however, he displayed by no means the same
discretion; for, though united to a very excellent and lovely
woman, he had the weakness to attach himself to one of quite an
opposite character, upon whom he bestowed a large portion of
his wealth, while at the same time he displayed equal kindness
and liberality towards his wife. The latter observing him one
day preparing for a journey, and laying aside a variety of
articles, intended as presents for his mistress, and being aware at
the same time that his simplicity of character was by no means
qualified to cope with female arts, requested of him, with a very
serious countenance, that he would have the goodness to bring
her back a small purse full of sense, which would give him very
little trouble, as he was going to the fair of Troyes, and that
even a single pennyworth would be enough. This she said, in
the hope of awakening him, by a gentle hint, out of the amorous
lethargy in which he lay bound. But he, imagining that she
alluded to some species of herb, or medicine, failed to perceive
her drift, and contented himself with assuring her that he would
fulfil her wishes.

Now as he ventured not to set out without taking leave likewise of his beloved Mabilia (so the other lady was named), she
on her part entreated him to purchase for her a rich and beautiful mantle, and this also he undertook to do. On his arrival,
therefore, he proceeded to dispatch his business, in order to

attend to the commissions of the ladies, and so successful was he in his speculations, that after realizing more than he expected, he purchased a variety of rich presents besides the mantle, and was enabled to expedite his return. As he was on the point of setting out, he recollected the purse of sense, and inquired of one of his old correspondents on change where he was most likely to meet with it. The other being very much of the same leaven as his friend, quite a matter-of-fact man, recommended him, in the same serious tone, to apply at an apothecary's shop, believing it must be some kind of herb or spice brought from the Levant. The apothecary, with as much simplicity as his customer, assured him that he had none, and referred him to an old Spanish chemist, a little better acquainted with the rare production of which he was in want. Though this tradesman resided at some distance, Ranieri, with a proper regard for his wife's wishes, persevered in his application, and begged to know whether he sold any of this rare article, or had any portion of it to spare. The good man, surprised at this singular demand, began to suspect that there must be some deception in the case, if indeed Ranieri himself did not wish to make a fool of him. 'There is mischief here,' he said to himself, as he began to question our hero more particularly on the point, until he artfully extracted from him a long account of himself and of his fair, discreet young wife, who had desired him to purchase a little sense, while he learned that articles of a very different kind had been purchased for the other lady. Upon this account, being a sensible, humane man, and seeing how the affair stood, he began to vend him a little of the article he so much wanted, in the shape of some good advice upon the subject. He described in pretty lively colours the folly and injustice of which he had been guilty, in preferring a vile mercenary creature to the gentle affections of so kind, so judicious, and lovely a wife, sacrificing her peace and happiness for the sake of a blind and illicit passion for another. 'And if you wish,' continued the kind old man, 'to experience the truth of all I have said, only consent to put to the trial their respective affection and regard for you, which I sincerely advise all such infatuated men to do, and you will soon find which of the two will remain most loyal and faithful to your love.'

Ranieri, who had listened very attentively to the old gentleman's discourse, without once interrupting him, or testifying
the slightest offence, for the first time began to consider the
matter seriously, and to feel impressed with the truth of what he
had heard. So, taking the good sense offered him by the old
Spaniard in good part, he professed himself ready to follow his
advice, would he only point out in what way he could satisfy
himself as to the different degrees of affection entertained by
his wife and the mistress; indeed, nothing would please him
better than to put their tempers to the proof. 'There can be no
difficulty,' continued the good Spaniard, 'in ascertaining this;
only despoil yourself of your gentlemanly attire, assume a very
plain, poor dress, and send before you tidings, of your complete
downfall in the world.' ('Heaven forbid!' cried the poor merchant, horrified at the idea.) 'Then,' continued the old man,
smiling, 'follow them yourself soon afterwards on foot. In this
plight, visit the respective houses of the ladies in question, and
I think I may give you permission to take up your residence at
that which, of the two, receives you the most kindly and hospit-
ably; but never, if you value your own happiness, visit the other
again.'

Perceiving the kind and judicious nature of this advice,
Ranieri promised to obey; he instantly proceeded to the execution
of his plan, and instructed his attendants as to all that was
necessary for its completion. Setting off alone, he arrived in his
poor habiliments, about sunset, in his own district: and apparently overwhelmed with grief and shame, as if he had barely
escaped with life, he knocked at the door of his adored Mabilia.
It so happened that the lady, being close at hand, came herself
to let him in; upon which, in a most alarmed and piteous tone,
Ranieri entreated her to grant him an asylum in her house from
the rage of his angry creditors, who would not be long in over-
taking him. For some time the mercenary woman was at a loss
to recognize her lover in his poor garb, and stood as if doubtful
what to think. At length, beholding him in so destitute a condition, and hearing the fatal tidings of his losses as it were confirmed, she at once assumed a bold and arrogant tone, inquired
who he was, and what he did there, and affected complete
ignorance of there being such a person in the world. At the

same time she shut the door in his face, and went murmuring away. Such was the sudden shock to the feelings of the poor merchant, that it was with difficulty he restrained his rage: he left the place, heaping upon her all the reproachful epithets that she so well deserved.

With sensations it is impossible to describe, he next proceeded towards his own house, whither the report of his ruin had already preceded him: but the moment the door opened, he felt himself encircled in the arms of his wife, who mingling consolations with her tears, conducted him into his room, where she had prepared every thing for his reception likely to alleviate his woes. Such, indeed, was the sweetness and kindness of her manner, that the delight he now felt amply repaid him for the disquiet and pain which the opposite conduct of his mistress had excited in him. Accordingly he found himself, as the good Spaniard had predicted, one of the happiest men in the world, and ever afterwards appreciated, as they deserved, the charms and virtues of his noble consort. Nor did her affection, courage, and devotion stop here; for believing that the whole of her husband's fortune was lost, she generously brought her private allowance, her jewels, and other ornaments, in order to supply his more immediate wants. For he, desirous of ascertaining the extent of her attachment to him, continued to feign the utmost difficulty, in what way to escape the vengeance of his creditors, and incessantly lamented the bitter fate that awaited him. His noble-minded consort, unable to witness his unhappiness, made over to him, without hesitation, a very considerable fortune, left to her by one of her relations. 'Take it, take it all, my dear Ranieri, if it can be of the least service in protecting you from the severity of the law: only let me behold you a little easier and happier in your mind. Let us recollect that fortune comes and goes; that "riches make themselves wings, and fly away",' and in this manner she would invite him to take heart, and induce him, by every means in her power, to partake of refreshment and repose. When these however, appeared to fail in their effect, she, for the first time, began to indulge her grief, declaring that she would rather die than witness his continual sorrow and lamentation; and with this she burst into a flood of tears. No longer proof against this last appeal, her delighted husband, soothing and caressing her in the most affectionate manner, acquainted her with the real circumstances of the case, and assured her that he was far more wealthy than he had ever before been. While he was yet speaking, and a crowd of incensed creditors besieged his door, there came tidings of the arrival of wagon loads of goods, with merchandise of every description, purchased with the immense profits he had realized in his last sales; a sight which, delightful as it was to his creditors, was surpassed by the pure and exquisite pleasure felt by his wife, who saw herself thus unexpectedly restored to affluence, and to the undivided affection and esteem of her repentant husband.

PART II

MODERN

Giovanni Verga

THE SHE-WOLF

TRANSLATED BY
GIOVANNI CECCHETTI

DON LICCIU PAPA

TRANSLATED BY
D. H. LAWRENCE

GIOVANNI VERGA

GIOVANNI VERGA (1840–1922) came from Catania, Sicily, and was the greatest exponent of a school of writing which aimed at an objective, pitiless realism. He has often, and with some justification, been compared to Thomas Hardy. He is at his best when writing of the Sicilian peasants and villagers. His two best-known novels are *I Malavoglia* (*The House by the Medlar Tree*) and *Mastro Don Gesualdo*; among his numerous short stories, the best known are the collections entitled *Vita dei Campi* (*Life in the Fields*) and *Novelle Rusticane* (*Rustic Stories*), the former including the famous 'Cavalleria Rusticana'. The two novels mentioned have been translated by Eric Mosbacher and D. H. Lawrence respectively. Verga is represented in various English short story anthologies, including A. Colquhoun and N. Rogers' *Italian Regional Tales of the 19th Century*, 1961. D. H. Lawrence translated both volumes of short stories mentioned above.

THE SHE-WOLF

She was tall, thin; she had the firm and vigorous breasts of the olive-skinned – and yet she was no longer young; she was pale, as if always plagued by malaria, and in that pallor, two enormous eyes and fresh red lips which devoured you.

In the village they called her the She-wolf, because she never had enough – of anything. The women made the sign of the cross when they saw her pass, alone as a wild bitch, prowling about suspiciously like a famished wolf; with her red lips she sucked the blood of their sons and husbands in a flash, and pulled them behind her skirt with a single glance of those devilish eyes, even if they were before the altar of Saint Agrippina. Fortunately, the She-wolf never went to church, not at Easter, not at Christmas, not to hear Mass, not for confession. Father Angiolino of Saint Mary of Jesus, a true servant of God, had lost his soul on account of her.

Maricchia, a good girl, poor thing, cried in secret because she was the She-wolf's daughter, and no one would marry her, though, like every other girl in the village, she had her fine linen in a chest and her good land under the sun.

One day the She-wolf fell in love with a handsome young man who had just returned from the service and was mowing hay with her in the fields of the notary; and she fell in love in the strongest sense of the word, feeling the flesh afire beneath her clothes; and staring him in the eyes, she suffered the thirst one has in the hot hours of June, deep in the plain. But he went on mowing undisturbed, his nose bent over the swaths.

'What's wrong, Pina?' he would ask.

In the immense fields, where you heard only the crackling flight of the grasshoppers, as the sun hammered down overhead, the She-wolf gathered bundle after bundle, and sheaf after sheaf, never tiring, never straightening up for an instant, never raising the flask to her lips, just to remain at the heels of Nanni, who mowed and mowed and asked from time to time:

'What is it you want, Pina?'

One evening she told him, while the men were dozing on the threshing floor, tired after the long day, and the dogs were howling in the vast, dark countryside.

'It's you I want. You who're beautiful as the sun and sweet as honey. I want you!'

'And I want your daughter, instead, who's a maid,' answered Nanni laughing.

The She-wolf thrust her hands into her hair, scratching her temples, without saying a word, and walked away. And she did not appear at the threshing floor any more. But she saw Nanni again in October, when they were making olive oil, for he was working near her house, and the creaking of the press kept her awake all night.

'Get the sack of olives,' she said to her daughter, 'and come with me.'

Nanni was pushing olives under the millstone with a shovel, shouting 'Ohee' to the mule, to keep it from stopping.

'You want my daughter Maricchia?' Pina asked him.

'What'll you give your daughter Maricchia?' answered Nanni.

'She has all her father's things, and I'll give her my house too; as for me, all I need is a little corner in the kitchen, enough for a straw mattress.'

'If that's the way it is, we can talk about it at Christmas,' said Nanni.

Nanni was all greasy and filthy, spattered with oil and fermented olives, and Maricchia didn't want him at any price. But her mother grabbed her by the hair before the fireplace, muttering between her teeth:

'If you don't take him, I'll kill you!'

The She-wolf was almost sick, and the people were saying that when the devil gets old he becomes a hermit. She no longer roamed here and there, no longer lingered at the doorway, with those bewitched eyes. Whenever she fixed them on his face, those eyes of hers, her son-in-law began to laugh and pulled out the scapular of the Virgin to cross himself. Maricchia stayed at home nursing the babies, and her mother went into the fields to work with the men, and just like a man too, weeding, hoeing, feeding the animals, pruning the vines, despite the north-east and levantine winds of January or the August sirocco, when the mules' heads drooped and the men slept face down along the wall, on the north side. 'In those hours between nones and vespers when no good woman goes roving around,' * Pina was the only living soul to be seen wandering in the countryside, over the burning stones of the paths, through the scorched stubble of the immense fields that became lost in the suffocating heat, far, far away toward the foggy Etna, where the sky was heavy on the horizon.

'Wake up!' said the She-wolf to Nanni, who was sleeping in the ditch, along the dusty hedge, his head on his arms. 'Wake up. I've brought you some wine to cool your throat.'

Nanni opened his drowsy eyes wide, still half asleep, and finding her standing before him, pale, with her arrogant breasts and her coal-black eyes, he stretched out his hands gropingly.

'No! no good woman goes roving around in the hours between nones and vespers!' sobbed Nanni, throwing his face back into the dry grass of the ditch, deep, deep, his nails in his scalp. 'Go away! go away! don't come to the threshing floor again!'

The She-wolf was going away, in fact, retying her superb tresses, her gaze bent fixedly before her as she moved through the hot stubble, her eyes as black as coal.

But she came to the threshing floor again, and more than once, and Nanni did not complain. On the contrary, when she was late, in the hours between nones and vespers, he would go and wait for her at the top of the white, deserted path, with his forehead bathed in sweat; and he would thrust his hands into his hair, and repeat every time:

'Go away! go away! don't come to the threshing floor again!'

Maricchia cried night and day, and glared at her mother, her eyes burning with tears and jealousy, like a young she-wolf herself, every time she saw her come, mute and pale, from the fields.

'Vile, vile mother!' she said to her. 'Vile mother!'

* Translator's note: An old Sicilian proverb, which refers to the hours of the early afternoon, when the Sicilian countryside lies motionless under a scorching sun and no person would dare walk on the roads. Those hours are traditionally believed to be under the spell of malignant spirits.

'Shut up!'

'Thief! Thief!'

'Shut up!'

'I'll go to the Sergeant, I will!'

'Go ahead!'

And she really did go, with her babies in her arms, fearing nothing, and without shedding a tear, like a madwoman, because now she too loved that husband who had been forced on her, greasy and filthy, spattered with oil and fermented olives.

The Sergeant sent for Nanni; he threatened him even with jail and the gallows. Nanni began to sob and tear his hair; he didn't deny anything, he didn't try to clear himself.

'It's the temptation!' he said. 'It's the temptation of hell!'

He threw himself at the Sergeant's feet begging to be sent to jail.

'For God's sake, Sergeant, take me out of this hell! Have me killed, put me in jail; don't let me see her again, never! never!'

'No!' answered the She-wolf instead, to the Sergeant. 'I kept a little corner in the kitchen to sleep in, when I gave him my house as dowry. It's my house. I don't intend to leave it.'

Shortly afterwards, Nanni was kicked in the chest by a mule and was at the point of death, but the priest refused to bring him the Sacrament if the She-wolf did not go out of the house. The She-wolf left, and then her son-in-law could also prepare to leave like a good Christian; he confessed and received communion with such signs of repentance and contrition that all the neighbours and the curious wept before the dying man's bed. And it would have been better for him to die that day, before the devil came back to tempt him again and creep into his body and soul, when he got well.

'Leave me alone!' he told the She-wolf. 'For God's sake, leave me in peace! I've seen death with my own eyes! Poor Maricchia is desperate. Now the whole town knows about it! If I don't see you it's better for both of us...'

And he would have liked to gouge his eyes out not to see those of the She-wolf, for whenever they peered into his, they made him lose his body and soul. He did not know what to do to free himself from the spell. He paid for Masses for the souls in purgatory and asked the priest and the Sergeant for help. At Easter he went to confession, and in penance he publicly licked more than four feet of pavement, crawling on the pebbles in front of the church – and then, as the She-wolf came to tempt him again:

'Listen!' he said to her. 'Don't come to the threshing floor again; if you do, I swear to God, I'll kill you!'

'Kill me,' answered the She-wolf, 'I don't care; I can't stand it without you.'

As he saw her from the distance, in the green wheat fields, Nanni stopped hoeing the vineyard, and went to pull the axe from the elm. The She-wolf saw him come, pale and wild-eyed, with the axe glistening in the sun, but she did not fall back a single step, did not lower her eyes; she continued toward him, her hands laden with red poppies, her black eyes devouring him.

'Ah! damn your soul!' stammered Nanni.

DON LICCIU PAPA

The goodwives were spinning in the sun, and the fowls were scratching among the rubbish in front of the doorsteps, when suddenly there arose a squealing and a scampering all down the little street, as Uncle Maso was seen approaching from the distance, Uncle Maso the pig-snatcher, with his noose in his hand; and all the fowls scuttled away squawking, as if they knew him.

Uncle Maso got sixpence from the Town Council for every fowl, and half-a-crown for every pig which he caught breaking the bye-laws. He preferred the pigs. Therefore, seeing Goodwife Santa's little porker stretched out peacefully with its nose in the mire, he threw the running noose round its neck.

'Oh, holy, holy, Madonna! What are you doing, Uncle Maso?' cried Aunt Santa, pale as death. 'For mercy's sake, Uncle Maso, don't have me fined, it'll be the finish of me!'

Uncle Maso, the traitor, in order to gain time to get the young pig on to his shoulders, began to reel off pretty speeches to her.

'My dear good woman, what am I to do? It's the Town

Council's orders. They won't have pigs in the street any more. If I leave you this young sow I lose my own daily bread.'

Aunt Santa ran behind him like a madwoman, her hands clutching her hair, screaming all the time:

'Ah, Uncle Maso! don't you know she cost me five shillings at the fair of San Giovanni, and I care for her like the apple of my eye! Leave me my little pig, Uncle Maso, by the souls of those that are dead and gone! Come the New Year, with God's help she'll be worth thirty shillings!'

Uncle Maso, with never a word, his head dropped, and his heart as hard as a stone, only minded where he put his feet, so as not to slip in the muck; the young pig over his shoulder twisting up to heaven and grunting. Then Aunt Santa, desperate, in order to save her pig fetched him a solemn kick in the rear, and sent him rolling.

The goodwives no sooner saw the pig-snatcher sprawling in the mud than they were upon him with their distaffs and their wooden-soled slippers, eager to pay him out for all the pigs and fowls he had on his conscience. But at that moment up ran Don Licciu Papa with his sword-belt over his paunch, bawling from the background like one possessed, keeping out of reach of the distaffs:

'Clear the way! Clear the way for the law!'

The law condemned Goodwife Santa to pay the fine and the costs, and in order to escape prison they had to turn for protection to the baron, whose kitchen window looked on to the little street, and who saved her by a miracle, demonstrating to the court that it was not an instance of rebellion, because that day the pig-snatcher hadn't got his cap on with the Town Council badge.

'You see now!' exclaimed the women in chorus. 'It takes a saint to get into Paradise! Who was to know that about the cap?'

However, the baron wound up with a sermon: those pigs and fowls had got to be cleared out of the street; the Town Council was quite right, their place was a pigsty.

After that, every time the baron's manservant emptied the garbage into the street, on to the heads of the neighbours, not a woman murmured. Only they lamented that the hens, shut up in the house to escape the fine, didn't rear good chicks any more; and the pigs, tied by the leg to the bed-post, were like souls tortured in purgatory — at least they used to cleanse their streets before.

'All that muck would be so much gold for the Grasshopper Closes,' sighed Farmer Vito. 'If I'd got my bay mule yet, I'd wipe up the street with my own hands.'

And this also was a bit of Don Licciu Papa's work. He had come with the bailiff to seize the mule for debt, since Farmer Vito would never have let the bailiff by himself take the mule from the stable, no, not if they'd killed him for it, he wouldn't, he'd rather have bitten off the fellow's nose and eaten it like bread. Then before the judge, who sat at the table like Pontius Pilate, when Farmer Venerando prosecuted him to recover the loan advanced on the half-profits, he couldn't find a word to say. The Grasshopper Closes were fit for nothing but grasshoppers; the fool was himself, he had himself to blame if he'd come home from harvest empty-handed, and Farmer Venerando was quite right to want to be paid back, without all that talking and spinning things out, though that was what he'd paid a lawyer to talk for him for. But when it was over, and Farmer Venerando was going off gleefully, rocking inside his great boots like a fattened duck, he couldn't help asking the clerk if it was true that they were going to sell his mule.

'Silence!' interrupted the judge, who was blowing his nose before passing on to another case.

Don Licciu Papa woke up with a start on his bench, and cried, 'Silence!'

'If you'd brought a lawyer, they'd have let you say something more,' neighbour Orazio told him for his comfort.

In the piazza, in front of the Town Hall steps, the crier sold his mule for him.

'Nine guineas for neighbour Vito Gnirri's mule! Nine guineas for a fine bay mule! Nine guineas!'

Neighbour Vito, sitting on the steps with his chin between his hands, wasn't going to let out a word about the mule's being old, and its being over sixteen years that he'd worked her. And she stood there as happy as a bride, in her new halter. But the moment they'd really led her away, he went off his head, think-

ing of that usurer of a Farmer Venerando who was getting nine
guineas out of him just for one year's half-profits on the Grasshopper Closes, and the land wasn't worth as much to buy it out-
right, and without his mule he'd never be able to work them,
and next year he'd be in debt again. And he began to shout like
a maniac into Farmer Venerando's face:

'What shall you want of me when I've got nothing left?
Antichrist that you are!'

And he'd have liked to knock the baptism off his brow, if
it hadn't been for Don Licciu Papa, who was there with his
sword and his braided hat, and who began to shout as he drew
back:

'Halt in the law's name! Halt in the law's name!'

'What law?' squealed neighbour Vito, going home with the
halter in his hand. 'Law is made for them who've got money to
spend.'

Which was what the Shepherd Arcangelo knew, who, when
he'd gone to law with his Reverence because of his bit of a
house, which his Reverence wanted to force him to sell to him,
had everybody saying to him:

'Are you out of your mind going to law with his Reverence?
It's the tale of the pitcher and the stone. His Reverence with all
his money will hire the best lawyer's tongue among them, and
will leave you penniless and senseless.'

His Reverence, since he'd got rich, had enlarged the paternal
house, this way and that, like the hedgehog does when he swells
himself out to drive his neighbours away from his hole. Now
he'd widened the windows looking on to Shepherd Arcangelo's
roof, and he said he needed the other man's house so as to build
a kitchen above it and turn the window into a doorway.

'You see, my dear neighbour Arcangelo, I can't manage without a kitchen! You must be reasonable!'

Neighbour Arcangelo didn't see it, and kept on saying he
wanted to die in the house where he was born. As a matter of
fact, he only came there of a Sunday; but the stones knew
him, and if he thought of the village, when he was away on the
wild pastures of Carramone, he never saw it as anything except
that patched-up little doorway and that window without any
glass.

'All right, all right,' said his Reverence to himself. 'Pig-headed peasants! We've got to knock the sense in.'

And from his Reverence's window rained down broken pots, stones, and dirty water on Shepherd Arcangelo's roof, till the corner where the little bed stood was worse than a pigsty. If Shepherd Arcangelo shouted, his Reverence began to shout louder than he, from the roof above: 'Couldn't one keep a pot of basil on his window-sill nowadays? Wasn't a man free to water his own flowers?'

Shepherd Arcangelo had a head stubborner than his own rams, and he went to law. There came the judge, the clerk, and Don Licciu Papa, to see whether a man was free to water his own flowers or not, so of course on that day the flowers weren't there on the window-sill, and his Reverence had only to take the trouble to remove them every time the law was coming, and put them out again as soon as they'd turned their backs. As for the judge, he couldn't spend his days playing watchman on Shepherd Arcangelo's roof, or patrolling up and down the narrow street; every visit he made was expensive.

Remained only to decide whether his Reverence's window should or should not have an iron grating, and the judge, the clerk, and all the lot looked up with their spectacles on their noses, and took measurements so that you'd have thought it was a baron's roof, that bit of a flat mouldy housetop. And his Reverence brought forth certain ancient rights for a window without a grating, and for a few tiles which leaned out over the roof, till you could make nothing of it any more, and poor Shepherd Arcangelo himself stared up in the air as if to find out whatever his roof could be guilty of. He lost his sleep at nights and the smile from his mouth; he bled himself in expenses, and had to leave his flock in charge of the boy while he ran round after the judge and the bailiff. So of course the sheep began to die like flies, with the first cold of winter, which showed that the Lord was punishing him for falling out with the Church, so they said.

'Take the house, then,' he said at last to his Reverence, when after so many law-suits and expenses he hadn't enough money even to buy a rope to hang himself from one of the beams. He wanted to sling his saddle-bag over his neck and go off with his daughter to live with the sheep, for he didn't want to see that accursed house again, as long as he lived.

But then his other neighbour, the baron, came forward, saying that he too had windows and jutting tiles above the roof of Shepherd Arcangelo, and seeing that his Reverence wanted to build a kitchen, he himself had to enlarge his pantry, so that the poor herdsman no longer knew whom his house did belong to. But his Reverence found the means to settle the quarrel with the baron, dividing the house of Shepherd Arcangelo between them like good friends, and seeing that the latter had this other obligation as well, the price of the house was reduced by a good quarter.

Nina, the daughter of Shepherd Arcangelo, when they had to leave the house and depart from the village, simply never stopped crying, as if her heart was fastened to those four walls and to the nails in them. Her father, poor fellow, tried to console her as best he could, telling her that away up there, in the Caves of Carramone, you lived like a prince, without neighbours and pig-snatchers. But the goodwives who knew the story winked among themselves, murmuring:

'Up at Carramone the Young Master won't be able to come to her, at evening, when neighbour Arcangelo is with his sheep. That's why Nina is weeping like a fountain.'

When neighbour Arcangelo got to know this he began to swear and shout:

'Hussy! Now who'll you get to marry you!'

But Nina wasn't thinking of getting anybody to marry her. She only wanted to stop where the Young Master was, so that she could see him every day at the window, as soon as he got up, and make him a sign if he could come to her that evening. This had been Nina's downfall, seeing the Young Master at the window every day, who had begun by smiling at her and sending her kisses and the smoke from his pipe, and the neighbour women were bursting with jealousy. Then bit by bit love had come, so that now the girl had quite lost her senses, and she said straight and flat to her father:

'You go where you like. I shall stop where I am.'

And the Young Master had promised her that he would look after her.

Shepherd Arcangelo wasn't swallowing that, and he wanted to fetch Don Licciu Papa to take away his daughter by force.

'Anyhow, when we've gone from here nobody will know of our misfortunes,' he said. But the judge told him that Nina had already reached years of discretion, and she was her own mistress to do as she pleased and chose.

'Ah! her own mistress?' muttered Shepherd Arcangelo. 'Well, I'm master!' And the first time he met the Young Master, who blew smoke into his face, he cracked his head like a nut with a wooden cudgel.

After they had tied him up fast, Don Licciu Papa came running up shouting: 'Make way! Make way for the law!'

They even gave him a lawyer to defend him before the judge.

'At least the law will cost me nothing this time,' said neighbour Arcangelo. The lawyer succeeded in proving, as easy as two and two make four, that Shepherd Arcangelo hadn't done it on purpose, wilfully seeking to murder the Young Master with a cudgel of wild pearwood, but that the cudgel belonged to his profession, and was used by him to knock the rams on the head when they wouldn't hear reason.

So he was only condemned to five years, Nina remained with the Young Master, the baron enlarged his pantry, and his Reverence built a fine new house above Shepherd Arcangelo's crumbling one, with a balcony and two green windows.

Luigi Capuana

THE REVEREND WALNUT

NEWLY TRANSLATED BY
BRUCE PENMAN

LUIGI CAPUANA

Luigi Capuana (1839–1915), also from Catania, Sicily, collaborated with Verga in the 'naturalist' school, though he never quite achieved Verga's sheer evocative power. He wrote numerous volumes of short stories, including some for children, and several novels. His stories feature in various English anthologies, though no full volume appears to exist.

THE REVEREND WALNUT

He seems to have had the nickname of 'Walnut' from the very day of his birth. Apparently he was in a hurry to enter the world, a month or so ahead of time; and the midwife quickly wrapped him up and sprinkled a little holy water on his forehead so that there should be no risk of his dying unbaptized on her hands, and then put him in his mother's arms with the words:

'He's just like a walnut! If he lives, it'll be a miracle!'

Seeing how tiny he was, people remembered and repeated the phrase about his resemblance to a walnut, until the nickname stuck to him. It stuck more tightly, in fact, than his family surname, which was Fiorito.

Fiorito * hardly seemed the name for him, poor little fellow. But his thin, wizened little body contained the kindest and gentlest of souls. His family had him trained as a surveyor, but none of his fellow-citizens ever made use of his services – partly because they knew him to be incapable of the slightest irregularity in the measurement and valuation of their lands. Luckily his parents left him enough to live on, together with his sister, in the little village where he was born. She was a member of a religious order, but acted as his housekeeper. He managed his property himself, and was very popular – because he was so easy to cheat – with the tenants who worked his land in return for a fixed share of the crop. Every year was a bad year for both grain and olives, according to them; and Don Lucio Fiorito, who never noticed anything and was incapable of suspicion, encouraged them to accept the will of Heaven and hope for better things in the future. The tenants dried their crocodile tears, resigned themselves to the will of God, and cheerfully continued to rob him.

From time to time Sister Celeste grumbled about it.

'This bad harvest!' she would say. 'It only seems to be bad for us!'

* A roughly equivalent English surname would be 'Fairchild'.

'What can we do?' her brother would reply. 'It's the way things are!'

And the good lady went off to church and said prayers to her Saviour, to the Madonna and to all the saints in heaven, to remind them about the state of her fields and her brother's land, which seemed to have a curse on them.

'Keep your eyes open, and remember that all peasants are robbers!' she would say to Don Lucio, as he set off to watch the sowing of his fields, the reaping of his grain, the gathering of his olives, or the operation of extracting the oil, which was carried out at a neighbour's mill.

But her advice did no good. The tenant's wife would distract his attention with her chatter, and the grain disappeared from the winnowing floor, or the oil vanished from the vat, while the miller's men turned a blind eye.

'Why don't you get married, your Honour?'

She knew that this was a subject near to his heart, the cunning peasant, and as soon as Don Lucio got off his mule, she would get him on one side and repeat the insidious question, putting forward suggestions and listening to his confidences.

'Yes ... yes. I've been thinking about it for some time. But, you know, I don't like to ask ...'

'What, *you*, your Honour? Why, a single word would be enough, coming from you! There's Miss Forti now; or Miss Lovico, with her fine dowry.'

She mentioned a string of names, with special emphasis on Miss Rizzo, the daughter of a lawyer who owned a neighbouring estate.

'It'd be a fine thing for her too, your Honour, now she's getting on for thirty. If you'd agree to my doing something for you, now!'

'Yes ... yes. Do whatever you can.'

The tenant's wife was cunning enough to keep him in suspense for nearly a year.

'Miss Rizzo's keen enough,' she would say. 'It's her father that's against it. And yet, you know ...'

'I'll get a friend of mine to talk to them about it,' said Don Lucio.

'That's right, your Honour! Get it settled as soon as you can.'

Miss Rizzo roared with laughter when she heard of his offer, saying that she had no use for walnuts. The news was a cruel blow to Don Lucio, and the tears came into his eyes.

His whole world seemed to have fallen in ruins. He had built so many castles in the air during the previous twelve months! Walled in by his own timidity, fully aware of his miserable appearance and his thin, withered little body, he had never before even dared to think of approaching a woman.

Finally he confided in his sister.

'You *have* been silly!' she said. 'There are so many women in the world. . . . Why didn't you tell me all this before?'

And Sister Celeste, who was fond of her brother, began to make inquiries herself. She spoke to her confessor about it, and to her friends – women who, like her, passed their days in church, reciting Pater Nosters and Ave Marias.

But that nickname was the bane of his life!

After a dozen unsuccessful attempts, Don Lucio followed the example of those women who give themselves to God, because no one else wants them. At the age of forty, he began to study for the priesthood, and took holy orders.

In his priestly robe and his shovel hat, he remained just as timid as before, and just as ingenuous. He believed that it was now his duty to lead every lost lamb back to the sheepfold of the Saviour, and he made a nuisance of himself. Spiritual grace was a very fine thing, no doubt; but other people had to think of the life of the body, as well, and could hardly join him in saying his rosary, attending endless masses and sermons, and making offerings to every saint in the calendar! Even the Prior urged him to use more moderation.

'This world of ours sometimes needs a worldly approach! Think more about winning your own way to Heaven. Enough is enough!'

The Reverend Walnut, as everyone called him now, was mortified by this, and shocked as well. He resigned himself to fasting and doing penance for himself and for all other sinners, without annoying other people by trying to get them to do the same.

The peasants cheated him more than ever, though they always kissed his priestly hand with the utmost respect when he went to see them. When the old mule died, that had carried him on his rounds for so many years, they wished a donkey on to him which was so useless that he did not know what to do with it. It was a fine enough beast to look at – tall and robust, with a shining coat. It might have been taken for one of the famous Pantelleria breed of asses. But it was so obstinate, so unreliable, such a terrible biter and kicker, that the unfortunate priest used to recommend his soul to God every time he mounted it.

'Your Honour must have spoiled its temper,' said the tenant's wife.

And he believed her, in good faith. But how could he have spoiled its temper, when he always let it do what it liked? The wretched brute seemed to enjoy embarrassing him – and what a cunning animal it was, too!

It would trot sedately for a certain distance, ears pricked, head up, as if proud to carry a worthy servant of God on its back. But the first patch of grass by the roadside would stop it in its tracks, and down would go its head – as if its belly were not already full of hay and barley! The unfortunate priest tugged at its bridle and kicked it in the ribs with his heels – he never wore spurs. All in vain – the donkey grazed on to its heart's content. When the delicious meal was finished, it brayed, and brayed again, and did all manner of fancy steps – round and round, sideways, backwards and forwards – before going on again along the well-known road to the farm. But when it reached a fork, the donkey insisted on turning left instead of right, showing great determination, and struggling with the priest, who pulled stoutly but ineffectively on the right-hand rein. More bucking and braying followed, together with a further display of fancy steps, until a passing peasant took the brute by the bridle, and led it round on to the right road.

'This is no animal for you, your Honour!'

The Reverend Walnut heard this last phrase so often that finally he decided to get rid of the donkey. Together with his tenant, he took it to Belverde Fair, and stood waiting for a buyer, among the throng of people and the hundreds of beasts.

The donkey attracted plenty of attention. It seemed to want

to find a buyer too, to judge by the spirited way it switched its tail, held up its head, and pricked its ears. The tenant began to sing its praises to a group of people who had stopped to look.

'Strong as a mule – lively as a horse! Never known him to get tired! And gentle – you can let a child look after him!'

He prodded its muscles, and stroked its back as if to improve the shine of its coat; he trotted it up and down to show off its fine, clean legs and pulled back its lips so that the onlookers could see its teeth and satisfy themselves that it was really only just four years old.

The priest stood by, with his green sunglasses, and his red parasol open against the rays of the sun. His eyes were lowered, and his lips were pursed. He seemed embarrassed by the praise lavished on his donkey, and when a buyer came forward, he listened attentively to the final discussion about the price.

'Say ten ounces, then! He's a real gift at that price!'

'No, my friend! Make it eight!'

'You don't like my price, and I don't like yours – make it eight and three-quarters, then! Here's the owner – you can pay him now.'

The Reverend Walnut raised his eyes, smiled gently and opened his lips to say something.

'No!' said the buyer quickly. 'Not a farthing more!'

'Yes ... yes. That's all right. But I feel I ought to warn you ...'

'Not another word!'

'No, wait. I must in conscience tell you ...'

'You just take the money, your Honour,' said the tenant. 'A bargain concluded before witnesses is as good as a legal contract.'

'That's all right,' said the priest. But he took the buyer by the arm, and led him to one side.

'Listen,' he said, 'it's true enough that the donkey is strong, untiring, and so on – but gentle! That's another matter. As a matter of conscience, I must tell you that the animal is obstinate, unreliable, unmanageable, and given to kicking and biting. But if you want it ...'

'That damned crook!' shouted the other.

And the witnesses had to intervene and stop him beating up the tenant.

The donkey began to bray, as if in mockery of its master, and everybody laughed.

When Sister Celeste went to Heaven, the Reverend Walnut was robbed more freely than ever by the peasants, and besieged in his own house by hordes of supposedly destitute beggars, who regarded him as a useful source of free meals. He began to find himself fasting far more often than he intended.

The Prior, who was a man of the world, and quite fond of him, in his own way, often spoke to him about it, when they met in the vestry.

'Be a saint if you want to – why not? But even saints ought not to be silly! Charity towards the poor ... yes, of course, an excellent thing – the poor are the brothers of Jesus Christ. But some distinctions are necessary. I never give a farthing in charity without asking myself at least twice if the recipient deserves it. There are some beggars who are better off than you or me. Not that that means much, in your case. You're an absolute skeleton! And your tenants are so fat they can hardly walk. They're all buying land and livestock. ... Your eyes are fixed on the heavens – why don't you lower them for a moment, and take a good look round? Be a saint, but don't be silly.'

With repetition, this sank into the ingenuous soul of the Reverend Walnut, and undermined his confidence in himself and everyone else.

'What must I do?' he said to the Prior. 'Tell me what to do!'

The Prior looked him over from head to foot, as if weighing him up and inspecting him inside and out, and then thought for a minute or two. Not for nothing was he a man of the world – a money-grubber too, according to some people. At the moment, however, he was thinking how to get this poor idiot out of his difficulties – by means of a practical business arrangement.

'You ought to take out an annuity,' he said.

'An annuity? With whom?'

'With me, unless you have anything against it. A full valuation of your estate ... correct calculation of capital and interest ... the house to be yours to live in for the rest of your life. You know Mr Stella, the notary? We'll go and see him, and have a proper talk about it. You've already earned your place in

Heaven — several times over, I should think! Now you must change your ways. Be a saint, but don't be silly! You must admit I'm right.'

Poor Father Walnut! He had had no luck with his matrimonial projects, and no luck with his dedication of himself to the service of God. Would he have any more luck with the annuity, he wondered, as this further change confronted him. He dared not think of himself as a saint — he knew himself to be a great sinner, and humbled himself accordingly before God. But he had certainly been silly, and still was. Perhaps he had been too long over admitting it to himself.

Sleepless nights followed, during which he indulged the fantasy of using the annuity only for the bare necessities of life, and saving up the rest to start a charitable foundation, if it pleased Heaven to grant him length of days.

He mentioned this to the Prior, after signing the annuity deed ...

'If Heaven grants me length of days,' he repeated.

'Heaven forbid!' said the Prior under his breath.

But Heaven punished the Prior by granting many more years of life to the Reverend Walnut. He remained a worthy priest, though not exactly a saint. He had given up the idea of winning sanctity at all costs by means of fasting and penitence. He began to get fat, in fact, and really started to look as round and plump as a walnut, as if to justify his nickname — though the Prior glared at him every time they met with a malevolence that might have been expected to blight his health.

Every six months, when the priest came to draw his half-yearly instalment under the annuity agreement, the Prior looked at him in consternation, unable to believe his eyes — unable to recognize in this bladder of lard (as he expressed it to himself) the withered little frame which had so deceived him.

'You're getting fatter and fatter!' he cried.

It sounded almost like a snarl.

'Yes ... yes. It seems to be the will of Heaven,' replied the Reverend Walnut, with all humility.

'You eat too much! Something's going to happen to you. Be careful! See how short your neck's getting! It's a bad sign! Be careful!'

He wanted to frighten him, to give him something to think about.

'Here we stand, awaiting the call of Providence,' said the priest, quietly pocketing his money.

Providence seemed to be having a little joke at the expense of the money-grubbing Prior.

The Prior was the first to be called away – whether to Heaven or elsewhere remains undecided. A week later the summons came for the Reverend Walnut, and certainly took him straight to Paradise.

Renato Fucini

THE CUCKOO CLOCK

NEWLY TRANSLATED BY
GRAHAM SNELL

RENATO FUCINI

RENATO FUCINI (1843–1922) came from near Pisa, Tuscany. He wrote a fair number of stories about Tuscan rustic life. The story here translated is from *Le Veglie di Neri* (*Neri's Vigils*). No volume of his stories exists in English, but he figures in one or two anthologies, including A. Colquhoun and N. Rogers' *Italian Regional Tales of the 19th Century*, 1961.

THE CUCKOO CLOCK

At last they came – those three conventional cracks of the whip from the sturdy arm of Fiore; faithful old Gigia broke into a gallop, joyfully shaking her damp, steaming rump; Fiore yawned as he thought of supper, and Signor Pasquale, lifting for a moment his right hand, deadened with cold, from the package he was holding jealously on his knees, wiped his nose with a rapid movement, just as rapidly put it back in its place, and mumbled a satisfied 'Ah!' which meant 'At last we're here!'

At that same moment the calm which, as usual, had reigned since midnight in Signor Pasquale's house was broken by a loud din. The children started shrieking, Toppa rushed barking up to the master's gig, and Signora Flaminia ran into the kitchen to throw everything in. Into the saucepan she threw the *taglierini* made with her own hands; into the pot which had stood simmering for some time she threw the cauliflower grown in her kitchen garden by the well; into the frying-pan she threw four handfuls of live leaping gudgeon, caught that morning by her sons; she also threw in the measure of ill humour that had brewed inside her while she waited for her husband's return, forty minutes later than usual, from Cutigliano market – and now she hovered expectantly before putting the last touches to this her favourite chore.

Five minutes later Gigia, who had been taken straight into the coach-house so as not to be left out to sweat in the biting wind from the mountains, was snorting and twitching her ears as the rascal boys roughly stroked her and Toppa licked her, though Toppa wasn't one for jumping up at his master, or at Fiore or at the mare's nose.

But that evening, or at least just at that moment, Signor Pasquale was in no mood for affectionate greetings from children or dog: he asked what the time was, grunted a good evening to his children, gave Toppa a blow with his umbrella, and hurried with his mysterious parcel straight into his room.

Signora Flaminia, who had been expecting him to come and thaw out near where the supper was cooking, was surprised when he failed to appear in the kitchen; but thinking he had gone straight in to take off his wet clothes, she continued blowing on the fire and getting on with the supper which that day, as on all market days, was going to be a really good meal.

'Now leave your father alone this evening,' said Fiore to the boys as he put down straw in Gigia's stable. 'Leave him alone because tonight isn't his night.'

'What's wrong with him? What's wrong with him?'

'Nothing, so far as I know; but I think he's got something on his mind – quite a lot, in fact.'

'Did he shout at you on the way back?'

'No, not shout – but every time I opened my mouth he called me a big oaf for no reason at all. I just let him go on because I know he's like that anyway. But it took all the patience I had! Can you imagine – he snapped my head off because I told him I wouldn't swap the old clock at the top of the stairs for half the world.

'And there he was telling me I was a big oaf, and I said I'd been in his house for twenty-four years and I'd never seen it at the repairer's or lose a minute. ... After all, hasn't he said so plenty of times himself? But not tonight! He said it wasn't true, any of it, so I just let him say so. And he was grumbling on! Oh, heaven knows what's got into him tonight ... Cecchino, stop that – leave the mare alone! ... And yet only the other day ... he should have remembered ... Natale, leave that wretched dog! There, what if he bit him! Wouldn't that serve him right? Oh no, Peppe, then you'd have to whip him off ... oh, goodness me!'

'Boys! Pasquale!'

'Do you hear? The mistress is calling you to supper. Go on, off you go.'

'Pasquale! Boys! Come and sit down!' repeated Signora Flaminia.

'Damn those boys!' mumbled Fiore, and as he put the whip back in its holder on the gig he showed it to Toppa who got the message and went galloping into the house with his tail between his legs.

It was all that was needed to free the animals, the eternal victims of those four scoundrel boys, who ran pushing and tumbling into the living-room, and plonked themselves down at the table, sniffing and all ready to give their usual response when the minestrone was served – 'Is that all?'

They were astonished to see it still wasn't served out; they looked at one another, coughed, sniggered, wiped their mouths and everywhere else with their napkins; and fidgeting on their chairs, they all asked together, 'Where's papa?'

Meanwhile Signora Flaminia, ladle in one hand and the first of the soup plates in the other, waited, looking towards the door through which her husband should have appeared.

For nearly two minutes the tureen sent its cloud of appetizing steam billowing round the petrol lamp which hung from a beam over the table; then Fiore came into the room.

'Where's the master?' he said as soon as he stepped in.

'But good Lord, where's he gone? What's he doing?' Flaminia cried impatiently. 'Give him a call – go on, Fiore. I think I heard him up in the study.'

'Yes, ma'am. Listen! He's up there doing something. It sounds as though he's knocking in some nails – but there's no knowing.'

'Yes, yes. Go and call him and tell him I'm serving out, because otherwise these *taglierini* are going to be awful.'

At that moment Signor Pasquale was happy. He had unburdened himself of the mysterious package that he had brought with such care, in the cold and sleet, over fourteen miles of mountain roads; and now, before he went downstairs to eat, he gazed up at the study wall where hung a very ordinary cuckoo clock which some rogue had palmed off on him as an object of fabulous rarity. As he savoured in advance the joyful surprise he was preparing for his children, for the local mountain folk, for the parish priest and for Signora Flaminia (who was thinking her husband must have his head full of one of his crazy ideas) – as he savoured in advance, as I said, the joy of their surprise, he forgot even the bad mood that had come upon him in a café where some people had called his cuckoo clock good for scrap and reckoned it was worth twelve lire when he had paid forty-five, thinking he had got a bargain.

'Here I am, here I am, Fiore. I'll be straight down!' he replied fondly to the servant calling him; and as happy as Paschaltide, the season after which he had been named, and with his clothes still spattered and his boots all muddy, he went down to join his family.

In the flurry of gladness among the boys at the sight of their father — which just then meant 'food' — a glass went flying, splashing wine all over the tablecloth before smashing in the middle of the room, accompanied by a roar of laughter from Signor Pasquale who, two nights before, at exactly the same time, had nearly dislocated his right thumb smacking Cecchino for a similar accident.

And that made Signora Flaminia all the more certain that Pasquale must have done something really crazy.

'Heaven knows,' she thought to herself, 'heaven knows what they've talked him into buying this time!'

And Signora Flaminia's fears were all too justified, because from the three markets he had been to that year he had never returned empty-handed. From the first he came back with a dozen silk headscarves all made of cotton; from the second, with a *Diodati* Bible for the priest who had asked him to get a *Martini* edition; from the third, with a fine pair of 'English' cashmere trousers from Prato which, when he tried them on, came half-way up his calves.

'And this time? God help me!' thought Signora Flaminia; and she looked with pity at Pasquale's mud-splashed clothes as he noisily sucked up his minestrone and chuckled to himself under his moustache. 'God help me!'

She blew on her first spoonful, and as she waited for it to cool she said to Pasquale, who was looking at his pocket watch, 'By the way — the chestnut man, did you see him?'

'Who? Oh! Be quiet, be quiet, never mind!' Pasquale answered irritably. 'Do you have to bring that up now?'

'But didn't you go to the market specially?'

'Fiore!' Signor Pasquale called, 'Fiore!' And in reply to his wife — 'Yes, you're right, but I believe Fiore saw him ... Fiore!'

'At your service, master ...'

'Tell me, Fiore, did you speak to Luc' Antonio?'

'No, sir – since you told me you wished to speak to him yourself ...'

'But didn't I also tell you ...?'

'Yes, sir, that if I saw him I was to send him to the tobacconist's – which in fact I did at exactly ten o'clock ...'

'You didn't send him!'

'Yes, sir, I did! But they told him that you ...'

'You're right, yes, you're right! With all these business matters on my mind ... But wasn't there something else I had to remember this morning? I had to see Luc' Antonio ... I had to see Luc' Antonio, and then I had to ... in fact I had so many things to do that this one must have slipped my mind. Well, anyway – enough's enough! This is no time to worry about that! Fiore, go and make that wretched dog shut up, or I'll murder it. Who's he barking at?'

'It's the new tenant-farmer ...'

'Well, tell him to be quiet too.'

Signora Flaminia was sitting quietly, not looking up from her soup plate.

'Off you go,' she told Fiore. 'I myself had a word with Luc' Antonio. I sent Cecco out to the main road to meet him and bring him here.' Then, plucking a piece of paper from out of her corset, she showed it to her husband and said, 'By the way, the nuns' bailiff sent you back this receipt for you to put the date on.'

That dismayed Signor Pasquale. He looked at his wife, looked at the receipt, slowly put his watch back in his pocket, gave a quick shrug and, for lack of a better reply, told everybody to be quiet. Nobody breathed.

The great moment, meanwhile, was fast drawing near.

Signor Pasquale had put the clock up on his study wall, exactly facing his armchair, and had then synchronized it with his pocket watch, which he had carefully set at midday by the clock at Cutigliano. In two minutes it should strike six o'clock, and in two minutes his family would enjoy the marvellous surprise, and his victory over the eternal sceptics, and over the nagging bad temper of his wife, would be achieved.

He wanted to sit quietly in his chair, but he couldn't; he wanted to eat and drink casually, but he couldn't: so much so

that he put a cork in his mouth, mistaking it for a piece of
bread; and then he emptied the vinegar bottle into Cecchino's
glass, thinking he was pouring him some vermouth. He also
wanted to keep quiet, and that was the most important, but he
didn't manage that either.

'Boys, it won't be long now!' he said, unable to hold out any
longer. 'It won't be long now!' He gave a chuckle and slily
tucked his chin into his chest, like a hedgehog when you touch
its back. 'It won't be long now!'

'What for? What for?' they all shrieked, thinking they were
authorized by this confidence from their father to raise the
devil's own din. 'What for? What for?'

'For nothing!' bleakly replied Pasquale, wounded by a specially loud sigh from his wife.

'For nothing,' repeated Signor Pasquale; then, having taken
his watch out of his pocket again, he felt an easing of the pain
caused by that sigh when he saw there was only half a minute to
go to six o'clock.

'Now then – quiet, and I mean it!' he said in a shaking voice,
and he threw a piece of meat under the table to stop Toppa
whining. Then, one hand raised, he looked almost in ecstasy at
Signora Flaminia – who was eating unconcernedly and with a
more severe expression than before – and waited.

What a tempest of thoughts must have raged through his
head in that half minute! Twice he changed colour, he smiled,
he frowned aghast as if he were looking down into a precipice,
his eyes moistened with tenderness, he became stern again; he
held his breath, but the others could see his heart thumping
under his lambskin waistcoat, when suddenly he let out a
hoarse shout, and the boys shrieked like souls in torment. Toppa
started barking wildly but was quickly quietened by Signor
Pasquale's big boot, and then the cuckoo after a brief interval
sent out its second *cu-ckoo*, round and clear, into the general
silence; and then it let out its third, and Signor Pasquale let out
a gasp of simple joy; and the cuckoo called out for the fourth
time ... and then stopped.

The clock at the top of the stairs, punctual as ever, at that
moment struck six o'clock.

Signora Flaminia looked at Pasquale, and seeing the wide-eyed look on his face she could no longer contain herself and she exploded in such a paroxysm of laughter that for a good half minute she sprawled on the back of her chair, her arms thrown open, her fresh mouth agape, gasping for breath.

Signor Pasquale looked thunderstruck. The boys would have liked to laugh and be merry, but a glance from their mother was enough to keep them in check – besides, there was that new noise from upstairs next to the room where Uncle Nastasio had died and it brought a certain foreboding into their minds which already were full of the stories they had heard from the old woman who used to come to make the butter.

Meanwhile it was the turn of Signora Flaminia, having sung her hymn of victory with that Homeric burst of laughter, to feel suddenly dismayed by the look of pain on the face of her Pasquale who was droopily gazing now at his sons, now at his wife, lost for words to express his profound distress.

Fiore broke the painful silence by appearing in the doorway. Thoroughly alarmed, he asked in a low voice, 'Did you hear anything? What's happened?'

'Fiore, light me a lamp,' said Signor Pasquale, making as if to stand up. But Signora Flaminia anticipated him: she got up and fondly said, 'Where do you want to go? You're tired out – I'll go.' And she picked up a lamp and went off to the study.

A few moments passed, by the end of which Signora Flaminia had corrected the mistake Pasquale had committed in his excitement and had put the clock to the right time: the cuckoo gaily sang out six o'clock.

Then Signor Pasquale gave vent to all his good humour. He ate very little, smiled at his wife, patted his children, had Cecchino – who was sitting next to him – almost suffering from indigestion by continually filling his plate and his glass; and even Toppa, warmed by the meat and fish bones that Signor Pasquale gave him and made the others give him, that night dirtied the best room and then spent all the next day in the vegetable garden eating the grass pushing up under the snow.

The new tenant-farmer, who had come to talk about the yield from the crops, was invited into the sitting-room, and with him too Signor Pasquale really let himself go. He addressed him all the time like a gentleman, three or four times he chucked him under the chin, he gave him wine to drink, and then talked to him about this and that: about politics, clocks, history, geography, the new calendar; he told him that the stars were worlds like ours, that down inside the earth there is a fiery furnace like a charcoal pit; and he told him lots of other things, all muddled up, but with fair good sense. He went to pieces only when the farmer started going into the estimates for the new crops; from then on he mixed up estimates and yield and cuckoos – and it all went until the children, who had begun falling asleep on their chairs and on the table, were picked up one by one, like wounded soldiers on the battlefield, by Fiore and Signora Flaminia, who carried them off to bed.

Then Signor Pasquale subsided; he dismissed the farmer, blew out the lamp on the table and, taking up his own little lamp, went off contented and as red as a tomato to his bedroom where Signora Flaminia was waiting to see if she could at least worm out from him how much he had paid for the thing.

How the years have flown! And how everything has changed in that family of good country folk! What fine days those had been for Signor Pasquale! What boundless pleasure he got when he sat quietly in his study listening to the farmhands as they stood in a group discussing his clock – signed by the maker it was – and the fabulous sum it must have cost him, and how impossible it would be to find another one to match it because it must certainly have come from America, from over the sea. And what hearty laughs he gave when he heard the men teasing the women and children who, every time the cuckoo sang, ran away and hid behind the beech tree by the dairy, with their fingers stuck in their ears! What a lark! And when the parish priest saw it for the first time! Or when he showed it to the chaplain, who took fright! Or to the mayor, who couldn't believe his eyes! And that field – the way that field was on a Sunday after the service! One needs to have been there, otherwise it's no good talking about it.

And now in that same field a flock of young sparrows are

pecking about in the grass and squabbling to their hearts' content, for no noise comes from that house to disturb them.

The years fly! Fifteen have passed already since that evening when the good Pasquale was in such a tizzy; but everything has changed in that kindly, cheerful household. The two middle sons, Natale and Gosto, are dead; Peppe is secretary in a far-away town in Garfagnana, and only Cecchino, now a young man of twenty-two, is left at home, destined to carry on running the little family estate.

And poor old Toppa has gone! He died of old age five years ago, and now he lies at rest under the wild cherry tree where Fiore sadly buried him, telling himself that for two years at least he wouldn't need any sheep manure for that piece of ground.

Everything has changed! Fiore is grey-haired now; and old Gigia, who was bought by a carter from Pracchia, has never been heard of since; Signora Flaminia has lost nearly all those lovely white teeth she used to show, right to the ones at the back, when she threw her head back and laughed; and Signor Pasquale is up in bed and ailing: today he is a little better, but he is gravely ill.

His robust constitution, which had looked like taking him well into his seventies, was badly shaken when his first son died, though at the time it was his morale that took the worse battering and he grew melancholy and taciturn to the point where he stirred from the house only one or two days a week; all the other days he stayed, except for the odd hour or two, shut away in his study, reading and thinking. Then, on the death of his second son, he fell ill. He spent several months between his bed and his armchair, and after that he was never himself again.

A strange fixation had entered his already disturbed mind. It was brought on by one of those miraculous coincidences that could be taken for supernatural if events did not continually produce them.

Whether it was from a door being slammed, or whether somebody forgot to wind the clock up, or whatever other ill-starred stroke of fate, the fact is that his incomparable cuckoo clock — which, be it said in parenthesis, had turned out a real gem —

stopped twice in two years, and those two occasions were the death of the first son and that of the second.

'When it stops again, it'll be my turn!' poor Signor Pasquale used to say with a sigh every night as he wound it up before he went to bed. 'The next time it will be for me!' And he used to say it with such conviction that nobody could get the idea out of his head and little by little it became a veritable fixation and ruined his already failing health.

Spring was well advanced, and with the first warm breezes of May his laboured breathing worsened to such an extent that the doctor deemed it his duty to advise Signora Flaminia to have a word with the priest. Signora Flaminia sighed and said she would. But it was hardly necessary because for a fortnight already the taciturn Don Silvio had been spending nearly all day at the bedside of his old friend, keeping him affectionate company when the others in the house had to go about their business.

'But what a clock, Don Silvio!' Pasquale said one morning after several hours during which he had been struggling for breath and had not uttered a word. 'What a little clock that's been! Did you hear it strike ten? Now look at the one on the bedside table.'

'It's ten o'clock exactly,' said Don Silvio.

'Do you see? It's twenty days now since I set it, when I got up, and it hasn't lost a minute. But when it does stop . . .'

Don Silvio begged him to be quiet, and making some excuse he went off, very pleased, to look for Signora Flaminia – who had gone down to warm a cup of broth for Pasquale – and tell her that Pasquale had been talking away and that he really seemed much better. He went back upstairs behind her, and she went into the bedroom with the cup and gestured, smiling, to her husband not to talk. She found him, in fact, a little brighter; but an hour later Fiore ran panting to call the doctor, for the master was worsening every minute in an alarming way.

When the doctor came in, Pasquale smiled and said, 'I'm sorry they've troubled you.' Then turning to his wife and Cecchino, he said, 'Make sure it doesn't run down and don't worry about anything . . .' Turning back again to the doctor, he said, 'Would it do me any harm to have that door and the window open?'

'Not in the least,' replied the doctor.

Cecco and Signora Flaminia rushed to fling everything open; and as the gust of wind swept into the room, Pasquale let out a sigh of contentment and said, 'Ah, that does me good!'

The woodcutters were singing down in the beech grove, and the doctor and the priest stood at the window looking silently out at the horizon that stretched in a vast arc across the distant plain.

After a few moments the priest, hearing his church clock strike noon, suddenly remembered it was lunchtime and turned from the window to take leave of Pasquale. He saw that his eyes were staring out of his head and that he was struggling to speak, and he was pointing with one trembling hand towards his pocket watch at the head of the bed.

They all rushed over, for they understood, and they took the watch and showed it to him. Signor Pasquale sat up in bed, his eyes glued to the watch, then fell back exhausted and gasped out, 'Now Pasquale's hour has struck ... it's struck ... it's struck!'

It was two minutes past twelve; the clock at the top of the stairs had struck and the cuckoo had remained silent.

The following evening the church bell rang out the *Ave Maria* over the mountain ravines, and the sun sent its last rays down on to the warm glistening foreheads of a group of woodcutters as they knelt on the trunks of some felled beeches, beside their gleaming axes, and said the first *De profundis* for the blessed soul of poor Signor Pasquale.

Giuseppe Giacosa

IN COMPETITION

NEWLY TRANSLATED BY
ANDREW HALE

GIUSEPPE GIACOSA

GIUSEPPE GIACOSA (1847–1906) was born at Ivrea, below the Val d'Aosta, Piedmont. He was a dramatist of considerable renown in his day, and also published two volumes of short stories about the mountain people of the Val d'Aosta: *Conti e Cose della Montagna* (*Mountain Tales and Things*) and *Novelle e Paesi Valdostani* (*Val d'Aosta Stories and Villages*), from which the story here is drawn. Neither volume exists in an English translation, though the author features in a couple of English anthologies of Italian short stories.

IN COMPETITION

Giacomo flung the bag of oats on to the foot-rest and gripped the reins; when he raised his foot to climb on to the coach, the four old hacks bridled and reared like thoroughbreds. The coach lurched forward, shot out of the gate with a masterly right-angle turn, and the horses broke into a jingling trot; at the same time, with one leg on the running-board and the other dangling in the air, he turned round and with insolent nonchalance tossed a last quip at the stable-boy. Then he climbed on to the coach-box and for some time turned his back on the horses, with the reins between his knees, while he rummaged amongst the travellers' legs to find a secure place for the bag of oats and the innumerable parcels and bundles. He took not the slightest notice of the complaints of those who had been woken up in the middle of the night and were muttering and tossing about in the stuffy darkness of the upper deck.

He had to go over the worst stretch of the whole road – all ups and downs, hairpin bends and potholes, with a surface as firm as shingle; it was a hell of a road, here and there wedged between the mountain and the river, covered with ice during the whole winter and in summer flooded at certain points thigh-deep at the first storm which swelled the Dora. He did two runs in twenty-four hours, one going up at night, and the other coming down in the day. Before him, there had been either a horse crowned or an axle or spoke broken every two months on that stretch of road; since he had taken hold of the reins not even a piece of harness had been broken in three years. Everyone along the road knew him. Wagoners, peasants, priests, innkeepers, shopkeepers, carabinieri, beggars, organ grinders, navvies, travelling pedlars, locksmiths, ribbon sellers, all called him by name and gave it a certain, trenchant abbreviation which perfectly suited his restless and determined character. He had the habit of echoing his own name with a similar sounding syllable, and when someone called him 'Giac', he invariably replied with a 'crac', as sharp as a whiplash.

His habit had been adopted by others and in the valley the pairing of those two sounds had almost become a sign of recognition which confirmed the right of citizenship and established between him and every other person a tacit pact of friendship and mutual respect. He was obliging, had an excellent memory and was always good humoured. His slim figure and pleasing appearance allowed him to be gracefully familiar even with people above his station. He had a way with women; he made the girls and women smile and used to catch them unawares with surprise embraces. As he went through the villages, he would give a quick nod, which made his hat slide on to the back of his head, to those watching from the windows, while his lips would signal such a sudden and unexpected kiss that they would barely have time to see it, let alone take offence. He had a joke for every kind of person and gave each one the sort of news likely to interest him. Since he was always on the road, how did he manage to know even the friends of his friends? The fact was that he did know them and called them by name, to such an extent that Lasquaz, the gate-keeper, used to say: 'He's a census.'

In winter when the coach was empty, he was an expert at the subtle art of luring pedestrians to get in. Before reaching them he would rein in, accost them as he went past and then ask them to do some small favour: to disentangle the reins which were hooked up on something, to shorten a bridle, or to adjust the bit; in the meantime, he would start up a conversation, which would be prolonged as long as possible, at the same time dropping hints that at the end there would be the juicy part of some piece of gossip or of a spicy joke, until finally he finished with a: 'Come on up,' which might have appeared as the payment for services rendered; and when the trapped friend took his seat, Giac would whisper into his ear: 'I'll let you come along for half price as long as you don't tell the boss.'

The boss did know all about it and laid his hands on the money. That stretch of road was now paying a good third more than it used to in the past.

At night during the winter he used to whistle four or five notes of just one song for the whole of the run; in summer, he used to chat with the horses, especially with those nearest him.

Those in the lead, he would say, don't have time to listen to me. I pat the ones nearest me, and give the others a crack of the whip.

His pace-makers were a white mare called Forca and a big bay called Rancio.

'Rancio, what are you looking at? It's mules piss making all that froth. Yes. Prick up your ears. Ciac, ciac (two cracks of the whip). Well then? Does it smell good? Keep your head up, Forca, Forca, Forchetta, Forchina, my beautiful white lady; you like your stable, eh? Look out or you'll get wet; lift up your hooves or I'll lift off your skin. Move, Rancio, shame on you! It's a grey stone shining in the moonlight; it was there yesterday too. Do you want another crack of the whip, Forca? Tell me that you do, is it true? Is it true? Here I am, here I am, it is in the air, the castigator of jades and hacks and beasts of burden, ciac, ciac, can you hear it? Oh, oh, no, not with me! You can't fool around with Giac! Giac's a good man! Will you get a move on, you rabble? Do these two old things here have to do all the pulling? There are gentlemen in the coach, do you realize? This is no winter shack full of beggars and bugs. Bravo, Forca! I knew it, now she is beginning to gallop – ciac, ciac, ciac. Ah, my beauties, I'll teach you your job.'

At certain times he used to teach his job to the travellers who were seated near him, and then there were exaggerated eulogies for his animals, his four little lambs, ciac, ciac, whom he never needed to touch.

With the gentlemen, all of the hack journalist type, he would call his whip a pen and his leather sheath, in which the whip was housed when not in use, an inkstand, and so on and so on.

Giac's boss, the landlord of the 'Golden Cannon', had held the mail contract for fifteen years and had grown rich and fat on it. He was a large man with sagging rolls of fat, a pallid appearance due to a weak heart, and as ponderous as an elephant. He was from Monferrat, had arrived twenty-five years previously in Val d'Aosta as a dealer in wine, had set himself up as a butcher, then established himself as an innkeeper and had afterwards risen to the dignified position of hotel proprietor and postmaster.

He had achieved two good things in his life: a lot of cash,

and a beautiful, buxom daughter; the former for himself, the latter – at least so she hoped – for others.

Now that he was old he no longer did anything; his daughter, who had been born when her father was already prosperous, looked after the hotel; she was called 'Mademoiselle' by strangers and 'Soura Gina' (Miss Giovannina) by the regulars, while the boss, who had risen from nothing, was unable to have the titled 'Sour' added to his name of Péro (Pietro) and it was only by special favour, due more to his stomach than to his worth, that in recent years he had acquired the name 'Barba Griz' (Grey Uncle).

'Soura Gina' was endowed with a firm, fresh plumpness; she was blonde, clear-skinned, with a pert nose, small lively eyes, a wide mouth, full smiling lips and a dazzling set of teeth. She took care of everything, including the horses; she was everywhere at all times, but especially in the stables when she knew she would find Giac there. Once, when Giac had received a vicious kick from a mule, she bandaged his wounded leg and kept him in grand style at the hotel for more than a week. Another time, when Giac and the stable-man had come to blows, the latter was given a week's pay and instant dismissal by Soura Gina. Barba Griz attributed these kindnesses to administrative prudence: Giac was a pearl of a coachman and it was natural that his daughter should treat him well: but Giac put a different value on these kindnesses, although nothing would induce him to earn them by his own endeavours; he was on easy terms with all women, but at a more intimate level he became a cold and haughty sultan, gracefully consenting to let himself be adored.

One day the village café-owner and tobacconist went to the innkeeper to confide in him that his niece and heiress had fallen in love with Giac and wanted him for her husband at all costs.

Unseen by either man, Giac was listening to their conversation.

'What do you think about it?'

'Give him to her. It's a lucky stroke which may make the family's fortunes.'

There followed a string of commendations.

In the evening Giac returned from the run, and, dressed as he was, in his blue canvas shirt and still holding his whip, took Barba Griz to one side and without further ado asked him for the hand of Soura Gina.

The big man glared at him, snatched the whip out of his hands and replied:

'Is this the pen with which you want to sign the marriage contract? Get out, or I'll lay it across your rump.'

'You're against it? Well, you're the boss!'

And he went to have his supper and then to sleep in the hayloft. Around midnight Gina came and woke him.

'Come with me.'

She took him to the kitchen, made him sit down, opened a bottle of Carema, sat down beside him, filled two glasses, raised her glass to touch his and said:

'To our marriage!'

Giac gave an imperceptible shrug. She went on:

'Here are two thousand seven hundred lire which I have scraped together during the four years I have been in charge. They are mine. My father has told me everything; we have to force his hand. If I marry you without his consent, he'll cut me out of his will: he's a swine.'

'And you won't marry me.'

'You set yourself up in competition with him; buy four horses and the omnibus which "The Red Cross" at Ivrea is putting up for sale. As for the money – you obtained it from A Benefactor. Leave immediately. In a week's time sweep in suddenly with the omnibus, freshly painted: call it the "America" and write "Competition" on it in a yellow which looks like gold. Use only three horses, the fourth will be a replacement; in six months you will have driven them into the ground, but between now and then things will have started happening. You will call in here to bring profits to the hotel. And not one sharp word to father. Are we agreed? Then off you go.'

Giac watched all the fire of her youth pour from her dry eyes and consume him; he felt that he could take her by just stretching out his hand. In that abrupt, premeditated and cunning speech, in which no words except of business were spoken, there vibrated an ardent passion equally disposed to immediate concessions and to long periods of waiting. Every word took on

additional force from the tone of her voice and from the emphasis she put on it. Each word passed through her brain, a merchant's quick, tidy brain, but sprang directly from her heart.
She spoke well-ordered phrases and betrayed disjointed
emotions; her expressions were those of a business letter, her
voice was full of impetuosity and alluring intimacy. Her eyes
seconded her voice; they were piercing and restlessly inquiring
and sought, in the inscrutable face of the young man, an
acquiescence which would give her a triumph, like that of an
unexpected victory.

The money was lying on the table. She went on:

'You'll find a horse at Donas, the grey one belonging to
Loutrier; it's eight years old; at the moment it's worn out, but
we'll pull it together. Loutrier bought it three months ago from
the Jew, now he's selling it as he's giving up his shop because of
the death of his son. There's another at Verres which the baker,
the tall one with the straggly beard, is selling: for three hundred lire they'll push it at you; you can try Viano, the dealer, to
see if he'll sell you La Bella: she's bad-tempered and will bolt,
but in your hands . . . !'

There was a distinctly admiring caress in those words 'in your
hands', and to emphasize it she grasped one of those powerful
hands and gripped it vigorously in a squeeze in which she com-
pressed all the fire of her impatient virginity and all the tenderness of her soul.

And the young man continued to look at her impassively; he
was already resolved to accept, but unconsciously he was convinced of the irresistible power which he derived from his
coldness.

Gina picked up the glass that he had put down and held it
out to him.

'Don't you want to touch glasses?'

'To us,' replied Giac, touching her glass as if he were a
cymbal player. Then he downed his drink in one gulp, stood up
and slowly put the cash in his pocket.

'Good day, Soura Gina.'

'When are you coming back?'

'As soon as I've put the wagon in order; but I don't want the
horses you told me about. If I was seen buying them there would

be too much gossip in the valley; I've got to arrive here out of the blue with this world-shattering "America".'

'You're right: buy them where you want to; but do it soon.'

'What if I throw the money away?'

Gina shrugged her shoulders, quite certain that he wouldn't. Giac moved off, followed by the girl. When he reached the door, she put a hand on his shoulder; he turned round sharply, lifted her up bodily, and holding her motionless in his arms, planted a long, biting kiss on her mouth until Gina wriggled out of his grasp like a fish and, standing stiffly very close to him, she eyed him languorously and 'Do you want to?' she breathed.

'Pas de bêtise,' he replied in French and hastened away.

So the competition began. At the beginning the 'America' used to discharge a load of tattered travellers into the courtyard of the 'Golden Cannon', and Barba Griz would laughingly say to Giac:

'How much do you pay them?'

'A lot,' the coachman would reply. The horses were three wretched nags, with no flesh and moth-eaten coats, which even left their stables reluctantly; with all the coughing and blowing and their muzzles on the ground, it took him an hour to release their harness.

Giac had bought them for their carcasses, just to see him through the dead spring season and then to surprise people, especially the innkeeper, with an unannounced fresh supply at the beginning of the summer.

The stable-boys laughed at them; Barba Griz in his triumph took care to praise them for more than they appeared to be and commended Giac for having started up on his own, because to serve a boss, he said, was to sell your birthright. And Giac replied modestly that they had put him up to it, that he was already regretting it, but that as long as the jades lasted out he felt he had to go on pulling the cart, but once they packed up ...

'I won't take you back, though; I'm afraid your place has been taken.'

'Can't be helped, I will look elsewhere; I left you and I'll have to pay for it.'

To Gina he never spoke one word, neither openly nor in secret: she had guessed his game and was giving him full support; only when he was sitting at the stable-boys' table did she stand in the doorway and gaze with tender pride at her man, so gay and handsome, so shrewd and persevering.

Barba Griz had not even reduced his fares.

'I'm doing it for you,' he told Giac, 'so as not to ruin you completely.'

The first nag cracked up at the beginning of June, collapsing dead in the courtyard, still attached to the coach which had just arrived; the schedule was continued for two weeks, crawling along at the pace of the remaining two horses. Meanwhile the innkeeper had published a broadsheet with his summer fares and had had it displayed in all the cafés and hotels of the area.

It was June 23rd, the eve of St John's Day, when Giac, like Brutus and Pope Sixtus before him, threw off his mask of humility and revealed his true colours. This time it was the real 'America' with its alluring coat of gold, a high slender frame which shone like a mirror, a green coach-box with red stripes, and wheels with spokes painted green. And the word 'Competition', written in white letters on a black background, blared out from a placard on the top, while the name 'America' emblazoned on the door, bathed in the glory of the gleaming gold.

The new coach was at the station for the arrival of the last train. The early summer had brought forward the flow of visitors; an urchin had been brought in as a tout and from the coach door was shouting: 'Leaving for Val d'Aosta immediately.' A porter was going around collecting the baggage tickets. On the coach-box, Giac was goading and restraining three large black horses which filled out their halters with flesh acquired in fifteen days of forced feeding in the stables. The omnibus was filled to the brim in an instant and noisily departed with resounding cracks of the long whip, which stripped the leaves off the trees along the avenue, as if there was a hailstorm.

At dawn, Barba Griz, who was kept awake by his heart condition, heard the coach burst into the courtyard; the frenzy of the horses and the muffled, even drum of the wheels made him think that it was a nobleman's coach. He dressed, went downstairs with the slow haste to which he was constrained, and found his daughter already busying herself serving coffee to the new arrivals.

His expert eye immediately told him that these gentlemen were not a party of friends and he deduced from this that it must be a public service coach. He went out, feeling uneasy. The coach was standing under the lean-to, without the horses; the bare shaft was planted in the ground, like a spear in the stomach. He circled it in silence as if identifying the scent of an enemy; he did not read the word 'Competition', which was written too high up, but the name 'America' made him raise his eyebrows. He stood for a moment, deep in thought, then murmured to himself: 'Never again, never again!' and went into the stable. Giac and the stable-boy had gone out, one for water and the other for hay. In the half-light of the low-roofed stable, poorly ventilated by a tiny window with an iron grating and illuminated only by a red, flickering charcoal lamp, he walked straight through to the stalls for visiting horses; there, he listened to them panting, and made a rough calculation of their size; a slap on the rump of the first one made a solid 'thwack', indicating firm, well-nourished flesh; he carefully felt the rumps of the other two, found them as taut as a drum, and stood thoughtfully mulling over his doubts and dispelling them with the usual: 'Never again, never again.'

But at the door he ran into Giac, who had a bucket and sponge in his hand.

'You've found a boss.'

'It's all mine, it's all mine!' the young man sang out without stopping.

Barba Griz had to sit down on the drinking-trough; his heart was pounding in his chest just as the wheels of the coach in the courtyard had done, a short while before; he was gulping like a fish out of water, while listening to Giac in the stable calling the horses by name and stroking them with his hand, as if they were brazen women, at the same time happily whistling the tune of a light infantry march. When he had recovered his breath, he shouted through the doorway: 'Where did you steal the money from?'

'My old uncle's will.'

At that moment the horn of the mail-coach was sounded outside in the street; the old coach rolled slowly through the gate-way and with groans of protest went over to the door of the dining-room. A carabiniere and a cook, who had come from a hotel in San Remo to do the summer season at the 'Golden Cannon', alighted from it.

'Thief!' muttered the innkeeper, as he went off to his room, where he shut himself up for the whole day. And Giac thus found the opportunity of giving Gina the takings of the first run, on June 24th, St John's Day, which was her saint's day.

The competition was soon fierce and ruthless. The mail-coach too now went to the station to pick up people, stridently announcing its reduction in prices; but it always took them half an hour to take on the mail bags, while Giac left immediately. The mail-coach changed horses at the half-way stage, while Giac did the whole run without a break; it is true that the time lost in the change-over was recovered through the strength of the fresh horses, but this was not enough to make up for the first delay. All the same, when he had completed two-thirds of the run, Giac would sometimes hear the rumble of the mail-coach behind him, and he would turn round and see the winking eye of its lamp shining high up in the darkness. Then, instead of keeping to the side of the road, in order to find the firm ground and avoid the ruts, he would take the 'America' straight down the middle of the track, raising clouds of dust; and this would give an easier, freer run for the three horses harnessed abreast than for the long train of coupled horses. The downhill stretches always ended in a victory for Giac, whose wrists of iron kept the horses on a tight rein, while whiplashes and shouts of encouragement and the weight of the coach precipitated them into a furious but steady run.

In the beginning Barba Griz would listen every morning from behind the blinds in the hope of hearing the horn of the mail-coach first, rather than the jingle of its rival; then when he became disheartened he changed his room, moving into the most remote one in the house so that he would hear neither of them; his daughter had persuaded him not to make a clean break with Giac, so as not to estrange him from the 'Golden Cannon' and therefore at least not to lose clients for the hotel. The excessive reduction of prices by which the old man had tried to win the competition, had backfired financially and had brought him humiliation, since by filling his coach with local people, he had deterred the visitors. As soon as the cut-price rabble got out of the coach, they dispersed all over the place, going back to their houses and their occupations, while the gentlefolk from the rival concern put up at the hotel. When Giac became aware of this, he reinstated the full tariff, so that the 'America' half empty yielded more than the mail-coach stuffed full of people, and it never was half empty.

What a thorn in the heart of the old man! The money lost was nothing compared with the humiliation; he would have squandered the lot if he could somehow have his way. He even thought of starting a service to Switzerland, but that wasn't something which could be set up overnight. His health suffered from it and his asthma became stronger and more frequent; he no longer spoke and only went down to the courtyard to walk across it to join the little group of card-players at the café, where he could vent his bitterness which came out in the form of laboured mockery.

Gina was filled with pity and was thinking of making a full confession, hoping that peace would come from it.

One night, at the beginning of August, a violent storm burst over the valley. As dawn broke, with the sky already brightening, a pedlar arrived and told of serious damage along the road. A few minutes later, Lasquaz the gate-keeper brought the news that the driver and two horses of the stage-coach had been struck by lightning. He did not know whether it was the mail-coach or its rival, as the news had come from Fort Bard, which had been asked to send help.

The innkeeper felt his legs give way and sat down on the kitchen steps, looking around and clutching his chest. The asthma was suffocating him. Gina, ashen-faced, would have liked to rush out along the road to verify the news, but the exhausted appearance of her father held her back : the courtyard was full of people and they kept on coming in. By that hour both coaches were long overdue. The crowd stood still and waited; the carabinieri had gone off towards Bard.

After a long silence, Barba Griz said:

'The mail-coach has the horn, and the "America" has harness bells.'

And he fell silent again.

There was another period of anxious silence. The baker's dog, from the other end of the village, was barking loudly as if it were night time; the water in the fountain trickled noisily into the horse-trough.

From far off there came the sound of the horn.

Then the old man rose up as if propelled by a spring, gasped for a moment, and the words: 'It's mine, it's mine!' escaped from his lips; he hurled himself into the centre of the courtyard amongst the people, who backed away in a startled circle, and took up a dancing posture, shaking his arms above his head in a ponderous and painfully unseemly dance.

The sound of the horn drew nearer, then the coach shot into the courtyard. Still dancing, the old man moved forward to meet it with sobbing cries of joy. When he saw it, he opened wide his arms and his cries of joy turned to an agonized 'oh' of amazement; he collapsed on to the ground with a thump like a heavy sack.

Just in time, Giac reined in the three horses which were almost on top of the old man. The 'America', unscathed, had picked up part of the load and the badly bruised postillion of the mail-coach. As he was approaching the village, he had sounded the horn as a sign of joy for having escaped the danger.

Barba Griz was dead.

Three months later, Gina and Giac were married.

Matilde Serao

DONNA CATERINA AND DONNA CONCETTA

NEWLY TRANSLATED BY
ANDREW HALE

MATILDE SERAO

MATILDE SERÁO (1856–1927) was born in Greece but was
Neapolitan by adoption. In addition to lush romances, which
brought her a large readership, possibly at the expense of her reputation with the serious critics, she wrote some very well-observed
stories featuring the women of the lower and middle classes. A good
one is translated in A. Colquhoun and N. Rogers' *Italian Regional
Tales of the 19th Century*, 1961.

DONNA CATERINA AND
DONNA CONCETTA

The two sisters, Donna Caterina and Donna Concetta, sat facing each other across the dining-table; they were eating in silence, with lowered eyes, leaning forward now and then to wipe their greasy lips on the edge of the tablecloth stained with bluish wine spots. Standing on the table between them was a large dish of macaroni, seasoned with oil, salted anchovies and garlic, all of which had been lightly fried and spread over the boiled pasta just before serving. From time to time the two women sank their forks into the macaroni and scooped some out on to their plates, and then started eating again. On the table there was also a large ring-shaped piece of whitish, underbaked bread – the *tortano* – pieces of which they broke off from time to time and used as an aid in eating the macaroni; a greenish bottle full of reddish wine which gave off bluish reflections; two large glasses and a salt-cellar also of glass – and nothing else at all. The two sisters were using forks made of lead and uncouth knives with black handles. Occasionally they broke off a piece of bread and soaked it in the fried oil at the bottom of the serving dish. Caterina, the *lotto* organizer, who was rather more coarse, who saw fewer people and led almost a furtive sort of life, dipped the bread into the macaroni dish with her hand: Concetta, who was more refined, who was always out and about, who dealt with so many people, delicately placed her piece of bread on the end of her fork before dipping it in the oil and garlic, and then when she had taken a quick look at it, ate it in little mouthfuls. In fact at a certain moment she discovered a piece of garlic which had turned red in frying, and discarded it with a gesture of disgust. Apart from this the sisters preserved their air of perfect similarity which was created more by their clothes, their gestures, and by their way of speaking than by their features. Both went to the same local hairdresser – it cost two pennies a time – and both had their hair drawn back into a bun at the top of the head and held in place by large mock

tortoiseshell hair grips, with a fringe drooping over their lightly
powdered foreheads; both wore dresses in the style of the Neapolitan well-to-do with a tunicless skirt and a simple tight-fitting
bodice, which still retained its Spanish name of *baschina*; round
the neck both wore a large gold chain from which they were
never parted and which was a sign of their formidable power;
both wore high leather boots with noisy wooden heels; and for
the purposes of eating both had left their regular work – a large
cotton counterpane, red one side and green the other, stuffed
with cotton waste, which was stretched over a large frame and
which they were embroidering with patterns of wheels, stars and
lozenges. They worked rapidly, one seated on one side and the
other on the other side, with lowered heads and noses close to
the design, raising and lowering the needles with a monotonous
movement of the arm; the frame had been pushed to the back
of the room and one could see the two chairs which had been
moved out of the way.

Now a servant girl of fourteen, with red hair and a very white
face covered with freckles, had come to bring in the second
course, a piece of that cheese from Basilicata, the *provola*, which
is more like a dried milk product, together with two large sticks
of celery. With an inquiring look, the servant girl questioned
Donna Caterina about the fate of the macaroni which lay in the
bottom of the dish :

'Keep one or two for Menichella,' said the *lotto* organizer,
cutting a large slice of cheese.

'Yes, ma'am,' murmured the maidservant as she went out.

Menichella was a poor old woman of sixty whose son, a
watchman, had died in a street-brawl in Piazza della Pignasecca
with a revolver bullet in his belly. She lived off alms and every
Friday she came to the house of the two Esposito sisters, who
gave her a hot dish, half a ring of bread and some item of cast off
clothing. This was the Esposito sisters' homage to the beautiful
Madonna of the Sorrows whose day is Friday. On Wednesdays
they gave similar alms to a poor blind man called Guarattelle –
the puppet man – because for many years he had run a puppet
show, and they dedicated this act of charity to the Madonna del
Carmine whose day is Wednesday. Similarly on Mondays they
fed an abandoned boy of ten who was looked after by everyone

in the Vicolo Rosariello di Portamedina, while the Esposito sisters helped him on that particular day as a prayer for the souls in purgatory, to whom Monday belongs. In fact, on any day of the week it was difficult for some down-and-out to knock on that door and then go away empty-handed.

'Do it for Saint Joseph, whose day it is today.'

'Praise be to the Holy Trinity, today is Sunday so give us some alms.'

Something to eat, a glass of wine, a rag or two was what the supplicants took away: but money, never. The Esposito sisters had too great a respect for their 'brass', as they called money, ever to give it away; and they explained that it was more charitable to give food than to pander to vice by giving money. The supplicants always stayed outside on the landing: the Esposito sisters did not let them come in as they feared for the valuables in the house; they took the plate of macaroni or vegetables or salad outside; sometimes the supplicant would eat, seated on the staircase, mumbling benedictions.

Now they ate the smoked cheese and the bread with a slow slightly goat-like movement of the jaws; they broke off stalks of celery and munched them noisily, like fruit, to remove the taste of oil from their mouths. When they had finished they stayed almost motionless, their hands lying limp in their laps, looking at the blue stains on the tablecloth, engrossed in the silence of their digestions and of their long businesswomen's mental calculations. The maidservant, Peppina, whisked everything away and the clatter of her down-at-the-heel slippers could be heard as she moved about in the kitchen washing the few plates, stopping now and again to stir the macaroni which she was heating up in the frying pan, seeing that it was cold.

The two sisters now stood up, shook the crumbs off their skirts and went to take up their posts again at the frame; they prepared themselves for embroidering, bowing their heads and methodically lifting their well-ringed right hands while keeping the left ones underneath the frame. The doorbell rang: the sisters rapidly exchanged glances and went on with their work, which apart from earning them money also served as a moral and material screen.

Two young girls, both seamstresses, came in, hustling each

other through the door. The first one, who was the braver of the
two, was the blonde Antonietta who worked in a dressmaker's
in Via Santa Chiara and used to go and buy lunch for herself
and her companion Nannina from the *osteria* opposite in the
lotto hall; both were wretchedly dressed with shabby, thread-
bare skirts, gaudy but tattered jackets of a different colour and
black shawls which they let fall over their arms to show off the
bodice and a little bow of pink ribbon at the neck. The smaller
one, Nannina, was a relative of the two Esposito sisters but she
had a holy terror of her aunts, with their money and jewels, who
always received her with such studied and deliberate coldness.
They even let their niece kiss their hands. The two young girls
remained standing near the frame with a mortified look on their
faces as they watched the deft handiwork.

'Didn't you go to work today?' Donna Caterina asked Nannina.

'I went to work,' the girl replied with a rush, urged on by
Antonietta's elbowing, 'but the mistress sent us out to buy some
things near here, and as my friend wanted to ask you a favour
– well, that's why we came . . .'

'From whom did she want the favour?' asked Donna Concetta, raising her head from the counterpane.

'From you actually, aunt . . .' stammered her niece.

'Huh !' exclaimed Concetta in an ironic tone of voice as she
smiled and shook her head.

The girls looked at each other in silence: they had got off to a
bad start. The *lotto* organizer quickly lost all interest in the question and cut off the back-stitching of the counterpane which she
was embroidering with a pair of scissors. The small white
threads dropped into her lap and covered the brown wool
skirt.

'Well, have you lost your tongue? What is it all about?'
Donna Concetta asked laughingly.

'All right, Donna Concettina, I'll tell you all about it,' replied the blonde Antonietta, biting her lips to make them red-
der. 'I would like to make myself a new dress for Easter, and a
pair of boots, and buy myself some muslin to make three or four
blouses. At the very least, and if I myself do all the sewing after
my day's work at the dressmaker's, I'll need forty lire. I haven't

got forty lire and it would take me a year to put that sum aside. As I've heard that you're so kind and do so many favours for poor people, I thought that you might lend me these forty lire ...'

'You thought wrong,' said the usurer, coldly.

'But why? I can pay off this debt at so much a week; I earn twenty-five pennies a day; I don't owe a penny to anyone; ask Nannina, your niece, she can be my guarantee ...'

'Nannina should find someone to be her own guarantee ...' muttered Donna Concerta. 'But what do you need this dress for? The one that you've got on – isn't that enough for you? When there's no money, you don't make yourself dresses! When my sister and I had no money, we didn't make ourselves dresses! You're all crazy, you girls today ...'

'Oh aunt, do her just this favour. She has a boyfriend and is ashamed of being seen with him like this,' said the niece, putting in a word for her friend.

'I've had a boyfriend too,' replied Donna Concetta, 'and I didn't feel ashamed when I was badly dressed.'

'Men today are rather different ...' murmured Antonietta, 'so will you do this favour for me?'

'My dear girl, I don't even know you ...'

'I work at Cristina Gagliardi's, Via Santa Chiara, number eighteen, first floor. I live at Strettola di Porto, number three. You can check up.'

There followed a silence during which the girls once again exchanged a look of alarm.

'At the most, at the very most,' said Donna Concetta, lifting her head, 'I can give you some cheap wool on credit for you to make a dress and some muslin for your blouses ... I will ask a merchant who knows me ... a good man ... but it'll cost you more ...'

'It doesn't matter, it doesn't matter,' Antonietta cut in quickly, 'you look after it ...'

'What colour does this wool have to be?' Donna Concetta asked maternally.

'Navy blue or bottle green ... I prefer navy blue ...'

'Navy blue suits you better. You'll look marvellous in it,' put in Nanna with an air of importance.

'And it doesn't fade so easily ...' concluded Donna Concetta. 'How many metres do you need?'

The girl made some quick calculations, using her hands as a tape measure and looking at her figure, at the same time counting and recounting.

'Ten metres, yes, ten metres will be enough ...'

'Five rolls? Good Lord! So you want to be in fashion?'

'Donna Concettina, bear with me ...' Antonietta replied smiling.

'All right, all right. For each blouse you'll need four metres of muslin, that'll be sixteen metres in all ...'

'And the shoes?' asked the girl, hesitantly.

'I don't know any shoe-makers, my girl.'

'Would you give me the rest of the forty lire in cash?' the seamstress ventured to ask.

'Listen, my girl,' said Donna Concetta, 'I'll come tomorrow, Saturday, to the dressmaker to find out if they really do give you twenty-five pennies a day and if you have had any money in advance. I'll arrange with the dressmaker to have two lire deducted for me every Saturday as the interest on the forty lire, instead of her giving you your whole weekly wage.'

'Two lire?' exclaimed the girl in dismay.

'That's right. I should ask for four, one penny per lira per week, but you're a poor young girl and I really want to help you. The dressmaker gives me the two lire as the interest: then you can pay off from the rest however much you want of your debt – five lire, three, two, as it suits you. Is that clear?'

'Yes, yes ...' exclaimed the girl, who by now was thoroughly frightened.

'The sooner you pay, the better it is for you. I should like nothing better. But I warn you that if you should get the dressmaker to pay you first, or run away, or play any other sort of trick, I'll arrive on your doorstep, sweetheart, and you'll very soon find out who Concetta Esposito is. I don't care about going to prison for my own blood ... do I explain myself?'

'Yes, ma'am, yes ma'am,' stammered Antonietta with tears in her eyes.

'But you've still time to refuse my offer,' concluded Donna Concetta icily, as she lowered her eyes to her embroidery.

'No, no,' the girl cried, 'anything you want. Promise me that you'll come tomorrow to Via Santa Chiara, number eighteen?'

'We'll see each other tomorrow,' said Donna Concetta, dismissing her.

'And will you bring the materials? And the money?'

'I'll see about that.'

'Good-bye aunt,' murmured Nannina, who was even more white-faced and frightened than her friend.

'May the Madonna be with you,' said the two Esposito sisters in chorus, returning to their work.

The girls went out in silence with bowed heads, so drained of strength that they could neither speak nor smile. A woman who was coming up the stairs in a hurry bumped into them, muttered a hasty 'sorry' and went on up to knock at the door of the Esposito sisters. It was Carmela, the cigarette woman, with large eyes full of sad thoughts, and a ravaged face. Before going inside she sighed deeply and a flush spread rapidly over her emaciated cheeks.

'Can I come in?' she said in a faint voice from the hallway.

'Come in,' was the reply from within.

'Oh, it's you, good Christian woman,' said Concetta recognizing her. 'Tell me the truth; have you come to pay off your debt? Your conscience has finally pricked you, has it? Give it here, then.'

'You must be joking, Donna Concetta,' said the wretched woman with a wan smile. 'If I had thirty-four lire, I would give thirty-four jumps for joy.'

'Thirty-seven and a half lire including last week's interest,' the usurer corrected coldly.

'If that's what you want, who am I to say no? You say thirty-seven and a half, and I say so too.'

'Have you at least brought the interest?'

'Nothing, nothing,' the girl cried despairingly, bowing her head. 'Poverty keeps gnawing away at me. I manage to earn one and a half lire a day, and I can really live like a lady on that!'

'Well, where does all this money go to, then?' asked Donna Concetta, yielding to her need to preach wisdom to her debtors. 'You've got no sense, that's your trouble.'

'What do you mean, Donna Concetta?' exclaimed Carmela

disconsolately. 'Am I not to give a morsel of bread to my old mother? Am I to refuse my sister half a lira when she is starving, with three children and one of them on the point of dying? And for all his faults, am I to refuse Gaetano, my brother-in-law, the odd penny when he has got nothing to smoke? I wouldn't have the heart, Donna Concetta!'

'It's Raffaele who fleeces you, it's Raffaele!' said the usurer in a sing-song voice, as she threaded a needle with red cotton.

'And what do you want me to do about it?' retorted Carmela, flinging up her arms. 'He was born to be a gentleman. As for me, if I don't pay the landlord on Monday, he'll turn me out. I have to give him thirty lire; if I could only give him ten! Ah, if only you would do me just this one favour!'

'You're out of your mind, my girl.'

'Donna Concetta, Donna Concetta, what's ten lire to you? And I'll give it back, you know that; I've never taken a penny from anyone. Don't get me thrown out on the street, Donna Concetta, do it for your loved ones in paradise!'

'No, no, no!'

'Well, look then,' went on Carmela dispiritedly, 'these earrings that I'm wearing: my godmother paid seventeen lire, four ducats, for them. I'll give them to you, I've got nothing else, and you give them back to me when I've paid you back the ten lire.'

'I'm not a pawnbroker,' replied Donna Concetta, having had a surreptitious look at the earrings.

'But this isn't pawning; it's a favour you're doing me. If I had to pawn them, they would give me five or six lire: they would deduct an advance payment of the interest and with the ledger fee, the deposit box fee and the middleman's cut, I would be left with three or four lire. Do it just this once, Donna Concetta, the Madonna is watching you from heaven!'

Abruptly, she snatched off the rather elderly gold earrings, polished them on the edge of her apron and placed them delicately on the counterpane. She went on looking at them intensely, as if saying farewell to them. Donna Concetta picked them up with a grimace of disgust. She exchanged a look with her sister, who had raised her head. The *lotto* organizer appeared to say yes with a blink of her eyelids. Poker-faced and without a word, Donna Concetta stood up. She picked up the earrings and went into the adjacent room where the two sisters slept. There was the sound of keys grating in locks, and the opening and closing of drawers interspersed with periods of silence. Then Donna Concetta reappeared. In her hand there were two small, yellow paper packets.

'There's money inside: count it,' she said curtly, placing them in front of Carmela.

'No no, there's no need,' the poor woman replied, trembling with emotion. 'The Good Lord will keep you in good health for what you have done for me.'

'All right, all right,' concluded Donna Concetta, taking up her work again. 'But I warn you that I will sell the earrings if you don't pay up.'

'You needn't worry,' murmured Carmela as she went out.

For a few moments the two sisters remained alone, embroidering.

'The earrings are worth twelve gold lire,' said Caterina, who had a sharp eye.

'That's right,' said Donna Concetta. 'But Carmela will pay, she's a good girl.'

Once again the doorbell rang.

'It sounds like the midwife ringing,' remarked Caterina.

There was a sound of shuffling feet and a noise as if a trunk was being placed on the floor in a corner of the entrance hall. Then the deformed, hunchbacked figure of Michele, the shoe-shine boy, his stance lopsided as if still carrying his shoe-shine box, appeared in front of the two sisters. He greeted them in the Spanish way: 'With your kind permission,' while the thousand wrinkles on his boyish face, gnarled and wizened though it was, seemed to radiate malice. The sisters looked at him patiently while they waited for him to speak.

'I have been sent here by Gaetano Galiero, the glove cutter ...'

'A real gentleman!' exclaimed Donna Concetta as she stuffed a piece of paper into her thimble, which was too big for her.

'If you didn't get people to talk about you, how could we ever understand each other!' the hunchback remarked philosophically. 'Gaetano is under great obligation to you, but you are a beautiful lady who does not lack judgement, and you will surely pardon his shortcomings. Well, that which doesn't happen in one year, happens in one day; and just when you least expect it, Gaetano arrives on the doorstep with the money . . .'

'Yes, yes,' said the two sisters with a sneer.

'You just wait and see. But I came to talk to you about my own affairs. I practise, praise be to God, an art which is better than Gaetano's. I work by the café "De Angelis", at the Carità, and I can tell you without a word of exaggeration that I clean the shoes of Naples' top nobility. Whatever I feel like earning, I earn. I don't have to worry about lean times. When it rains, I move into the shelter of the café's door: and the more mud there is in the street, the more shoes I clean. Oh, my dear ladies, if I were more presentable, I would be a gentleman by now ! Right now I need a certain sum of money to bring off a big deal, which may well put me on the road to fame and fortune. And since you are always willing to help people, I have come to offer you a bargain. I need forty lire, which I'll pay back at the rate of three lire a week. I need the money just until I bring off this big deal; then I'll give you back capital and interest, and I'll give you a marvellous present as well . . .'

'Don't bother,' said Donna Concetta ironically.

'If you don't lend this money to me, who do you expect to lend it to?' the cripple boldly asked. 'If I spend a whole day in front of the café, I earn two lire, did you know that? Not even a barber's assistant can say that ! Besides, that pitch is worth a fortune to me, it's my shop. If I leave there, I can't earn a penny ! So you see I can't escape you ! Ask the café proprietor who Michele is. In my hands your money is quite safe. The proprietor will bear me out.'

'If the proprietor stands surety for you, I'll give you the money,' Donna Concetta said at once.

'In that case he would give me the money,' the cripple objected. 'No, no, Michele doesn't need a guarantor. Come and see the proprietor tomorrow morning, Saturday, at nine o'clock. Just listen to what he has to say, and you'll be giving me sixty lire, not forty. I'm a gentleman, I have my public, dear ladies.'

'All right, I'll see you tomorrow. Do you know what the interest is?' asked Donna Concetta.

'Whatever you want it to be,' the cripple replied gallantly. 'Even a cup of coffee with a roll dipped in it. At the café, what I say goes! Any orders?'

'Orders never, always requests,' the two women murmured as he was leaving. Caterina stopped working for a moment and remarked:

'You said yes to him too soon.'

'I'll get the café proprietor to guarantee the loan. And then, he is a hunchback; he brings luck,' added Donna Concetta.

'If he were to bring us luck, this back-breaking life of ours should come to an end,' replied Caterina, who was very fond of bemoaning her luck.

'Ah well,' said the other sister with a sigh, 'we don't have a strong man behind us; so there is no one else to see that we get our due. Ciccillo and Alfonso are two idiots, it's useless ...'

'What can you do about it!' sighed the other.

And the sisters put aside their work and, with their hands lying idle on the red counterpane, turned their attention to their secret burden, to that tormenting anguish which they confessed to no one, to those two fiancés of theirs, two honest dockyard workers, the brothers Jannaccone who loved them but neither of whom wanted to marry them because of the business the sisters were carrying on. For three years the sisters had been conducting their struggle between love and money, but Ciccillo and Alfonso Jannaccone just didn't want to know: to marry a *lotto* organizer and a money-lender would have disgraced them in front of the whole dockyard.

They were two good workers, simple and very taciturn, who didn't idle the days away, had put a little money on one side, and who came to spend their evenings with the two sisters. With that idea, one of the few in their simple brains, fixed firmly in their heads, no impetus of love or lust for money succeeded in overcoming their obstinacy. Several times the two sisters, in tenacious defence of their profits and bitterly offended by their refusal, had argued with their two fiancés and had chased them out of the house, but only for a short time: peace was restored quite naturally. Caterina and Concetta promised to stop. The two women must have had money, and a lot of it, put on one side but they never talked about it: and these same two, in spite of their love for Alfonso and Ciccillo, still kept putting off their marriage to earn still more lire, not knowing how to break the cycle of their money-lending business, not wanting to renounce old credits, and unable to resist the temptation of creating new ones; they did not understand the shame of their two lovers and complained about it as if it were an injustice. You see, to the two sisters it appeared as an act of humanity to lend money at interest, and to sell *lotto* tickets for a penny or two seemed to them to be an act of charity. After all, the good, honest, downtrodden and swindled people of Naples who took the money from Concetta to give it to the government and to Caterina, then thanked them with tears in their eyes and blessings! When they were alone and feeling communicative, the two sisters would complain about their fate: anyone except the brothers Jannaccone would have been very happy at the prospect of such assiduous and industrious wives with a dowry: but the two workers were unmoved and invincible in their insistence that they would never, never marry them unless they ceased earning money in that way. Above all, Ciccillo, the fiancé of Caterina the *lotto* organizer, was as hard as a stone; now and again he even used to say:

'One of these days, Caterina, you'll end up in prison.'

'I'll bail myself out! And the lawyer will get me off,' she would say, revealing her knowledge of the law and its intricacies.

'If you go to prison, that will be the last you see of me,' Ciccillo would retort, as he lighted a cigar stub.

Yes, when the two sisters were absolutely alone they gave way to despair. But love of money was so strong that it always made them postpone the day of the double wedding. The two workers waited patiently and with their savings they slowly bought, between them, the furniture for the house, which was to be shared as they were never separated from each other.

'At Easter,' said the two sisters, thinking that they would terminate their obligations by then.

'At Easter,' consented the two brothers.

'In September,' said the two women when April came and

they found themselves even more ensnared than ever in that mesh of sordid transactions. And always when they were alone, the two sisters complained of being illtreated by fate, of being unappreciated by the men they loved, and ended up by saying:

'Ciccillo and Alfonso are two idiots.'

But even on that day they didn't stay alone for very long. The sad business went on until evening. There came a painter of saints, a painter in the sense that he used to paint the faces, hands and feet of the wooden and stucco saints in the thousand churches in and around Naples: he was a sickly painter and when he asked for money it was granted to him if he would promise to bring, the next day, a statuette of the Immaculate Conception, the protectress of Concetta the usurer, in a blue dress sprinkled with stars. Annarella, the sister of Carmela, came in desperation to ask for a loan, as an urgent act of charity, of two lire for that day; she wanted to make a little broth for her sick child. A horrible scene took place as the two women didn't believe what Annarella was saying: she wanted to make a fool of them, yet again, since she and her husband Gaetano had accumulated a huge debt and weren't ashamed of squeezing the last drop out of poor people and not giving it back. Annarella screamed, cried, shouted that she would go and bring her child, burning with fever, for the two sisters to see; that the child would make even stones have pity; and sobbing, she shouted that they too were right, that everyone was right, but that they should be moved to have pity on that poor little creature who was not to blame, and now that it was weaned she would find a part time job as a maid, if only the Madonna gave her some help. Finally, tired of it all and from a wish to be rid of the shouting and weeping, Concetta gave her those two lire, swearing by the Lord above that they were positively the last, however true it might be that it was perhaps on this Friday in March that Our Lord had died – after all, no one knows on what Friday in March Our Lord did die! Other people, either embarrassed, enraged or grief-stricken, came to pay off old interest instalments, to offer belongings as security, to ask for more money; and the discussions passed from humility to acrimony, from threatening to pleading, from solemn promises to cowardly concessions.

Discussing, arguing and threatening, Concetta continued working opposite her sister until evening: and she never tired, always being ready with the right word, with a lucid turn of phrase, with immediate intuition of the good or the bad payer. Only for one discreet and respectably dressed visitor with the clean-shaven face of a servant from a good household, did she get up and then accompany him into the adjacent room, where they chatted in a low voice for some time. The usual noise of keys grating in locks, of drawers opening and closing, was heard; the servant came out, encased in his air of discretion, followed by Concetta.

'Was that the Marquis Cavalcanti's majordomo?' Caterina asked when he had left.

'Yes,' said Concetta briefly.

That hard, wearisome Friday was slipping away. Now that it was growing dark, the two sisters had stopped embroidering the counterpane. And Caterina was preparing a number of large ledgers, written in anonymous handwriting, all figures which she understood extremely well, for the great day of Saturday which was hers. Under the oil lamp, she bent over the ledger, thinking and moving her lips. Concetta saw that she was immersed in her solemn weekly task and kept silent out of respect for this astute preparation, feeling that from it would be disgorged piles and piles and piles of money on the following day.

Gabriele d'Annunzio

THE END OF CANDIA

NEWLY TRANSLATED BY
BRUCE PENMAN

GABRIELE D'ANNUNZIO

GABRIELE D'ANNUNZIO (1863–1938) came from Pescara in the Abruzzi. Poet, dramatist, novelist and man-of-action, he was in his time the most flamboyant, indeed Byronic figure on the Italian literary scene. He was an air ace and national hero in World War I, and after the war he led a commando incursion to restore Fiume to Italy. His stories about the Abruzzi vividly illustrate the more repulsive traits of human nature; his style is very reminiscent of de Maupassant. The *Novelle della Pescara* were published in 1902. No complete English translation appears to exist, but twelve stories from it, translated by G. Mantellini, were published as *Tales of My Native Town*, 1920. Numerous anthologies include stories by d'Annunzio, one of the best known appearing in A. Colquhoun and N. Rogers' *Italian Regional Tales of the 19th Century*, 1961.

THE END OF CANDIA

I

The great Easter dinner party was always a magnificent affair in Donna Cristina Lamonica's house, with crowds of guests. Three days later, she used to count the cutlery and check the table linen, as everything was neatly put away and locked up for use on future occasions.

She always had two helpers with her – Maria Bisaccia, her maidservant, and the laundress, Candida Marcanda, generally known as Candia. The great baskets, full of fine linen, stood in rows on the floor. On a sideboard lay a glittering display of silver dishes and cutlery. The handiwork of country silversmiths, they were a little heavy in their decoration, but with something almost sacramental about their shape, like most of the silver handed down from generation to generation in rich provincial families. The room was full of the fragrance of freshly washed linen.

Candia lifted the tablecloths and napkins out of the baskets, holding each of them up so that Donna Cristina could see that it was perfect and undamaged, and handed them one by one to Maria, who packed them away in the drawers. Her mistress added a sprig of lavender after each layer, and marked them off in her book.

Candia was in her fifties, tall, bony and tough; her back was somewhat bent by the habitual position of her trade, and her arms were very long. She had the head of a bird of prey on the neck of a tortoise.

Maria Bisaccia came from Ortona. She had a plump body, a milky complexion, and very bright eyes. Her voice was soft, and she had the slow, delicate gestures of a woman whose hands are always busy with pastry, syrups, sweets and preserves.

Donna Cristina also came from Ortona, where she had been educated by the Benedictines. She was on the short side, with a sagging bosom. She had reddish hair, a freckled face, a long, thick nose, bad teeth, and very beautiful eyes, with an intensely decorous expression in them. She looked like a priest dressed up in female clothing.

The three women devoted the most scrupulous care to their task, which generally took them most of the afternoon.

One day, just as Candia went off with her empty baskets, Donna Cristina found a gap in one of the sets of cutlery she was checking.

'Maria! Maria!' she cried in horror. 'Come and look! There's a spoon missing. Check the things yourself!'

'There can't be a *spoon* missing, Madam,' said Maria. 'Let's have another look.'

And she rechecked the cutlery, counting aloud as she did so. Donna Cristina looked on, shaking her head. A clear, tinkling sound came from the silver.

'Yes, it's true!' cried Maria finally, with a despairing gesture. 'What are we going to do now?'

Maria herself was above suspicion. Her honesty and loyalty had stood the test of fifteen years service in the family. She had come from Ortona with Donna Cristina after the wedding, like part of the furniture which the bride had brought with her. Now she enjoyed a certain authority in the household, thanks to the special regard of her mistress. She was full of religious superstitions, full of devotion to her patron saint and the chime of his church bells – and full of cunning too. She and her mistress had formed a sort of hostile alliance against Pescara and all its works, but especially against its patron saint. Maria never missed a chance of mentioning her native town, with its beauty, its treasures, its splendid basilica, its priceless relics of St Thomas, and its magnificent church services – all in contrast with the wretched St Cetteo of Pescara and his single miserable silver arm.

'Better look in the other rooms,' said Donna Cristina.

Maria went out and searched every corner of the kitchen and the verandah, but came back with empty hands.

'No sign of it, Madam!' she said.

Then they both tried to think the question out, to search their memories, to put two and two together. They went out on to the verandah where the washing was done, overlooking the courtyard, for a final search. As they were talking loudly, faces began to appear at the windows of the neighbouring houses.

'What's happened, Donna Cristina? What is it?'

Donna Cristina and Maria told their story, at great length, with many gestures.

'God forbid! Are there thieves among us, then?'

The news spread rapidly through the neighbourhood, and then through all Pescara. Men and women alike eagerly discussed the case, wondering who the thief could be. By the time the story reached the far end of town, it was not just one spoon that had been stolen, but all the Lamonica family's silver.

The weather was fine, the roses round the verandah were coming into flower, and the goldfinches sang in their cage. The pleasure of gossiping in the agreeable warmth of the sun kept the neighbours at their windows. They peeped out between the pots of basil on their window-sills, and the sound of their chatter seemed to fascinate the cats sitting on the tiles over the eaves.

Donna Cristina folded her hands together as if in prayer.

'Who can it have been?' she cried.

Donna Isabella Sertale, nicknamed the Weasel, who had the quick, furtive movements of a small, predatory animal, spoke up in her squeaky voice:

'Who was with you, Donna Cristina? Didn't I see Candia?'

'Aha!' exclaimed Donna Felicetta Margasanta, who was known as the Magpie because of her continual chatter.

'Aha!' repeated the other neighbours.

'Didn't you think of her?'

'Didn't you notice anything?'

'Don't you know about Candia?'

'We'll tell you about Candia!'

'Yes!'

'We'll tell you all right!'

'She washes the clothes well enough, that can't be denied. She's the best laundress in Pescara, no doubt of that. But ... light-fingered. Didn't you know, Donna Cristina?'

'I've been two table-napkins short before now!'

'I lost a tablecloth, once.'

'I lost a shirt.'

'I lost three pairs of socks.'

'I lost two pillow-cases.'

'I lost a new shirt.'

'One time I couldn't get anything back at all!'

'Nor could I!'

'Nor could I!'

'I never got rid of her, of course — who else is there? Silvestra?'

'What an idea!'

'Angelantonia? Babascetta?'

'They're all one worse than the other.'

'You just have to put up with it.'

'But a spoon's another matter.'

'A spoon's too much of a good thing.'

'Don't you lie down under it, Donna Cristina.'

'Lie down, indeed!' snorted Maria Bisaccia. For all her calm, good-natured appearance, she never missed a chance of damaging or discrediting anyone else who served her mistress. 'Leave it to us, Donna Isabella — you just leave it to us.'

The stream of gossip flowed on, from verandah to window. And the story against Candia spread quickly from mouth to mouth through the whole town.

II

The following morning Candia was standing at her wash-tub when a policeman appeared at her door. It was Biagio Pesce, who was known as the Little Corporal.

'The mayor wants to see you, up at the town hall, at once,' he said.

'What was that?' asked Candia with a scowl, not interrupting her work.

'The mayor wants to see you, up at the town hall, at once.'

'The mayor? What for? Why? Why?' asked Candia. She spoke rather tartly, not being able to imagine the reason for this unexpected summons. She had the air of a horse preparing to shy at a shadow.

'How should I know why?' said the policeman. 'I'm just carrying out an order.'

'What order?'

She was an obstinate woman. She kept on questioning him — she could not believe the message was really for her.

'The mayor wants me. Why? What for? What have I done? I won't come. I haven't done anything.'

The policeman began to get impatient.

'You won't come, eh? You'd better watch out!'

He went away, with his hand on the hilt of his old dagger, grumbling under his breath.

Various neighbours, who had heard the conversation, came out and stood at their doors, staring at Candia, who was working away at her wash-tub again. They had already heard about the silver spoon, and began to laugh, and to make remarks with a hidden meaning. Their laughter and their incomprehensible words made her feel uneasy. Her discomfort increased when the policeman reappeared, accompanied by a colleague.

'Come on!' said the Little Corporal resolutely.

Candia dried her arms without a word, and went off with them. People stopped to watch them as they crossed the square. Rosa Panara, an old enemy of Candia's, came out of her shop, laughed ferociously, and screamed:

'Scornful dogs will eat dirty puddings!'

The washerwoman had no idea what lay behind this persecution, and was bewildered, not knowing what to reply.

In front of the town hall stood a group of people who had come to see her taken inside. Candia hurried angrily up the steps, and made her way breathlessly into the mayor's office.

'What do you want me for, Don Silla?' she demanded.

The mayor was a man of peace. He was disturbed for a moment by the harshness of the washerwoman's voice, and glanced at the two faithful guardians of his mayoral dignity. Then he took snuff from a little box made of horn, and said:

'Sit down, Candia.'

Candia stayed on her feet. Her curved nose was swollen with rage, and her wrinkled cheeks trembled with the working of her jaw muscles.

'What is it, Don Silla?'

'Yesterday you delivered some washing to Donna Cristina Lamonica?'

'Well, what about it? Is anything missing? We checked every single item. Nothing was missing. What about it?'

'Just a moment, Candia! The silver was in the same room ...'

Candia guessed what was coming, and began to look like an angry hawk, ready to pounce. Her thin lips started to tremble.

'The silver was in the same room, and now there's a spoon missing. ... Do you understand, Candia? Did you pick it up ... by mistake?'

Candia jumped like a cat on hot bricks at this undeserved accusation. She was completely innocent, in point of fact.

'Who, me? Who says so? Who saw me touch anything? I'm very surprised at you, Don Silla! I can't believe my ears! Me, called a thief! Me, of all people!'

She went on and on like this. She was all the more deeply wounded by the unjust accusation because she knew that she was quite capable of the crime attributed to her.

'So you didn't take it, then?' interrupted the mayor, prudently retreating into his big official chair.

'I can't believe my ears,' she gabbled again, stiffly waving her long arms.

'All right, you can go. We shall see ...'

Candia left the room without taking leave of the mayor, and bumped into the door-post as she went. Her face was green; she was beside herself with fury. When she reached the street, and saw the crowd that had assembled, she realized that public opinion was against her, and that no one would believe that she was not guilty. None the less she began to scream at them, proclaiming her innocence. They laughed, and dispersed. She went home in a rage, which suddenly turned to despair. She began to sob, sitting on her doorstep.

'You'll have to cry louder than that if you want people to hear you,' was the mocking comment of Don Donato Brandimarte, who lived next door.

There was a pile of washing still waiting for her, and in the end she calmed down, rolled up her sleeves, and got back to work. As she laboured away, she was thinking about clearing her name – planning her defence and exhausting her resources of feminine cunning to find some trick that would prove her innocence. The subtlest quibbles passed through her mind, and she drew on all the treasures of popular logic and eloquence as she put together a speech designed to convince the sceptical.

When her work was finished, she went out. The first person she wanted to see was Donna Cristina.

But Donna Cristina was not available. Maria Bisaccia listened to the many things that Candia had to say in silence, shaking her head, and withdrew in a dignified manner.

Then Candia went round to see all her customers. She told her story to each in turn, proving her innocence, bringing in a fresh argument with every repetition, adding to the length of her oration, getting more and more excited, desperate at the incredulity and distrust that greeted her. It was all in vain. She realized that defence was no longer possible. A grim depression came over her. What more could she say or do?

III

Donna Cristina Lamonica sent for La Cinigia, a woman of the people, who made a good thing out of white witchcraft and quack medicine. La Cinigia had found stolen property for the owners several times before. Some said that she had dealings with the world of petty thieves.

'You find me that spoon,' said Donna Cristina, 'and I'll give you a good reward.'

'Very well,' said La Cinigia. 'I can do it by this time tomorrow.'

She came back exactly twenty-four hours later.

'The spoon is in a hole in the ground, near the well in the courtyard,' she said.

Donna Cristina and Maria ran down to the courtyard, and there was the spoon, much to their amazement.

The news spread rapidly through the whole town.

Candia Marcanda strode proudly through the streets. She seemed to have grown taller. She held her head high, and looked everyone smilingly in the eyes, as if to say:

'Have you heard the news? Have you heard?'

When people in the shops saw her go by, they muttered to each other and sniggered meaningly.

Filippo La Selvi, who was drinking a glass of the potent local spirits in Angeladea's café, called her over to his table.

'Another of the same for Candia !' he said.

Candia smacked her lips – she loved strong liquor.

'You deserve it – there's no doubt about that,' he went on.

A crowd of idlers gathered in front of the café. All of them had the air of participating in a joke.

While Candia was having her drink, Filippo La Selvi turned toward his audience.

'She knows what's what, eh? The old fox ...'

And he gave the washerwoman a familiar pat on her bony back.

Everyone laughed.

Magnafave, a half-witted little hunchback with an impediment in his speech, began to say something, stumbling over the syllables:

'Ca – Ca – Candia ... La – La – Cinigia ...'

At the same time he held out the forefingers of both hands in the pointing position, turned them towards each other, and dabbed the tips together. He went on cunningly stammering and gesticulating for some time, the whole performance expressing the opinion that Candia and La Cinigia were very old friends. The crowd were roaring with laughter now.

Candia was bewildered for a moment, and stood there with the glass in her hand. Then, suddenly, she understood. These people did not believe in her innocence. They were accusing her of complicity with La Cinigia – of hiding the spoon where it had been found, to avoid further trouble.

A blind fury came over her. Speechless with rage, she attacked the weakest of her tormentors, the little hunchback, punching and scratching him. With cruel joy, the crowd gathered round in a noisy circle, as if watching a dog-fight. They cheered on both the contestants, shouting and waving their arms.

Overwhelmed by this unexpected, frenzied assault, Magnafave tried to get away, his little legs working like a monkey's; but he was held tight in the washerwoman's powerful hands, and whirled round and round with increasing speed, like a stone in a sling, until he finally crashed face downwards on to the ground.

A couple of men ran to pick him up. Candia withdrew, pursued by hissing, and went home. She locked herself in and threw herself on her bed, sobbing and biting her hands in an agony of grief. This new accusation hurt even more than the previous one. How could she clear her name now? How could the truth be brought to light? She realized, to her despair, that the trick of which she was accused had no material difficulties that she could bring forward to discredit the idea. Access to the courtyard was perfectly easy; an open door led straight in from the street to the foot of the main staircase, and people were coming and going all the time – dustmen, tradesmen and so on. She could not silence her accusers by saying 'How could I have got in?' The trick could have been carried out quite easily in any one of a number of ways – in fact its easiness was the foundation for the popular belief that it must have happened.

Candia searched her brain for persuasive arguments, using all her cunning. She invented three, four, five explanations that would account for the spoon being found where it was. She had recourse to every kind of artifice and quibble, displaying great subtlety and ingenuity. Then she went round all the shops, and visited all the houses, trying every possible device to overcome the general incredulity. People seemed to enjoy listening to her elaborate arguments. When she had finished, they would say:

'Yes, yes! Of course!'

But the tone in which they uttered the words drove Candia to despair. So all her efforts were in vain! No one believed her! No one! With wonderful resolution, she returned to the attack. She spent whole nights inventing new arguments, constructing new edifices of proof, answering new objections. This continual effort slowly began to weaken her brain, which had no room for any thoughts except the thought of the spoon, and lost almost all awareness of everyday life. Later on, the cruelty of the people around her drove the poor woman almost out of her mind.

She neglected her work, and was reduced almost to starvation. She washed her clients' clothes badly, or lost them, or tore them. When she went down to the river bank, under the iron bridge, where the other washerwomen congregated, she sometimes let go of the garments she was washing and watched the current carry them away beyond recall. She talked all the time, untiringly, always about the same thing. When they got tired of hearing her voice, the younger washerwomen would sing a song, often mocking Candia with new, improvised verses. This made her scream and gesticulate like a madwoman.

Then people stopped giving her work. Her old customers occasionally sent her something to eat, out of charity. She slowly got used to the idea of begging. She toiled through the streets, a ragged, bent, bedraggled figure. The street urchins shouted after her:

'Tell us about the spoon, Candia! We don't know the story — tell us about the spoon!'

Sometimes she stopped complete strangers in the street, to tell them the story, and elaborate her defence. Young fellows used to call her and give her sixpence to tell her tale three or four times over. Sometimes they raised objections to all her arguments; sometimes they listened quietly to the very end, and then wounded her deeply with a couple of well-chosen words. She shook her head, and walked on; she often joined a group of other beggar-women and talked on in their company with the same unending, indefatigable, immovable loquacity. Her favourite companion was a deaf woman, who had a reddish, leprous infection of the skin and a lame leg.

In the winter of 1874 Candia was struck by a lingering, malignant fever. The leper-woman did what she could for her. Donna Cristina Lamonica sent her a bowl of broth, a brazier, and some fuel.

As she lay on her straw pallet, the invalid went on raving about the spoon, hoisting herself up on to her elbows, trying to use her hands to lend emphasis to her peroration. The leper-woman held her hands, and tenderly laid her back on to the bed.

In the agony of death, her huge eyes already darkening as if muddy water were flowing into them from the back, she was still stammering:

'The spoon, Madam ... it wasn't true ... you see, the spoon ...'

Luigi Pirandello

LIMES FROM SICILY

TRANSLATED BY
V. M. JEFFERY

LUIGI PIRANDELLO

LUIGI PIRANDELLO (1867–1936) was a Sicilian, from Agrigento. As a playwright (*Six Characters in Search of an Author* is his most famous play), novelist, and prolific short story writer, he has enjoyed constant popularity: his plays are still everywhere performed, his books are kept in print. The majority of his stories were collected and published in the multi-volume edition *Novelle per un Anno*, 1922–37. He writes with equal genius of the rustic peasantry and of the urban upper middle classes; he can handle both tragedy and farce with ease and authority. His trade mark, like Chesterton's, is the paradox. Pirandello has had more attention from English translators than any other Italian prose writer except Boccaccio. Frederick May's *Luigi Pirandello – Short Stories*, 1965, includes a ten page bibliography of stories published in English. Volumes include A. and H. Mayne's *Better Think Twice About It*, 1933, and *The Naked Truth*, 1934, and S. Putnam's *The Horse in the Moon*, 1932. W. Strachan's *Modern Italian Short Stories*, 1955, includes one of his most-translated stories.

'Does Teresina live here?'

The manservant, still in his shirtsleeves though already half-strangled by a very high collar, stared the young man up and down as he stood in front of him on the landing. He looked a real country bumpkin with the collar of his coarse overcoat turned up to his ears. His hands were stiff and blue with cold. In one he held a dirty little canvas bag, and in the other, by way of counter-balance, a shabby little suitcase.

'Teresina? And who might she be?' asked the other in his turn, raising bushy eyebrows that met in the centre and looked for all the world like a moustache that had been shaved off his lip and stuck on up there so as not to get lost.

The young fellow first shook his head to remove a dewdrop from the tip of his nose, and then he replied:

'Teresina, the opera singer.'

'Well! Well!' exclaimed the manservant, with a sarcastic smile of amazement. 'Do you think she can be called Teresina, just like that, and nothing more? And who might you be?'

'Is she in, or not?' asked the young man, frowning and giving a long drawn out sniff. 'Tell her it's Micuccio and let me come in.'

'But there is nobody in at this time of day,' replied the manservant, his smile frozen on to his lips. 'Signora Sina Marnis is still at the opera house and . . .'

'Aunt Martha too?' Micuccio interrupted.

'Oh, you are her nephew?'

The manservant immediately turned obsequious.

'Come in then, please come in. There is nobody in. Yes, your aunt is at the opera house too; they will not be back before one o'clock. They are celebrating tonight. Your . . . What relation are you to Madam? Your cousin then . . .?'

Micuccio hesitated for a moment and looked awkward.

'I'm not – no, not her cousin really. I'm . . . I'm Micuccio Bonavino, you know. I have come up from home on purpose.'

At this reply the manservant thought fit to moderate his obsequiousness. He showed Micuccio into a small dark room near the kitchen, where somebody was snoring noisily, and said to him:

'Sit down here. I will bring a light in a moment.'

Micuccio looked first in the direction of the snoring, but he could make out nothing. Then he looked into the kitchen, where the cook was preparing supper with the help of a pantry-boy.

The mingled smell of cooking overwhelmed him. It went to his head and made him giddy, for he had hardly eaten anything since morning. He had come from the province of Messina, a whole night and a day in the train.

The manservant brought the lamp, and the person who was snoring, behind a curtain hung from a cord running right across the room, muttered in her sleep:

'Who's there?'

'Here, Dorina, get up!' called out the manservant. 'Look, here is Mr Bonvicino.'

'Bonavino,' Micuccio corrected him, breathing on his fingers.

'Bonavino, Bonavino, a friend of Madam's. You're sleeping like a log. The bell's been ringing, but you can't hear it. I've got the table to lay, I can't do everything. Do you hear? The cook doesn't know his job. How can I keep an eye on him and answer the door as well?'

A long noisy yawn prolonged into stretching of arms and legs, and ending in a little whine and a chilly shudder greeted the manservant's protest. He went off exclaiming:

'All right, you wait.'

Micuccio smiled and watched him pass through the half-light of another room, till he came to the big brilliantly lit dining-room at the end where stood a richly-laden table. He stayed watching in amazement until the sound of more snoring made him turn round again towards the curtain.

The manservant, with his napkin under his arm, kept going by, grumbling now about Dorina who was asleep again, now about the cook. He was evidently new, called in specially for the party and he kept on bothering him with requests for explanations. Micuccio in order not to be a nuisance too, thought it best to swallow all the questions he wanted to put to him. He ought, of course, to have told him or let him guess that he was Teresina's fiancé and he did not want to, though he himself did not know why: except perhaps for this reason, that the man-servant would then have had to treat him, Micuccio, as his master; and he, seeing him so self-assured and elegant although still without his coat, could not manage to overcome the embarrassment he felt at the mere thought of such a thing. At a certain moment, however, seeing him pass, he could not help asking him:

'Excuse me ... who does this house belong to?'

'It's ours, so long as we are in it,' the man replied in his hurry.

Micuccio stayed there shaking his head.

Heavens! It was true then! Her fortune was made. Things were flourishing. That manservant with his lordly air, the cook, the kitchen-boy. And Dorina over there snoring – all of them servants at Teresina's beck and call. Who would have thought it!

In his mind's eyes, he saw once more the squalid garret, far away in Messina, where Teresina used to live with her mother. Five years ago, in that far-off garret, if it had not been for him, mother and daughter would have starved to death. It was he, he who had discovered the treasure that existed in Teresina's throat! She used to sing all day long then, like a sparrow on the house-tops, quite unaware of the treasure she possessed. She used to sing out of vexation, she used to sing in order to forget the poverty which he tried his best to alleviate, in spite of the campaign of nagging that his parents and particularly his mother kept up about it. But how could he abandon Teresina to that state of affairs after her father's death? Abandon her because she had nothing, while he, for good or ill, had at least a small job as flute-player in the town band? A fine reason! Had he no heart?

Ah, it had been a veritable inspiration from Heaven, a real stroke of luck that he should have seen the value of her voice when nobody else gave it a thought, that lovely April day when they were sitting by the attic window that framed so vividly the deep blue of the sky. Teresina was singing snatches of a little

Sicilian air, full of passion. Micuccio could still remember the
fond words of the song. Teresina was in a sad mood that day,
partly on account of the recent death of her father, partly because of the unyielding opposition shown by his relatives. He
too, he remembered, had felt sad, so much so that his eyes had
filled with tears as he listened to her singing. He had heard it
very often, that little song, but sung as she sang it, never once.
He had been so much impressed by it that the day after, without
warning either her or her mother, he had taken up to the garret
the conductor of the band, a friend of his. And so she had begun
her first singing lessons, and for two years on end he had spent
on her almost the whole of his wages. He had hired a piano for
her, bought sheets of music for her, and he had made some
friendly payments to her singing master. Lovely days of long
ago!

Teresina was burning with longing to fly off, to launch herself on that career which her singing master promised her would
be so brilliant; and meantime what burning kisses she showered
on him to show him all her gratitude! What dreams of happiness together!

Aunt Martha, however, used to shake her head bitterly. She
had seen too much in her day, poor old woman, and now she
had no faith left in the future. She was afraid for her daughter,
and did not want her even to think of the possibility of escaping
from the poverty to which she had resigned herself. And then
she knew – she knew what it was costing him, that mad and
dangerous dream.

But neither he nor Teresina listened to her, and it was in
vain that she protested when a young composer who had heard
Teresina sing at a concert declared that it would be an absolute
crime not to give her a better teacher and a complete musical
training. Naples, they must send her to the Conservatoire at
Naples, no matter what it cost.

Then he, Micuccio, without thinking twice about it, had
broken with his relatives. He had sold a little farm left him as a
legacy by his uncle, the priest, and he had sent Teresina to
Naples to finish her studies.

He had not seen her again since that time. Letters, yes ... he
had had letters from her from the Conservatoire, and those

which Aunt Martha had written him, when Teresina was already launched on her career as a singer, when she was already being fought for by the chief theatres, after the uproarious début at the Saint Charles Opera House. At the foot of these shaky indistinct letters scratched out anyhow by the poor old woman, there were always a few words from Teresina, who had not had time to write to him: 'Dear Micuccio, this is to say the same as Mother. Take care of yourself and love me ...' They had agreed that for five or six years he should leave her free to make her way in the world untrammelled. They were both young, and they could wait. During the five years that had already passed he had always shown those letters to anyone who asked to see them, to put an end to the malicious reports his relatives spread against Teresina and her mother. Then he had fallen ill. He had lain at death's door. At that time, unknown to him, Aunt Martha and Teresina had sent a substantial sum of money to his address. Part of it had gone during his illness, but what was left he had snatched out of the greedy clutches of his relatives. Now he had come to hand it back to Teresina. Money, no, he didn't want it. Not because he thought it given out of charity, for he had already spent so much on her, but ... no, he wouldn't hear of it; why he couldn't say himself, still less now that he was here in this house ... but money, no he wouldn't hear of it. He had waited for so many years, he could wait a little longer. For if Teresina had money and to spare, it was proof that her future lay clear before her, and consequently it was high time the promise of long ago should be kept, no matter who else refused to believe in it.

Micuccio rose to his feet, frowning as if to strengthen his own resolution. He blew once more on his frozen hands and stamped his feet on the ground.

'Cold?' the manservant asked, as he passed. 'They won't be long now. Come along into the kitchen. You'll be more comfortable.'

Micuccio would not take the advice of the manservant. With his lordly air, he disconcerted and annoyed him. He sat down again and began to think, full of consternation. A little while later he was startled by the loud ringing of the bell.

'Dorina, it's Madam!' yelled the manservant, thrusting his

arms into his coat as fast as he could. He rushed to open the door, but seeing Micuccio about to follow him, he stopped short and said to him:

'You stay here. I'll tell her you are here first.'

'Oh, oh, oh,' wailed a sleepy voice behind the curtain. Then a moment later there appeared a stumpy fat woman, slovenly dressed. She was limping a little, and could hardly keep her eyes open. She was huddled up to the eyes in a woollen shawl, and her hair was bleached golden.

Micuccio stood and gaped at her, all eyes. She too, taken by surprise, stared wide-eyed at the stranger.

'It's Madam,' repeated Micuccio.

At that Dorina recovered her wits immediately. 'Here I am, here I am,' she said, removing the shawl and flinging it behind the curtain. As fast as she could she propelled her heavy bulk towards the door.

The sight of that hag with dyed hair, together with what the manservant had said, suddenly gave Micuccio a painful sense of foreboding, sick at heart as he was. He heard Aunt Martha's shrill voice:

'Out there in the dining-room, in the dining-room, Dorina.'

The manservant and Dorina went by carrying magnificent baskets of flowers. He put his head out to watch the brilliantly lit dining-room at the end and he saw a number of gentlemen in evening dress and heard a buzz of talk. A mist swam before his eyes. So amazed was he, so agitated that not even he knew that his eyes had filled with tears. He shut them, and in the darkness he huddled himself up as if to ward off the pain which a peal of silvery laughter caused him. Was it Teresina? Oh Lord, why was she laughing like that out there?

A stifled cry made him open his eyes, and he saw standing before him – barely recognizable – Aunt Martha. Her hat was on her head, and the good soul was weighed down by a sumptuous velvet cloak.

'What! Micuccio – you here?'

'Aunt Martha ...' cried Micuccio, half in terror. He stood and looked at her.

'How is this? What made you come?' went on the old lady, all upset. 'Without letting us know? What has happened?

When did you get here? Today, of all days. ... Oh dear, dear ...'

'I came to ...' stammered Micuccio, and did not know how to go on.

'Wait,' Aunt Martha broke in. 'What's to be done? What's to be done? Don't you see all these people, my dear boy? It's Teresina's party; she is giving a party. ... Will you wait? Wait a little while here ...'

'If you think,' Micuccio tried to say, choked with grief, '... if you think I ought to go ...'

'No, wait a bit, I say,' the kind old lady hastened to reply awkwardly.

'You see,' went on Micuccio, 'I don't know anywhere to go in this city at this time of night.'

Aunt Martha left him, bidding him wait with a wave of her gloved hand. She went into the dining-room, and there it seemed to Micuccio a moment later an abyss opened. Silence fell all at once. Then he heard, clearly, distinctly, Teresina say these words:

'Excuse me one moment, gentlemen.'

Again a mist swam before his eyes, as he waited for her to appear. But Teresina did not appear, and conversation began again in the dining-room. Instead, after a few minutes which seemed to him an eternity, Aunt Martha came back without her hat, without her cloak, without her gloves, seeming less upset.

'We will wait a bit here, shall we?' she said to him. 'I will stay with you. They are having supper now. ... We will stay here. Dorina shall lay this table for us and we will have supper here together. We'll talk over old times, shall we? ... You can't think how glad I am to be here with you again, laddie, here, all to ourselves. ... You see, there are such a lot of men there in that room. ... She, poor girl, can't help it. ... Her career, you know. ... Ah, well, what can you do! You've seen the newspapers? Big successes, my boy! But I ... to me it's like walking on water all the time. ... You can't think how pleased I am to be here with you this evening.'

And the kind old woman who had gone on talking and talking so that Micuccio should have no time to think, finally

smiled and rubbed her hands together as she looked at him
fondly.

Dorina came in to lay the table in a great hurry because
supper had begun already in the dining-room beyond.

'Will she come?' gloomily asked Micuccio, his voice full of
anguish. 'I mean, just for me to see her?'

'Of course she will come,' the old lady answered at once,
striving to hide her awkwardness. 'As soon as she has a moment
to breathe. She told me so.'

They looked at each other, and smiled as if at last they understood each other. Over and above the constraint and emotion
their spirits had found a way of greeting in that smile. 'You are
Aunt Martha,' said the eyes of Micuccio. 'And you, Micuccio,
my dear good boy. You are just the same as ever, poor lad,' the
eyes of Aunt Martha were saying. But immediately the kind old
woman lowered them, so that Micuccio should not read more.
She rubbed her hands again and said:

'Let's have something to eat, shall we?'

'I'm hungry, I am!' cried Micuccio, cheerful and reassured.

'Grace first. I can say it in front of you, here,' added the old
woman roguishly. She winked an eye and made the sign of the
cross.

The manservant came in to hand them the first course.
Micuccio watched carefully to see how Aunt Martha helped
herself from the dish. But when his turn came, as he raised his
hands, it struck him that they were dirty from his long journey.
He blushed, turned awkward, and looked up at the manservant
who, all politeness now, gave him a slight nod and smiled as if
to encourage him to help himself. Fortunately Aunt Martha
stepped in to save him.

'Here, here Micuccio. Let me help you.'

He could have kissed her, so grateful he felt. When he had
his plate in front of him, as soon as the manservant had gone
away he crossed himself hurriedly.

'There's a good lad!' Aunt Martha said to him.

And he felt he was in Heaven. Everything was all right and
he fell to as if he had never eaten before in all his life, without
another thought for his hands or the manservant.

Yet, every time the manservant entered or left the dining-

LIMES FROM SICILY 241

room, closing behind him the long glass door, there filtered through in a wave snatches of talk or bursts of laughter. Micuccio would turn round anxiously and then encounter the sad, fond gaze of the old woman, as if seeking an explanation there. But instead he read there the request that he would not ask anything for the time being, that he would postpone explanations till later. And they would both smile again at each other, and begin to eat again, and to talk of their far-off village, their friends and acquaintances, about whom Aunt Martha went on endlessly asking him for news.

'Won't you drink something?'

Micuccio stretched out a hand to the bottle, but at that moment the door of the dining-room opened again. The rustle of silk, hurried footsteps, and as if the room had been abruptly filled with light, a sudden glitter blinded him.

'Teresina.'

His voice died on his lips, in his amazement. Ah, what a queen!

His face aflame, eyes staring, mouth agape, he stayed looking at her stupidly. How was it she looked like that ... like that!

Her bosom was bare, her shoulders bare, her arms bare ... all gleaming with jewels and fine silk. ... He could not see her, he no longer saw her a real living being standing before him. What was she saying to him? It was not her voice, nor her eyes, nor her laugh. Nothing, he recognized nothing of her in that dream-apparition.

'How are you? Are you better now, Micuccio? That's good, that's good. ... You were ill, if I remember rightly. We shall see each other again presently. ... In any case you have Mother here with you. ... All right?'

And Teresina slipped away into the dining-room, a rustle of silk.

'Won't you have anything more?' asked Aunt Martha timidly, a few minutes later, to break into Micuccio's bewilderment.

He barely looked at her.

'Eat something,' the old woman urged, pointing to his plate.

Micuccio ran two fingers round his crumpled, travel-stained collar and pulled it down, trying to take a deep breath.

'Eat something?'

He waggled his fingers several times up and down near his chin, as if he were greeting somebody, and he meant, 'I don't want any more, I can't eat.' He remained silent a long time, stricken, absorbed in the vision that had just vanished, then he murmured:

'How she has changed....'

He saw that Aunt Martha was bitterly shaking her head. She too had stopped eating, as if she was waiting for something.

'It's no longer to be thought of,' he added, as if to himself, shutting his eyes.

He saw now, in that darkness that enfolded him, the gulf that had opened between the two of them. No, it was no longer she, that woman there: she was not his Teresina. It had all ended a long time ago, and he, fool that he was, idiot that he was, he only saw it now. They had told him so in the village, and he had obstinately refused to believe them. ... And now, what sort of a fool did he look, staying here in this house? If all those fine gentlemen, if that manservant even, had only known that he, Micuccio Bonavino, had taken all that trouble, had come all that way, thirty-six hours in the train, seriously believing himself to be still engaged to that queen, how they would have laughed, all those fine gentlemen and the manservant, and the cook and the kitchen-boy and Dorina! How they would have laughed if Teresina had pulled him into their midst, there in the dining-room, and said, 'Look! this poor fellow, this flute-player, says he wants to be my husband!' She herself had promised, it was true. But how could she know that one day she would turn into this? It was also true, yes, that he had made clear the path before her feet and had given her the means of treading it. But, there, she had gone so far, so very far, that he who had stayed where he was, always the same, playing his flute on Sundays in the village market-place, how could he ever catch up with her? It was not even to be thought of ...

Then what, after all, were those few miserable pounds he had spent on her, now she had become a great lady? He was ashamed at the very thought that somebody might suspect that he, by coming there, might have wanted to put forward a claim on account of those few miserable pounds. He remembered then that he had in his pocket the money sent him by Teresina, while he was ill. He blushed. He felt ashamed, and he thrust a hand into the breast-pocket of his jacket, where he kept his wallet.

'One of my reasons for coming, Aunt Martha,' he said hurriedly, 'was to give you back this money you sent me. What did you mean it to be? Payment? Restitution? I see that Teresina has become ... yes, she looks to me like a queen! I see that. ... No, it's nothing. It can't even be thought of! But this money – no: I did not deserve this from you. It is all over and we shan't say any more about it ... but money! No, I am only sorry that it's not all there ...'

'What are you saying, my dear boy?' Aunt Martha, distressed, tears in her eyes, tried to stop him.

Micuccio signed her to be silent.

'I didn't spend it. My people spent it while I was ill, without my knowing anything about it. But it can stand for that miserable little sum I spent then. ... You remember? We won't think any more about it. Here's the rest. Now I'm off.'

'What? Rush off like that?' cried Aunt Martha, trying to hold him back. 'At least wait till I see Teresina. Didn't you hear her say she wanted to see you again? I'll go and tell her ...'

'No, it's no use,' Micuccio answered her firmly. 'Let her stay with those gentlemen. She belongs there, it's her rightful place. I'm only a poor wretch. ... Well, I've seen her. That's enough for me. ... In fact you should go too: go and join her too. Can't you hear her laughing? I don't want her to laugh at me. ... I'm going.'

Aunt Martha put the worst interpretation on this sudden decision of Micuccio's: it must be an outburst of anger, a fit of jealousy. She thought it inevitable, poor thing, that now when they saw her daughter, everyone must immediately suspect the worst. She herself spent hours weeping inconsolably over this same suspicion. She was ceaselessly tormented by this burden of secret grief, as she moved on in the ferment of this life of hateful luxury which was so hideously dishonouring her weary old age.

'But I ...' the words slipped from her lips, 'I can no longer keep an eye on her, my boy ...'

'Why?' asked Micuccio then, suddenly reading in her eyes the suspicion which had so far not entered his head. His face darkened.

In her grief the old woman lost her head. She hid her face in her shaking hands but she could not keep back the flood of tears that welled up in her eyes.

'Yes, yes, my boy, you had better go,' she said, her voice choked with sobs. 'You are right, she is no longer for you. ... If only you two would have listened to me.'

'So that's it, then,' Micuccio burst out, bending over her and roughly tearing away one hand from her face. But the look she gave him was so pathetic and heart-broken as she laid a finger on her lips as if to say, 'For pity's sake,' that he checked himself and went on in a changed tone, forcing himself to speak softly.

'Ah, so she ... she is no longer worthy of me. Enough, enough. I'm going just the same: in fact all the more reason now. ... What a fool I am, Aunt Martha! I hadn't understood! Don't cry. ... Besides, what does it matter? It's fate, they say ... fate ...'

He took his little suitcase and his bag from under the table, and he was on the point of leaving when he remembered that there in the bag were those splendid limes he had brought from home for Teresina.

'Oh look, Aunt Martha,' he began. He undid the string of the bag, and holding out his arm in front to stop them, he tipped out on to the table the fresh sweet-smelling fruit.

'What if I were to start throwing all these limes at the heads of those fine fellows in there?'

'For Heaven's sake,' groaned the old woman through her tears, with a gesture again begging him to be quiet.

'No, of course not,' went on Micuccio with a harsh laugh, as he stuffed the empty bag into his pocket. 'I had brought them for her, but now I'll leave them for you and no one else, Aunt Martha.'

He took one and put it to Aunt Martha's nose. 'Can you smell it, Aunt Martha? Can you smell the scent of home? ... To think that I even paid excise duty on them. Enough. They're for you and no one else; mind that. ... Just wish her good luck from me ...'

He took up his suitcase again and went. But on the stairs an agonizing feeling of being lost overcame him. It was night, and he was alone, forsaken, in an unknown great city; far from home: disillusioned, sick at heart, humiliated. He reached the outer door and saw that it was pouring with rain. He could not summon up the courage to venture into those strange streets in that downpour. He crept back softly, climbed to the first landing, and sat down on the bottom step. He planted his elbows on his knees, dropped his head into his hands and began to weep quietly.

When supper was nearly over, Sina Marnis paid another visit to the little room. She found her mother weeping all alone, while those gentlemen were all shouting and bawling.

'Has he gone?' she asked in surprise.

Aunt Martha nodded without meeting her eyes. Sina stared into space, lost in thought, then she sighed.

'Poor fellow ...'

But almost at once she broke into a smile.

'Look,' her mother said to her, taking away the dinner napkin from her streaming eyes. 'He brought you these limes ...'

'Oh, how lovely!' exclaimed Sina, giving a little skip. She held an arm close to her side and heaped against it as many of them as she could carry.

'No, you are not to take them in there!' her mother protested sharply.

But Sina shrugged her shoulders and ran into the other room calling out, 'Limes from Sicily! Limes from Sicily!'

Italo Svevo

TRAITOROUSLY

TRANSLATED BY
BEN JOHNSON

ITALO SVEVO

ITALO SVEVO (1861–1928) came from Trieste. His real name was Ettore Schmitz. Most of his work was published late in his life, some of it posthumously. His reputation outside Italy, even more perhaps than within the country, has been growing in recent years. His novels, philosophical and meditative, have enjoyed particular favour in England. They are translated as: *Confessions of Zeno*, *As a Man Grows Older* and *A Life*. His stories and fragments are collected in *The Nice Old Man and the Pretty Girl*, and *Short Sentimental Journey*, 1967.

TRAITOROUSLY

Signor Maier set out for Reveni's home still not completely decided whether to ask for help and solace. The two men had been good friends all their life; they had both started from the bottom, and, by working every day from morning till evening, had both succeeded in making a great deal of money. Dealing in two entirely different lines, there had never existed the slightest competition between them, and despite their never having worked as partners, their friendship, which dated back to early youth, had remained firm and unchanged until their declining years. Unchanged but lifeless: their wives never called on each other, and they themselves met daily only for a quarter of an hour in the Stock Exchange. Both had now passed their sixtieth year.

After a sleepless night, Maier had decided to write to his old friend for an appointment. And now, as he was on his way to it, he turned over a vague plan by which his old friend should be asked to help him, but in such a way (as he would try to present it to him) that Reveni would be running no personal risk. Of course, in his own eyes help was due to him. So many years of honest successful work swept away by a moment of thoughtlessness! It was intolerable. Seeking to branch out, the old merchant had let himself be talked into a contract putting him in the hands of a third party; and they, having squeezed every last bit of credit from Maier's signature, had pulled up stakes and quit Trieste, leaving behind nothing but a few pieces of worthless furniture. At first Signor Maier had determined, as honesty required, to meet all his obligations. But it had now come to seem unjust that he should have to assume responsibilities not his own. If Reveni, who was a notoriously decent man, would relieve him at least for the time being of part of the burden, Maier's prospects for the future would be rosier. Maier could not recall having turned down a similar request himself. He remembered (and very clearly) having signed that contract — another gesture of confidence in human nature, as it seemed to him now, forgetting that the original motive for drawing up the contract had merely been to make money.

If Fate meant to favour him, it would certainly act through Reveni, who, without even being asked, would offer to help him. He expected this of Fate. And then – but not until then – he could lay his plan before his old friend who, if he was in a mood to take such risks, would accept it. Maier himself felt no risk was involved. He was only asking for the long-term credit he knew he deserved. Despite his old age, he was still an enterprising man, and against that one time when he had let himself be swindled he could cite hundreds of instances in which he had escaped from similar traps. So there was really no question of risk.

Reveni's home was in the centre of the town. Maier mounted the staircase, and from the moment the butler opened the door he felt nothing but envy. At present he also had a large heavily furnished anteroom hung with tapestries, and a small thickly carpeted chamber within, like the one in which Signor Reveni and his wife were waiting to offer him coffee. Ah, but he wouldn't have them for long! His poor wife was already out looking for a smaller, more modest flat. Here everything had the solid, confident look of a home that had existed for a long time and would long so continue. At his own home, on the other hand, everything was about to fly out of the window. Except for his wife's jewellery everything was still there, but it looked as if the rest were all ready to take flight.

Though the two men were the same age, Signor Reveni was much heavier and sallower than Maier. And seated as he was in a large armchair opposite Maier, who was himself sitting in an equally large chair, but timidly, perched on the edge of it, he – this man who had accumulated and accumulated without ever letting himself be tricked into signing an instrument like the one that had ruined Maier – seemed awe-inspiring.

Signora Reveni served the coffee. She was a woman who dressed with a certain ostentatiousness, all frills and lace, even at home. She was wearing a morning dress that would have looked ravishing on a younger, more beautiful woman.

Maier began to sip his coffee, thinking, 'Is she going to leave us to ourselves?'

It soon appeared that the Signora felt she had to let him know that she did not intend to leave them alone together: she told him that her Giovanni had not been well for some days and that he spent the afternoons at home, being looked after by her.

Maier thought it strange that a man who looked healthy enough, and had just got up from lunch, not only had to stay at home but to be continually watched over by his wife. From this, he felt, he must deduce that Reveni and his wife had already decided not to help him. He recalled that the wife was notoriously the more close-fisted of the two and that Reveni himself had once told him how she had managed to rid him of a poor relative who had been pestering him for money. And now, no sooner had Reveni received Maier's request for an appointment, than here she was hurrying to help him.

He felt humiliated – downright offended. Maier could not imagine being classed with a poor and insistent beggar. Quite the contrary, considering he had come with a business proposition that would benefit Reveni if he agreed to have a hand in it. In an effort to pull himself together, to cleanse himself of every trace of inferiority, Maier settled back into his own armchair too, in direct imitation of Reveni's posture. With a slight nod, he thanked the Signora as she handed him another cup of coffee. And the effort he made was such that feelings of inferiority actually seemed to have been purged from his system. He would propose nothing to Reveni. He would pretend instead that he had asked for the appointment for an altogether different reason. But what reason? It was hard to find one, because these two old friends had very rarely met to talk about business. Business was no good, then. But was there some other field in which he might need Reveni's advice? Then he remembered that a few weeks before a friend had vaguely asked whether he would accept a post as a town councillor. Perhaps he could ask Reveni for advice about this.

But Reveni immediately brought up the very topic that had brought Maier to him.

'Why, that Barabich!' he exclaimed. 'To think that Barabich, the scion of a fine old Triestine family, has stooped to such a thing! And where is he now? They say he's already had time to reach Corfu.'

To Maier that didn't sound at all like the prelude to the offer of help he was expecting from Fate — something else entirely! Reveni, in fact, sounded as though he sympathized more with the swindler than with the victim.

Maier once again settled himself somewhat more comfortably in the armchair, taking care, with his hands trembling as they were, not to drop his cup. He forced himself to wear an attitude of resolute indifference.

'You understand of course,' he said, 'I *had* to denounce him. Now it hardly matters to me if he gets off scot-free.'

The Signora had poured her husband another cup and was passing it to him; with her eyes on the cup, she took a step or two in order to reach him and then immediately turned to Maier.

'Think of the mother in the case!' she said, pained. As in her dress, in the sound of her voice, and every movement of hers, the Signora was determined to inject great sweetness into her words. So, in this affair that meant ruin for Maier, her first thought was for the culprit's mother. And to think that she, for all her airs of a *gran signora*, had been a cabaret singer in her youth, undressing in public as long as anyone would pay her to do so. Had she nurtured this ill will for him because, years ago, Maier had tried to stop Reveni from marrying her?

It was no longer possible to feign indifference. Flushed with anger, and with a bitter smile, Maier exclaimed: 'You will understand that I don't give a damn about that mother, considering that her son is about to make another mother — I mean, my wife — suffer terribly.'

'I see, I see,' the Signora murmured, still as sweetly as ever. And she sat down beside the table and filled her own cup from the steaming coffee-machine.

It was as if she were only now beginning to see; and she obviously still didn't see everything, for then it would have been up to her to say either that she or her husband were prepared to help him or that they didn't want to hear any more about it.

Reveni broke in. He seemed to feel that the affair could be considered from only one angle — that of his poor friend. A little uneasily, he stretched himself out in his armchair, looked up and grunted, 'An ugly business!' He sighed and, finally looking

Maier in the face, added, 'You've had a stroke of really bad luck.'

In other words, this meant that the matter was so serious that any intervention on his part to ease the situation was entirely out of the question. So, no help, and Maier could spare himself the humiliation of asking. He rose, set down the demitasse, which he had emptied without even tasting the coffee, and, settling back in his chair again, said with an offhand gesture, 'To be sure, there's money involved – and quite a good deal – but not all the money I had. It's unpleasant to think that I'll have less to leave my son, but at least he'll get more from me at my death than I got when my father died.'

Reveni's aloof attitude, of a man who did not wish to hear any more than suited him, changed, and he exclaimed, evidently genuinely delighted: 'Then I was right! Your difficulties have not set you back as much as they're saying about town. My good friend, let me shake your hand! I'm happier to hear this than if I'd just made I don't know how much!'

Reveni was wide awake now. He had even got out of his chair to go and shake Maier's hand. Maier found himself unable to show much gratitude for such a demonstration of joy and he let his hand lie limply in his friend's, so that the other returned to his chair. Maier thought: 'They're ready to share my joy, but they weren't ready to share my pain.' His mind flashed back over his day's activities: his fortune had been completely wiped out by that speculation – completely! – and he was still not sure that in the drawer of some unknown party there might not be more engagements than he could meet. His son stood to inherit absolutely nothing if, in the few years left to him, Maier couldn't continue in active business. On his own he had been able to take stock and make some exact calculation. But now, in his friend's presence, everything seemed more confused. Wouldn't it perhaps be wise to conceal his true position even from Reveni so as to regain the credit he needed to stay in business? This tactical scheme, though not properly thought out yet, restored his courage a little. The Signora, as if to show her own joy at such good news, offered him another cup of coffee, which he accepted with a grateful smile – a smile that cost him some effort. Meanwhile, in token of his gratitude, he swallowed the whole cupful of coffee, though it was more than he usually took.

Now that it was clear that Maier's situation was not too grave, Reveni seemed to find himself able to speak his mind:

'I confess I would never have trusted Barabich myself. I heard about your partnership only after it had all been settled. But everybody in Trieste knew that all Barabich's previous deals had ended badly.'

'Yes, but never to this extent!' Maier protested. 'It always looked as if he managed things perfectly well, but that everything he undertook was dogged by bad luck.'

Reveni gestured dubiously:

'I don't trust a man who's been set afloat so often and has always sunk. It's pretty clear he doesn't know how to swim. Barabich's career began ten years ago, with that business everybody talked so much about at the time, all those loads of Chinese rice. Remember how much money went overboard then! Then, all of a sudden, he was an industrial promoter. Now, it's true that some of the concerns he promoted actually prospered; but they prospered without him, because at a given stage people would feel it was time to cut free from him. Nothing bad was said about him – quite the contrary. In fact, there was a great deal of talk about his honesty; but still nobody was able to explain how it was that he wasn't connected with the businesses any more. And then how did he live? Until he snared you, all he did was talk, talk, talk. He talked about developing the Argentine, and the Klondike – both of them schemes that couldn't have brought in much, seeing that he never actually went in for them. And then he discovered another distant land – motor-car manufacture. It strikes me as incredible that a man of your experience would want to follow him there.'

For Maier it was terrible, the fact that Reveni was right. He remembered how he had been lured by visions of enormous quick profits. But now, in order to defend himself, he remembered also how much he had liked Barabich, who was younger than himself and so self-confident and bubbling over with ideas – they gave him the air of an expert. He wanted to remember only his fondness for him.

'I was led into it out of a desire to help Barabich, too. I felt sorry that a talented man like him should have to remain such a mediocrity.'

For a moment, seemingly hesitant to reply, Reveni said nothing. Then he gave Maier a searching look, as if trying to determine if he was really serious. Presently he remembered something that made up his mind for him, and he spoke, laughing and trying unsuccessfully to make Maier laugh too.

'Remember old Almeni? It was because of him that we had our first and last business conference – remember? After lots of insisting on his part he managed to get us – you, me and two friends of ours – all together to decide whether to lend him the money to open a bar, in the middle of the town, to be run by him and his son. It had to be luxurious, and so he needed considerable funds, for only by making it a *de luxe* place would he have been certain of a return. Neither you nor I fully understood businesses of that nature, but another of our prospective partners did and explained it to us, seriously doubting whether such a venture would be successful in this town. And the upshot was we decided that the main thing about the deal was the enormous help it would be to Almeni, who was a fine old chap, with a family to support, and who had never, despite his many excellent qualities, managed to raise himself out of the rut. Then we two broke in – you and I – and agreed with one voice that in this world of ours there have to be business dealings and there have to be good deeds, but that a good deed in the guise of business was bad business – all the more because it would no longer be a good deed. We finished by all agreeing to give the old fellow a little immediate help, simply because he deserved it, but nothing more. I remember our arguments perfectly, and I'm surprised you've forgotten them.'

Maier felt he must defend himself vigorously. It was too much for Reveni not only to refuse help but to make out that he was justified in doing so.

'There's a great difference between Almeni and Barabich; Almeni was simply an old fool, whereas Barabich was a shrewd and cultivated young man, with the single defect of being a thief.'

Maier had spoken so heatedly, and his face had flushed so red with anger, that Signora Reveni felt she ought to intervene. The day before, she had seen Signora Maier with her daughter:

'What a little darling your daughter is, with those innocent gazelle-eyes of hers!' (The gazelle being a sweet animal, Signora Reveni included it in her vocabulary.)

Maier would not have been placated, even if she had called him himself by the name of some charming animal! A thought struck him. Not only did he recall the Almeni episode, but he was also pretty certain that he had been the one who had thought of the arguments which Reveni was expounding as if they were his. What insight he had had in those days! He was reminded of his one-time intelligence only to be hit all the more by the shame of his recent mistake.

And moved by self-pity, with actual tears in his eyes, he said to Reveni: 'Life is long, too long; it is made up of so many days, in every one of which there's time to make the error that will cancel out the wisdom and effort of all the other days. Only one day . . . compared with all the others.'

Reveni gazed into space, perhaps to search his own long life for the day when he had made a mistake that might have jeopardized the work of all the other days. He agreed with Maier, but perhaps only to calm him. He did not seem particularly concerned by either the dangers he had faced or those he was likely to face. 'Yes,' he said, 'life is long, very long, and full of dangers.'

Maier felt Reveni was incapable of putting himself in his shoes and he couldn't blame him, because everyone knows how hard it is to think of the cold which others suffer when one is warm and cosy oneself; but he noticed that while Reveni was speaking, his wife looked at him with a smile of perfect confidence, of abandon, a look that seemed to say, 'Why, what a strange fancy! No, no, *you* couldn't make mistakes!'

And because of that, his dislike for the woman mounted to the point where he felt he could no longer stand her presence. He got to his feet and forced himself to make a courteous gesture towards her: he extended his hand, saying that he had to leave because of pressing business. He had decided to visit Reveni at his office the next day, not to ask for help, just to convince him that life really was long and that he should not condemn a man for one day's rashness – one day out of so many. Having shaken the Signora's hand he turned his back to Reveni. Reveni suddenly let out a peculiar sound. In a voice pitched somewhat lower than usual, he softly mumbled some incomprehensible word; Maier tried to catch it but failed, as it is hard to retain a series of meaningless syllables. Curious, he turned round. The Signora had already rushed terrified to her husband's side, crying: 'What's the matter?'

Reveni lay sprawling in his armchair. But after a moment he was still able to say to his wife, quite clearly and as though he had recovered: 'I've got a pain here.' And he moved his hand which, incapable of making the desired gesture, simply rose from the arm of the chair. Then, for a while, nothing more: he lay motionless, his head lolling upon his chest. He let out another sigh, like a lament, and no more. The Signora propped him up, screaming into his ear: 'Giovanni, Giovanni! What is it?'

Maier dabbed away the tears prompted by his own distresses and turned to his friend. He instantly guessed what was happening, but was still so wrapped up in his own affairs that his first thought was: 'He's going! He couldn't help me now even if he wanted to.'

He had to make a violent effort to throw off his abject self-centredness and act like a man. He went over to the woman, saying gently: 'Don't be frightened, Signora. It's only a fainting-spell. But would you like me to call the doctor?'

She was down on her knees in front of her husband. A tear-stained face looked up at Maier, obviously relaxing in the hope his words had inspired. 'Yes, yes! Call the doctor!' And she gave him a telephone number.

Maier rushed off in the direction from which he had entered, but the Signora, still on her knees, called out: 'No – the other way!' – an outcry softened by a sob. Then, opening the opposite door, Maier found himself in a dining-room in which two maids were clearing the table. He ordered them into the next room to help their mistress and, quickly locating the telephone, dialled the number she had given him.

He did not get connected at once, and, trembling with impatience, he anxiously asked himself: 'Is he dying – or already dead?' Then, as he waited, he felt himself filling with compassion. 'So this is how one dies!' And then: 'He can't agree to help any more, but he can't refuse either!'

The doctor promised to come at once. Maier put the receiver

back and paused a little before returning to Signora Reveni. He glanced round the room. What luxury! His relations with Reveni had been very tenuous after Reveni's marriage, and their wives had never had anything to do with each other. He was seeing their dining-room now for the first time: light flooded in from the great windows and gleamed from the marble skirting along the walls, from the gilt mouldings of the doors, from the crystalware still on the table. Everything was solidly in place, irremovable, because the poor devil in the next room had never done a foolish thing. Nor would he.

'Which of us two is the better off?' Maier thought.

With the maids' help, Signora Reveni had laid her husband's body out on the sofa. She was still busying herself over him. She had soaked his face with vinegar and was holding a little bottle of smelling-salts under his nose. He was now – there was no doubt about it – a corpse. His eyes had shut of their own accord, but the left eyeball protruded visibly.

Feeling himself such a stranger to the woman, Maier did not dare say anything to her. He remembered the address of Reveni's daughter and considered going back to the telephone; on second thoughts, however, he decided to go and see her in person, as she lived not very far away.

'I think,' he said hesitantly to Signora Reveni, 'I think I'll go over to Signora Alice's and tell her that her father is not feeling well.'

'Yes, do!' sobbed the Signora.

Maier flew out of the door not so much because he was in a hurry, for no one could help Reveni now, as to escape the presence of that corpse.

And once down in the street he questioned himself again: 'Which of us two is the better off?' How peaceful he looked, laid out on the sofa. Strange! – it was all over, his gloating over his own successes, which were magnified by Maier's errors. He had rejoined the great majority, whence, unmoving, he was staring now with that one protruding eye of his, free of joy and free of pain. The world ran on, but what had happened proved its utter pointlessness. The fate that had befallen Reveni made his own fate of perfect unimportance.

Corrado Alvaro

JEALOUSY

NEWLY TRANSLATED BY
GRAHAM SNELL

CORRADO ALVARO

CORRADO ALVARO (1895–1956) came from Reggio (Calabria) in the very south of Italy. He was a considerable novelist but also a prolific short story writer, and at his best when writing about the South. He established his reputation in Italy with *Gente in Aspromonte*, 1930, stories set in his native Calabria. One of his stories is translated in W. Strachan's *Modern Italian Short Stories*, 1955.

JEALOUSY

A friend of mine, himself a doctor, told me, when I met up with him after many years, that in Calabria there are several ways of using a doctor and his prescriptions. One way, perhaps the oldest, among the country folk there, consists of putting the prescription under the sick person's pillow: the evil spirit, intent on deciphering the doctor's hieroglyphics, is thus lured away from the sufferer. Now this is nothing to laugh at: many of modern man's prejudices have little more to recommend them. But that remedy is hardly used any more now, to tell the truth. A more widely used remedy consists of placing the prescription under a holy picture until the person recovers. At this stage of humanity's development, when questions on man's destiny are interspersed with statistics on his sexual habits and with competitions in female exhibitionism which can often lead to a situation where one is paying one's regards to a lady who has in the pages of a newspaper displayed her *os sacrum* to three hundred thousand strangers, I want to tell you of one of the dramas of jealousy and modesty that can still occur.

Before settling down in the city I spent several years as a general practitioner in a number of provincial towns. You know what the people are like out there, and how they judge a person by his behaviour and decide on his worth. Theirs is rather a primitive yardstick, but one that would be acceptable in the best schools of manners: to speak in clear, measured tones, not hesitantly, not drawling one's words, not talking down one's nose; to dress neither eccentrically nor yet shabbily; to wear one's hat squarely on one's head; to have a calm, assured presence, not letting oneself be carried away by fits of anger. These people like to give their deep respect to those in responsible positions. 'Eat to please yourself and dress to please others' is one of their mottoes.

On one occasion I was called here in Aspromonte. A boy came to tell me that his mother was ill: she had a pain in her side, he said, which had been troubling her for two days. We went together on foot – in those days there was no road other than a mule-track. I knew the boy by sight, but though he told me several times his name and surname and his father's nickname, I could not recall what his father looked like. The family had been out gathering the sparse wheat and corn which ripen late in the mountains, up in those fields you spot suddenly on a summer's day standing yellow in a clearing among the woods on the mountainside, and there in the middle you make out a fruit tree by the shadow it casts on the yellow and you have a feeling of ancient peace. The boy looked after a small flock of goats, he informed me. He belonged to the sort of people who are reasonably well off, who don't get themselves talked about, and who have a reserve and dignity which among the mountain clans (shepherds or farmers, or both in most cases) amount almost to nobility. The boy led the way, respectfully leaving me to my thoughts. The breeze up on the plateau seems straight away to announce that this is another kingdom; the mountains and the valleys are a gigantic shell that echoes with the wavy humming of all the vegetal world traversed by the roaring waters. For three hours I walked on air. Everything was clean and pure, like that morning.

First to come out and meet us were the dogs, the sort of scrawny creatures reduced to a voice and a bark, and they stopped behind the heather hedge round the huts. Then a young woman appeared and she too stopped at the hedge. 'I'm sorry to have brought you such a long way, and maybe for nothing,' said the woman. 'For nothing – how's that? Where's the sick woman?' I asked. 'There inside,' she replied, pointing to a hut at the end where a soldier's mess-tin was hanging outside in the sun. 'Can I see her?' I asked, since she showed no sign of moving from the hedge. She replied, 'No. Her husband isn't back yet. She's my sister.' I said, 'But in the meantime I can be seeing her.' 'No,' she countered, 'she's a young woman.' I replied, 'I'll wait for her husband.'

I hadn't been practising long, but I had seen several of those women who, when they are old, make up their minds to go to a doctor and reveal an illness they have been concealing for years and that sometimes has become incurable. For such women old age is a liberation from everybody, starting with their husbands: from the retiring creatures they once were they become bright and witty and talk as bold as brass; they look you straight in the face, with not a suspicion of the old dramas; they become masculine, freed from the nightmares of jealousy, freed from temptation and advances – almost as if they have lost all sense of shame. At last they can show the doctor their ailments, and whatever part of the body that gives them pain. These women go early to seed, shortly before their forties if not their thirties, and they seem to belong to a third sex, vigorous, free, superior.

The roads up on the plateau give a sense of infinity, as if they led on into the sky and, in Calabria, on into the sea which merges at the horizon with the sky. And when you look down there on the sea, in summer, it is steely white. I lingered there enjoying a world that was far above everything, and I heard from the hut those words which our peasant folk utter incessantly when they are ill: 'I'm dying, I'm dying, I'm dying,' meaning they are alive and chirpy. In the triangular entrance to the hut I noticed a pitcher hanging from a branch, and in a ray of sunlight a sparkling drop forming on the damp clay bottom. The sick woman must have measured the passing time by those drips. It was a new pitcher. They had recently bought it, and a man – the husband or son – would have taken the first sip, when it was used for the first time, because they say that if a woman takes the first sip, she stamps the fresh clay with an ineradicable feminine essence. Jealousy, that too? I don't want to comment here on the life of our peasant women. If the husband is kind, good-hearted and not poverty-stricken, there is a patriarchal relationship that can be even elegant: in public the couple call each other '*voi*', in the old style, and as still happens among certain elements of the French bourgeoisie; but if the husband is harsh, then you see one of those women who snatch at the smallest kindness, the slightest consideration or sign of gentleness towards the weak – children, animals – with a thirst for affection that finds an outlet in song and in passionate outpourings to the Madonna at the altar. The Madonnas of southern Italy must know all the words these poor women would like to hear addressed to them just once, and not while they are virgins but in the pain of their womanhood.

I had taken shelter in a hut near the road. I was determined, as soon as the husband arrived, to carry out my duty and treat the woman and face up to the man's prejudice and jealousy. I was going over in my mind the arguments I would use: my professional secrecy, which I would honour; the fact that I could report him to the legal authorities for murder – for that was what his opposition would amount to; and since the woman was complaining, according to what her son had told me, of an unbearable pain in her right side, I feared the worst. I waited for a time in the hut. From the heights of Aspromonte a storm began raging, as happens in August, and lightning came hurtling down on some of the old trees in the forest. Up there, at two thousand feet from the summit, I felt as if I had entered into the secrets of a great power, into nature's workshop. Suddenly the rain was teeming down, and with the same abruptness it cleared. At that sudden smile from nature I stepped out of the hut, into a happiness that hung in every glistening drop on the branches; the scene sparkled from its deepest recesses, giving the impression that everything passes and is forgotten, and joy was in that very moment. Only man's obstinate waywardness is tireless. A conference was going on in the sick woman's hut: I dragged my feet to warn of my approach.

I stood at the entrance experiencing an emotion such as I have rarely felt, waiting for somebody who must come to me to be saved – and there I was waiting. The husband appeared at the entrance: I recognized him. Some people stay stamped in one's memory because of their quietness and reserve; one remembers them for their brief and rather distant greetings, as if they hesitated to say anything, to utter a word out of the ordinary. He turned back to the bed where the woman was lying, though I could not see her, and said, 'The doctor's here. Do you want him to examine you? To let him see you?' Her voice replied, 'It's not for me to say. It's for you. I'm your wife. You must decide.' In the meantime two men came out of the hut, together with the sick woman's sister. She it was who spoke next. 'The doctor gentleman has been here since this morning,' she said. The husband, nodding towards the two men, said 'Let her two brothers decide. She's their sister, they know whether or not a stranger should see how their sister is made.'

I was stirred to indignation by those calm, calculated words, spoken as if in a market-place while a fellow human was in danger of her life, and this helped me to express with force the arguments I had prepared: my professional secrecy, the possibility of having to report him for murder; and I added that soon I would be leaving the practice in the local town, and that even if I was going to see another man's wife I would take that secret away with me. In the end I stepped resolutely forward to go into the hut but the sister barred my way, throwing up her hand in a dramatic gesture. 'Don't go in,' she said. 'She's the one who'll pay for it. Her husband will torment her with jealous scenes; he'll remind her that another man has seen how she's made, that another man has touched her. And there'll be blows too.' She spoke as if of some fatal madness, the madness of men. I looked at this man I had imagined so meek. He lowered his eyes and said, 'If her brothers allow it, it will be their responsibility.' Then the younger of the brothers snapped back, 'No. Afterwards you'll blame us. She's *your* wife.'

The wife's sister had advanced the only objection I had not anticipated: the suffering I would cause the sick woman so long as she remained a young wife. 'If you swear you won't illtreat her, that you'll respect her, that you'll never remind her that anybody else has seen her the way you see her – all right. Otherwise it will be up to me to protect her,' the elder brother said threateningly. The husband, brooding already over the torments he saw in store, said, 'No, I can't promise that.' From within, the voice of the sick woman, a childlike voice on the verge of delirium, said, 'Go in peace, Doctor sir. Perhaps this is God's answer to my sins.'

I went away after telling them I would be at the hotel all that night, until dawn, should they decide to call me. It was the big hotel which had just been completed and was not yet open. The freshly-built walls still had the vast breath of the mountains in them, the rigour of those heights still vibrated like an echo in the rooms, in the corridors, in the lounge where there hung an old picture of a woman coming down a flight of steps, while a man bowed and looked slily at the little foot she revealed as she stepped. Today it is a big hotel round which a rich holiday village has sprung up. A kilometre further on over the plain there are still huts where a scene of this sort can occur. I set off at dawn. On my way past the hut I asked how the sick woman was doing. They called back, 'A little better. God's will be done.' Whether the woman recovered or died, I leave to your imagination.

Alberto Moravia

THE STRAWBERRY MARK

TRANSLATED BY
ANGUS DAVIDSON

ALBERTO MORAVIA

ALBERTO MORAVIA was born in 1907 and lives in Rome, the *doyen* of Italian letters. He has written an imposing opus – novels, short stories, critical works – and is probably the one living Italian writer with a world-wide reputation. His fictional works are largely set in working-class and bourgeois Rome. Virtually all of them have been translated into English by Angus Davidson, and no English anthology of Italian short stories is regarded as complete without one of his. Among his best-known works are *The Woman of Rome, Two Women, The Empty Canvas,* and *Roman Tales.*

THE STRAWBERRY MARK

As far as my brother-in-law Raimondo was concerned, things were bound to finish like that: I am sorry for my sister, but it wasn't my fault. The first hot day, then, in the morning, I made my bathing costume and towel into a bundle, tied it on to the saddle of my bicycle, and started off with the bicycle across my shoulders towards the stairs, with the idea of creeping off unobserved and going to Ostia. But – talk about bad luck! – who should I meet on the landing but Raimondo, Raimondo himself, of all the many people who sleep in our house? He immediately eyed my bundle and asked: 'Where are you going?' 'To Ostia.' 'And what about the work?' 'What work?' 'Don't be a fool. . . . You can go to Ostia on Monday. . . . We're going to the shop now.' To put it briefly, Raimondo is a big, tall young man and I am small and thin. He took the bicycle forcibly away from me, shut it up in a cupboard in the wall and then, taking me by the arm, pushed me downstairs, saying: 'Come along, it's late.' 'Never late enough,' I answered, 'for what *we* have to do.' He said no more, but I could see from his face that I had touched a tender spot. With my poor sister's money he had opened a barber's shop; but business was not going very well – in fact, to tell the truth, it was going extremely badly. There were the two of us in the shop, himself and me; but, for all the clients who turned up, we might as well have gone out for a walk, both of us, leaving the boy, Paolino, to look after the shop – just to prevent people stealing the razors and brushes into the bargain.

We walked off in silence, beneath a sun which was already scorching. The shop was only a short distance from the house, in the heart of the old part of Rome, in the Via del Seminario; and this had been the first mistake, because it was a street through which nobody passed, in a quarter where there was nothing but offices and poor people. When we arrived, Raimondo pulled up the roller-blind, took off his jacket and put on his apron; and I did the same. Paolino also arrived, and Raimondo at once put the broom into his hands and told him to sweep the place carefully, because, as he said, cleanliness is the first essential for a barber's shop. Yes indeed, you may well sweep the floor; but that won't help you turn tin into gold! For not only was the street an unhappy choice, but the shop itself was a wretched-looking place – small, with a dado round the walls painted to look like marble, with cheap wooden chairs and shelves painted pale blue, stained, chipped china that had been taken over from another establishment, and clothes and towels hemmed and embroidered by my sister so that you could tell from a mile off that they were home-made. Well, Paolino swept the floor – a very accommodating kind of floor, being made of greyish tiles – while Raimondo lay back in a chair and smoked his first cigarette. When the sweeping was done, Raimondo, with a lordly gesture, gave Paolino twenty-five lire to go and buy a newspaper; and when the boy came back with it, he plunged into a close study of the sporting news. And so the morning began – with Raimondo lying back in the chair, reading and smoking; Paolino squatting in the doorway, amusing himself by pulling the cat's tail; and I, sitting outside the shop, stupefying myself with watching the street. As I have already said, it was an unfrequented street: in an hour I must have seen, all in all, about ten people go past, almost all women coming back from the market with their shopping-bags. Finally the sun, having gone round behind the roofs, came into the street; then I retired into the shop and sat down in another of the chairs.

Another half-hour went by, and still no customers. All of a sudden, Raimondo threw down the paper, stretched himself, yawned and said: 'Come on, Serafino ... as the customers don't come, you might as well keep your hand in: give me a shave.' It was not the first time he had asked me to act as his barber, but that day, with the thought of his having prevented me from going to Ostia still running in my head, it annoyed me more than usual. Without saying anything, I seized a towel and stuffed it under his chin, in a very rude sort of way. Anyone else would have understood, but not he. Conceitedly, he was now leaning forward to look at himself in the glass, examining his chin, feeling his cheeks with his fingers.

Paolino zealously handed me the wooden soap-bowl; I

worked up a lather and then, whisking the brush round and round as though I were beating eggs, soaped Raimondo's face right up to the eyes. I worked away furiously with the brush, and in a very short time made two enormous balloons of foam on his cheeks. Then I grasped the razor and started shaving him with big, vigorous strokes, from the bottom upwards, as though I wanted to cut his throat. At this he was frightened, and said: 'Gently now ... what's come over you?' I made no answer, but, thrusting back his head, removed the lather, with a single sweep of the razor, from the base of his throat to the dimple in his chin. He didn't breathe a word, but I knew he was fuming. I also shaved him against the lie of the hair, using the same method; and then he bent forward over the basin and rinsed his face. As I dried him I gave him a few good slaps in the face which, if I had had my way, would have been real blows, and then, at his request, I sprayed him thoroughly with talc powder. I thought I had finished with him; but he, lying back in the chair again, said: 'And now a haircut.'

I protested: 'But I cut your hair only the other day.' He replied calmly: 'Yes, you did, it's true ... but now you must trim the edges; the hair's beginning to grow again.' Once more I had to swallow my annoyance, and, after shaking out the towel, I fastened it under his chin again. Raimondo, it must be admitted, has magnificent hair, thick, black and glossy, growing down low on his forehead and brushed back thence in long locks right down to the back of his neck; but that day I felt a strong dislike for this splendid hair, which seemed to have in it all the laziness and conceit of his caddish nature. 'Now, be careful,' he warned me; 'just a trim, don't shorten it'; and I answered between my teeth: 'You needn't worry.' As I snipped off the tiny, almost invisible ends of his hair I thought about Ostia, and a great longing came over me to cut a big slice out of the glossy mass with my scissors: but I did not do it, for my sister's sake. As for him, he had now taken up the paper again, and was enjoying the twittering sound of my scissors just as if it had been the song of a canary. At one moment, casting a glance at the mirror, he said to me: 'D'you know, you've got the makings of a very good barber?' 'And you' – I should have liked to reply – 'you've got the makings of a man who manages very well on the immoral earnings of women.' Well, so I trimmed the edges of his hair; then I took the hand-mirror and held it at the back of his neck to show what I had done, and asked in an insinuating tone: 'And now, shall it be a shampoo? ... or a nice friction?' I was joking, but he, with an impassive face, replied: 'Friction.' This time I couldn't help exclaiming: 'But, Raimondo, we've only got six bottles altogether, and you want to waste one on a friction for yourself!' He shrugged his shoulders. 'Mind your own business ... It's not your money, is it?' I wanted to answer him: 'It's more mine than yours, anyhow,' but I said nothing, again for the sake of my sister who was dying of love for this man; and I obeyed. Raimondo insisted, shamelessly, on choosing which perfume he would have. Violet was the one he preferred; and he then instructed me to rub his scalp thoroughly and massage his head with the tips of my fingers, beginning at the bottom and working upwards. While I was giving him the massage I kept looking at the door to see if a customer would come in and interrupt this buffoonery; but, as usual, no one appeared. After the friction, he made me put some solid brilliantine on his hair – the very best kind, out of the little French pot. Finally he took the comb from me and himself combed his hair, with a care which I will not attempt to describe. 'Now I feel fine,' he said, getting up from the chair. I looked at the clock: it was almost one. I said to him: 'Raimondo ... I've given you a shave and a haircut, I've given you a friction. ... Now let me go to the sea ... there's still time.' But all he said, as he took off his apron, was: 'I'm going home for lunch now ... if you go too, who's to mind the shop? ... I tell you, you can go to Ostia on Monday.' He put on his jacket, gave me a nod and went off, followed by Paolino who was to bring me my lunch from home.

Left alone, I felt like kicking the chairs, breaking the mirrors, and throwing the brushes and razors into the street. But, with the thought still in mind that, really and truly, all this stuff belonged to my sister and therefore to me too, I overcame my anger and lay back in a chair, waiting. There was no one at all passing along the street now; the paving-stones were blinding in the sunshine; inside the shop all I could see was myself, with my scowling face reflected in all the mirrors in turn; and partly from hunger, partly from the effect of these mirrors, my head

was going round and round. Luckily Paolino arrived with a
plate done up in a napkin; I told him to go home too and retired into the room at the back of the shop, a little cubby-hole
hidden behind a semi-transparent curtain, so as to eat my food
in peace. At that same moment, at home, Raimondo would be
turning up his nose at the good things my sister had been preparing for him; but I, when I undid the napkin, found nothing
but a plate of half-cold spaghetti, a roll and a small bottle of wine.
I ate slowly, if only to pass the time; and all the time, while I
was eating, I was thinking that Raimondo was in clover and that
it was a bitter shame that my sister had taken up with him. I
had only just finished eating when the sound of a voice made me
jump – 'May I come in?'

I came hurriedly out of my cubby-hole. It was Santina,
daughter of the porter in the building opposite. She was dark
and small but with a good figure, and a pretty little face that
was rather broad in its lower part, and two very knowing black
eyes. She often dropped into the shop, with one excuse or another; and I, in my ingenuous way, imagined it was for me that
she came. Her visit, at this moment, gave me pleasure; I told
her to make herself at home and she sat down in one of the
barber's chairs: she was so small that her feet didn't reach the
floor. We started talking, and I, to get the conversation going,
remarked that it would be a lovely day to go to the seaside. She
sighed and answered that she would be delighted to go, but,
alas, that afternoon, she had to hang out the washing on the
roof. 'Would you like me to come and help you?' I suggested.
'Come up on the roof with me?' she said. 'Why, I'd be crazy if
I let you. ... My Mum would soon be after me, if I did.' She
looked round, trying to find something to say, and at last remarked: 'You haven't many customers, have you?' 'Many?' I
said, 'none at all.' 'You ought to open a hairdresser's shop for
ladies,' she said, 'then I and my friends would come to you for a
perm.' In order to ingratiate myself with her, I suggested: 'I
can't give you a perm – but, if you like, I *have* got a scent-spray.'
She replied at once, coquettishly: 'Really? And what scent is
it?' 'A very good scent,' I said. I took the bottle with the atomizer
and began spraying her here and there, all over, for a joke,
while she cried out that I was making her eyes smart, and put

up her hands to protect herself. At that moment Raimondo arrived.

'That's fine; you're having a great time,' he said severely, without looking at us. Santina had risen to her feet, apologizing; I replaced the bottle on the shelf. Raimondo said: 'You know I don't want women in the shop. . . . And the spray is for the use of customers.' Santina protested, in an affected sort of way: 'Signor Raimondo, I wasn't doing any harm,' and off she went, without hurrying herself. I noticed that Raimondo cast a lingering glance after her, and this annoyed me because I saw that Santina had attracted him; and, from the way in which she had protested, the idea came into my head, all of a sudden, that he had attracted her too. I said sulkily: 'The violet friction for you – that's all right, of course ... but a little whiff of scent for that girl, who at least was kind enough to keep me company – oh no, that's not allowed. ... Where's the sense in it?' Raimondo said nothing, but went to take off his jacket in the back shop. And so the afternoon began.

A couple of hours passed, in heat and silence. At first Raimondo slept for nearly an hour, his head thrown back, purple in the face, his mouth open, snoring like a pig; then he woke up and, taking a pair of scissors, amused himself for a good half-hour by snipping off the hairs in his nostrils and ears; finally, not knowing what to do, he offered to give me a shave. Now, if there was one thing I disliked more than shaving him, it was being shaved by him. As long as it was I, the assistant, who was shaving *him*, it seemed to me in order; but that he, the boss, should shave *me* – that could only mean that we were a couple of failures without so much as a dog to make use of our services. However, since I too was bored at having nothing to do, I accepted his offer. He had already cleared the lather from one side of my face and was preparing to start on the other, when suddenly, from the street, came Santina's voice again: 'May I come in?'

We both turned round, I with my face half covered in soap, Raimondo with the razor poised in the air: and there she was smiling, provoking, with one foot on the doorstep and the basket full of wrung-out washing resting on her thigh, looking at us. 'Excuse me,' she said, 'but as I knew you hadn't any customers at this time of day, I was wondering whether possibly Signor Raimondo, who is so strong, would help me to carry this basket of washing up to the roof? ... Please excuse me.' If you could have seen Raimondo ...! He put down the razor, said to me: 'Serafino, you must finish shaving yourself,' threw off his apron, and off he went, like a rocket, together with Santina. Before I could recover myself, they had already vanished into the entrance of the building opposite, laughing and joking.

Then, without hurrying, for I knew I had time, I finished shaving, I washed and dried my face, and then I told Paolino: 'Go to the house and tell my sister Giuseppina to come here at once. ... Go on, run.'

Giuseppina arrived shortly afterwards, half fainting with fright. Seeing her so crooked and ugly, poor creature, with that strawberry mark on her cheek in which lay the whole story of the shop that had been started with her money, I almost took pity on her and thought of not telling her anything. But it was too late now, and besides, I wanted to get my revenge on Raimondo. So I said to her: 'Don't be frightened, there's nothing wrong. ... It's just that Raimondo has gone up on to the roof to help the porter's daughter, over the way, to hang out her washing.' 'God help me!' she said, 'now there's going to be trouble,' and she went straight to the big entrance-door across the street. I took off my apron, slipped on my jacket, and pulled down the roller-blind. But, before I went away, I hung up a printed notice which we had taken over, with the wash-basins, from the other establishment, and which said: 'Closed on account of family bereavement.'

DON VINCENZO AND
DON ELIGIO

NEWLY TRANSLATED BY
GUIDO WALDMAN

GIUSEPPE MAROTTA

Giuseppe Marotta (1902–63) was a Neapolitan. His stories about the Neapolitan tenement-dwellers are amongst the most charming and humorous in Italian literature: in addition, they provide a highly authentic key to the elusive, impulsive Neapolitan character. The stories in *Neapolitan Gold* (*L'Oro di Napoli*), *Enchanted in the Sun* (*Gli Alunni del Sole*) and *Slaves of Time* (*Gli Alunni del Tempo*) have been published in English. (Vittorio de Sica's film, *The Gold of Naples*, derives from the first book.) He also features in John Lehmann's *Italian Short Stories Today*, 1959.

DON VINCENZO AND DON ELIGIO

There is a saying in Naples: I have shared my sleep with a friend. Indeed, there used to be a song with a refrain which practically became a proverb: 'Three vices there are with which men are born and die – gambling, friendship and first love.' I fully believe it; I have had friends for as long as I can remember and I hope it will be a friend who closes my eyes for me. I should like him to be Neapolitan, and that his fingers should close my eyelids in the most intimate and simple of ways, in dialect; to lull me into my last sleep I would have him think of paraphrasing the lullaby with which mothers sing their babies to sleep in our back streets: 'Everybody is ugly and Don Peppino is beautiful,' he would, in his mind, sing to my corpse. And I should wish that only when the last recollection of light had faded from my eyes, only then would my friend turn away from me to drop genuine tears on my bedhead.

The temperature of Naples is that of a handshake, a long drawn out, affectionate handshake; there is in the air the vital, animal warmth which came down on the manger where Jesus was born. Does it seem right to you, beneath this sky, or rather this soft roof, in these alleys which come tumbling together down the steep hillside, chattering and ribald like torrents (not the prolix straight lines of the cities of the plain, of the North, all cold and unsociable – they'd never go off arm in arm, or play leap-frog like Via Chiaia and Via Nicotera); does it seem to you conceivable, I ask, to live so pleasantly up against a volcano without entrusting yourself to a friend?

In Naples friends share not only their sleep, but their one cigarette, a handful of pumpkin seeds, a shrivelled and wizened oatcake, the triple on the Lottery and the clouts in a brawl, their debts, incarceration, hope, raiment, everything – except for women, of course: and too bad if the wife, sick and tired of taking second place in her husband's affections, storms off and has a fling with his friend instead. Then the blood will flow, a sacrilegious, black blood which cries to Heaven – and to the

ballad-monger. But on one thing the street-corner poets and
the Good Lord are undoubtedly agreed: the more unworthy
are friends, the lovelier, the more desirable a thing is friendship.

When I was a small boy and enjoyed listening to stories, I
heard of a legendary, an unblemished friendship. Don Vincenzo
and Don Eligio were the names of the two singular friends.
They did in fact share their sleep, belonging as they did to the
category of foundlings who live on nothing and on everything,
like the mouse and the fly. They are little boys clad in almost
nothing but their dark skin; they lean against the walls next to
the pizzerias, and their eyes and hands exhort the customers to
throw them the odd crust; periodically a waiter swoops on to the
pavement and puts them to flight, producing a flurry of rags
which flap like wings; but a second later the whole swarm is
back in the strategic positions, and eventually some blackened
pizza crust falls into an outstretched hand. And where did the
two friends sleep, after having thus nourished themselves? Any
wall with a recess, any railway wagon or abandoned watchman's
hut would serve to shelter them from the tramontana or the
sirocco. When day finally broke, the one friend would extricate
his limbs from those of the other, and they would go to the
Galleria to earn a couple of brass farthings as buskers, slapping
their bare feet on the glassy-polished pavement (a terrible, compact sound, as it were a desperate, sacrosanct slap on the face of
the earth), or by blowing raspberries. This then is how the pair
grew up, until temperament and physical strength had turned
them into two thoroughly promising recruits for the under-
world.

There were several ways to achieve distinction here, assuming,
of course, the requisite courage, the inclination, and the desire to
risk hospital or gaol. Here they are in their prime, Eligio and
Vincenzo. They are wearing dark, slick, natty suits, highly revealing, which show up their lank, knotted muscles, and they
betray a wicked hint of a moustache; their eyes are severe and
sad (suggestive of trouble, the trouble incurred by anyone who
makes bold to meet their gaze); the cane between their
fingers is alive, like a flower; and up the sleeve or in the hat is

warmly secreted, oh, most secretive, the grey flick-knife. They are taciturn and lazy; like the great cats, they save their vital energy for the moment of action: does the powder in the cartridge open its mouth and bellow and spring out before the firing-pin strikes home?

Eligio preferred gambling: not in the sense we normally give to the word. A cigarette between his lips, he would make his way, quiet as a wraith, into some tavern on the outskirts, where artisans and labourers, peasants and simple layabouts frittered away their souls; propping himself against a wall, faraway and fully there, for an hour or two he would observe from beneath his shaggy brow everyone and everything, just like a cat. Generally in a corner there was (no less slow and silent) the 'protector' of the place. Fair or dark, slender or massive, of recent or ancient vintage, his only concession to mobility would be when he approached the tables to collect the statutory tariff due to him from the players on each new hand. It was the tribute which the wolves required from the lambs – known in professional circles as the rake-off. The possessor of this singular privilege – which was, after all, one of the sacred laws of the back streets – retained it so long as he managed to live up to his reputation; to aspire to deprive him of it was quite admissible, but it had to be won like a sporting trophy, confronting the champion in the proper way, and reducing him to a pulp. Eligio, then, leaned against the wall, appearing and disappearing in the cloud of smoke from his cigarette, and made an exact calculation of the available takings and of the force, the unknown reactions, the 'temper' of the rival grafter; eventually he would approach him and with terrifying suavity, almost with elegance, he would whisper to him, pointing vaguely in the direction of the door and the street: 'May I trouble you? Only a moment.'

The other would have no illusions about this *souplesse*, about this menacing and courteous ceremony. 'I'm at your service,' he would say, straightening his jacket and getting up.

They might have been on their way to call on a lady. They made their way, without a word, to where the shadows were deeper. Rheumy old walls, a street lamp, a cat, the rustle of paper caught by the wind, a raindrop, a hint of moon. They stopped. A hard stare; a silent scrutiny. Then to the game of out-facing, brief and modulated:

'D'you know who I am? Eligio, alias "Red", from Porta San Gennaro.'

'Flattered. But so what?'

'You can do something for me.'

'Well, here I am.'

The temerity, the irony of that 'Here I am' at once added pace to the conversation. Eligio's voice hardened and imperceptibly he stepped back. 'Good, then we won't beat about the bush. I'm after your rake-off. Let's have a straight answer – yes or no.'

'You kidding?'

An unrepeatable insult exploded, and a mighty clout. But Eligio was a target never to be found, never to be destroyed. To the alloy, to the solidity of his metal many things had contributed: hunger and thirst, nights in the open, the arid tears of his dreams, the bug-ridden straw pallets of the prison cell, the endless slaps received in his utterly destitute childhood. A cold and sagacious hatred guided his hand; he gained over his opponent without the smallest expenditure of blows; he was attentive and accurate, nothing more; he was almost surgical. The next day the tavern had changed protectors, that was all. 'A glass of wine?' asked the players obsequiously; and Eligio, absent, hieratic, deigned to dip his lips into their inky Mondragone, black as pitch.

Vincenzo, sad to say, frequented ladies of easy virtue. He would spend days on end sitting on the edge of a divan, studying those unhappy, those brittle women. Who would have dared address a question to him, invite him to leave? Who he was could be read on his face. A breath of tragedy would wrinkle the diaphanous skirts of those courtesans – the life of these traders, these conjurers of joy is anyway inconceivable without dramas. Suddenly Vincenzo would lean a fraction towards the best endowed of them and, his glance barely resting on an elbow or a knee, he would murmur: 'What's your name?'

'Olga.'

'Olga, who is your boyfriend?'

She would tell him, meekly; his name, let's say, frequently

accompanied by some illuminating nickname in dialect, was Luigi. Vincenzo would nod and depart. A few days later he would be back, only to say: 'Olga, are you pleased? Luigi is no longer your boyfriend.' And with a light caress on a shoulder, or on a temple, he would annex her.

Who can understand this sort of love? Can the contempt these poor creatures feel for the endless men who buy them – can it be gently healed by the awesome myth of the one man with power to force them to buy him? I remember (I was brought up in the back streets and tenements of Naples, and the things I saw are nobody's business) I remember instances of prostitutes who were sister, wife and mother to their tyrants, and who even gave their lives for them. I've no opinion to offer about this. A curse on the man who first paid for the embrace he did not deserve; now he lies deep in the well of centuries; he it was who brought forth the art of Vincenzo.

This art did not suit Eligio. Saving the infinite superiority – or, better, the regality of his sex – he always had a lofty and romantic idea of woman. He obviously reverenced the maiden whose honour was still intact, but could still feel a clouded, mute pity for the prostitutes. At all events, judge your friend and he is your friend no longer. Not once did Eligio rebuke Vincenzo; besides, their career was all that counted with either of them. Their notoriety gradually spread. They assumed the title 'Don'. From the local tradesmen they began to receive spontaneous offerings. Friars and policemen would not pass before their ornate living quarters, contiguous on one of the less peaceful piazzettas round the Sanità, without paying their respects. In that happy period, Don Vincenzo and Don Eligio cemented their ancient bond of affection with the sacrament of confirmation. In Naples, bosom friends regard each other as blood-relatives. Holy water, and an enigmatic, sumptuous intervention from above effect the bond. Don Eligio was either alone, or with Don Vincenzo. At table in the famous trattorias which gleam and smile over the sea from Pozzuoli to Vesuvius, or in a gala carriage at Montevergine, or on a tribune at the feast of the Carmine, or at a table at Gambrinus, never did the two have other company. They ate and drank and enjoyed themselves silent as idols; but each knew that the other was at his side, to reinforce his own confidence in fate and in the future.

Don Vincenzo and Don Eligio were now to enter into legend. No longer was it a question of confronting the small-time hoodlums, but of unseating the king-pins who ruled in each quarter, individuals of legendary ferocity and invincibility, the very stuff of epic. This had to be done in the most theatrical and original of ways; Naples had to shudder and to exult, to gasp with horror and amazement. The good folk of Vicaria, of Pendino, of Porto expected thugs of genius, of finesse, thugs to put in a class with the Greek heroes – filigree-workers, not mere machines, of violence. Decidedly so. Don Vincenzo gallantly yielded to Don Eligio the Heap-big Chief of the Sanità, one Don Gregorio Demma, otherwise known as the Bull (for his formidable build, but also because of his bovine habit of using his head in order to splinter the ribs of his opponents). Don Eligio gratefully accepted his friend's offering, which he greatly prized. He let a couple of weeks elapse: perhaps he was awaiting inspiration. And it was a delicate, mild April noon-tide when, hands in pockets, the lightness of an archangel in his gait and in his Swabian profile, he turned into Vico Lammatari. Down this canyon, sitting on the front step of his cavern, with a chair set between his knees, Don Gregorio was preparing to devour a mountain of spaghetti.

Don Eligio who, according to the rules, should have stopped to inquire tenderly after the health of the Bull, addressed an inscrutable leer in his direction and passed on. The Chief frowned, put down his fork and called out hoarsely, 'Hey! Sonny boy!'

Don Eligio turned back. 'You called me?' he crisply asked, removing the lighted cigarette from his lips and throwing it into the glistening red tangle of spaghetti.

'You're dead and still talking!' bellowed Demma, and he jumped to his feet.

In a trice doors and windows slammed shut, Vico Lammatari was deserted. Calliope, help me! Don Gregorio was seething. He was, of course, armed; but he craved to feel Don Eligio beneath his fingers – this proved his undoing. His adversary played him for all the world like a matador – he faced him the whole time, while the famous bandit, groping and lashing out and trotting about like a bear for interminable minutes, was simply unable to lay hands on him. Executing a graceful sideways flick, oh, a bare centimetre, or suddenly dropping flat as though the earth had swallowed him, Don Eligio eluded him. 'He was not a man, he was a melody,' as a baker explained to everyone the following day – from a spy-hole in his lair he had observed every phase of the magical duel. Anyway, when, panting and sweaty, the Bull resigned himself to drawing his revolver, eye and wrist betrayed him. That is just what Don Eligio had been counting on. He did not move; he did not bat an eyelid. Don Gregorio kept firing, and Don Eligio was quietly lighting a cigarette. Oh no, there's nothing spacious about the atrium of Legend. The bullets shattered window-panes and splintered shutters; Don Eligio smoked. He heard the trigger click uselessly; unhurriedly he in turn drew a pistol. Don Gregorio tried to shelter indoors; he was hit six times in the ankle and fell flat on the ground.

'Good,' murmured Don Eligio, touching a cheek with the toe of his glistening shoe. 'I've spared you for this. This is how you must be when I pass: flat on your face. You hear me?'

'Just as you say,' moaned Don Gregorio, lame and enslaved for life. He became one of Don Eligio's lackeys, bringing him the first fruits from the market, coddling him like a nanny; he took a perverse delight in being the living witness to the might of his despoiler.

That same year, 1920, if I'm not mistaken, Don Vincenzo rid himself of the top gangsters of Montecalvario, Porto and San Ferdinando. He judged them unworthy to be disposed of individually. After all, he was working for his biographers – in the taverns and on the quayside, at the street corner and on the fore-deck. He wanted a chapter which would make every barroom brawler's heart shrivel like a gnarled kernel, and which would send voluptuous icicles through the veins of his women. Late the previous evening, he had confided in his friend as they drove in a carriage down Via Partenope. Just a word or two, freshened a little by a breath of wind carrying seaweed and tufa from the Castel dell'Ovo. Don Eligio stroked his chin and said: 'I'll be there too.'

Don Vincenzo's jaw contracted imperceptibly.

'Only to watch your back, of course,' explained Don Eligio.

Don Vincenzo replied, gentle but firm, 'I won't have anything at my back.'

'But ...'

'Listen, friend,' put in Don Vincenzo, 'if I say no to you, then it's no, don't you see?'

Don Eligio nodded, closing his eyes and abandoning himself to the swaying movement of the carriage (the result of some trick of the wheels), gentle as an infant's game.

The three bandits to which Don Vincenzo had staked a claim were to meet the following day in a cheap café on Via Nardones. They had a slight difference to sort out (in peace, devoutly hoped the proprietor with tears in his eyes). They talked slowly with Spanish arrogance, turning over each sentence before pronouncing it. One glance from them and the other customers had cleared off. A good idea. Next, a sudden, metallic clatter filled the air. Most sinister. Don Vincenzo had come in, pulling down the shutter behind him. When he had told Don Eligio that he would have nothing at his back, this is what he meant.

'What the hell are you doing?' exclaimed the boss of San Ferdinando. 'We're in conference.'

'Without my permission?'

For the next month the local population was admiring the bloated and riddled shutter of the café, as it reconstructed and recited the phases of the memorable encounter. Don Vincenzo landed in gaol, his opponents, believe it or not, in hospital, crippled for life. The luxurious fare which was sent in to Don Vincenzo at Poggioreale prison was a little daily tribute from Don Eligio to his friend. He also took care of the pearl of Don Vincenzo's harem. He would throw open his glass-paned front door (so that everyone could see them), and sit, mute, still as a statue, at some distance from her – and smoke. One evening, while a curtain of hail cut them off from the street, which had suddenly emptied, she, Donna Concetta Frezza, laced her arms round Don Eligio and entreated him to take her. He floored her with a swipe. When Don Vincenzo returned, fear prompted her to attack in order to defend herself.

'Not true,' Don Vincenzo decided at once; and he floored Donna Concetta twice, I regret to say, with two swipes.

The following year, while cleaning up the suburbs (Giugliano, Marianella, Secondigliano), Don Eligio was machinegunned from a hay-rick. Twenty orderlies had to throw themselves on top of Don Vincenzo to prevent his breaking into the operating theatre at the Pellegrini. Of course he tracked down the aggressor – a rural thug, followed everywhere by a wicked great mastiff which would have made a lion turn tail. The man's name was Don Eugenio Pica.

'I'm coming for you,' said Don Vincenzo, closing in.

Pica had buried his weapon for obvious reasons. He unleashed the hound with the command, 'Go for him.'

You will find the memory is still fresh up there, at the Porta Piccola of Capodimonte. Some seventy-year-old will tell you, in the voice of one reciting from Homer: 'I saw.' Lord! Don Vincenzo, knocked down by a monster, grabbed it: and, anticipating it by a fraction of a second, got his bite in first, sinking his teeth into its throat. Poor dog. Poor Don Eugenio Pica. Would that I were inspired as a bard or a ballad-singer, to weep for you!

And so the time arrived when every crook in Naples and its province, right out to Sannio, to Irpinia, found himself paying allegiance either to Don Eligio or to Don Vincenzo. As by tradition the supreme power could not be shared, the two final contestants had to fight for it in one final, definitive round. *Noblesse oblige.* One July night, therefore, Don Eligio and Don Vincenzo went off, just the two of them, almost arm in arm, to enjoy a breath of air in a deserted clearing at San Martino. They were not, as one might suppose, laden with arms or pondering base expedients. A razor concealed in a handkerchief, a handful of pepper to throw at the eyes, an accomplice in the shadows: they had nothing like that in mind, by no means – the facts themselves are guarantees.

They sat down on the grass; below them, at their feet, they could see Naples glittering, the wonderful realm which one of them was to inherit. How fragile and enchanted the city looked beneath the enormous moon: it might have been painted on a banner, it might have been a trophy.

Eventually the friends stood up, godfather and godson, Don Vincenzo and Don Eligio.

'Good-bye, Eligio,' said Don Vincenzo.

'Good-bye,' said Don Eligio.

They made the sign of the cross and kissed each other on both cheeks. They stepped back a pace or two. Each aimed his revolver at the other. They had wasted an hour or two quietly discussing the opportuneness of punishing one of the Mafia bosses from Sicily, who had broken his journey at Avellino and done some poaching. As dawn was almost at hand, they agreed to fire simultaneously, at the first stroke of the bell.

That is all I remember. The survivor, a somewhat perforated Don Eligio, got Naples but envied and longed for Don Vincenzo (more alive than he in legend) as long as he lived. It's a stupid thing, in fact it's downright shameful, that this story about friendship should have afforded me so much pleasure as a child, that I could easily imagine myself as Don Eligio or as Don Vincenzo. Today, all I need say about the two celebrated criminals is: what abject men, what noble friends!

Cesare Pavese

WEDDING TRIP

TRANSLATED BY
A. E. MURCH

CESARE PAVESE

CESARE PAVESE (1908–50) was a Piedmontese, from near Cuneo. His was a frustrated and tortured life which burnt itself out quickly: he committed suicide at the age of forty-two. He left behind a considerable opus – novels, stories, critical works, and a number of translations, especially of American authors. He wrote the present story when he was in his twenties. He is one Italian twentieth-century author who is well represented in the English language, nearly all his major fiction, including *Festival Night*, *Summer Storm*, and *The Moon and the Bonfire*, having been published in translation. He features in the Penguin bilingual *Italian Short Stories*.

WEDDING TRIP

I

Now that I, shattered and full of remorse, have learned how foolish it is to reject reality for the sake of idle fancies, how presumptuous to receive when one has nothing to give in return, now – Cilia is dead. Though I am resigned to my present life of drudgery and ignominy, I sometimes think how gladly I would adapt myself to her ways, if only those days could return. But perhaps that is just another of my fancies. I treated Cilia badly when I was young, when nothing should have made me irritable; no doubt I should have gone on illtreating her, out of bitterness and the disquiet of an unhappy conscience. For instance, I am still not sure, after all these years, whether I really loved her. Certainly I mourn for her; I find her in the background of my inmost thoughts; never a day passes in which I do not shrink painfully away from my memories of those two years, and I despise myself because I let her die. I grieve for her youth, even more for my own loneliness, but – and this is what really counts – did I truly love her? Not, at any rate, with the sincere, steady love a man should have for his wife.

The fact is, I owed her too much, and all I gave her in return was a blind suspicion of her motives. As it happens, I am by nature superficial and did not probe more deeply into such dark waters. At the time I was content to treat the matter with my instinctive diffidence and refused to give weight or substance to certain sordid thoughts that, had they taken root in my mind, would have sickened me of the whole affair. However, several times I did ask myself: 'And why did Cilia marry me?' I do not know whether it was due to a sense of my own importance, or to profound ineptitude, but the fact remains that it puzzled me.

There was no doubt that Cilia married me, not I her. Oh! Those depressing evenings I endured in her company – wandering restlessly through the streets, squeezing her arm, pretending

to be free and easy, suggesting as a joke that we should jump in
the river together. Such ideas didn't bother me – I was used to
them – but they upset her, made her anxious to help me; so
much so that she offered me, out of her wages as a shop assistant, a little money to live on while I looked for a better job. I
did not want money. I told her that to be with her in the evenings
was enough for me, as long as she didn't go away and take a
job somewhere else. So we drifted along. She started telling me
fondly that what I needed was someone nice to live with; I spent
too much time roaming the streets; a loving wife would know
how to contrive a little home for me, and just by going into it
I should be happy again, no matter how weary and miserable
the day had made me.

I tried to reply that even living alone I barely managed to
make ends meet, but I knew this was no argument. 'Two
people living together can help each other,' said Cilia, 'and save
a bit. If they're a little in love, George, that's enough.' I was
tired and disheartened, those evenings; Cilia was a dear and
very much in earnest, with the fine coat she had made herself
and her little broken handbag. Why not give her the joy she
wanted? What other girl would suit me better? She knew what
it was to work hard and be short of money; she was an orphan,
of working-class parents; I was sure that she was more eager
and sincere than I.

On impulse I told her that if she would accept me, uncouth
and lazy as I was, I would marry her. I felt content, soothed by
the warmth of my good deed and proud to discover I had that
much courage. I said to Cilia: 'I'll teach you French!' She
responded with a smile in her gentle eyes as she clung tightly to
my arm.

11

In those days I thought I was sincere, and once again I explained
to Cilia how poor I was. I warned her that I hardly ever had a
full day's work and didn't know what it was to get a pay-packet.
The school where I taught French paid me by the hour. One day
I told her that if she wanted to get on in the world she ought
to look for some other man. Cilia was really upset, and offered

to keep on with her job. 'You know very well that isn't what I want,' I muttered. Having settled things thus, we married.

It made no particular difference to my life. Already, in the past, Cilia had sometimes spent evenings with me in my room. Lovemaking was no novelty. We took two furnished rooms: the bedroom had a wide, sunny window, and there we placed the little table with my books.

Cilia, though, became a different woman. I, for my part, had been afraid that, once married, she would grow vulgar and slovenly — as I imagined her mother had been — but instead I found her more particular, more considerate towards me. She was always clean and neat, and kept everything in perfect order. Even the simple meals she prepared for me in the kitchen had the cordiality and solace of those hands and that smile. Her smile, especially, was transfigured. It was no longer the half-timid, half-teasing smile of a shopgirl on the spree, but the gentle flowering of an inner joy, utterly content and eager to please, a serene light on her thin young face. I felt a twinge of jealousy at this sign of a happiness I did not always share. 'She's married me and she's enjoying it,' I thought.

Only when I woke up in the morning was my heart at peace. I would turn my head against hers in our warm bed and lie close beside her as she slept (or was pretending to), my breath ruffling her hair. Then, Cilia, with a drowsy smile, would put her arms around me. How different from the days when I woke alone, cold and disheartened, to stare at the first gleam of dawn.

Cilia loved me. Once she was out of bed, she found fresh joys in everything she did as she moved around our room, dressing herself, opening the windows, stealing a cautious glance at me. If I settled myself at the little table, she walked quietly so as not to disturb me; if I went out, her eyes followed me to the door; when I came home she sprang up quickly to greet me.

There were days when I did not want to go home at all. It irritated me to think I should inevitably find her there, waiting for me, even though she learned to pretend she took no special interest; I should sit beside her, tell her more or less the same things, or probably nothing at all. We should look at one another uneasily and smile. It would be the same tomorrow and the next day, and always. Such thoughts entrapped me whenever the day was foggy and the sun looked grey. If, on the other hand, there was a lovely day when the air was clear and the sun blazed down on the roofs, or a perfume in the wind enfolded and enraptured me, I would linger in the streets, wishing that I still lived alone, free to stroll around till nightfall and get a meal of some sort at the place on the corner. I had always been a lonely man, and it seemed to me to count for a great deal that I was not unfaithful to Cilia.

She, waiting for me at home, began to take in sewing, to earn a little. A neighbour gave her work, a certain Amalia, a woman of thirty or so, who once invited us to dinner. She lived alone in the room below ours, and gradually fell into the habit of bringing the work upstairs to Cilia so that they could pass the afternoon together. Her face was disfigured by a frightful scar — when she was a little girl she had pulled a boiling saucepan down on her head. Her two sorrowful, timid eyes, full of longing, flinched away when anyone looked at her, as if their humility could excuse the distortion of her features. She was a good girl. I remarked to Cilia that Amalia seemed to me like her elder sister. One day, for a joke, I said: 'If I should run away and leave you, one fine day, would you go and live with her?' 'She's had such bad luck all her life. I wouldn't mind if you wanted to make love to her!' Cilia teased me. Amalia called me 'Sir' and was shy in my presence. Cilia thought this was madly funny. I found it rather flattering.

III

It was a bad thing for me that I regarded my scanty intellectual attainments as a substitute for a regular trade. It lay at the root of so many of my wrong ideas and evil actions. But my education could have proved a good means of communion with Cilia, if only I had been more consistent. Cilia was very quick, anxious to learn everything I knew myself because, loving me so much, she could not bear to feel unworthy of me. She wanted to understand my every thought. And — who knows? — if I could have given her this simple pleasure I might have learned, in the quiet intimacy of our joint occupation, what a fine person she really was, how real and beautiful our life together, and perhaps Cilia would still be alive at my side, with her lovely smile that in two years I froze from her lips.

I started off enthusiastically, as I always do. Cilia's education consisted of a few back numbers of serial novels, the news in the daily papers, and a hard, precocious experience of life itself. What was I to teach her? She very much wanted to learn French and indeed, Heaven knows how, she managed to piece together scraps of it by searching through my dictionaries when she was left alone at home. But I aspired to something better than that and wanted to teach her to read properly, to appreciate the finest books. I kept a few of them — my treasures — on the little table. I tried to explain to her the finer points of novels and poems, and Cilia did her best to follow me. No one excels me in recognizing the beauty, the 'rightness' of a thought or a story, and explaining it in glowing terms. I put a great deal of effort into making her feel the freshness of ancient pages, the truth of thoughts and feelings recorded by men who had lived before either of us was born: how varied, how glorious life had been for so many men at so many different periods. Cilia would listen with close attention, asking questions that I often found embarrassing. Sometimes as we strolled in the streets or sat eating our supper in silence, she would tell me in her candid voice of certain doubts she had, and once when I replied without conviction or with impatience — I don't remember which — she burst out laughing.

I remember that my first present to her, as her husband, was a book, *The Daughter of the Sea*. I gave it to her a month after our wedding, when we started reading lessons. Until then I had not bought her anything — nothing for the house, no new clothes — because we were too poor. Cilia was delighted and made a new cover for the book, but she never read it.

Now and then, when we had managed to save enough, we went to a cinema, and there Cilia really enjoyed herself. An additional attraction, for her, was that she could snuggle up close to me, and now and then ask me for explanations that she could understand. She never let Amalia come to the cinema with us, though one day the poor girl asked if she could. She explained to me that we had first met in a cinema, and in that blessed darkness we had to be alone together.

Amalia came to our place more and more often. This, and my well-deserved disappointments, soon made me first neglect our reading lessons, and finally stop them altogether. Then, if I was in a good mood, I amused myself by joking with the two girls, and Amalia lost a little of her shyness. One evening, as I came home very late from the school with my nerves on edge, she came and stared me full in the face, with a gleam of reproof and suspicion in her timid glance. I felt more disgusted than ever by the frightful scar on her face, and spitefully I tried to make out what her features had been before they were destroyed. I remarked to Cilia, when we were alone, that Amalia, as a child, must have been very like her.

'Poor thing,' said Cilia. 'She spends every penny she earns trying to get cured. She hopes that then she'll find a husband.'

'Trying to get a husband? Is that all you women can do?'

'I've already found mine,' Cilia smiled.

'Suppose what happened to Amalia had happened to you?' I sneered.

Cilia came close to me. 'Wouldn't you want me any more?' she faltered.

'No.'

'But what's upset you this evening? Don't you like Amalia to come up here? She gives me work and helps me . . .'

What had got into me – and I couldn't get rid of it – was the thought that Cilia was just another Amalia. I felt disgusted with both of them and annoyed with myself. My eyes were hard as I stared at Cilia, and the tender look she gave me only made me pity her, irritating me still more. On my way home I had met a husband with two dirty brats clinging round his neck, and behind a thin worn-out little woman, his wife. I imagined what Cilia would look like when she was old and ugly, and the idea brought a lump to my throat.

Outside, the stars were shining. Cilia looked at me in silence. 'I'm going for a walk,' I told her with a bitter smile, and I went out.

IV

I had no friends and I realized, now and then, that Cilia was my whole life. As I walked the streets I thought about us and felt troubled that I did not earn enough to repay her by keeping her in comfort, so that I needn't feel ashamed when I went home. I never wasted a penny – I did not even smoke – and, proud of that, I considered my thoughts were at least my own. But what could I make of those thoughts? On my way home I looked at people and wondered how so many of them had managed to succeed in life. Desperately I longed for changes, for something fresh and exciting.

I used to hang around the railway station, thrilled by the smoke and the bustle. For me, good fortune has always meant adventure in faraway places – a liner crossing the ocean, arrival at some exotic port, the clang of metal, shrill, foreign voices – I dreamed of it all the time. One evening I stopped short, terrified by the sudden realization that if I didn't hurry up and travel somewhere with Cilia while she was still young and in love with me, I should never go at all. A fading wife and a squalling child would, for ever, prevent me. 'If only we really had money,' I thought again. 'You can do anything with money.'

'Good fortune must be deserved,' I told myself. 'Shoulder every load that life may bring. I am married but I do not want a child. Is that why I'm so wretched? Should I be luckier if I had a son?'

To live always wrapped up in oneself is a depressing thing, because a brain that is habitually secretive does not hesitate to follow incredibly stupid trains of thought that mortify the man who thinks them. This was the only origin of the doubts that plagued me.

Sometimes my longing for faraway places filled my mind even in bed. If, on a still and windless night, I suddenly caught the wild sound of a train whistle in the distance, I would start up from Cilia's side with all my dreams reawakened.

One afternoon, when I was passing the station without even stopping, a face I knew suddenly appeared in front of me and gave a cry of greeting. Malagigi: I hadn't seen him for ten years.

We shook hands and stood there exchanging courtesies. He was no longer the ugly, spiteful, ink-spotted little devil I knew at school, always playing jokes in the lavatory, but I recognized that grin of his at once. 'Malagigi! Still alive, then?'

'Alive, and a qualified accountant.' His voice had changed. It was a man speaking to me now.

'Are you off somewhere, too?' he asked. 'Guess where I'm going!' As he spoke he picked up a fine leather suitcase that toned perfectly with his new smart raincoat and the elegance of his tie. Taking me by the arm he went on: 'Come to the train with me. I'm going to Genoa.'

'I'm in a hurry.'

'Then I leave for China!'

'No!'

'That's what they all say. Why shouldn't a man go to China? What's wrong with China? They should be wishing me luck. I may not come back! Are you the same sort of cissy, too?'

'But what's your job?'

'I'm going to China. Come and see me off.'

'No, I really can't spare the time.'

'Then come and have coffee with me, to say good-bye. You're the last man I shall talk to, here.'

We had coffee there in the station, at the counter, while Malagigi, full of excitement, told me in fits and starts all about himself and his prospects. He was not married. He'd fathered a baby, but luckily it died. He had left school after I did, without finishing. He thought of me once, when he had to take an exam a second time. He'd gained his education in the battle of life. Now all the big firms were trying to get hold of him. And he spoke four languages. And they were sending him to China.

I said again that I was in a hurry (though it was not true), and managed to get away from him, feeling crushed and over-whelmed. I reached home still upset by the chance meeting, my thoughts in a turmoil induced by this unexpected throw-back to our drab boyhood and the staggering contrast of his brilliant career. Not that I envied Malagigi, or even liked him; but to see, unexpectedly superimposed on his grey background, which had been mine, too, his present colourful and assured existence, such as I could glimpse only in dreams, was torment to me.

Our room was empty, because now Cilia often went down-stairs to work in our neighbour's room. I stayed there a while, brooding in the soft darkness lit only by the little blue of the gas-jet under the saucepan bubbling gently on the stove.

V

I passed many evenings thus, alone in the room, waiting for Cilia, pacing up and down or lying on the bed, absorbed in that silent emptiness as the dusk slowly deepened into dark. Noises from below or in the distance – the shouts of children, the bustle of the street, the cries of birds, the occasional human voice – reached me only faintly. Cilia soon realized that I was ignoring her when I came home, and she would put her head out of Amalia's room, still sewing, to hear me pass and call to me. I didn't care whether she heard me or not, but if she did I would say something or other. Once I asked Amalia, quite seriously, why she didn't come up to our room any more, where there was plenty of light. We felt obliged to turn out of our room and spend our evenings at her place. Amalia said nothing; Cilia looked away and flushed.

One night, for something to say, I told her about Malagigi and made her laugh gaily at that funny little man. I felt dis-gruntled, through, that he had struck it lucky and was going to China.

'I should like it, too,' Cilia sighed, 'if we went to China.'

I gave a wry grin. 'In a photograph, perhaps, if we sent one to Malagigi.'

'Why not one for ourselves?' she said. 'Oh, George, we haven't ever had a photograph of us together.'

'A waste of money.'

'Do let's have a photograph.'

'But we're not going to leave each other! We're together day and night, and anyway I don't like photographs.'

'We are married and we have no record of it. Let's have just one!'

I did not reply.

'It won't cost much. I'll pay for it.'

'Get it done with Amalia.'

Next morning Cilia lay with her face to the wall, her hair over her eyes. She would not take any notice of me, or even look at me. I caressed her a little, then realized she was resisting me, so I jumped out of bed in a bad temper. Cilia got up, too, washed her face and gave me some coffee, her manner quiet and cautious, her eyes downcast. I went away without speaking to her.

An hour later I came back again. 'How much is there in the savings book?' I shouted. Cilia looked at me in surprise. She was sitting at the table, unhappy and bewildered.

'I don't know. You've got it. About three hundred lire, I think.'

'Three hundred and fifteen and sixty. Here it is,' I flung the roll of notes on the table. 'Spend it as you like. Let's have a high old time! It's all yours.'

Cilia stood up and came over to face me. 'Why are you doing this, George?'

'Because I'm a fool. Listen! I'd rather not talk about it. Money doesn't matter any more when it's down to this. D'you still want that photograph?'

'But, George, I want you to be happy.'

'I am happy.'

'I do love you so much.'

'I love you, too.' I took her by the arm, sat down, and pulled her on to my knee. 'Put your head here.' My voice was indulgent and intimate. Cilia said nothing and leaned her cheek against mine. 'When shall we go?' I asked.

'It doesn't matter,' she whispered.

'Then listen!' I held the back of her neck and smiled at her. Cilia, still trembling, hugged me and tried to kiss me.

'Darling!' I said. 'Let's stop and think a minute. We have three hundred lire. Let's drop everything and go on a little trip. Right away! Now! If we think it over we'll change our minds. Don't tell anyone about it, not even Amalia. We'll only be away a day. It will be the honeymoon we didn't have.'

'George, why wouldn't you take me away then? You said it was a silly idea, then.'

'Yes, but this isn't a honeymoon. You see, now we know each

other. We're good friends. Nobody knows we're going. And, besides, we need a holiday. Don't you?'

'Of course, George. How wonderful! Where shall we go?'

'I don't know, but we'll go at once. Would you like us to go to the sea? To Genoa?'

VI

Once we were on the train, I showed a certain preoccupation. As we started, Cilia was almost beside herself with delight, held my hand and tried to make me talk. Then, finding me moody and unresponsive, she quickly understood and turned to look wryly out of the window. I remained silent, staring into nothingness, listening to the rhythmic throb of the wheels on the rails as it vibrated through my whole body. There were other people in the carriage, but I scarcely noticed them. Fields and hills were flashing past. Cilia, sitting opposite and turned towards the window, seemed to be listening to something, too, but now and then she glanced swiftly in my direction and tried to smile. So, for a long time, she spied on me.

When we arrived it was dark, and at last we found somewhere to stay, in a large, silent hotel, hidden among the trees of a deserted avenue, after going up and down an eternity of tortuous streets, making inquiries. It was a grey, cold night, that made me want to stride along with my nose in the air. Instead, Cilia, tired to death, was dragging on my arm and I was only too glad to find somewhere to sit down. We had wandered through so many brightly-lit streets, so many dark alleys that brought our hearts into our mouths, but we had never reached the sea. No one took any notice of us. We looked like any couple out for a stroll, except for our tendency to step off the pavements, and Cilia's anxious glances at the houses and passers-by.

That hotel would do for us: nothing elegant about it. A bony young fellow with his sleeves rolled up was eating at a white table. We were received by a tall, fierce-looking woman wearing a coral necklace. I was glad to sit down. Walking with Cilia never left me free to absorb myself in what I saw, or in myself. Preoccupied and ill at ease, I nevertheless had to keep her beside me and answer her, at least with gestures. Now, all

I wanted — and how I wanted it — was to look around and explore this unknown city for myself. That was precisely why I had come.

Feeling on edge, I stayed downstairs to order supper, without even going upstairs to see our room or discuss terms. I was attracted by that young fellow with his auburn moustache and his vague, lonely manner. On his forearm was a faded tattoo mark, and as he left he picked up a patched blue jacket.

It was midnight when we had our supper. At our little table, Cilia laughed a great deal at the disdainful air of the landlady. 'She thinks we're only just married,' she faltered. Then, her weary eyes full of tenderness, she asked me: 'And so we are, aren't we?' as she stroked my hand.

We inquired about places in the neighbourhood. The harbour was only a hundred yards away, at the end of the avenue. 'Let's go and see it for a minute,' said Cilia. She was fit to drop, but she wanted to take that little walk with me.

We came to the railings of a terrace and caught our breath. The night was calm but dark, and the street-lamps floundered in the cold black abyss that lay before us. I said nothing, and my heart leapt as I breathed the smell of it, wild and free. Cilia looked around her and pointed out to me a line of lights, their reflection quivering in the water. Was it a ship? The breakwater? From out of the darkness we could hear the breath of the sea, the gentle wash of the waves. 'Tomorrow,' she cried ecstatically, 'tomorrow we'll see it all.'

As we made our way back to our hotel, Cilia clung tightly to my side. 'How tired I am! George, it's lovely! Tomorrow! I'm so happy! Are you happy, too?' and she rubbed her cheek against my shoulder.

My mind was almost a blank, as I strode along with clenched jaws, taking deep breaths and letting the wind caress me. I felt restless, remote from Cilia, alone in the world. Half-way up the stairs I said to her: 'I don't want to go to bed yet. You go on up. I'll go for another little stroll and come back.'

VII

That time, too, it was the same. All the hurtful things I did to Cilia, which even now fill me with remorse, come back to me as I lie in bed at dawn, when I can do nothing about it, cannot even escape the memory. Yet I couldn't help it! I always did everything like a fool, a man in a dream, and I did not realize the sort of man I was until the end, when even remorse was useless. Now I can glimpse the truth. I become so engrossed in solitude that it deadens all my sense of human relationships and makes me incapable of tolerating or responding to any tenderness. Not that I found Cilia a handicap: she just did not exist. If I had had any idea of how much harm I was doing to myself by cutting myself off from her in this way, I should have made it up to her with deep gratitude and cherished her presence as my only salvation.

But is the sight of another's suffering ever enough to open a man's eyes? Instead, it takes the sweat of agony, the bitter pain that comes as we awake, lives with us as we walk the streets, lies beside us through sleepless nights, always raw and pitiless, covering us with shame.

Dawn broke wet and cloudy. The avenue was still deserted as I wandered back to the hotel. I saw Cilia and the landlady quarrelling on the stairs, both of them half dressed. Cilia was crying. The landlady, in a dressing-gown, gave a shriek as I went in. Cilia stood motionless, leaning on the banisters. Her face was white with shock, her hair and her clothes in wild disorder.

'Here he is!'

'Whatever's going on here, at this time in the morning?' I asked harshly.

The landlady, clutching her bosom, started shouting that she had been disturbed in the middle of the night because of a missing husband; there had been tears, handkerchiefs ripped to shreds, telephone calls, police inquiries. Was that the way to behave? Where had I been?

I was so weary I could hardly stand. I gave her a listless glance of disgust. Cilia had not moved. She stood there breathing deeply through her open mouth, her face white and drawn. 'Cilia,' I cried, 'haven't you been to sleep?'

She still did not reply. She just stood there, motionless, making no attempt to wipe away the tears that streamed from her eyes. Her hands were clasped at her waist, twisting at her handkerchief.

'I went for a walk,' I said in a hollow voice. 'I stopped by the harbour.' The landlady seemed about to interrupt me, then shrugged her shoulders. 'Anyway, I'm alive, and dying for a sleep. Let me throw myself on the bed.'

I slept until two, heavily as a drunkard, then I awoke with a start. The light in the room was dim, but I could hear noises in the street. Instinctively I did not move. Cilia was there, sitting in a corner, looking at me, staring at the walls, examining her fingers, starting up now and then. After a while I whispered cautiously: 'Cilia, are you keeping an eye on me?' Swiftly she raised her eyes. The shattered look I had seen earlier now seemed engraved on her face. She moved her lips to speak, but no sound came.

'Cilia, it won't do to keep watch on your husband,' I said in a playful voice like a child's. 'Have you eaten yet?' The poor girl shook her head. I jumped out of bed and looked at the clock. 'The train goes at half past three,' I cried. 'Come on, Cilia, hurry! Let's try to look happy in front of the landlady.' She did not move, so I went over and pulled her up by her cheeks.

'Listen,' I went on, while her eyes filled with tears, 'is it because of last night? I could have lied, said I had got lost, smoothed things over, but I didn't, because I hate lies. Cheer up! I was on my own all the time. Besides,' and I felt her give a start, 'I haven't enjoyed myself at Genoa, either. But I'm not crying.'

Carlo Emilio Gadda

THE FIRE IN VIA KEPLERO

NEWLY TRANSLATED BY
ANDREW HALE AND
GUIDO WALDMAN

CARLO EMILIO GADDA

CARLO EMILIO GADDA was born in 1893. He is a Milanese. His ribald, macaronic sense of humour, depending for much of its effect on spoken idiom and working-class dialect, is virtually impossible to preserve in translation, but the effort is worth making. He has enjoyed a kind of 're-discovery' in England. There is a story of his in the Penguin bilingual *Italian Short Stories*. His novel *That Awful Mess on the Via Merulana* was published in English in 1966.

THE FIRE IN VIA KEPLERO

There were all kinds of stories going round about the fire at Number 14. But the truth is that not even His Excellency Filippo Tommaso Marinetti could have reconstructed the events that the fire managed to produce within the space of three minutes inside that heaving ant-hill – viz. that suddenly all the women, in a state of considerable undress because of the August heat, and their innumerable progeny, were liberated from the house, out of the stench and the sudden terror; they were followed by various males, then by some poor ladies, generally considered to be somewhat doddery on their legs, who appeared, bony, white and dishevelled in white lace petticoats instead of their customary church-going composure and black clothes, then by some gentlemen who were also rather patched up, then by Anacarsi Rotunno, the Italo-American poet, then by the maid of the expiring Garibaldi-veteran on the fifth floor, then by Achille with the child and the parrot, then by Balossi in his underpants with la Carpioni in his arms, sorry, la Maldifassi, who appeared as if the devil was hot on her heels, she was screaming so much. Then finally, amidst continuous howls, wailing, tears, children, shouts, agonized yells, forced landings, bundles thrown to safety from the windows, and when the firemen could already be heard arriving hot foot and two lorries were already spilling out three dozen policemen in white uniform and even the Red Cross ambulance was on the point of arrival, then at last, by the two windows on the right on the third floor and shortly afterwards on the fourth floor, the fire released its own terrible pent-up sparks – and they had been expected for so long! – and red tongues of flame which abruptly shot up in snake-like coils, vanished and then reappeared together with black spirals of smoke so thick and greasy that it seemed to come from some infernal roast and was only interested in coiling itself up sinuously into ever tightening balls like a contortionist black python emerging from the depths of the earth amidst ominous glares of light; and there were fiery

moths, or so they seemed, perhaps of paper or more probably
of burnt cloth or cardboard, which fluttered all over the sky
tarnished by that smoke and which provoked even more terror
amongst those rumpled women, some with bare feet in the
dust of the unfinished street, others in slippers oblivious of the
dung and horse piss, amidst the shrieking and wailing of their
countless offspring. They already felt as if their heads and
fruitlessly permed hair would burst into flames in a dreadful,
living torch.

The sirens from the smokestacks or from the near-by fac-
tories howled at the scorched sky: and these electric shrieks
blended symbolically with the desperate cries of anguish. The
doors of remote fire stations were flung open and fire engines
raced out, eager to give prompt and speedy assistance at every
sudden outbreak of fire. Executing a flying leap, the last fire-
man of the fifth squad managed to clutch with his left hand
the last rung of the ladder on the last fire engine, which was
already turning out of the gateway, while with his right hand he
finished doing up the row of buttons on his uniform jacket.

The drowsiness of the sleek, slick motorists, slumped, all
vacuous bovinity, inside their vehicles but appearing from outside to be crazy firebrands, who with their bumpers scythe off
the knees of aged pedestrians hobbling at street corners and
tear away the edges of the most Garibaldosanct pavements of the
metropolis, was rudely shattered by the sound of the warning
bells, which brought them to an abrupt halt by the curb, just
in time to let the sirens fly past. The trams were riveted to the
spot; the horses, held on the bit by the drivers who had come
down from their seats, pressed their rumps hard against the
wagons and the corners of their eyes showed white in their
terror of the unknown.

There on the spot, the effects of the fire were terrifying. A
three-year-old child, Flora Procopio, daughter of Giovan Battista, who had been hoisted into a highchair, strapped in, and
left alone in the house with a parrot, was desperately calling for
her mother and was unable to get down from the chair; large
tear-drops like pearls of hopelessness trickled from her eyes and
rolled down her cheeks on to her sodden bib with '*Buon Appe-
tito*' written on it, and dripped into the pappy slush of her milky

coffee in which she had gradually immersed a whole stick of French bread, evidently none too well baked, plus some 'Novara' biscuits – or perhaps 'Saronno' – one or the other, but they too a good three years old in any event. 'Mamma! Mamma!' she yelled, terror-stricken. There, meanwhile, beyond the other end of the table, was the motley-plumed bird with its beak like a duchess's nose – he'd go into raptures and swoon blissfully the moment the urchins called him from the street, 'Loreto, Loreto,' when he would strike an arrogant posture or assume an air of melancholy, of hopeless lethargy; but if they egged him on, 'Come on, Loreto, sing! Give us ... *Viva Italia!* ... Come on you stupid bird!' then as soon as he heard the word 'sing', he would squawk with a rich gurgle 'sing-it-yourself!'; but not this time, poor creature – oh no! For, Good God! Yes! The fact is the bird, poor thing, had definitely noticed a certain smell of burning even though it hadn't worried him too much. But when he saw those sinister, bewitching petals dart obliquely past the open window and then flit into the room like so many red-hot bats, and start licking up the tattered folds of the meagre curtains and the yellow slatted ash-wood blinds, rolled up and secured by their frayed cords, he too suddenly began to squawk out, from the bottom of his crop, everything that came into his head, everything at once as if he were a cacophany of radio stations. In a panic he flustered and fluttered towards the little girl with sudden dashes which were cut short after a couple of feet of frantic flapping by the inexorable treachery of the chain which secured him by one leg to his perch.

It was said that in his youth he had belonged to General Buttafava, veteran of Moscow and the Beresina crossing, and had then been passed on to the late-lamented nobleman Emmanuele Streppi, with whom he had spent a restful but not unstimulating youth in Borgospesso; he is supposed to have succeeded in outliving not only Streppi but all the most venerable scions of the Lombard nobility, about whom, be it said, he tended to make scurrilous remarks to any passers-by. But this time, faced with this deluge of red-hot coppers which seemed to have come spinning out of Beelzebub's private mint, he went clean off his head: '*Hiva-i-Ita-ia! Hiva-i-Ita-ia!*' he began to screech frenziedly as he flapped wildly about on the taut end of his chain, amidst a shower of feathers and a great cloud of charred paper and soot, in the hope of conciliating Fate, while the little girl was yelling, 'Mamma! Mamma!' and shouting terrified cries between sobs and beating on the table with the handle of her spoon. Until a certain Achille Besozzi, thirty-three years of age, due for trial on charges of theft and kept under special watch by the police, unemployed, and obliged by reason of his unemployment to sleep by day so as to be available to bring off the odd job by night, in case his services were called on and in spite of the watch kept on him, so that even he, poor chap, could earn himself the odd crust of bread; so it was a real stroke of fortune, a great mercy on the part of St Anthony of Padua – there's no getting away from it so let's admit it – the way this man under watch happened to be sleeping right on the floor above and in the room above, in Signora Fumagalli's flat; on a family settee; as soon as he realized the danger, he immediately took his courage in both hands, 'midst the terror and the smoke, a smoke which blew up the stair-well as if it were a chimney, and all those women in their dressing-gowns or nightdresses rushing headlong down the stairs, and the shrieks, and the children and the sirens of the approaching fire brigade. He broke down the door of the Procopios' with kicks and shoulder charges and rescued the child and the bird and also a gold watch sitting on the chest of drawers, which last item he forgot to restore, and everyone attributed the loss to the firemen's water, with which they inundated the house from attic to cellar to put out the fire.

Besozzi had heard the shouts and knew that the little girl was alone, since five o'clock was precisely the time at which he was accustomed to disembark from the settee on to the wharf of wakefulness regained, with all that tedious embroilment with the police; he would rub his eyes, scratch himself here and there, especially inside his shock of hair, and end up by putting his head underneath the kitchen tap; he would then dry himself – with a towel the colour of a sewer rat – comb his hair – with the remaining half of his green, celluloid comb – and then, with great delicacy, extract the hairs, one by one, which had stuck to it, count them and consign them one after another to the sink,

which was overflowing with piles of greasy bowls and plates
from the homely cooking of Isolina Fumagalli's 'boarding-
house'. Then with a yawn he would pull on his handful of
tatty garments and climb into those two cavernous old shoes,
half rotted away by the sweat of his feet; after that he would
saunter out, yawning yet again, on to the landing and wearily
drag himself up and down the endless stairs on one pretext and
another, now and again shooting out a liquid dart of saliva on
to the steps or the wall from between his bulbous lips; his body
still relaxed from the softness of the settee, he would be listless
and at the same time alert in the hope of some happy encounter. Oh, you know, some of those women in the building,
they were ready waiting, amply proportioned and no nonsense
about them – then they'd be away, clickety-clack down the stairs
and out into the street. No doubt a few such women lived at
Number 14, for all that the upper crust of the tradesman classes
had started moving into the street with their families. That's
how he met the mother – what a bitch she was! – on that day,
and therefore knew that the little girl had been left alone with
the parrot. And so he saved her. And Loreto too. People would
learn who he was and the stuff he was really made of. And
how he rewarded them for their arrogance, notwithstanding
the police making a nuisance of themselves day and night.
All right then, so there was the watch – but that's quite
another story: more fool them for leaving it out on the chest of
drawers just at the moment when the house chose to burst into
flames.

'Fire,' they all said afterwards, 'is one of the most terrible
things there is.' And it's true: what with the generous excesses
and the indecision of those invaluable firemen: the cascades of
good drinking water all over the mouldy, pee-stained settees,
threatened this time by ugly red flames, and over the dressing-
tables and sideboards, custodians, possibly, of an ounce or two
of sweating gorgonzola, but licked already by the flames – a
roebuck confronted by a python; the spurting jets and liquid
shafts of water from the swollen, sodden, serpentine coils of
tubular hemp and long, stabbing lances from the brass hydrants,
ending in a white spray of haze in the torrid August sky; half
burnt-out porcelain insulators disintegrating in mid-air and

shattering crash-bang against the pavement; burnt telephone
wires fluttering away in the evening air from their scorching
brackets, along with flying strips of cardboard and charred
drapes floating like hot-air balloons; and below, between the feet
of the men and behind the extending ladders, the twisting,
turning, prancing hoses spurting out parabolic jets of water
from every direction into the mire of the street: splinters of
glass in a marsh of water and slime and enamel chamber-pots,
full of 'sausages' thrown out of the window – yes, even at a time
like this – to land against the top-boots of the rescuers, the
leggings of the civil engineers, of the *Carabinieri*, of the fire
marshals; and the insolent, ceaseless clickety-clack of the women's
slippers as they went around collecting bits of combs, and fragments of mirrors, and holy pictures of San Vincenzo de' Liguori,
squelching about in the devil's own wash-tub.

A pregnant woman, another extremely lamentable case – she
was already in her fifth month! – was overwhelmed by all the
panic-stricken *sauve-qui-peut* and fainted away right on the
landing while attempting to escape, though perhaps she had
been suffocated on the staircase by the smoke which came in
billowing all over her in frightening gusts the moment she
opened the door. Miraculously she was saved by a certain
Gaetano Pedroni, son of the late Ambrogio Pedroni, thirty-
eight years of age and a porter at the main station, where he
was due to begin his shift at half past six. Clearly he was sent
by God, if you consider that to shift a baggage of this kind
there is no substitute for experience. Whistling away like a
blackbird, he was about to go out of the door on the floor above
Isolina Fumagalli's, having just brought off a robust piece of
gallantry, towards which the Good Lord will almost certainly
have turned a blind eye. Having taken his leave he felt liberated
and carefree and more inclined than ever to the protection of the
feeble and the forsaken; he picked up his straw hat, put it on
his head, lit a cigar stub, and dreamed of being put in sole
charge of all the twenty-five trunks, suitcases and hatboxes of
some eager American amazon, one of those tall, spindly, over-
bearing women who strut around the station with those men's
walking sticks, waiting for the train to Venice, to the St Got-
thard, Bologna and all points south.

But instead of his American woman, there he was faced with the smoke and shrieks and utter chaos the moment he opened the door, and he could scarcely see in front of him at times. It was an ugly moment, he recounted that evening, one of the most terrible in all his life. He immediately shouted back to the woman, who was still wrestling with the tap, with some sort of bucket-type bidet and with minute pots and pans and great gushes of water; but she dropped everything on the spot, soap, towel, pans and water and all, and in the twinkling of an eye had slipped on a kind of Chinese house-gown, or maybe it was Japanese, and straightway began to yell, 'Holy Mother of God! My fur coat! My fur coat!' and she wanted to get her handbag out of the chest-of-drawers but he took her by the arm and dragged her outside as she was, in her flea-market kimono-affair and without even her knickers on, in her bedroom slippers, one of which, however, made its own way down the stairs; pulling her along behind him, they both plunged into that breathless vortex in search of an escape. Then with a couple of casual kicks he shattered the first glass panes he passed, and the smoke poured out through there, too. Further down they stumbled into the woman who'd passed out, propped up in a doorway; the other woman, limping along in her one slipper, wanted to escape on her own account, come what may, but he grabbed hold of her, held her tight and shouted into her face, 'You bloody well lend a hand!' Together they managed, panting and sweating and terrified, to carry her right down to the bottom where, by the grace of God, there was already a stretcher and the ambulance men from the Red Cross, and by that time the firemen too.

But Signora Arpalice Maldifassi, cousin of the famous baritone Maldifassi, Eleuterio Maldifassi – yes, of course, the very one ... you know – yes, he had sunk at La Scala in 1908 ... in *Mephistopheles* ... the Spring season ... a triumph! a real triumph! adding new lustre to our own Milan! well, as she tried diving headlong to safety along with all the others, she was knocked and pushed about 'by the selfishness', as she later asserted, 'of the tenants from the fifth floor', who came scampering down the stairs like so many hares. Isn't that how she caught her shoe – the dirty cowards! – between the marble step

(marble from Carrara) and the rickety wrought-iron bannisters?
Exactly so! And that was why she had broken her leg, so she
said, but the fact is she had only wrenched her ankle on the
first step because she had slipped in her panic and didn't know
where to put her foot, what with her high heels all bent on
giving her those extra five inches of elevation that women seem
to want. Anyway, it all happened because, poor woman, she had
wanted to save at all costs the portrait of her Eustorgio and her
valuables, which were also a souvenir of her poor Eustorgio, and
she had dashed back to rescue them from the chest of drawers:
she had only ransomed them from the pawnshop that very
morning, with the money repaid her by la Menegazzi. Talk of
everything coming at once! Just imagine how she must have felt
– dear God, it doesn't bear thinking about, let alone describing –
when, caught up in a situation of utter, horrifying chaos, she
found herself slammed first against the banisters and then
against the wall by the 'pitiless egoism of human nature', and
then once more against the banisters, with the risk of being
hurled into the void; and then, to add to the panic and to the
frailty of her sex, she suddenly wrenched her foot – a sudden
stab of pain followed by a horrible ache which shot up her leg –
as a result of which she fell into a sitting position on the edge of
a step and then slid down the stairs for a bit on her bottom –
talk of a sleigh-ride – getting one big bruise after another at
each touchdown on her *os sacrum*, or *coccyx* if you prefer,
which was so poorly protected owing to the meagre cushioning
of her glutinous parts, a deficiency from which she had suffered
ever since the days of her youth, poor Signora Maldifassi! She
was coughing and spluttering in the acrid fumes and shrieking
'Air! Air! Aaaoou, my leg! My leg! Save me for the love of
God! Oh my leg, Holy Mother, I'm choking!' So she continued
her endless invocations, her dirge, the vocal outlet for her terrified soul and her tormented body. She had to be dragged down
the stairs through the horrendous smoke, amidst spine-chilling
cries of pain and bouts of coughing, by a plucky apprentice
bricklayer, a very *avant-garde* youth of seventeen, in underpants,
Ermenegildo Balossi, son of Gesualdo, from Cinisello, who, pale
as death, was at the moment concerned only with saving his
own private jewels – not the kind you could pledge at any

pawnbrokers, alas! At least, I don't think so. Here too the finger of the Lord was clearly in evidence, for Balossi had come hurtling down bare-foot from the roof where he was busy repairing the battered tiles after the furious hailstorm of the previous week which had descended on various roofs of the area with impartial solemnity, as do all calamities which put on the air of descending by divine providence, or justice as the case may be.

He was working in the early evening, as in the heat of siesta time one would be cooked to a turn on those red-hot tiles, as well as getting sunstroke; a red and yellow handkerchief was bandaged round his head, which was even better protected by the density of his hair, which was like a sheep's fleece well pomaded with lime dust; he was, as we have seen, lightly clad: on his back he had a faded blue vest made of transparent nylon, which was full of holes and resembled tissue paper soaked in sweat. His enormous size-twelve feet, with fleshy stumps of toes, which were spread out like a fan, enabled him to maintain an uncanny grip on the baked porousness of the tiles, which was specially appreciated by site foremen and contractors all over Milan and there was therefore no one more suitable, in all the Milan bricklaying and apprentice trade, to send up on to steep roofs for seven lire a day, slipping round the chimneys like a phantom or slinking along the gutters and eaves like an intrepid cat. He had therefore won his 'place in the world', to use the words of Virgilio Brocchi, by his own deeds, unfettered by recommendations or any other dubious paths to glory. And in the course of this sweated labour the four ribbons supposed to fasten his trouser-legs round his ankles kept coming loose, giving him the air of some Hermes of Cinisello with trailing ribbons on his ankles instead of wings.

His foreman, with lime-spattered moustaches and wrinkled face sporting a fine crop of warts, had been exhausted by the pandemonium and admitted defeat; he stood at the bottom of the stairs calling out mournfully, 'Balossi! Balossi!' and dolefully explained to all those frenetic women fleeing in their slippers, burdened with terror and bundles and screaming children, that there was still a boy on the roof, 'my mate's up there, my mate! ... Gildo ... up on the roof ... the lad from Cinisello ...' and he had another go at Balossifying up the smoky

well of that hellish staircase but was drowned in the chorus of
screams. Certainly no one got the idea of turning back for the
man's mate – most of the women did not even hear him. Then
the lad himself appeared on the bottom flight of stairs, dishevelled, red-faced, bathed in sweat, with that red and yellow strip
of a handkerchief around his head, a black smear on his cheek
and in his arms Signora Maldifassi shouting 'Aaou! my leg!
my leg! Holy Mother of God help us!' She was still clutching a
canvas bag from which, it was clear, she refused to be parted
on any account; and he, with his underpants at half-mast and
unlikely to remain even there for much longer, tripped on each
step as his great spread-eagle feet, his gaping rows of toes like
a pair of combs, kept treading on the ribbons trailing round his
ankles. He had picked her up and held her by the armpits from
behind and, bracing one knee or the other under her thin,
scrawny bottom, had made her a sort of momentary seat to
lower her, one step at a time, taking care to keep a steady
balance lest they tumbled down the stairs one over the other right
to the bottom. Such was his courage that they gave him the
highest commendation for civil bravery on Constitution Day.
Poor boy, plucky boy! He deserved it!

And there was also another poor devil, who only escaped by
the skin of his teeth. Zavattari, the poor old man, had been
suffering from asthma and bronchial catarrh for years. It was
such a serious case that not even the Milan August could miti-
gate his suffering, and everyone was convinced by now that he
was incurable. He got some sort of mild relief from his misery
by observing a regime of bed until midday, then the dinner table
until six in the evening; this was permanently laid, with a filthy
tablecloth and a bottle of Barletta wine; he called the wine 'my
medicine', and took no notice of the wine-, tomato- and coffee-
stains; nor was he in the least put off by the prevailing litter –
tooth-picks snapped neatly in two, a mess of gorgonzola and
miscellaneous cheese crumbs which lingered on the table until
all hours of the night. Seated at the table, with one elbow on
the tablecloth and his left hand dangling limply over the edge,
the old man would help himself to one snifter after another
throughout the lazy, sleepy afternoon – 'just a little nip' and
'just one more little nip' – and his palsied right hand would

raise the glass up under his moustaches from time to time; so there was no end to his sipping and savouring the wine (with much swilling round on his palate and smacking of lips) – it might have been nectar and ambrosia though in fact it was such a full-bodied red, fermenting in the cellars of Martesana under the August heat, that it left him with a thick purple slime on his clammy tongue, great red dew-drops on his drooping moustaches and a permanent snort of catarrhal retching. So red and lustrous were the drops, they might have been drops of blood in a 'Sacred Heart' or 'Madonna of the Sorrows' by Cigoli. Even his look, glazed, melancholy and fixed on the far, far distance, inside a heaven of total apathy, with the upper halves of his eyeballs hidden by drooping brows in a kind of outward sleep, even his look had about it something of those 'Sacred Heart' pictures, in a local setting; but no, it was simply the Sacred Bottle in constant use. Thus he would sit for hours on end, his elbow resting on that dung-heap he called a tablecloth, all tomato smears and wine stains, one hand dangling in the void and the other one, when not employed in pouring or sipping, absently scratching his knee; thus he would sit, grunting and snorting, for hours on end, as the afternoon gently declined, sweating inside that stuffy room, all dust and stench, with the bed still unaired and the pillow-case the colour of a hare; his trousers, from which the tip of his nightshirt peeped out, would be unbuttoned, his bare lichen-hued feet would be thrust into a pair of tattered, down-at-heel slippers; his breath came in short rasps, and seemed to glide over ball-bearings of mucus; tenderly he would coddle his precious catarrh, buried catacomb-deep in his body, like a glue bubbling slowly in a long-forgotten cauldron on a fire.

Zavattari was a partner in the firm of Pasquale Carabellese, in Via Ciro Menotti 23, which dealt in cut-price Atlantic fish, the fish being brought in by the two fishing smacks *Stefano Canzio* and *Gualconda*, and occasionally also by the *Doralinda*; but they also sold oysters from Taranto at bargain prices, and seafood packed in ice from both Italian coasts. And the firm didn't do so badly retailing these green monstrosities from the depths of the sea to the bewildered housewives of Via Ciro Menotti, whose main concern was to economize, and who didn't have the first idea how to cook such far-fetched zoological specimens.

But all this is by the way: what I was meaning to say was that the old boy, whatever state of stupefaction and comforting torpor he may have achieved by this time, at the first hint of burning and at the first cries of terror from the stairs and court-yard, tried to move towards the window, prompted by some unconscious physical impulse, to attempt to open it because in his besotted condition he believed it to be closed while in fact it had been open all afternoon: it was a primordial, physical fear which hovered like an *ignis fatuus* around the stunted remnant of his instinct: but all he succeeded in doing was to knock over the bottle of Barletta, which was no less vapid and vacuous; instead, his bronchial cataracts suddenly opened wide while at the same time the more valiant of the inhibitory rings of his anal duct acted similarly; so amid a terrible attack of coughing and pitch black, acrid smoke beginning to filter into his flat through the keyhole and under the door, he was seized with terror through being alone and finding his legs as weak as putty at the very moment when he needed them most. As a result, he first released a generous excremental expulsion into his night-shirt, and then brought up such quantities of green matter from the depths of his lungs that I am sure that not even the sea off Taranto, with all its oysters, would have been able to throw up anything comparable.

The firemen, wearing their masks, broke down the door with their axes and rescued him. 'Looks as though the fire got his bowels moving,' observed the squad leader when they had completed the rescue operation.

The case of the *Cavaliere* Carlo Garbagnati, the Garibaldi-veteran on the fifth floor – he was one of the original Thousand who landed at Marsala, one of the fifty thousand present at the fiftieth-anniversary celebrations – was heart-breaking and, alas, fatal. The trouble was that, in spite of the cries of his maid, Cesira Papotti, he refused, contrary to every normal criterion of expediency, to make a move without first salvaging his medals, as well as his daguerrotypes and two small portraits in oils dat-ing back to his youth, that is to the battle of Calatafimi. Now the transportation of a Garibaldi-veteran's collection of medals, especially at a time of utter panic as this was, is not such a simple problem as it might appear at first sight. He too finished by being asphyxiated or something like that, and the firemen had to go in and carry him out bodily in order to save him, at the risk of their own lives. But unfortunately what with his age – eighty-eight – a weak heart and a painful contraction of the urethra from which he had been suffering for some time, his situation rapidly deteriorated. So that before the Red Cross ambulance, which was making its fifth journey, had even reached the first-aid post at Via Paolo Sarpi, it was obliged to turn back hurriedly and proceed towards the mortuary at the University hospital at the far end of the university campus, behind the new Polytechnic ... no, not in Via Botticelli! further on, further on, in Via Giuseppe Trotti, yes ... that's it ... no, beyond Via Celoria you come to Via Mangiagalli, then Via Polli, Via Giacinto Gallina, then Via Pier Gaetano Ceradini, Via Pier Paolo Motta, then to the back of beyond.

Italo Calvino

THE ADVENTURE OF
A READER

NEWLY TRANSLATED BY
GUIDO WALDMAN

ITALO CALVINO

ITALO CALVINO was born in Cuba in 1923. He lives in Rome, where radio and journalism, as well as his work as a novelist and short story writer, keep him employed. His work is distinguished by the strong vein of fantasy running through it. Among his novels published in English are *Baron in the Trees*, *The Non-Existent Knight* and *The Cloven Viscount*, translated by A. Colquhoun, who also translated a number of his stories in *Adam, One Afternoon and Other Tales*. One of his stories is included in John Lehmann's *Italian Short Stories Today*, 1959, and one in the Penguin bilingual *Italian Short Stories*.

THE ADVENTURE OF A READER

The coast road, on the cape, ran high above the sea which lay vertically below and all around, way out to the misty horizon. The sun also was everywhere, as though the sky and the sea were two lenses enlarging it. Down below, against the jagged outcrop of rocks on the point, the calm water was lapping without foam. Amedeo Oliva went down the steep flight of steps with his bicycle on his shoulder; he set it down in the shade, after securing the locking device. He continued down the steps between landslides of dry yellow earth and Agaves hanging over the brink, and as he went he looked out for the most convenient dip in the rocks where he could lie down. He carried a rolled-up towel under his arm, and, wrapped in the towel, his bathing trunks and a book.

The cape was an unfrequented place: a scattering of bathers were diving, others sunbathed, hidden from each other by the broken contours of the place. Between two outcrops which sheltered him from view, Amedeo undressed, put on his trunks, then set to jumping from rock to rock. In this way he negotiated half the reef, leaping on slender legs and occasionally flying almost past the noses of unsuspecting couples reclining on their bathing towels. Beyond a last outcrop of sandy rock with a rough, porous surface, the rocks became smooth and rounded; Amedeo took off his sandals and held them in his hand as he ran on barefoot, confident in his eye for the distance from rock to rock and in feet with insensitive soles. He reached a point sheer over the sea; the rock wall was crossed half-way down by a sort of ledge. Here Amedeo stopped. On a flat shelf he laid out his clothes, carefully folded, placing his sandals on top, soles up, in case a gust of wind carried off the lot (as it happened there was barely a breath of wind, off the sea, but this must have been one of his regular precautions). A little bag he had with him was in fact a rubber cushion; he blew it up, chose a place for it, and next to it, where the rock had a slight downward slope, he laid out his towel. He dropped backwards on to it while his hands opened the book at the mark.

There he lay full length on the rock, in the sun which reverberated on all sides; his skin he left dry (he had the deep, irregular tan of the haphazard sunbather who is immune to sunburn). On the rubber cushion he laid his head, clad in a white cloth hat which first he had soaked (scrambling on to a lower rock and dipping his hat into the water). He lay there motionless, only his eyes (invisible behind dark glasses) pursuing down the lines of black and white the horse of Fabrizio del Dongo. Below him there was a little inlet of blue-green water, transparent almost to the bottom. The rocks, according to their exposure, were white and calcined or covered with seaweed. The inlet ended in a little pebble beach. Amedeo would now and then raise his eyes to the surrounding view, taking in the sparkle on the surface of the water and the slanting progress of a crab; then his attention would again be absorbed by the page where Raskolnikov counted the steps between him and the old woman's door, or Lucien de Rubempré before putting his head into the noose, contemplated the towers and roofs of the Conciergerie.

Amedeo had long tended to reduce to the minimum his participation in active life. Not that he disliked action – his whole character and his tastes had thriven on a love of action; and yet, his urge to be himself a man of action diminished yearly, till he had to ask himself whether such an urge had ever really been his. His interest in action survived, however, in the pleasure of reading; he always loved narrative, history, the woven thread of human events. He enjoyed nineteenth-century novels best of all, but memoirs, too, and biographies, and so on down to thrillers and science fiction, which he by no means scorned though they afforded him less satisfaction: they were on the short side, for one thing, whereas Amedeo liked fat tomes, pitching into them with all the physical pleasure inherent in tackling a major undertaking. He liked to weigh them in his hand, these thick, compact, solid books, and consider, a shade apprehensively, the number of pages, the length of the chapters. Then in he would plunge, offering some initial resistance, reluctant to face the business of grasping names, of picking up the thread of the story; he would, however, let himself go at last, gliding along the lines, crossing the regular grid of the page and, beyond the characters cast in lead, the flames and fire of battle would appear – and the cannon-ball whistles through the air and lands at the feet of Prince Andrey; or the shop crammed with prints and statues – and Frédéric Moreau, his heart a-flutter, makes his entrance among the Arnoux. Beyond the surface of the page one entered a world in which life was more life-like than here, on this side of it – like the surface of the sea, which separates us from that world of blue and green with its crevices as far as the eye can see, its stretches of fine undulating sand, its creatures half animal, half plant.

The sun beat down, the rock was scorching and Amedeo soon tended to feel himself a part of the rock. When he reached the end of the chapter, he would shut the book, putting in the publicity leaflet to mark the place, take off his cloth sunhat and glasses, get up half dazed, and go bounding down to the tip of the point, where a group of little boys was always diving in and climbing out of the water. Amedeo would stand on a ledge overhanging the sea, not too high, a couple of metres above the water and, with eyes still dazzled, contemplate the luminous transparency beneath him, then suddenly plunge in. It was always the same dive, like a fish, correct enough but somewhat rigid. The change from the sun-warm air to the tepid water would be scarcely noticeable were it not so sudden. He did not surface at once; he liked to swim down through the water, almost grazing the bottom, as long as his breath held. He loved physical exertion, the challenge of difficult tasks – for which purpose he would come out to the cape to read his book, peddling furiously up the hill on his bicycle under the noonday sun. Every time he swam under water he would try to get as far as a reef of rocks sticking out from the sand of the sea bed at a certain point, all covered with a thick undergrowth of seaweed. He would surface among those rocks and swim about a little, starting with the crawl executed with method but also with superfluous exertion and soon, tired of swimming blind, face immersed, he would change to the freer overarm sidestroke. As he derived more satisfaction from seeing than from moving, he would shortly abandon the sidestroke and swim on his back, his

progress ever more irregular and interrupted until he stopped
and just floated. And so he made his way, turning and turning
again in that sea as in a boundless bed. He would choose some
reef for an objective, or he would set himself a certain number
of strokes, and he had no peace until he had accomplished his
task. He would wallow lazily awhile; or head out to sea, incited
by the prospect of having around him nothing but sea and sky;
or he drew into the rocks scattered about the point so as not to
overlook a single one of the many possible paths through the
little archipelago. As he swam, though, he noticed that the
curiosity uppermost in his mind was that of knowing what happened next — for instance — in the story of Albertine. Would
Marcel find her again or wouldn't he? Whether he swam
furiously or floated inertly, his heart was among the pages of the
book left on the shore. With rapid strokes he would regain his
rock; he would look for the place to climb out, and the next
thing was he would be up there again, rubbing his shoulders
with his towel. He would cram his hat on his head, stretch out
again in the sun, and there he was, already into the next chapter.

Not that he was a frantic, hungry reader. He had reached an
age when the second, third or fourth reading gives more
pleasure than the first. And yet he still had many continents to
discover. Every summer, the most elaborate preparations prior
to departure for the sea centred on the heavy suitcaseful of
books: each year, according as the trends and discussions of his
day-to-day life in town suggested, Amedeo chose a number of
well-known books to re-read and certain authors to broach for
the first time. Here on the rocks, then, he would absorb them,
poring over the sentences, frequently raising his eyes from the
page in order to ponder, to collect his thoughts. Looking up
like this at a certain point, he saw that the pebble beach at the
end of the inlet was now occupied — a woman lay there.

She was deeply tanned, slender, not in her first youth, not all
that beautiful, but her nudity favoured her (she was wearing a
brief bikini much cut away at the sides to give maximum exposure to the sun), and Amedeo's eye was drawn to her. He
realized that, as he read, his eye was tending to leave the book
and hover in mid-air — in mid-air, that is, between this woman
and himself. Her face (she was lying on the sloping shore, on a

rubber lilo, and Amedeo at each fleeting glance noted her legs, not opulent yet graceful, her belly, beautifully smooth, her breasts, on the small side, not unpleasingly so but probably a trifle flaccid, her shoulders, somewhat on the bony side, her neck and arms, and her face masked by dark glasses and by the brim of her straw hat) – her face was delicately featured, alive, knowing, ironical. Amedeo placed her in the category of independent women who take their holidays on their own and shun the crowded beaches in favour of the less frequented rocks, where they like to tan themselves black as pitch. He appraised the element of lazy sensuality, of chronic dissatisfaction there must be in her; he considered fleetingly the possibilities she held out of a short-term *affaire*, but weighed these up in the perspective of the small-talk to be made, the evening to be programmed, the logistical problems which would doubtless arise, the effort of attention needed in getting to know a person even superficially: and he went on reading, secure in the conviction that the woman could not begin to interest him.

Whether he had been lying too long, though, on that particular rock, or whether these fleeting thoughts had somehow unsettled him – at all events he was aware of feeling cramped; the uneven bed of rock beneath the towel on which he lay was becoming distinctly uncomfortable. He got up to find somewhere else to lie. He had a moment's uncertainty as between two places which seemed equally suitable: one further away from the beach with the sun-tanned woman (indeed, beyond a spur of rock which cut off his view of her); the other, closer to it. The idea of moving closer to her, with the possibility of being drawn by some unforeseen circumstance into conversation with her, thus having to break off his reading, led him naturally to favour the more remote location; but on second thoughts it would look as though no sooner had she arrived than he decided to leave – which could appear a trifle discourteous. So he settled on the nearer place; in any event, he was so wrapped up in his book that the sight of that girl – not all that stunning anyway – was unlikely to prove a distraction. He lay down on his side, holding his book up so as to shut her out, but it was a tiring position for his arm and in the end he lowered it. Now each time his eye moved to the beginning of the next line, just a fraction outside the margin it would encounter the legs of the solitary bather. She too had shifted slightly in search of a more comfortable position; she had raised her knees and crossed her legs in Amedeo's direction, a development which enabled him to give closer consideration to certain of her proportions, which were by no means unpleasing. Amedeo, then (for all that the rock was cutting into one hip), could not have found a better position: the pleasure he could derive from the sight of the tanned girl – a marginal, accessory pleasure, but not one to be sacrificed, enjoyable as it was without effort – did not inhibit his pleasure at reading; the one blended into the other, so he could continue reading now safe from the temptation to raise his eyes.

Stillness reigned; the reading followed in a framework provided by the motionless landscape – and the tanned bather had become a necessary part of this landscape. Amedeo took for granted his own capacity for long periods of total immobility; but he had not allowed for the restlessness of the woman, who was already getting to her feet and picking her way over the pebbles to the water's edge. She had gone, he realized at once, to have a close look at a large jellyfish which some boys were bringing to shore, pushing it with sticks. She was leaning over the upturned body of the jellyfish and questioning the boys; her legs rose on wooden-soled wedges much too high-heeled for these rocks; seen from behind, as now Amedeo was seeing it, her body was that of a younger, more attractive woman than had been evident at first. He thought that a man in search of a pick-up would have seen a classic opening in this conversation between her and the little boys: approach, comment on the capture of the jellyfish, get into conversation. Not for all the gold in the world! he told himself, plunging back into his book. This behaviour, though, did prevent him from satisfying his natural curiosity about the jellyfish which was, he could see, of unusual size, and of a strange shade, somewhere between pink and violet. This curiosity of his about marine fauna was by no means an irrelevance: it derived from the same order of interests as did his reading; furthermore his attention was slackening at that point – it was a long page of description; anyway, it was absurd that to ward off the danger of getting into conversation with the girl he should deny a spontaneous and perfectly justifiable impulse such as that of taking a few moments off to have a close look at a jellyfish. He shut the book at the mark and got up. His decision could not have been better timed: the young woman was just moving away from the huddle of boys to return to her lilo. Amedeo realized this as he was approaching and felt impelled to say something at once out aloud. He shouted to the boys: 'Careful! It can be dangerous!'

The children, crouched around the animal, did not even look up; they went on trying to lift it up and right it with their sticks. But the woman jerked round and made for the water-side again, her face evincing curiosity and distaste.

'Ugh, does it bite?'

'It burns if you touch it,' he explained, and realized that he was making not for the jellyfish but towards the girl, who had inexplicably drawn her arms over her breast in a needless shudder, and was darting almost furtive glances first at the supine creature, then at Amedeo. He reassured her, thus engaging in conversation, as was to be anticipated, but it did not matter, for he would be going straight back to the book which awaited him; all he wanted was a glance at the jellyfish, so he drew her back to lean over the huddle of children. She looked down with disgust, her knuckles pressed against her teeth, and at a certain point as they stood side by side their arms came into contact and a moment elapsed before they drew apart. Amedeo started talking about jellyfish: his direct competence was limited, but he had read books by famous underwater fishermen and explorers, which soon brought him, skipping over the lesser fry, to mention the notorious manta ray. The girl listened to him with rapt attention, dropping in irrelevant interjections periodically, as women habitually do: 'This red patch on my arm? Is it from a jellyfish?' Amedeo felt the place, a little above the elbow, and said no. It was a little red because she had leaned on it when she was lying down. That was all. They took leave of each other, and she returned to her place, he to his – and to his book. It had been an interval of just the right length, neither more nor less, a human contact which was pleasant enough (the girl was courteous, docile, discreet), exactly because it remained superficial. He found in the book a much more concrete, a much fuller correspondence now with reality, everything had meaning, importance, rhythm. He felt in perfect fettle: the printed page divulged life, real, boundless, fascinating life, and he would raise his eyes to register a casual but pleasant awareness of colours and sensations, an accessory, decorative world which could make no demands on him whatsoever.

From her lilo the girl with the suntan smiled at him and nodded a greeting; he answered with a smile and a vague gesture and at once dropped his gaze. But she had said something.

'Mm?'

'Always reading?'

'U-huh!'

'Interesting?'

'Yes.'

'Well ... happy reading!'

'Thanks.'

The thing was not to look up again – not till the end of the chapter, anyway. He read it at a gulp. She had a cigarette between her lips now and was signalling to him and pointing to it. Amedeo had the impression that she had been trying for some time to attract his attention. 'Pardon?'

'... a match, by any chance?'

'I'm afraid I don't smoke.'

The chapter was finished, and Amedeo quickly read the first lines of the following one, which he found remarkably enticing, but in order to attack the new chapter without distractions he would have to settle the match question straight away. 'Wait!' He got up and jumped from rock to rock, half dopey with the sun, till he came upon a group of people smoking. He borrowed a box of matches, hastened back to the woman, lit her cigarette, doubled back to return the matches, was told, 'Go ahead and keep it,' hastened back to the woman again to leave her the matches, and she thanked him; he waited a moment before taking his leave, but realized that this pause necessitated his saying something further, and said: 'Aren't you bathing?'

'In a while,' she said, 'what about you?'

'I've been in already.'

'Aren't you going in again?'

'Yes, I'll read another chapter and then go for another swim.'

'Me too, I'll smoke this cigarette then plunge in.'

'Well, see you later.'

'See you later.'

This implicit appointment restored to Amedeo the peace of mind which, as he now realized, had eluded him ever since he first became aware of the woman sunbathing. He now no longer felt it incumbent upon him to carry on some kind of rapport with her; everything could wait till bathing time – and he would have had another bathe anyway, whether she had been there or not – and now he could abandon himself without inhibition to the pleasure of reading. Hence he did not notice that at a certain point – before the end of his chapter – his sunbather, having finished her cigarette, had got up and approached him, to invite him to bathe. He saw the wedges and the straight legs a little beyond the edge of the book; he raised his eyes, then dropped them again to his page – the sun dazzled – hastily read a few lines, then looked up again and heard her say: 'Isn't your head bursting? I'm diving in!' How nice it was just to go on reading, glancing up from time to time! As there could be no delaying, however, Amedeo broke a rule: he skipped a good half page to the close of the chapter, which he read most carefully, then he got up. 'Good! Are you diving off the point?'

After all this talk of diving, the girl descended cautiously from a ledge at water level. Amedeo plunged off a higher rock than usual. The decline of the sun was still gentle at that hour. The sea was gilded. In this gold they swam, a little apart. Amedeo occasionally submerged for a few strokes under water and amused himself frightening the girl by passing underneath her: amused himself in a manner of speaking – it was childish, of course, but what was there to do? Bathing in pairs was a fraction more tedious than bathing alone – the difference was marginal, however. Beyond the golden shimmer, the water veered to a deep blue, as though an inky darkness were surfacing from the depths. It was no use, nothing equalled the flavour of life to be found in a book. As Amedeo glided over some half-submerged, bearded rocks and directed her apprehensive movements (to help her up on to a reef he grasped her by the hip and bust, but his hands had become almost insensitive from their immersion, and his fingertips were white and puckered), he kept looking more frequently towards the shore, where the coloured cover of the book showed up conspicuously. There was no other story, no other suspense possible beyond the one whose outcome lay amid the pages where the marker was; everything else was a blank interval.

Returning to shore, however, helping each other out of the water, getting dried, rubbing each other's shoulders, all this created a sort of intimacy, so that Amedeo felt that to withdraw on his own again would now be impolite.

'Well,' he said, 'I'll stay here and read; I'll just get my book and cushion.' *And read*, he had taken care to say.

'Fine. I'll smoke a cigarette and take a look at *Annabella*.'

She had one of those women's magazines, so there was reading matter for both of them. Her voice reached him like a drop of cold water on the back of his neck, but she was only saying: 'Why stay there where it's hard? Come on to the lilo, I can make room.' It was a kind suggestion; the lilo was comfortable and Amedeo readily accepted. They lay head to foot. She said no more, but leafed through her illustrated pages, and Amedeo managed to lose himself in his book. The sun was suggestive of a delayed sunset, the heat and light scarcely fading, but remaining, rather, gently muted. The novel that Amedeo was reading had reached the point where the biggest secrets of the characters and of their environment are revealed, and the reader moves in a familiar world, and a sort of equality, of complicity has been established between author and reader — they go forward together and could continue indefinitely.

It was possible, on the lilo, to make those little movements needed to prevent the limbs from going to sleep, and one of his legs, pointing one way, came to rest against one of hers pointing the other. He had no objection to this, and kept it there; neither, evidently, did she, for she did not move. The contact deliciously enhanced his reading and, so far as he was concerned, made it more complete; for her it must have been different, for she got up, sat down again and said: 'But ...'

Amedeo was constrained to look up from his book. The young woman was looking at him, with a bitter look.

'Something wrong?' he asked.

'But don't you ever get tired of reading?' she asked. 'You're

not exactly the companionable type! Don't you know that one
should make conversation with ladies?' she added with a faint
smile which doubtless was meant to be merely teasing but which
to Amedeo, who would have given the earth to avoid inter-
ruptions at that point, seemed frankly menacing. 'Why the
blazes did I move here?' he reflected. It was obvious that with
this woman at his side he was not going to read another line.

'The thing is,' he thought, 'to make her see that she's got me
wrong, that I'm simply not the type to make a beach playmate,
that I'm the type to leave alone.' 'Conversation?' he asked.
'How do you mean?' and he stretched a hand out towards her.
'Supposing I grab her,' he thought, 'she's bound to find such an
ill-conceived move offensive – perhaps she'll slap me and go
away.' Whether it were his natural reserve, however, or simply
that his aim had a different, more gentle direction, at all events
his caress, far from being brutal and provocative, was timid,
sad, almost suppliant: he brushed her neck with his fingers,
lifted a necklace she was wearing, and let it drop. She replied
with a move which was initially slow, suggesting resignation
and a shade of irony – she lowered her chin on one side so as to
imprison his hand – then swift, as in a calculated attack: she bit
him on the back of the hand.

'Ouch!' cried Amedeo. They drew apart.

'Is this how you make conversation?' she asked.

'Clearly my conversational approach is not to her liking,' he
was quick to assure himself, 'therefore no conversation, therefore I'll read,' and he was into the next paragraph. He was only
trying to deceive himself, though. He knew perfectly well that
they had already gone too far, that a tension existed between
himself and the tanned girl which could no longer be broken;
he also realized that he was the first to want to preserve it – in
any case he would no longer have been able to isolate the tension
of the book alone, a tension all recollected and interior. He
could, though, try to establish this external tension on a parallel
course, so to speak, and thus avoid having to choose between the
woman and the book.

As she sat down with her back against a rock, he sat down
beside her and passed an arm round her shoulders, holding his
book on his lap. He turned to her and kissed her. They drew

apart and kissed again. Then he lowered his head to his book
and resumed reading.

He wanted to read on as long as he could. He was in terror
of not being able to finish his novel: the start of a seaside *affaire*
could mean the end of his peaceful hours of solitude, a completely different rhythm gaining control of his holiday routine;
and it is common knowledge that when a person is wrapped
up in a book, most of its value is lost if he has to set it aside
only to take it up again some time later: so many details are
forgotten, it is not easy to pick up the threads.

The sun was gradually sinking behind the next cape, and
behind the one beyond, and behind the one beyond that, leaving
them bereft of colour, dark silhouettes. The bathers had all
deserted the nooks and crannies of the point. Now they were
alone. Amedeo circled the girl's shoulders with one arm, and
read; he planted kisses on her neck and ears – which she seemed
to like – and now and then, when she turned to him, on her
mouth; then he went on reading. Perhaps this time he had
discovered the ideal balance: he might have gone on like this
for another hundred pages. But it was she once again who
wanted to change the situation. She started stiffening, almost
repulsing him, then said: 'It's late. Let's leave. I'm getting
dressed.'

This abrupt decision opened different prospects. Amedeo
momentarily lost his bearings, but wasted little time in weighing up the situation. He had reached a culminating point in the
book, and her words: 'I'm getting dressed,' at once suggested
these others to his mind: 'While she's getting dressed, I'll have
time to read a few pages without interruption.'

But, 'Hold up the towel, please,' she requested, calling him
tu for perhaps the first time, 'so that no one will see me.' The
precaution was needless for the rocks were quite deserted, but
Amedeo complied with good grace, as he could hold up the
towel while remaining seated and continuing to read the book
which he held on his lap.

The other side of the towel, the girl had slipped off her bras-
sière, heedless of whether he were looking or not. Amedeo did
not know whether to look at her while pretending to be reading,
or whether to go on reading while pretending to be looking at

her. Both were of interest to him: to look at her, though, could suggest too much indiscretion on his part, while to go on reading could suggest too much indifference. The girl did not go in for the usual system women have for getting dressed in the open, whereby first they put on their clothes and then take off their bathing costume underneath. No: bare-breasted as she was, she now took off her briefs. It was then that for the first time she turned her face towards him: and it was a sad face, with a bitter slant to the mouth, and she shook her head, shook her head and looked at him.

'Since it must happen, it may as well be now!' thought Amedeo as he launched himself at her, his book in hand, a finger in the pages. But what he read in her eyes – reproach, pity, dejection, as much as to say: 'All right, idiot, let's do this if that's the best we can manage, but you haven't understood, you no more than the others ...' – or rather what he did *not* read (for he was incapable of reading expressions), but only surmised, unleashed in him such a powerful feeling towards the woman that, as he hugged her to him and fell with her on to the lilo, he barely turned his head towards his book to see that it did not end in the water.

It had landed, open, right next to the lilo, but some pages had turned over, and Amedeo, without relaxing his embrace, tried to leave a hand free to put the marker at the right page: nothing is more irritating, when you are in a hurry to go on with a book, than having to thumb through the pages looking for where you left off.

Their amorous response was perfect. It could perhaps have been drawn out further; but had not everything about this encounter happened in a flash?

It was growing dark. Below, the rocks sloped down to a little cove. She was down there now, standing in the water. 'Come along, one last dip!' Amedeo, biting his lip, was counting how many pages there were to the end.